Dedalus Original Fiction in Paperback

Apparel

Arthur Mauritz was born in Bristol in 1989. In the past two decades he has played rugby for a local team, lead guitar in a local thrash-metal band and studied at university, all without leaving the confines of what he regards as the world's greatest city. During this time, he has worked as a shoe salesman, a pint-puller and a kitchen porter, pursuing his hobbies of writing, rugby and music as much as he can while meeting the demands of a full-time job.

Apparel is his first novel.

Arthur Mauritz

Apparel

Dedalus

Supported using public funding by
**ARTS COUNCIL
ENGLAND**

Published in the UK by Dedalus Limited,
24-26, St Judith's Lane, Sawtry, Cambs, PE28 5XE
email: info@dedalusbooks.com
www.dedalusbooks.com

ISBN printed book 978 1 910213 40 7
ISBN ebook 978 1 910213 43 8

Dedalus is distributed in the USA & Canada by SCB Distributors
15608 South New Century Drive, Gardena, CA 90248
email: info@scbdistributors.com   web: www.scbdistributors.com

Dedalus is distributed in Australia by Peribo Pty Ltd
58, Beaumont Road, Mount Kuring-gai, N.S.W. 2080
email: info@peribo.com.au

First published by Dedalus in 2016
Apparel copyright © Arthur Mauritz 2016

Printed in Finland by Bookwell
Typeset by Marie Lane

A C.I.P. listing for this book is available on request.

←
→

↓↑

←
→

A cigarette. That's what he wants. Light-ignite and all the world is a safer place. He drags a deep lungful and immediately feels safer, his growing rage calming by the second, by each inhalation, each taste of the grey smoky goodness, until it is diminished before taking any real shape. Cheap suit and cheaper sunglasses protect him from being known as the cheap person that he is not. Clothes, to him, look the same, and he is not mug enough to spend more than the minimum for any look. Especially one which every mid-class consumerist licker aims for and, guess what, achieves.

His cigarettes, however, aren't cheap. Each packet of twenty costs more than his trousers, and three packs cost the same as his suit jacket. But here, you see, is where taste really speaks and money has value. That gimp over there with the suit and that old bastard by the coffee shop's shitty cheap plastic chairs: they both look identical, regardless whether their clothes cost the same or less or whatever. These little babies, three-and-a-quarter-inch wonders, taste magnificently different to the cheap versions and the pea soup that they emit. By comparison, these are positively healthy from the internal angle. They actually are healthy for the mental mechanisms, Exhibit A testament to this.

And whilst he thinks this, he scuffs his right shoe on the upturned cover of a drain.

Time after work is always the wind down, the time to try and exorcise those whiny voices from the stuck record of the quotidian. Whoever coined the daily grind was a knowing so-and-so, probably a worker in a sweat-shop factory or something; every day in his job he has to listen to the same stylised nattering of the never content, the bodies who want everything with a golden spoon and are unwilling to do anything at all about it.

Scuffed shoe being led towards home, he stops by a newsagent's to pick up the evening and what he calls the next day's medicine.

Honestly, life wouldn't be worth living without smokes.

The man behind the counter is like all newsagents. He has a fixed smile betrayed by vacant eyes, although the retention of furtive observation, borderline paranoia, is still there. Like all of them. The man is also forty-something, pot-belly drooping ever so slightly over his too-tight belt, and balding with hair like a monk. Like all of them. This one, though, has less balding hair and looks a little too uncannily like Cadfael, and with a murmured thanks and a last, semi-reluctant glance, he gets back on the path.

Shit. Another cigarette will be perfect.

A habit, whoever they are say. Like chewing gum but without the chewing. Hell, they used to chew tobacco for sake of habit. Smoking is a lesser evil than the disgusting chewing gum habit anyway. Look at the bloody streets and those ink-black tar stains that are actually spat out gobbets of hygiene-unfriendly gum. He never tosses his butts on the road or the pavement, simply blowing a smoke ring or two into the carbon-starved air. Well. Maybe he does every now and again, but the point's the point.

Oh wait, the air is full of it. Overload. Stop. Or raise the tax rather than ban the little terrors. Taxes will save the ozone, the atmosphere, the stratosphere, the troposphere and the sphere of the planet itself. It's a spherical problem of spherical proportions, after all.

Fuck it. He doesn't even drive. Hardly ever.

His clip-clop of highly polished hand-made shoes makes a pretty percussive sound, evenly paced and repeated at perfect intervals. He is quite tall and whilst not big, lacks any impression of skinny weakness or frailty. He is not that old, either, but does not look young.

Walking is enjoyable, good for the legs, the heart, the lungs and the brain, if not for the feet. Those poor little feet of his, actually size eleven, had a blister the other week. A squishy padded plaster sorted that out pretty swiftly. He looks after his feet. Pumice, talc, wash three times daily. These fuckers hold you up for a modern average of seventy-odd years: look after them.

The walk from work is always the most enjoyable, as his back is turned towards the ominous fifties architecture of his workplace. He leaves the whiners, the naggers and those voices behind, still whining and nagging at shadows, probably. Or standing in the mirror and endlessly doing it, stopping maybe to escape into their selected soap operas and mind-numbing television, before standing back in front of their reflection and resuming their monotonous tirade. Moan for the sake of moaning, pessimism for the sake of pessimism, age for the sake of age.

Smoke because it relieves you. Smoke because it stops you from doing all of those things that you despise so much in others. Smoke because it's good for you.

Apparel

His suit jacket is a deep, full navy blue, with darker blue buttons and only one pocket on the right. It is always open and today reveals a summer's day sky-blue shirt, slightly darker blue shirt buttons, top button not fastened to reveal the bottom of his neck, the ridge of collar bones meeting. His hair is cut with a short, clipped back and sides and a thicker crop on the top, quiffed at the front toward the right. His shoes are black leather, and one of them is scuffed from recent contact with a drain cover. He polishes these every day, in the morning, before work. He does not work weekends.

The path seems empty of people today, which is strange because the sun's out, and that usually guarantees the hermits coming out. Where are the legs today, too? The heat always brings out those long-legged creatures who know what denim hot-pants do for their figures. They know what they do to appraising eyes and the male blood, too. Crafty, cunning, long-legged creatures. People fascinate themselves with the shit churned out in galleries these days. Childish nothings slapped on paper, not even canvas, and labelled modern for all the modern suckers. He knows art, and art is easily found in the female form. Someone had once told him that they'd had an eye for art, and if that was what they'd had then praise be to God that he doesn't.

What he does have, at this precise moment, is a sense of warmth and happiness. Tuesdays are always the worst days and God be thanked again that it is over. Monday mornings are easy to wake into, the exploits of the weekend infectious enough to last until midday, making the earlier rise painless and bearable. Come Tuesday, the realisation of four more early rises and no real allowance to debauch the evenings away settles in and holds its ground, dissipating only on Friday when, undoubtedly in a shroud of smoke, fifty-six hours is granted him until the next Monday. Hangovers always add to the easy transition back into the work cycle, the delicious irony of working whilst intoxicated to the point of illness bringing comfort. At least until midday, that is when he feels nauseous. That's not to say that he always drinks heavily on a Sunday, but sometimes he does, depending on the offers and wildlife of the night. Never liked the term nightlife.

He lives about half an hour's walk from work, apparently one-point-eight-seven miles, and he likes to walk no faster than average, enjoying the great outdoors and its urban sightseeing opportunities, most of which seem conspicuously absent today. He does own a car, but feeding petrol to its engine doesn't have the same allure as feeding a pint of cold lager down his throat. Funny thing on the radio the other day: petrol per pint is a helluva lot cheaper than lager per pint, even if bought from an award-winningly cheap, interchangeable supermarket that will undercut every other award-winningly cheap, interchangeable supermarket. It's not a bad motor, either. Sports car with electronic convertible roof in a mean shade of dark green and alloy wheels and a nought-to-sixty in less than five seconds. Purrs like a beast, too. The car is really for other purposes. He doesn't do the shopping in it or drive it on holiday or much at all really. It's a passenger vehicle only, for all intents and purposes and realities.

Like most days, he thinks about his Walkman. It's the third one that he's bought from the internet in the last decade, but his tapes have never needed replacing. It is like the world has really developed some sort of technophile virus, where every new model has to be worth more than its predecessor and all old models, whether two months or two days old, must be discarded as trash. One hundred pounds off bargain for the new Model XVI Technocrap, although machines that once did this thirty years ago and are unsung and oh so cheap on the miracle internet (credit where due) get forgotten. They do the same job. He thinks about why he doesn't bring his Walkman to work, but the reasons to leave it at home are far outweighing the reasons to wear it on his person and listen to it. Currently, it's twenty-one reasons to seven, a perfect 3:1 ratio. If it ever becomes 2:1, he promises himself often, he will bring it once a week. The principal, top of the food-chain reasons, consist of two points. The first is that hearing is a large part of alertness and awareness and he has seen things that, whilst being funny, could be embarrassing if it had been or was to be him. A dumb old woman had once been walking down the road with her nose buried in a book when her left elbow knocked into a lamppost and she was floored, sprawled on the pavement. He had put on his concerned face and swallowed his laughter as she cried and asked for an ambulance. It broke the predicted torpor of the evening ahead. He had sat in the back of the ambulance and walked with her into hospital, leaving when she was due a cast for what the paramedics assumed to be a fracture of some sort. He can't remember if they had said hip or arm. Whilst not actually because of music (same thing, he tells himself), the other four definitely were. All incidents involved dullard-unfortunates listening to some probably and ridiculously expensive gadget and then getting, in order of most recent viewing, run over and splayed across the road in an admittedly sickening display of hit-and-run, knocked from a bike (the car was loud, so God knows how loud the music was), shouted at aggressively from across a road and then punched from behind (an aggressive shout is a pretty good warning. If you hear it), and walking out into a road with a car turning into it. That last one pissed him off and still pisses him off the most. After the car stopped, the walking idiot nonchalantly put out his hand as if to ward the car away, and with no change of pace continued to reach the pavement across the road. That prick deserved to be road kill, and seeing him get away unscathed had annoyed and annoys him still. After ringing for an ambulance, Samaritan that he is, he had found out (and this no longer than half-a-year earlier) that the hit-and-run woman was dead, which just doesn't seem fair. The second reason: if electronics are worn on the person then they can be broken or stolen. He imagines some gangster wannabe with a three-inch blade demanding his Model XVI Technocrap, only to find out that it's an antique and stabbing him anyway for his troubles. Yep. He'll definitely keep leaving it at home for the foreseeable.

His briefcase is a gift from an old girlfriend and it was given to him about seven years ago to mark something that he cannot remember. One of those silly anniversary things that girls make up at different supposed stages of a relationship. Oh look, it's our one month anniversary or oh whatdyaknow, it's our seventy-fifth day of us. He supposes it is kind of cute in a teenaged American stereotypical kind of way, just like the word cute itself. The briefcase is brown leather, real ass-hide of cow and fastened with burnished gold-coloured metal. It is heavy and looks expensive and, knowing what she was like, probably is expensive. She did not last long: they never do. Wonders what anniversary she celebrated with the gift. The weight is pleasant in his hands and makes his arm ache slightly after ten minutes or so. He changes it back to his left hand, the one where it was when he departed the workplace. He is left handed and can carry it for longer in his left than in his right. He will make the rest of the trip home with it in his left.

He comes to a park and at the gate, a panting fat man runs across the path and he finds it comical and bizarre and ridiculous, unable to prevent grinning at the red face and

→

←

The smug bastard with his smug suit and handbag. Might as well have laughed at him with that face. He resolves to speed his pace. Don't stop now. It bloody hurts and it's bloody warm. If he keeps at this pace he will cut handbag man off at the other gate.

The expensive running trainers have saved him from blisters, but the purplish mottling of his arms and forehead have not been saved from the strength of the sun.

Oh god. Have a breather after the gate. Knock into the bastard.

He looks to his right to gauge the timings of creating a coincidence, slows and breathes deeply, a squeezing feeling affecting the right side of his stomach. Twenty more seconds, probably. Thinks it's funny to laugh at the fat man, does he? At least he doesn't carry a bloody woman's bag with him to work.

He slows to the pace of a walk, maintaining the jogging motion, and accelerates five yards from the gate as the man in the suit closes it behind him.

Perfect. He knocks against the man's shoulder, mutters *Dick*, and continues with a slow jog to move away, regarding the stumbled man with satisfaction.

←

→

The fat prick. The stupid fat waddling prick. Is his brain so filled with fat that he can't see where he's going? If he sees him again he'll skin the fat little pig. He is shaking in the adrenal grasp of anger, deliberating whether he will run back through the park or around the park or shout at the man.

He watches the man jog away and removes his cigarettes from his pocket and opens the lid of the carton and pulls out a cigarette and ignites it with his lighter, taking a long and steady drag. If he ever sees that fat prick again, he'll follow him home and slice the prick open.

He shakes his head and the small cloud of smoke clears his thoughts. A consciously constructed image of roasting the man on a spit causes him to laugh once in the form of a long sigh and he walks away from the park.

His house looms not far up the road, a terraced leviathan built just after the war, and he is looking forward to having a smoke in the garden with his latest book. The house is high-ceilinged and three-bedroomed, although initially it had five. One bedroom now hosts a library with a baby-grand piano and the other keeps his collection of vintage guitars. He likes the shabby exterior of the building, stained by age and dirtied a greyer shade of the pale grey it once had been. No decorative ivy or plant creeps upwards across the walls, and the paint on his door is peeled and the number six of his house number is slightly askew. Number one burglar deterrent: poverty. The idiots that broadcast their wealth are asking to be burgled, whilst other idiots invite the burglars in with an evident lack of security. A happy medium is needed. This is what he has. His garage faces the lane at the back of his house and again does not seem to offer much to the thief's eyes. His gardens are kept neat but not adorned with statues or water features or any pretentious ornamentation: a nice border of various plants for the front and a set of plastic chairs and table for the back. The reclining wooden sun-lounger is the most lavish item on show in either garden, and his shed has no windows.

He walks up to the front door and with keys already in his hand, places the briefcase on the cheap, coarse welcome mat. Obvious signs to protect the house. No wealth here. With his left hand turning the key in the lock and the right pushing forward, he is not met by the yelping of an excited dog, or the enquiry of a husband or wife. Instead he is met by the smell of lavender. It is faint and caresses the nostrils perfectly. It is not excessive and pungent like the perfume of some men and women. It is also not too faint. It is just noticeable and slightly accentuated by the smells of the outside. He bends down and slips his shoes off. He doesn't notice the scuff on the right shoe. He then places them inside on the cashmere rug underneath the hallway heater. His suit jacket is hung on the stand by the rug.

His carpets are underlayed and thick, spongy on the feet. These are the third carpets he has had laid in the last six years. Comfort of the feet, he knows, is very important.

He is quite hungry. It's a good feeling, hunger. If you eat without feeling hungry then you aren't going to enjoy the eating and the tastes so much. He makes a sandwich of cheese, pesto, smoked ham and real butter on granary bread and picks up the book that he has been reading.

After getting his book he opens the kitchen door, picks up his plate and puts them both onto the plastic table next to his sun-lounger before he sits on it. An oyster shell has the black stains of an ashtray on its white underside. He rests the plate on his lap and holds his book one-handed, the right, whilst holding a sandwich in his left. The sandwich is nice, and he focuses mainly on eating rather than reading. The book is at the top of the bestsellers and even people who don't read are reading it. He reads a lot. He has got to page one hundred and twenty nine, and the main character is a woman who is on the trail of a mystery perpetrator or killer or loved one or someone else intriguing. She is well-developed and full of nuances and mannerisms that make a character believable and he likes her, which he knows is the point. Every ten pages or so there's a turning into the unexpected or the incredible, the author's skill as not just a character writer evident as each abrupt turn leads into an exciting new find. Only, he knows that she is dead and is seeking peace of phantasmal mind or spirit or whatever it is they have, so the end won't be new or unexpected. As with all books that become sensations, mouths give away the story. It's kind of like that film where the kid sees dead people, only more adult and not horrific. Everyone had known about the end of that before watching, but it didn't really ruin the experience. He supposes it's literary art, but he enjoys it anyway.

With his sandwiches eaten he lights a cigarette and the smoke coats the greenness of the pesto and the peppery cheese that was stronger than expected. He really can't remember what eating must have been like as a kid, a time when he didn't smoke after eating. This is not to say that he eats and smokes all of the time (for instance, the impossibility due to work), but the simple pleasure and accentuation of the tastes through the smoke is just better. As he smokes and savours the mélange of tastes, he resumes reading, intently now. The woman (dead and ghostly, by all accounts but he doesn't know that) has just found a letter written to an ex-boyfriend of hers in another man's apartment that she's broken into and has just realised that it's in her own handwriting. Genius. He reads for an hour, forty-three pages, and from reluctance to finish too soon, puts the book down and closes his eyes with the sun baking him nicely from a late June angle, high up in the perfect, blue sky, all cotton-wool clouds having retreated for the night. His garden faces exactly south, a conscious factor for determining his residence. The north wind hits the front of the house with its cold hatred and the sun rises and sets on the garden, not that it's been windy for a while. It isn't too late yet – still another couple of hours of sun if he wants it.

His mind is filled with the dead protagonist from his book. She is Hungarian and calls herself Urs, although the smart writer dips into parts where Orsolya is goading her, playing on the language incompetence of a lot of readers. It's written from her perspective and he thinks that she has lost some or most of her memory through death so cannot remember her ethnic roots. It's smart, either way, and while the prose is quite complicated at times, he can see the easy appeal to the non-frequent reader. She's not really described in the book, though, which annoys him a little. Then again, it adds to the realism that when you follow a person through a book they don't say hi, I'm five-ten, dark brown hair down to my collarbone with elliptical eyes made-up with thin black eyeliner and I have a slim physique, size eight, thirty-four B breasts and bony hips. There's also a mole on my left forearm that I've had since I can remember so perhaps it's a birthmark. My lips are peach-coloured gloss and my thin face has angular cheekbones that are not unlike a classic catwalk model's. I have pierced ears and wear fake pearls in both. That's how he pictures her, with the glasses, of course. They have been a problem to Urs from page one as she can never seem to find them and her cases are always empty. Now where was that going to turn?

Pencil skirts and white blouses with thick rimmed glasses and contours of beautiful curves and hair pulled into a tight and shiny ponytail and his thoughts become erotic. He wonders if he's going to masturbate tonight but it really is too hot. He opens his lids and unbuttons his shirt and takes it off. He has a toned stomach, a six pack, not overly muscled but visible. His chest is hairless thanks to his genetic make-up and only a faint trail of hair leads up to his belly-button. His thoughts linger on official looking women in their late twenties, blouses showing cleavage and smiles promising a whole series of nocturnal explorations.

The sun is still raining down on him when he starts to feel sticky and decides that a shower is in order. Usually, he does a small routine of press-ups and crunches, sit-ups being bad for the back. He owns some free weights and would do fifteen-kilogram repetitions to keep a decent strength and shape to his arms. A range of leg stretches are usually carried out. This evening, he doesn't feel like it. He is not tired but his bed has a certain appeal tonight, the appeal of comfort and unwinding. Instead of working out, he has a cigarette, one from his new packet. The face of the newsagent smiles his dead smile at him momentarily before it evaporates with the first exhalation of smoke. Cigarette between lips, never between teeth, he walks up the straight stairs to the main bathroom, undoing his belt and carrying his shirt. Without much care, he drops all of his clothes on the tiled floor of the bathroom and drops his butt in the toilet, urinating on it and making it sail languidly around the bowl.

He showers, enjoying the feel of the soap on his skin. The soap is such a quality that it acts like a moisturiser, penetrating the stratum corneum. He knows this because the girl at the counter became his epidermal teacher for twenty minutes and because he loves skin. The girl who was extolling the wonders of the dead seas and the phospholipid-friendly natural components within her soaps had lovely skin, mahoganied until nearly black, a cross between a Mediterranean maiden and a Caribbean queen. The feel of someone else's skin is also incomparable. There is so much character within the body's largest organ, so much to be explored in the nocturnal rites between man and man, man and woman, and woman and woman. The expanse of the erogenous is an often guarded secret, locked behind an invisible and unreasonably enforced chastity. The sin should not be the sexual but the bringing to the grave of an unexplored body, for after all, an unexplored body is an unknown body. He turns the shower off, opens the sliding shower door and steps dripping onto the towels placed on the tiles of the bathroom floor. Without drying or allowing himself to drip most of the water onto the towels, he walks into his bedroom.

Central to attention in the bedroom is the bed. It is pretentious. Everyone who enters the room is struck by the size and the nature of it. It looks as if it should be in a royal residence, all four posters with billowing curtains bound in the middles of each post and splayed at the tops. Golden tassels keep them bound. Equally regal is their colour. They are burgundy. He is not too keen on the bed but knows the value of impression. The bed has yet to fail to impress. He considers jumping straight under the duvet and sleeping, but instead walks to the en suite and picks up his toothbrush, no gimmicky electro-crap toothbrush, and puts a perfectly round, pea-sized amount of toothpaste on it. He brushes for a minute and a half and gargles the minty foam that he produces before spitting the last into the basin. Now, with the good intention of reading a dozen more pages of the book, he does get into bed and enjoys lying in comfort. It is before the postmeridian nine o'clock. Before an hour of shifting shapes and comfortable positions and considering the death of the fat man in the park, he is asleep. He dreams of many things.

And he wakes to the undeniable conscious comfort that tries not to let him leave. He denies its hold on him. The alarm clock is programmed to sound at seven from Monday to Friday but he rarely needs to hear it, waking like clockwork five minutes before. It is six fifty-three. His fingers on each hand are locked with each other and he pushes up and out, making his body rigid by pointing his toes down and stretching them as far from his hands as possible. He tenses as many muscles as he can and then allows them to relax, aiding his circulation and waking his body up. The ridge on the bottom of his left foot starts to cramp and he welcomes full consciousness, even as his penis limps, and he quickly gets out of bed to place the cramping foot flat on the carpet, leaning forward to exercise the stiffness of the tendon or muscle and get rid of the pain.

For whatever activity and exercise that he carries out, he does not sweat. For this reason he does not shower again in the morning, but simply washes his feet and removes the crusts from his eyes with warm water and snorts salt to clear his sinuses, spitting some that enters the back of his mouth. He always feels like a Country and Western singer when he does this. His mouth tasting of brine throughout his dress routine, he walks down the stairs with slippered feet and without a tie and, in the kitchen again, the epicentre of the domestic world, he pours a cup of water into the kettle and flicks the switch. Tea won the war, lifting morale and warming up spirits and bodies, and each day in workdom is a miniature war against the pricks who can't do their jobs properly, and they far outnumber those who can. The start of every day requires a cup of tea. A splash of milk and a levelled spoon of Acacia honey makes it perfect.

He quickly wipes a drip of honey from the worktop with a dampened sponge and rinses the spoon. He unlocks the backdoor and puts the sponge on the plastic table, in the shade at the moment but soon to be in the early-morning sun. The morning is blue, hazy white clouds straddling it and warning of the heat to come. The only way to improve a morning like this is with a smoke. Tea, sun and smoke: can there be a more perfect way to start anything? His cigarettes are in the house and his still-slippered feet do not worry him. His patio is swept and hosed once a week and his house is cleaned meticulously twice a week. Good agency, too.

The decision to eat first solves the dilemma, cereals being drowned in full-fat milk and the leftovers poured down the sink. He never has sugar on cereal. The blue and white china bowl is placed in the sink. The dessert of a cigarette is tucked between his lips and his lungs gratefully welcome the smoke. He walks back to the garden and sits for a second, one hand, the left, curled with a warming palm around the cup as the right forks the cigarette. The red-embered stump meets the oyster's old home and with a sigh of spoilt bliss he stands and makes his way into the kitchen to lock the door and kick his slippers off and head upstairs for some socks.

The socks that he chooses are cotton, fifteen pounds for a pair, but look no different to any other socks that have ever existed. As a matter of fact they look less than plain, but whereas a suit or trousers can wear quite well, socks become more hole than fabric and you get what you pay for. There are no holes in these socks and they can stretch past the middle of the calf, which he makes them do. Never forget the importance of feet. They carry every burden that hits the soul and the body, all the way to the grave.

In the main bathroom he gargles mouthwash and rinses before brushing his teeth. He quickly moisturises his face with a cream from the exotic Caribbean-Mediterranean, rubbing the excess into the backs of his wrists. He is ready for the day ahead and will last the pressures of a scrutinising world without combustion. Today sees him in silver-grey trousers with a pale pink shirt. He wears this and a pair of marigolds and polishes his shoes in a mechanised manner. The yellow gloves have only the faintest sign of polish having hit them. He notices the scuffed leather of the right shoe and thinks shit, he'll have to buy a new pair at the end of the month. The polish masks most of the creases and covers every dulling patch of leather, which he buffers to a waxy shine. The scratched surface of the leather is obvious to his scrutiny. The gloves, brushes and polish are placed in the box and put in the cupboard under the stairs. He picks up his briefcase, untouched since being dropped yesterday. He puts on a purple tie with thin, diagonal yellow stripes, bought four-for-ten pounds at a local credit-crunch busting mini-version of an award-winningly cheap, interchangeable supermarket. He puts on yesterday's suit jacket and without double-locking, starts the walk to work. It is seven-thirty.

Thought patterns resume their daily musings and motions, starting with the bespectacled brunette receptionist, hair pulled tight in a bun this morning. Maybe he should have gone out last night, or at least masturbated. He hadn't bothered to check his emails. The thought-shift leads him to his brother in Australia, openly homosexual in a gladiatorial way, although intolerance levels these days can't possibly give him reason to be as antihomophobic as he is. Time appears soon after, tumbling along the domino trail of thought. It has been two years since he has seen his brother and he works out the equivalent of his life for which this accounts and places it in a ratio and forecasts when he will see him next and realises that time, for its never-constant, eternally altered speed, really does separate much more than it unites. This in turn makes him recognise his loss and that he wants to see his brother, his only brother. He is not sad. There is a sense of regret. They had been close as children. Children. The beautiful bane of a parent's life. The fat prick isn't here. Maybe he'll waddle around the park again later.

Closer to the newsagent's than the park, a woman is walking towards him. She has dyed-blonde hair that is arched around her face, too short to touch her shoulders. She has large breasts that move with an upwards bounce with each brisk, wedge-heeled step that she takes. Not that he notices her shoes. Good morning, this is better.

→

←

Well it is to be expected, for after all, she is Davina Devereux, perfect double-D, just like her boobs which she hasn't failed to notice him looking at, the sneaky, rather sexy, perv. Looking at him as she passes, she can smell a soft purple scent and notices that he is quite tall and a bit more handsome than she had first thought. They pass and she smiles back a mirror of his smile, slightly too assured and appraising in the same curve of the lips, cheeks and eyebrows.

She can hear his footsteps over her wedges, even though her steps are nearly two for everyone of his. Davina had found out, in her mid-teens, that small steps make her breasts move, but that was when she had had tiny little bumps, more nipple than boob, and nearly a decade before her father had relented and bought her the augmentation that she had wanted. It wasn't even because of bullying or because she thought they would make her look better; it was because she knew that men thought they made her look better.

She is on the way to the gym to keep her size six upper and size eight lower exact. She had been a size four before and had been proud of the way that she could lose weight from every part of her body but from her breasts. She knows now though, that men like contours not just on the front of a woman, but on her backside and hips too.

The gym is a small, privately owned members only, the current vogue, where rates are regarded by the average buff worker-outer as being high. She likes this though, as the clientele are generally more moneyed, more classy and more depressed with their wives of silvered years. She refuses to have the personal trainer, solely for the reason that his nineteen-year-old crush cannot be more evident and the juvenility possessing him also has control of his eyes, eyes that could not meet her eyes or stare at her boobs. Those kind of eyes are the worst. His fumbled attempts to be casual when showing her how to use each machine and their operating procedures had actually been quite cute, but cute isn't what she likes.

The walk is slow for the amount of steps that it takes her to get through the revolving doors of the gym, but she has all the time of anyone on the allowance that grants her nearly anything she could really want. She is not dressed expensively for all that money, wearing a zipped-up tracksuit jacket and a vest top beneath, with jogging bottoms and white trainers.

There is no need for her to talk to the receptionist as her plastic card speaks the admission codes and informs the system who she is and more importantly that she is a member.

At first, machines are overlooked for a range of rubber hand-weights. She picks up two kilogram blue hand-weights and extends her arms into an arabesque-standing shape, lowering them to her sides after five seconds in the air. Her arms are not overly muscly: small and taut yet definitely not weak for a woman who weighs just over eight stone. Next up is a series of bicep curls that sees her arms bent at a right-angle to her abdominals, elbows digging in, and then lifted up against her shoulders. She takes about ten minutes on this and then heads to the treadmills. Idiots running on pavements are more than just idiots for damaging their knees against the hard surface of concrete, they are idiots because they don't realise, or worse don't care, how they appear when exhausted, sweaty and flushed. The grimaces of displeasure and apparent pain on the majority of their faces, coupled with rasping or heavy panting, is nearly comical.

She runs at her usual twelve kilometres-per-hour for a time just shy of twenty minutes, slowing down a fraction before registering a round four kilometres. She has been to France on dozens of occasions and to most other countries of Europe at least once, but cannot remember the conversion scale into miles.

She turns the machine off by touching a monitor on the right-hand side and her walk slows to a stop. As she turns around, a familiar looking man in his early fifties is starting to programme his machine.

↓↑

It is her and he has an excuse. She probably does it every time, a force of habit.

Four kays is the perfect amount. I don't tend to do much more but I'm not as young as you. It wasn't the best ever thing and he hoped he didn't daddify it, but the phatics are in place. He thinks he needs to ask a question though and is lumbered with yet more of the nothing-talk. *Workout before work?*

She is bloody hot, with absolutely sensational tits and a slim but damned curvy rump. She can't be more than thirty, either, and her blonde hair makes her look really slutty.

↑↓

Davina looks over his body in his loose grey shorts and a-little-too-smart-for-the-gym white polo. *I'm not working today, on holiday. Keeping up routine is all.* Have some of that. A little hook for him to ask a question and no impression as to move. He has most of his hair and it's only faintly grey in places. His arms look quite strong, but his chest is big. Her eyes stay on his face.

↓↑

She doesn't look away from him, with her blonde-framed face and that pinky gloss on her lips. The only thing missing to make her look like a real slut was the mole somewhere on her cheek or lip that they all used to have, those pin-ups of his teenaged years. How pervert can he play this? He knows that his licence to be lecherous is fully owned now he is over fifty and he can get away with quite a lot, as long as he utters the immortal line or uses the laugh. *And it seems your routine is doing you fine, even on holiday.* A little pat of an actually non-existent belly and the laugh. Perfectly pitched. *This thing just gets bigger and bigger when I'm not working.*

↑↓

Looks fine to me. And smiles. She has seen him a few times before and sees through his veneer. He is one of those people who likes to learn a little bit about their probably perceived prey before initiating the interaction. She has caught a few of his downward glances and knows he would like to fuck her. No part of the opening was spontaneous but it had sounded so. Just to flummox him, she adds *And don't you know it,* followed by a very girlish giggle, sweet-coating and hiding a sexual minx beneath it. Davina lets her eyes work their way to his stomach and flicker across the area where his cock must be, none too slowly. She faces him again. *Well. See you later.*

He says goodbye and see you next time and she turns and leaves and can near enough feel his eyes trying to sodomise her as she overtly wiggles her way to the entrance/exit. The summer's light breeze is warmer than the air-conditioned gym and she immediately sweats, tiny beads lining her brow and armpits dampening. She doesn't really know why but she likes to sweat, feels cleaner for it, and even looks good. She doesn't take off her tracksuit jacket to cool down.

Having walked the fifteen minutes that it takes, she has not brought a bag and heads back to her apartment to play some music. She usually has her music-player with her, but ever since her bag was stolen at a bus stop she refuses to take it out in public. She also now refuses to use public transport, opting instead to use the incredibly swift to arrive and incredibly slow to transport taxi service. Thanks father. Even though she knows the gym does not admit that ilk, she leaves it at the apartment. She realises that she could actually have brought it with her today, but habit hasn't allowed her to until now, too late.

The man in the gym is on Davina's mind. She has never liked boys or men her own age, since growing up as a sexually-charged teenager to the present day. She has always found the slightly greying hair and the partially residualised strength found in the matured body as being a turn on. Cocks were always cocks, the bigger the better, but the way that they were used by men who had children and wives and not necessarily plenty of use, just happens to be better. Davina has a few theories pertaining to the causes of this irrefutable truth. Her first is that the mechanised sex with a partner of duration, let's say five or more years, cannot arouse the same libidinous desires or lust that it would when newly committed with a foreign body, a new land to explore, taste, savour and use to a mutually abusive eroticism. Time has control of sex as it has control of everything. Stagnation is always a by-product. Her second is that children are a dampener. Whereas a man can still have sex with his wife and enjoy it enough to ejaculate and plaster a genuine enough smile of (no, not animalistic greed for another go) gratitude, a child dampens the simple want for sex. The reason for this is simple enough: guilt. Some odd notion has been spread that sex sullies and damages, and that it is dirty, which in an equally odd paradox. It makes the children themselves see it as dirty for a good few years. It's not everyone's belief, but Freud has some interesting ideas about this himself. The last of her many-times-over thought-out reasons is ridiculous, but she likes it enough to try and believe it. She thinks that an older cock has a better taste than a younger one, and jokingly likens it to wine. The more aged and vintage it is, the better it tastes and more exquisite it is. At least until it gets too old and tastes like piss. Wine from experience, cock from conjecture.

She imagines him in the gym the next time, starting some more small talk and heading to the changing rooms and showers at the same time. There are two blocks of showers, male on the right at the bottom of the corridor past reception and female to the left. Once through the gendered doors, however, they are split into around twenty individual cubicles. He follows her down the corridor of her imaginative fantasy and walks in immediately behind her, pulling his polo off and pushing her into a cubicle. The rest is a mental montage of various positions and fellatio and rough kissing, no one image or chronology of events settling in her thoughts. She laughs inwardly that her shower had better be a cold one. She wonders whether she will masturbate when she gets in, but decides not to.

She moves past an old lady who pushes a wheeled hand-trolley in front of her, as if to cast aside anything in her way. Her hair is tobacco-smoke-stained sepia, a filthy habit and one that is not doing the old lady any good. Davina does realise the irony in her suddenly guilty face, stopping her thoughts in case they are less than hidden. The old lady's head is tilted at a near ninety degree angle facing the pavement and she does not seem to notice being passed.

The apartment blocks are in view and the electronic security gate can be seen along with the porter's shed of a day-office. He's never in it, instead coming when his buzzer goes off and a resident needs letting in because they are too drunk to remember their code. She has lived here for four months and has never forgotten her code, not even on the several occasions when she would have struggled to tell you her name. She does like to drink.

At the gate, she keys in 5 5 5 1 2 and the whirr precedes a click and the door swings inwards. The pink-orange of the apartments' walls are on her left, leading to a double-doored access hall. There are no stairwells inside the building that grant tenants passage to their homes. Electricity and laziness have taken over. This suits her just fine. Don't get her wrong; even though she might be athletic and fit enough, stairs and five flights don't much appeal to her.

Every part of the building is spotless. The ground floor's entrance halls are washed daily, buffered and shined, business folk's scuffed-leather polish removed when still removable and if found at a time when firmly set, ways are found to remove it still. The carpeted corridors that lead into the separate apartments are crimson and extensively vacuumed, also daily. A person is employed within the private cleaning company assigned to the building solely to wipe down the walls. There is CCTV in evident abundance, openly hiding in the corners of walls. Every door has the same silver numbering and spyhole, with a dull red-painted door.

One lift at each access point remains permanently on the ground floor, returning there after depositing its contents, and the other does the same but returns to the uppermost floor, the seventh. The only thing lacking is a porter, resplendent with the typical red and gold attired bellhop uniform and bell-boy hat and white gloves. If she pesters her father enough she can probably get one, but then she might have to live in a hotel. New faces might be fun, she reasons. The doors are open as usual and she walks in, presses the circle with 5 on it and looks at herself in the mirrored rear of the carriage. She is never unhappy with the way she looks and knows that this is because she is so many things: sultry is one, with the poutable expression never far away; pretty is another, the youthful hue and largish eyes currently a permanent feature; slutty comes easy with the large breasts and peroxide blond hair; sexy is, she supposes, the term that encompasses all of her aspects.

What is funny to her is that she can also quite easily pull off intellectual, bookish, superior, timid and a lot more of the not-so-stereotypical. Her days at Trinity were well spent and her father's money has not been wasted.

Out of the lift and in her apartment, she is in the mood for music.

The music system that she walks over to is of good quality. Music is important to her: classical overtures, simple grunge bridges, smoothly erratic percussion, varieties of voices, digitalised synthesisers, chicken-picked strings and tribal chants and... Limited only by time and perhaps its metaphorical counterpart, money, music is endless and eternally changing. Davina has no genre restrictions or dislike for a certain labelled form of aural art, even, somehow, avoiding the natural prejudice for the pop machine and its churned-out mechanicals. Her, an Oxbridge graduate, too.

She chooses now a little-known-outside-of-Ireland Irish singer, an angel by all accounts with a delicate voice that brings every word of one of her songs to life. She is also not sucked in to the necessity of liking all songs on an album or by a certain artist. Of the eleven tracks on the CD now being played, she likes one, enjoys two more and is completely indifferent to the lack of creativity, difference and poetry found in the others. It is the first three tracks on the disc and this is fortunate, because it gives her the twenty minutes that she needs to sift through her messages on FAFAF.com.

The song starts with the plucked strings from a violin before a melancholic, elongated note is played on a cello. Her voice is the next to be added, soft and high but full of power in an understated way. The whole song, rather ingenuously, crescendos until the end, with drums and cymbals and piano added to the earlier three instruments. The song is not a sad song, but an ominity is felt throughout, a sense of warning and danger coupled with the innocence of a delicate voice, a voice which finishes as the strongest of the combined sounds. She has just logged into her FAFAF.com account at the end of the song.

The next song doesn't change throughout its seven minutes duration and goes largely unconsidered as she reads the thirty-three messages on her account. Two are from what the website nominates as friends and the others by strangers. Some of these arouse her interests, largely through difference to the usual garbage she has to read and one through a clear indication of something intellectual on the other side of the cybersphere. Telling the reality behind the cyberface is not difficult at all, and only once has she been caught out. The content of messages is also informative of character. The ones who pour the real sleaze into their words are nearly always introverted fantasists. They rarely have the libertine abandon and casual nature needed to perform the intrigues in their minds. The shy and coy messages are as they seem, the most genuine of them all and without much doubt posted by teenagers, virgins and social outcasts. Messages that contained uncommon words or ones that are long (by letter, not syllable: variety has four) are often lacking real intelligence and thus are dumb, whereas the perfect and consistent use of text talk hints at a smart person. The use of basic language with perfect punctuation is when there is a real feel for a smart person. Davina's own style was inconsistent text talk with an exaggerated amount of xs and emoticons added to suggest girlishness. She replies in this manner to three of the messages, logs off, and heads to the shower.

In the bathroom she takes off all of her clothes, including the trainers that she did not remove and never does remove on entering the apartment, stands in front of the full-length, wall-mounted mirror and raises her arms directly above her to inspect her armpits, before turning her back to the mirror and continuing the inspection from her neck to her ankles. Lastly she faces the mirror, cups her breasts, pouts, bends slightly forwards from her back, legs kept straight, and then walks behind the curtain. Curtain drawn, she lets the water hit her immediately, gaining a gasp-shriek of shock as the cold water responds to her glowing and warm skin. Her gasp soon turns to a soothing sigh as it heats.

She lathers a shower gel over her whole body and firmly pushes her fingers against the top of her vagina, kneading her clitoris. She enjoys herself but stops after only two minutes and resumes the removal of the gel. Next she squeezes an almost run-out tube of peroxide-friendly shampoo into her left hand and works this through her hair. She scratches her scalp as she does so with fingers going rapidly in opposite directions to one another, before allowing the water to rinse most of it away. She finishes this ritual by pulling her hair into ropes and squeezing out as much of the absorbed water as she can. Her hands then create a warmth of friction by rubbing her hair between the folds of a cream towel that she proceeds to make into a turban, before wrapping another towel around her body, just above her breasts and all the way to her ankles.

In the living room again and the song that's being played

sounds different for a second and then resumes its familiarity. Another uninteresting song. She presses a button on the stereo and skips to track ten and takes off her towels, leaving them in a pile on the settee. She lightly stretches her legs, extending her left to the side whilst keeping her right knee bent and facing forwards. This is repeated with the right before she rests her body weight on the backs of her forearms and lifts herself on her toes, tensing her abdominal muscles deliberately and feeling them strain after ninety seconds. She turns on her back and tucks her chin up against her knees for twenty seconds and extends, lightly panting, pushing her head against the floor with a sigh.

Davina lies comfortably on her carpets for ten minutes in a blissed state of non-thought and daydream, hands spread cruciform in line with her shoulders, eyes open and only blinking occasionally. She has no cares or fears or worries, which in turn leads her to think of food and of the time and that she is meeting with Diane, Claire and Rachel for a lunch at Barucelli's at two.

Not unwelcome reality is brought back and the fugue is dispelled. Time to get dressed and straighten her hair.

She walks to one of her two walk-in wardrobes in her bedroom and selects a pair of skin-tight leggings and a white laced-front, sleeveless top. Cleavage visibility essential. Why have an augmentation otherwise? The straighteners are plugged in and she puts on a pair of plain-white knickers and a thin pink strapped bra. A pair of pink-white socks follows, adorned with girly red hearts around the frilly edges covering her ankles. The straighteners are hot and she irons her hair to a perfect flatness, deciding upon a fringe to brush over the right side of her forehead. She unplugs the straighteners, leaves them on a chest of drawers, struggles into her jeans and puts the pullover back in the wardrobe. Selected instead is a light-grey vest top for maximum breast display.

A light spray of fragrance, floral but alcoholic, and she walks out of her door with a purse-sized handbag containing only plastic and a pair of straps for her feet. She looks younger for no make-up and will apply some when she gets to Barucelli's, just enough time for her friends to remark on her youthful looks and hopefully get asked for ID when she orders a wine or vodka-tonic.

The mirror in the lift compliments her and she flutters her eyelashes and smiles cheekily. Her skin is glowing with the dull fleshy orange of energised blood and the remnants of her Barbadian tan from the holiday two months previously. As the lift doors opens she is greeted with the same empty cleanliness and no bellboy.

The air outside is at its summer hottest, with heat raining down upon her. The light breeze is barely there. It's odd to have such good weather for such a prolonged time and she isn't complaining. Most people she knows moan about the cold, then the heat, then the rain and then the lack of it, almost as if no weather exists that would satisfy them. Davina gave up caring years ago. She can understand the complainers in one instance, however: those who work outdoors or whose income is affected by the temperament of the skies. That must really be a pain in the ass.

She walks past more people as she comes closer to the rendezvous, which as she thinks this wonders why they hadn't chosen Rendezvous instead; the tapas are infinitely better and they have more chance of being seated outside. Not that she doesn't like Barucelli's, though. A mother with a pram attempts to ignore her with her eyes directed from their corners to her breasts, whilst a group of young men walk by and smile at her breasts and face with an easiness marking them out as students.

Her face is set in a pout that belies no emotion, although she feels like laughing from the jealousy and lust so obviously on show. It isn't even that she's pretty, which she is, but because of the silicone that sits proudly in her chest. She can relate and does. A penis to her is more valuable and exciting than what it's attached to, and just like the many men who boast about their size, she knows how to gain attention. From the upward rise with each step, a combination of bra, footwear and pace, and the lack of concealment, everyone knows and notices and feels something about them.

A few more varied appraisals are received and she sees Diane sitting with Rachel through the lightly tinted brown glass, the table closest to the open window on the left of the entrance. This isn't surprising. Claire is always late and Diane and Rachel early. Davina's always perfect. She angles towards the open doors as a man walks past her, nearly into her, walking quickly.

←
→

He's feeling good. No doubts at all. He's looking more at the pavement than what's ahead, nearly hitting that blonde chick, but that's his normal. Sometimes before the meet the nerves come bad and the adrenal fear sets in. So far, so good. The geezer on the phone sounded posh and talked damned well, so sure as sure there could be no problems. He sounded nervous, in fact, when he was placing his order, which is a big order too and right to feel nervous about, and after all a nervous customer is usually one who doesn't meddle in the unknown relationships of new dealers.

It sits in his back pocket, not conspicuous in the slightest but the knowing that it's there makes him immediately feel guilty. He knows a lot of other streeters that push the same as him, but most of them say they never feel guilty and he can't quite believe them. Sitting in his back pocket is a soon-to-be five hundred smackers, purchased at a quarter of the price from the Lab. Tonight is a good week's worth of work in a single sell. He has an inverted commas proper job, don't get him wrong, but his fun money comes from the streeting. After all, what type of life is it when work is solely done to pay for the utility bills and the two-channelled TV fucking licence? He loves TV, but still: to pay for it. In a nutshell, his streetjob pays for his clothes, his computer, his games, his beers, his music and his car. Shitty cheap clothes own their owners, so nothing shy of the labels suits him.

The man's name on the other side of the line hadn't been given, which demands respect. He'd given his name as Greg because that's a regular kinda name and the same regular kinda name he operates under. His name is Andrew, but no one knows that on the street and no one knows where he lives. (Plus, whoever goes by that anyway? It's Andy). He's okay as far as he knows. A few of his friends know that he does this on the so-called side but these are his real friends. The unnamed smart arse had also been smart enough to choose a decent part of town as a meet. The ridiculous amount of times he'd been asked to sell in an alleyway, usually at night, is likely down to film and television. The fact that it's daylight and the park is a middle-classed playground for successful families is another reason why he is so at ease.

There is another element to the deal that has been agreed and at the time it sounded like sense, too. Now, however, it seemed stupid. In the unnamed's attempt at keeping maximum identity unknown, he had asked to simply meet and not exchange a word. Andrew respected that and thought that the guy really was smart, but walking as he is towards the park he can't help thinking that the man sitting on the bench directly opposite the yellow-painted swings might be a vigilant father and not the unnamed. This does not worry him at all, but he is stupid for having agreed upon it.

His swift pace brings him to the top of the egg-shaped park in only a couple of minutes and he skirts the metal railings slowly, observant eyes taking in as much as possible and trying to locate or identify a potential. There is, at present, nobody else sitting alone on a bench. For this reason, Andrew spies out all of the single men in the park but this allows him to deduce nothing. What the fuck does a drugtaker look like anyway? A druggie? He sniffs a quiet laugh at his self-perceived humour.

He pulls out his phone to look at the time. It's two minutes past the agreed time. Shit. He decides to sit on the bench but he'll be damned if he's keeping the agreement. If anyone approaches he's going to say something. In a flash the fear hits him and he is completely nervous. What if the bastard is a cop and he's waiting ready to arrest him? Ensnarement or entrapment or summat but he can't remember. He wills and then forces his legs to carry him to the bench and oddly they feel light. A repeated mantra of encouragement is spoken in his head and he does his best to look calm and collected. He's just a student or some such, here to enjoy another beautiful sunny day and... The universities closed, or whatever it is they do, two weeks ago. It doesn't matter. He's just normal and in a park. Sitting on a bench. A pretty amazing park, mind. A helter-skelter slide and sand pit and a merry-go-round sort of roundabout thing and a kiddy pool. Nothing like the park he used to have when he was a kid, with tangled swings and condoms at the back by the bushes.

A man is walking towards him and where the hell did he come from? His tucked-in shirt and brown leather belt and impassive face makes him anyone but the unnamed and he sits next to him and doesn't look nervous so.

Hi how's it going? Good day yeah?

↓↑

The kid spoke. The bloody kid spoke. Couldn't he remember?

Greg. The kid can't be anyone else so he quickly takes out the moneybag and turns it round so it faces him from the safety of his palm. He is obviously nervous, and shuffles awkwardly to push his back against the back of the bench and lifts his backside in the air. He slips his hand into the elevated back pocket and pulls out a thin wad of papers. With the kid sitting back down, he decides that he'll sit too, to the right. The kid puts the paper to his right, so he puts his paper down next to it, casually folding his legs. The kid pockets the money and walks away with a

↑↓

Cheers. Bye. Easy breathing, resume easy breathing. It was actually painless and he is now in the throes of elation. He agreed with the unnamed to not count each other's offerings, but he is going to walk back to the gate, check it, and watch the man to see where he goes. Andrew's not a gangster wannabe or tough or foolish, insofar as he isn't foolish for streeting, and he isn't going to walk back up and demand any missing money, but he is intrigued by the posh man. The faint shadow of something troubling him is there but not for long.

At the gate, twenty-five blue-purple notes are found to be in the moneybag and he is happy. This does not abate his curiosity at all and so he circles the park slowly, eyes planted on the gate opposite the one he entered from. Unless the man is Houdini he can't have left the park, but there's no sign of him walking towards the avenues and cul-de-sacs outside of the fences. A glance at the bench shows he's not still seated and his interests are piqued further. Surely he's not...

But he has.

Bugger me. And a disbelieving giggle leaves the park with him.

He walks back the way he came with thoughts of the weird clientele he has and has had turning over in his brain. To be honest, it wasn't the weirdest, but still. Hands down the weirdest he'd had was the man baby. Sober, the man was a smart-talking accountant (by all accounts, and there were many afterwards) who lived in a stylish apartment on the Upper Banks. He wasn't married but those who knew him said he was successful with the ladies and often threw lavish parties at the expense of the company's plastic, although not altogether liked by many people. He drove a brand-new feline-sleek wagon and pulled in a hundred Ks standard with bonuses from those whom he represented. This isn't bad for any thirty-year-old. What turned out to be bad was the quality of the liquid he'd cooked up and shot into his thigh. In a poetically tragic way, the heroin he'd been served was a better quality to any he'd had before and hadn't been cut with the usual additives, flooding his opioid receptors and inducing a comatose state that anaphylactically shut his body down. He was found amongst a dozen images of breast-feeding mothers and wearing only a disposable nappy with the lace taut to his thigh. The police found him after a missing person's report was issued from his work and his neighbour had told the papers what the police respectfully refused to. Perhaps his copulatory exploits had kept her awake too often. The diggers dug and found their dirt and soon man baby was born of the media's outstanding artistry for names and a fuzzy mobile-phone photograph even managed to do the rounds. It says a lot really: even in death do they look for entertainment.

So no, he wasn't weird in comparison, but then in comparison no one was anything if there was a superlative form.

His front-left pocket has the moneybag in it and it is entirely to blame for the detour that he takes. With a late start tonight at the shit-factory he can get a good couple of hours in, so when he walks into the shop he is in no hurry and luxuriates in that funny smell that all of these shops have. It reminds him of childhood and the easy joys that came from being given a card with a twenty pound note in it or a trip to the stores to peruse before purchase as a reward for some school-related thing. The shops themselves have never seemed to change, only the merchandise, their shapes and sizes.

A true connoisseur, Andrew. He goes to the worlds on offer, places where he can determine the very fabrications of society and destroy them at the ever-changing winds of whim. The aisle he stops at says RPG above it, suspended on a sign with faux razor-wire cables, the hornet's casing of black and yellow the same as the other genre signs signalling their fans, clients, both.

A new game has come out recently where the landscape is twice the size of its predecessor, the second in the franchise, with cities and villages already sculpted and the potential to build his own townscape. All the reviews have given it the maximum rating and he, like nearly everyone switched on to the gaming world, has been exhorted sufficiently to buy it. The character selection is more expansive than ever and the species that he can play as beats its competitors hands down. And it's only the third in the series, too.

He takes a look at the other games and weighs the money up and at an average thirty pounds per game, he works out he can get eight more and still have enough for the other thing that he owes Charlie for. He picks up another two because three is a magic number and everyone knows that, and takes them to the till. He waits for twenty seconds staring at the poster of a virtual babe before a stereotype in everything gaming says

↑↓

Sorry about the wait. She wonders what he's got and he doesn't much look like a gamer, more like a wiry sportsman type. Quite cute though and a spotless face. *Did you get everything you're after today?*

↓↑

He supposes he did. *Yeah. Thanks.* The girl takes the cases from his hands and pulls out a drawer from behind her, searching for the discs. Her back is shapeless but he still likes her enough to focus on her backside and imagine the outline of a g-string as she turns around with a tap of the drawer and three white plastic sleeves in her hand. The sleeves on her black uniform top are pulled to the elbow and the blue tattooed stars reach the top of the back of her hand, twirling into something he can't make out past the wrist and leading up her arm.

↑↓

There we go. There's the buttons which she learnt quite quickly when she started but now she's confused because they updated the system and now it's all over the place. It's always been like this, since she can remember; she goes red and feels the customer's eyes on her telling her to hurry-the-fuck-up, the useless bitch. She's warm and then hot and... *Where is it.* Come on. *No.* That was the old button. She voids it but the seconds feel like minutes. *Ah yeah.* Found it. *There.* She feels relieved, still wishing that one of the others had noticed him first. Truth be told, she clocked him as soon as he arrived. *That's one hundred and four ninety-seven. Cash or card?*

↓↑

Cash, thanks. And plenty of it, too. He wants her to see the wad of notes as he pulls it out of the money bag, but it doesn't seem as much to him now he's spending it. He is disappointed that she doesn't remark on the amount he has on his person, but not much. He had it revised: dealing drugs chuckle chuckle chuckle, innocent grin. Instead she tells him there's his change and receipt, there's his games in a bag and have a nice day. She's actually quite cute and doesn't have any spots. The piercing on her lip is bearable, too. *Thanks. See you later.*

It's too hot for him really and he concedes that he's too heavily attired, but naked home time awaits. Wearing clothes is a luxury in public when they are luxury items, and equally, being naked at home is the same. Two domains and two different privileges. It makes him feel more attuned with the world he is living in. In the real world (he's not absorbed or mad; he knows the other is a game) he fits in by looking the desired way, just as a nobleman is accoutred in the liveries of his fiefdom. He wants to be noticed as fashionable on the streets; his denuded state when gaming allows him closer access to the virtual world. He was told this by a legend of the online-gaming circle and at first was rightly sceptical, just as the don himself had said he would. But, taking the advice of his elders and betters as every fifteen-year-old should, he had tried it. He couldn't help wondering if the man was some paedophile who preyed on the dumb kids through his legendary status, and as a kid who wasn't dumb, had been reluctant to do it. There are some sick bastards out there: that, he's sure of. At least until he was offline and in a different world. Now it is the normal. More people in his gaming circle were doing it than not.

Because it is hot he is walking quicker than usual, the bag in his hands is held tightly in the cup of his hands. It is also because the child feeling is in him, the feeling that can't really be described as anything other than anticipatory excitement.

When he was a kid and Father Christmas was coming and the wide eyes of reluctant, impossible sleep had taken over and the not-butterflies-but-somethings were in his chest, not his stomach, is exactly the same feeling that he has now. The repressions of this juvenile excitement on the adult is unfair and enforced. He would like this feeling all the time and he counts himself lucky for knowing how he can get it. He likes sex, of course, but the feelings aroused by it are purely physical and completely separated from the feeling of excitement itself, captured in the whole body and unqualifiable. He blames it on the dismissal of the wondrous myths that captured children's imaginations: Father Christmas, fairies to remove your teeth, aging as a good thing, sweets and toys. Shit, birthdays aren't anything to get thrilled about and he's not long out of his teenaged years. Perhaps this is what the religiosos get out of their colossal mythology on a Sunday morning or when facing the east. He doubts it. This game is going to blow his mind; the clips on the internet and the advert are his evidence. And don't forget the reviews.

In a blissful eagerness of what is to come he walks across the road at a zebra crossing without looking to see if anything is coming. There is not. The early-afternoon traffic is not congesting the residential roads, home to coffee houses, charity shops and newsagents. The bustling sound of summer is a background to his thoughts, hearing the bass drums leaking from opened windows and the compulsory whirr of power tools reconfirming obeisance to their saviour from the cold dust of inactivity. In an automatous state, he walks up the high grey-white steps and flashes his fob across the red light sentry, which turns green. Up the stairs and subconsciously putting the key in the door of the flat and he is naked in four minutes with the game loading in the console. The other two are placed at the top of a rack to the right of the big flat-screen, the proud centrepiece of the room. The bag is on the carpet, next to him. His legs are crossed and knees raised, backside on the carpet. His penis is pressed against the inner thigh by his right heel, flaccid.

This is it. He will lose another gaming virginity, the eternal chastity that will always exist as long as new games are created. The first taste of the apple after biting, the resealed hymen of virtuality being broken again, as with each time he has become novitiate. There is no contest that he is an excellent gamer, so to experience the unknown and be less than proficient for a few hours of a new world is a thrill. This game has the additional excitement of being a key component in his plan, too. It does not matter which game he chooses, but he has decided on this one. Every minute detail has been thought of, he thinks.

He selects the life mode and starts a new life, opting for a veritable babe of some exotic species and changing her dimensions, sculpting her every feature and spending the starting allocation of skill points on making her quick. He has never been one for fighting in the games early on, knowing to flee is more profitable in the long run. Much like life, where the bigger kids in school would beat up the smaller, or the big man at work (metaphorical, thanks authority) would get the little subordinates to scurry for the menials, or the tough bastards on the street got what they wanted, running is always the better option with far less health risk. He finally names her Athene after the obvious, his favourite from school, rejects a guided practice run, and begins playing.

Born in a barn. He chuckles. The starch-coloured pastures of tilled fields fill the screen and his character is in a scene that informs him he's become an old woman and needs to follow her destiny and the paths that it creates. She's soon off down a dirt-road that has a range of people with carts and horses and barrows, and he directs her to follow a lone rider cantering along on a horse. He soon finds out that the stream of people is a cavalcade and he is eager to see where they are heading. Little icons are floating above many of the people's heads and he knows that when she presses the right button he will interact with the chosen person. He never starts a game by taking advantage of the instructions or helpers that are inevitably offered on the menu screen. If a child came into the world and was told how to do everything every second of every day then there would be no use for experience and living, just doing. Life is trial and error and he has to work things out for himself, just like in a game. Making mistakes or even working out how to avoid mistakes, a mixture of logic and deduction, is what makes anything fun.

He is lost in the world and feels himself becoming Athene and he slips into her seamlessly, simply exploring the new lands and enjoying everything. He has long had the idea that if some sort of sensory exudor could be added then scents could be smelled and tasted as different places were visited. He is sure that there is money in the idea. The travellers he follows take him to the battlements of a fortified city's outer walls. He takes in the sheer size of the game and the detail gone into the artwork. He tilts the POV vision upward. The walls are immense and when he skirts the walls along the ridged bank of grass, he walks for a good half hour finding no weakness or accessways or anything much, really. Time in the game is five times quicker than that of time, and nearly half a day has already gone by.

The beep-beep of his watch is an unwelcome reminder to save the game, get something to eat and put on his uniform. It goes off two times before he's back and he saves the game, immediately reintroduced to the life where work is ruler and the job he's going to is the less interesting, lucrative and easy. It's also considerably more legal. He smirks.

Okay, fine. Before he goes to work, he'll finally give in to his self-enforced prohibition. He had promised himself that he'd only look at it, finally take it out of its box, when he had the money to pay Charlie, but it's gonna be used soon. Besides, the only reason he can think of for why Charlie had let him have it on credit is because he's scared to keep it at his house, anyway. As much as any transaction meant something is his, this is now his. He pulls out a little box and cautiously splits the tape sealing it shut with his thumb nails. He's a bit disappointed with it, in all honesty. In real life, it doesn't seem that special and it's smaller than what he'd expected, something for which replicas, games and images haven't prepared him. He thought it would be heavier than it is, too, again being proved wrong. Two hundred pounds is still a steal and he knows it is cheap, though. A bit disappointed, not a lot. It will suffice to do what he has to do. He still has the residual child in him and it's not fading, and knows to put it back in the box to keep the feeling alive until he has a closer inspection later. Not wanting a thief to choose this inopportune time for fortuity, he puts the box under the drapes covering his only sofa, an unused moving-in gift that could never beat the gaming chair or the floor two feet before the flat-screen.

He thinks about a time that seems long ago but that he knows is not. He thinks too of the future. He thinks of the box and its contents and the purpose for which he is going to use it. It should not be long. He will complete the computer game in the next two days easily and then only minor details will remain to evaluate and subsume in his plan of action.

There is a half of a pizza in the fridge and he nakedly eats it in a few bites: bites of necessity rather than enjoyment. A quick glass of tap water follows, before he gets dressed quickly in his already-laced trainers, before leaving the apartment.

Andrew has always appreciated being allowed to wear his own footwear at work. He gets swollen feet at the best of times and the calloused soles and heels are a layered hierarchy of varying degrees of blisters.

His car is parked on the path. It was second-hand when he bought it and his are the third hands. It is dullish red with a black rim around the trapezoid outlines of the doors and sides, as well as along the rectangular roof. There is no sunroof, which doesn't bother him at all, but the windows are electric. Miles on the clock is a round enough 130,000.

He disagrees. It does bother him. Especially when it's hot.

He has never had a problem with the car and he does not have one now, ignition chugging its usual sound in response to the key's turn and he pulls out in gear and it's a little bit early for work which is actually great because he needs petrol which isn't great but he'll top up with a tenner. He doesn't work too far away from home and used to cycle, but what's the point of having a car licence and not using it, what with road tax and insurance (fucking ridiculously sky-rocket high) and pure luxury when it rains? Plus, reminding himself to switch it on, music is legal to listen to. Once, headphones in on the bike, a volunteer fluorescent jacket wearing asshole had stopped him and attempted to issue a caution or something like that, just for having earphones in. He's never been knocked off from a bike.

The drive doesn't take five minutes, traffic oddly flowing. The petrol station is a takeover from the halcyon establishments that dealt only and specifically in fuel, a fucking monopoly war of supermarket feudality on show in garish, luminous signage, for the benefit of all those who have never heard of it or can't read the five-feet lettering otherwise. Very few, he imagines. Proud petrol prices are advertised on the boards stating how he is buying his petrol for a whole half-a-penny less than their closest rival. He'll save just over three pence. Cracking deal.

He slows the car to a stop and turns the engine off. Opening the door there is an old man filling his 4X4 and he nods at him.

$\rightarrow$

$\leftarrow$

A polite gesture, the nod. The kid seems okay and he's on his way to or from work, one of those logistics and delivery companies. He can't be more than twenty or so, so is probably a student or part-timer. Loads of them around here.

Always a fan of cash, he does not bother getting out his card and slotting it into the payment port on the machine attached to the pumps. He knows that he is traditional, old school, but this does not mean that he is outdated. His phone is the latest model and his television is four-foot long, flat-screened and highly defined. He looks slightly older than he is, again self-acknowledging, but that's the greyness that peppers his hair, camouflaging the black to near concealment. He is not balding though, a definite plus point.

Sandra had always liked that about him, his full head of hair that was similar to the fifties' Teddy boys only shined with pomade and combed backwards and to the side, any side. She had never seen his hair so greyed with apparent age, having left him two years ago.

His tank is near full, and he rattles the last drips from the nozzle and passes the kid on his way back from paying. Another nod matched by the kid's smile. These kids are all right. Curiosity betters him and he turns to see the illuminated red digits above the kid's pump and can't help finding a regretful humour in it all.

In the shop-come-station there is a girl with auburn hair waiting to ask him

↑↓

Hi. Which number are you? She reckons it's the one-ten.

↓↑

Three, thanks. Hi. He studies her button nose and can't help being reminded of Sandra as she asks him for one hundred and ten pounds and twenty-one pence. His wallet is leather and faded from the mahogany of its original hue to the dusty tan of a desert brown. Tucked inside the two now unfolded main compartments is five hundred and thirty pounds worth of notes. A buttoned pouch contains an assortment of coins. This usually lasts him a fortnight easily enough and is on course to do so. He hands her six notes, not feeling like counting out the shrapnel and coppering his fingers. He thinks of Sandra and looks at the girl, remembering only just to give her a smile of hidden wistfulness in receipt of her thanks and have a good day.

He finds this happening a lot recently and under the circumstances, it is nothing out of the ordinary. Her face, features, mannerisms and postures are imbued upon numerous faces and bodies. He finds himself seeing her in the billboard models' curves and the checkout girls' eyes, the clothes of a stranger and the voice of a friend. Not confident enough to recount this to a shrink, he does his own psychoanalysis and becomes his own doctor, providing his own psychotherapy. The results are variable. A face tells him that he has hope; the contours of a body, rekindled desire; clothes are the very fabric of memory, in many colours. What worries him is when the tragic muse is missing, vacant, yet the thoughts remain.

This he attributes to guilt.

A man can always do more and he could have done more. Honest to himself, he does not deny the loss and longing that he has. This comes frequently in the form of tears and does not oppose his masculine nature, or at least the supposed constraints attached to the fragility of masculinity. The role has enough dominion over him to repress overt showings in public and even to his adult children, family, and friends. What more could he have done? Lots. Simple things like picking her up from work, only a ten-minute drive, rather than allowing her to walk alone. Simple things like spending more time in the evenings with her, rather than squash sessions with Alan and Gareth and their associates. Simple things like music.

Music. That was always her favourite and he had tried so damned hard and that was ultimately its ruin, so much so that he threw all of her records, CDs and even cassettes away, along with the stereo they'd recently bought. He never listens to the radio any more.

But more than that, guilt. Guilt is not a fan of misappropriation or unfair allocation and he is the deserved, earned owner of all the trappings: shame, regret, remorse, and many more of the names familiar to perpetrators and wrongdoers. For that is what he is, the rightful recipient of his loneliness.

Guilt is also in residence for other reasons.

The GPS navigation system in his car directs him to a quiet road that leads to a small car park behind a block of flats and local shops. There's a newsagent, a chip shop, a launderette, and maisonettes sitting above them all, bearing the inarticulate and unrefined artistry of the juvenile graffitist along their sides. Happily authoritative signs inform him that anti-vandal paint perches on the ledges of the walls. He eyes the screen of the GPS and submits a few routes to memory before turning the engine off and stepping out. It's nearly seven and it's still bloody hot. Summer has definitely made up for its lack of blessing these last ten years. There is the noise of screaming children playing some game amidst the whirr of washing machines and unintelligible chatter. A television is played loudly and escapes through the opened windows of one of the buildings. There's a series of little ponds around here somewhere and he is intent on finding them.

Being early, he has time to kill, but he regrets his choice of expression soon after thinking it. Fencing leads him down a narrow path away from the local shops. The sign for the Community Ponds appears on a post with the council's logo stamped beneath it. The ponds are fifty square yards or so at their largest and there are four criss-crossed in a diamond shape from where he enters. Parents with their children throw balls and groups of adultless children run amok in pure happiness. Lovers, parents, wives and husbands hold hands in displays of love and commitment and maybe expectation and routine, but hold hands nonetheless. He sits on one of many black benches with dedications on them and thinks of the dead that they recognise and remember and couples the dead with that of memories of Sandra because she is dead.

It was told in a hurried manner and with as much sadness that could be emitted from one trying to remain impartial. Just gone eight o'clock and walking home from work. The little music player he'd bought her as a gift for their anniversary had been smashed into as many pieces as her hips and eye-socket. She'd been listening to it when the car that was speeding along at more than twice the limit had gone through a red light and upended her. The car was later found burnt out but the glass that had embedded itself into her had matched that of the glass of the burned-out wreckage. It was probable that she'd died within minutes and the eyewitnesses had said she was not moving which would have been difficult with snapped vertebrae and the angles of the limbs, but they had no real idea.

A young man had rung the ambulance and after the ten minutes it took to arrive, she was pronounced dead at the scene. Her teeth were collected from the road and sent with her body to a mortuary, the last place he had seen her and then through tear-stained lenses. He had declined an open casket, going against the Redlaw family funeral tradition. She had married into it, had been his argument. In truth, he could not look upon her in any state other than in life. His love was a real love, as real as anything that was not of the tangible world could be.

And guilt is there, waiting to be expunged, waiting for the welcoming arms of catharsis to pull it from him and cast it out, seed, root and all. But, he knows, the only way to do this is to remove it. It feels like a tumescent weight. It is an unwanted abstraction that for as much any emotion can take a physical form, it has. He breathes it, tastes it and hears it. His words are leaden with the heaviness of grief, falling from lack of warm timbre or the enthusiasm of honesty before reaching his intended destination. They are dry in his mouth, acridity sapping any emotion from them. They are unmelodious. Tuneless. He sits on the bench traversing his thoughts and thinking about what has happened and what is happening and what is about to happen and he cannot say he is unhappy. The happiness around the ponds and the picturesque scene of green-blues are undeniably pleasing. The summer's return is a wonder that deserves the never-ending conversation it receives. It's just that it's there, a proverbial monkey that silently keeps vigil perched by his ear, capable of advice yet withholding it.

The people are dwindling and the sun is still an inch above the buildings' tops in the cloudless sky. He sighs and puts his hands on his knees and leans forward, standing up. He glances at his watch and it is nearer eight than half seven but he does not know exactly. Time to head off, to be a little early or a little late.

He joins a funny procession of kids and adults and thinks of his children. Josephine works as some type of vet that isn't a vet and Rachel works as a beautician. Funny, the way their employment is always attached to them, as if it reflects a judgement on him by determining their successes. Just as his unshifting guilt is inextricably linked to them. He wonders what they'd think.

He leaves the wagon parked up and works from memory, the route and the usual unending loop. He knows where both head. The first is Weyland Street and the second is inevitable, just as it has been since the policeman finished his hasty monologue. He is agitated by the paradoxical obviousness of life's unfairness. In every waking moment and through frequent nocturnal visitations does she rest in him, a far cry from when living. A humourless recognition that the old adage is true. Only he did realise what he had had, every day, and he did appreciate her. The oddness is that he could go without her for days and not think of her, yet now he can go no more than minutes without her phantom sharing his actions.

The traffic is light, which does not mean that there are not many cars on the road but he does not need to press the button on the lights to call the green man. He does so anyway out of respect. Out of irony. He waits for each one to go green before walking, holding up the cars and paying them little attention, unaware of who they are or whatever faces they may be pulling. Green light of safety.

She walks with him all of the way to the gate and the shiny round buttons and the voice that comes and the elevators (for where are the stairs?) and then onto the pristine floor and the door with the little peephole, and he doesn't know what he's doing but she voices no complaint and so he knocks.

Dani meets him at the door and she is half hidden behind it as he walks in. *Hi. Nice to meet you in person.* She responds in kind and asks him if he wants a drink and he does. *Yes please. Water is fine thanks.* She closes the door and he sees that she is dressed in a black thong and matching bra, barefoot, and as she walks away from him to the kitchen, that is joined to the lounge, her buttocks move from side to side making his cock harden a little as he watches her. He watches as she takes a glass out of a pine-laminated unit above the sink, placing it on the draining board before crouching down by the fridge to pull out a bottle of water. From the side, her tits look fantastic, large and pushed upwards. She stands up and flips open the sports cap on the bottle before squeezing water into the glass. She leaves the bottle on the side and picks up the glass, making her way towards him, bright-blonde hair unmoving.

He has not expected this and does not know what to do as she stands there offering him the glass with a cheeky, naughty smile. He takes the glass and without really thinking puts his left hand on the right side of her waist, sipping a small amount of the cold water. He cannot help his breathing's sound and she takes the glass from him, moving away from the hand on her waist to put it on a little coffee table by the sofa. Her ass is magnificent. She walks straight back to him, and puts her arms around his neck and her tongue in his mouth and in reaction his hands grab firmly onto her buttocks, before pushing his fingers into the firm, soft flesh. His chest is beating and cock throbbing in seconds to the same rhythm, and when she breaks away and moves to the sofa, lying on her back with her head pillowed on a bundle of cream-coloured towels, he takes off his shirt and decides to leave his jeans on.

↑↓

What will drive him crazy now is easy. A soft purr in a sweet voice. *Come on baby, don't keep me waiting.* She'd been thinking about saying daddy I've been a bad girl, but he might be the sensitive-about-kids type. His body is slightly rounded but obviously strong, and short silver chest hairs pepper his pectorals. His plump belly is strangely bald and she imagines he shaves his pubic hair.

He tosses his shirt onto the floor and works his way on top of her, supporting his weight over her body on one of his arms and pushing his lips against hers. He is a good kisser and has that dominant weight behind his jaw, telling her that he's in charge now. To reinforce his message, his other hand is under her back and between two fingers and thumb he unclasps her bra. She can feel the hardness of his penis through his jeans, resting on her inner thigh. She is aroused and puts her hand on it and he puts his knees on either side of her before straightening his back away from her kisses. He tells her to unzip his cock and he pulls her brassiere off, following this by loosening the buckle of his belt. Being told what to do is perfect and she likes the roles they have adopted already. She knows that he isn't going to be soft on her. She unbuttons the solitary button and unzips his fly, the head of his penis visible over the top of his boxer shorts. Before she can put her hand around it and pull out the cock of her own volition, he takes her hand and does it for her, making it cup his testicles. He does not shave. Like this, he reaches forward again, this time resting his body on his elbows over her and puts his mouth back on hers with both his hands cupping her breasts. His cock reaches to the middle of her forearm. She likes the feel of his testicles and they are coarse and heavy, swollen large and firm. She squeezes them and he mutters in surprise. She slides her hands up and holds his penis, pulling his foreskin down from the tip and his teeth touch hers in his enjoyment.

She finds him teasing when he stands up again and kicks off his jeans and pulls off his boxer shorts. He leaves his watch on, as well as his socks. Without much warning, a thing that she likes, he puts his cock in front of her face, bending his knees. It looks bigger close up and feels big in her mouth, stretching her lips around it. She sucks it and it is tasteless, other than that of skin. He sighs words of encouragement and doesn't talk dirty, allowing her to move her neck and head back and forth without pushing his hips at all, for which she's grateful.

Slipping the cock out of her mouth it has to be doggy for his eyes were definitely on her ass when she got him the water. *Are you ready to fuck me?* she asks in a very inquisitive tone to which he replies that yes he is oh god he is, and so she rests her bent knees against the settee with her feet on the carpets and hands on the big, puffed cushions. The feel of his hands parting her ass and stroking both her asshole and vagina, using her wetness to moisten both, is nearly perfect. All too quickly she feels him using his penis in place of his hands, before he forcefully pushes it in her so deep as to make her feel his lower belly on her lower back.

Her mouth is covered by his left hand and he pulls her lower jaw down with two fingers dragging at her lower front teeth. This brings her head forward and he opens his mouth like a vampire on her shoulder, leaking spit down her collarbone and taking harder than pleasurable bites that leave the imprint of his teeth. His left hand smells like latex and she knows what this means. This is somewhat surprising to her. The right hand is being used to firmly squeeze her right breast and pinch her nipple. His thrusting pushes deep into her, hardly pulling out to cause any friction and pushing her bodily forward. The hand on her breast moves to her flat stomach to pull her in when he pushes at his hardest and she has the perfect pleasure of largesse bringing that tiny stab of pain. It feels amazing and the shadow of fear that his physical power brings, adds to the pain and accentuates her pleasure. She sucks at his fingers and he reaches along the back of her tongue, which is not good and she gags slightly. He realises this and although undoubtedly turned on by it, pulls his index and middle fingers out and cups her left breast with it, the new wetness on her nipple between the pinch that comes sending a shiver of excitement that is met by the orgasm from her vagina and mouth. Her little moan, sugar-sweet and high-pitched, tells him of her delight and he pulls out three or four inches each time to make a wet slapping sound.

It is good, so very good. He has taken his hands from her breasts and they are now on her hips and he spreads her asshole with his thumbs and she knows that he will ejaculate soon. She grinds against him, reducing the distance that he can pull out and theatrically moans to make him moan, much like a yawn in its contagious properties. It has the exact effect that she knew it would and he is pneumatically moving into her now and he groans and spasms with his hips and she can feel it inside her, even through the condom. The penis's throb of expulsion is her climax and equal in intensity to his. The yawn effect. They are both panting and he leans on her, not heavily, for a short while. His breathing is rapid and his heart is obvious on her back. She feels him pull out and stand up, so she slowly turns around, coquettishly smiling at him. He is already getting dressed and his boxer shorts are covering his genitals with his jeans being pulled up. If there was a record for speed dressing. What concerns her is his face, though; he looks pained and is deliberately avoiding looking at her. Without much more thought, compassion makes her say *What's wrong? Is everything okay?* He says that yes it's fine but is already leaving her behind on the settee. She notices the discarded condom.

At least he shuts the door on the way out. She laughs. Strange, but far from the strangest she has met. And of course, it has been well worth it. He was obviously satisfied with Dani, Davina laughs again. And she is happy with him, more so for his quick departure and therefore no need to pretend small talk or any other awkward post-coital dialogue. He is probably married and has a wife to answer to. She had not bothered to check for a ring and cannot remember feeling one.

Davina picks up the condom, coiled into a sleeping cobra and its venomous contents contained within, and heads to the toilet to flush it away. Walking past the clock mounted on the wall opposite the settee she sees that it is nearly half past eight. A definite quickie. It hits the water with a plop and she sits down to urinate before flushing. Her labia feel a little sore and sting in a more painful than pleasurable tingling, but this will go, she knows. Straight into the shower afterwards and she is out again before the oceanic sound of the flush has stopped. More towels are wrapped around her and they join those on the settee by being slung into the washing machine, in the kitchen. Some of her friends, Gemma and Diane for example, use a laundering agency to do theirs for them, which does nothing but compound the image of the bourgeoisie. Her mother had instilled a self-sufficient ethic in her and as much as possible, she did things for herself. That, surely, is the true face of feminism? Use of men for usury purposes and the lack of dependence or reliance upon them.

She hasn't eaten since the tapas (that was actually really nice) earlier at Barucelli's, but doesn't really feel hungry. One of the things she likes the most about her situation is that she has no set schedule in which to do things: no requirements or enforced routine. Already naked and feeling the fatigue that follows sex, she takes to her bedroom and burrows herself under the thin silk sheets. No insomniac she, sleep comes calling quickly.

A lovely warm dream broken by the vicious summer sun magnifying through the window. Her forehead is speckled with sweat and she knows she is not lying in for the heat. Not making the bed when she gets out, she stretches her legs by placing them in front and behind her on the bedroom carpets in a one-hundred and eighty degree line. She can feel her thighs ache, which she likes.

Showering shortly after, her labia sting with the hot water, a memory of the previous evening's activity. She dresses quickly after cleaning herself, a knee-length skirt and short-sleeved blouse today, and leaves the apartment.

It is a Thursday and yet, like most days, there is no one in the corridors leaving for work. This isn't because they don't work, but they perhaps leave later. To be honest, she doesn't know because she has kept very much to herself. Only on infrequent occasion has she crossed paths with her neighbours and they seem friendly enough. The outside world, the world impersonal to her, has never bothered her. They can think whatever they want, but prying eyes and ears and misconceptions are just as good unformed as when formed, and you don't proverbially defecate on your very own doorstep. And looking in the mirrored back of the elevator she finds no complaint. The make-up from yesterday, not faint, makes her look over thirty but today that's no problem. Beauty is a different thing at different ages and she in fact looks forward to the beauty of the forties. She lifts the vest top to inspect her flat, yellow-brown tanned stomach and smiles into her face as an afterthought. The lift judders a faint tremor to tell her to turn around, and the doors open and she exits.

Outside, the mid-morning sun is already cooking the pavements and heating the air with the smell of tarmac, wafting down the path to the security gate. She flashes a smile to the window of the porter's shed but sees that he is not there, instead smiling at the reflection of her smiling self. She giggles in realisation that she's vain, but this is no revelation. Vanity is not a bad thing as she doesn't see herself as better or worse than anyone else. In the cycle of vanity, arrogance, and modesty, she is a combination of vanity and modesty.

Only now, outside of the gate, does she select a playlist and put the music on randomly and place the earphones into her ears. She starts to jog, only slowly. The playlist that she has chosen is full of more raucous songs and she matches her pace to what she thinks is the around one-hundred BPM of the first song. She is already sweating for the warmth of her circulation and the sun, and wipes her forehead with the back of her right hand. She is going to work out her legs today, hence the jog to the gym and stretches this morning. At a zebra crossing she slows down and looks left and right and jogs across it, passing and glancing at a man standing at the other side.

$\leftarrow$
$\rightarrow$

She's back and bouncier than ever, what with her jogging in her tight-fit grey vest. Good morning, his smile says, but she pays him no attention. It will be one hell of a shame if she is added to the casualty list of musical calamities, run over to the detriment of hot-blooded libido worldwide. He wonders where she's heading and is pretty certain it's the gym: she's not a jogger per se, as she was walking a couple of days ago, and she carries no bag to be heading to work (unless, don't exclude, she's an instructor or trainer), and she seems dressed in the right attire. He discounts her being an instructor on the basis that she obviously doesn't routinise her morning journey and is most probably not bound by time. If she is he'll definitely sign up.

Work has the same tedium through the same routines. They had been a bit of fun when he'd started four years ago. The old bastards are resolute in their ways as to diminish all creativity on his part and the politics of the whole thing is one of those unfunny jokes because he is stuck inside it. Slipping a cigarette in his mouth he focuses back on blondie's body and imagines her working out and the plaintive faces of the oppressors, all those jealous balding egos, disappear down a valley of cleavage and he smiles at the image for both reasons. He inhales a long breath of grey-white ethereal nectar and chuckles to watch its swirling patterns. He knows their problem and it is the problem of the dinosaurs: so lost in their ways as to soon be extinct. The world moves on and unless they adapt to its changes and learn respect for their younger colleagues then they will stagnate and wither into the omniscient fucks they want to be, only the complete knowledge they always suspected they had is instead the misery of a solitary queue for death. He is getting irate and the cigarette is rapidly approaching the butt. Direction to think. He needs a direction to think now the distraction of breasts has gone. He finds it and he's there. He never smokes two cigarettes together because if the first didn't work why waste a second?

The email service on FAFAF is always a positive distraction and he thinks of whether she'll look like the middle-aged, trim-bodied brunette who's on the other side of the road, walking briskly in a very business-like way. Something about those pencil skirts does it for him. He checks out her wide hips and she glances across.

←
→

Reminds her of Drew when they first met, maybe a little older. Tall, suited and flicking the dog-end on the road, like she used to scold him over when they were flirting at uni. Last night's flirting was the usual bouquet and apology and ownership of the remote for the evening work's do. She loves the cooking programmes with the man from Australia, especially when he criticises them for the obvious mistakes they make. Last night, a girl from the North had made the obvious mistake with meringue. She can't believe people sometimes: why do they even bother going on them? If she went on she'd have a good chance but some of them are really good so who knows? Imagine her on the telly.

She dropped the twins off at the infant school a bit earlier than usual, but Lydia was there and the other girls whose names she doesn't know, and she said it was fine. She's a good girl, a bit younger than her, and her daughter is the same age as the twins. Lydia is seeing the caretaker and they seem to be getting on well, at least that's what she hears. He's a big Polish chap who whistles when he trims the hedgerows and he is hot. Muscly arms, too. The twins think he's a super-hero character from one of the cartoons that they watch before tea and Drew encourages this idea with them. He's brilliant with them. Drew picks them up around lunchtime. He'd wrangled it with his boss to let him work from home in the afternoons so he is out of the house earlier even than her and puts the children to sleep for a siesta of sorts after he picks them up. They are always up to watch the children's programmes though, just before she serves their tea.

Her house is on the left, a terraced four bedroom that they had inherited from Drew's grandmother when she'd passed away nearly a decade ago. It always makes her smug to know she owns over a half-million pounds' worth of property, or rather half of that, as it's a joint bequest. He is her one, anyway, so thoughts of divorce are out of question and seem horrid. She'll never be one to join that club.

She dressed for work earlier and has returned to collect the car keys. The school is a ten minute walk with the twins and five without, laziness never being part of her ethos. She is a constant ten with gymnast's thighs and only the smallest wobble of the stomach, although it has swollen of late. She does not overtly exercise, but she eats balanced and healthily and walks instead of drives as much as possible. The hospital is five miles away and Doctor Travers (please, call me Simon, no honorific) called her on her mobile surreptitiously with the rendezvous time, deliberately clear of her working schedule, exactly as she'd told him. Doctor Travers, Simon – even at their stage of the relationship she found it hard not to refer to his title – is only thirty or so and has a mild way about him but with the most intense eyes. She imagines he could work his way into any woman's heart. If Drew found out about the calls he would go spare, and he's not even the jealous type. She dreads to think what will happen if he finds out.

She is nervous and she can feel her hand shake when she unlocks the car. They have two, of course, and hers still requires the key to be put in the door. She doesn't mind about this and doesn't care much for cars anyway. Drew can tell her all about them and their engines, bless him. For all of his intelligence and lovely speaking, he is a typically boyish man beneath it all, his car a symbol of this.

In the car, she puts on the radio and on the only station she listens to. Well, this isn't quite true, but it's the most played of hers. It's an old classics as they call it, which isn't really fair because they are songs from her teenage years which are only just over two decades past. Old these days. Forty is the new twenty five, right? The song is midway already when the car starts and she is humming shaky notes to it, resisting the urge to actually sing. Her voice is good and she used to sing in the school talent shows. That is itself odd now, for the moguls on the telly have only capitalised on what schools have done for years. Genius is cheap these days. Drew compliments her on her singing when she's in the shower, usually before he joins her and holds her from behind, cleaning her shoulders. He is such a sweetheart.

The sun has been baking the car and the warmth is heavy. Electric windows are a godsend. There is only the breeze from her speed though and she never drives fast. Five below the speed limit at best. Drew could drive like a daemon and she often berates him for it, especially when the twins put their hands on their imaginary steering wheels on their booster seats.

The anxiety of the meeting feels like guilt. She is guilty, she realises.

The next song is a complete classic that her friends had once done karaoke to when she was not yet eighteen and in a bar in town: reckless, as teenagers, and memories to cherish forever. That night had made the song almost smell of vodka and vomit and she giggles with more comfort than before the song started. The group's combined voice is a synthesised sound and the disco beat is the infectious drum pattern of the era. She really doesn't feel any different from then, even two babies later and the years at the reception desk. Every word is known and she cannot help but sing, only quietly, along with it, tapping the steering wheel with the base of her hand.

Her heart is fluttering with the butterflies that she gets in these situations. Situations that merit their arrival include any that bring her worry, happiness, fear, jealousy, panic, arousal, doubt, nervousness, and excitement. She is not any of these things, rather a cocktail of many. When in school and still playing with dolls, a vivid memory, she can remember saying how she'd marry a doctor. Doctor Travers (Simon) has been her secret for the last four and half months and he is the reason for these feelings. She can remember the first time he placed his hand on her breasts and the feeling of erotic shame that had come with it. Hands off Drew's property, morbidly enough, had come to mind. On the subsequent occasions it was still there but intensified. She can hardly look at him in his deep, shocking-blue eyes when he touches her and not think of Drew. Like on the telly, maybe she should get a shrink. Imagine that, her on a leather couch or chaise longue and answering questions like an affluent woman who merely wants to indulge her sordid concealments for self-gratification whilst someone else vicariously gets off on it. That's what Drew had said, or something like it in his wordy way, after an episode of some American soap opera where all the couples were rich and had problems that weren't problems. Realism, he'd say, is here and now and we shouldn't model what we do on the constructions of the television world. He can be persuasive.

The songs keep coming and the music moves her to sing at regular speaking volume, oblivious to anyone who may look in on her but not exaggerating any facial expressions or head movements. The twins are the funniest when they pick up the cardboard toilet-paper tubes and pretend to be pop stars. They have a little old-man knee-bending move they do in an epileptic way, smiles plastered wide over their faces and their eyes widening as far as they can go. Their singing is more of a lengthy chuckle and gasp for breath from laughing, than any sensical words or tune.

School children are on the path and crossing the road nonchalantly, attired in the trendy manner of shortened ties and untucked shirts. Wasn't it long ties that were cool and garish, bright socks on show? She can't remember, but finds it amusing anyway. Fashion and its cyclical motion. She stops at a zebra crossing to let a slow stream of children across, some of whom are over six feet tall. She wonders how tall her boys will grow. Drew is five-eleven but she knows that this has little to no bearing on the size and height of her children. Not necessarily. A gap in the line allows her to go again, just before the frustrated cars behind her start to beep, no doubt.

The presenter of the show has just talked over the repetitive, faded part of the end of the song, mentioning the rise in online sales of the record recently due to the newly announced reunion tour. That's the fifth band from the same era coming back over the space of a year, he tells her. Nostalgia is unbeatable right now and perhaps we're all living in the past, us new oldies. Or, he adds, maybe the newbies are just not cutting that mustard the way they used to in the good old days. She once knew where that saying had come from, but can't remember now. Luckily, the presenter stops just before she goes to change the station and her absolute favourite comes on. Well, it's one of them at least, and she sings her loudest yet. The song takes her thoughts to a different place.

At the entrance to the hospital she turns the presenter off over the fade out and doesn't look at the signs that apparently help to navigate the network of roads. The hospital grounds are massive but she's been here many times now. Twice in the last month. What it is going to be like today she can't tell but can predict with the usual optimism she places upon the clandestine. The expectation brings adrenaline and is it her or are her hands visibly shaking? Focused on her hands she wills them to stillness and she regulates her breathing in the manner taught to her by the television. Slow breath in and breathe out quickly, doing neither for three seconds and resuming the pattern towards calm. When she finds a parking space in the usual, for some reason emptier, car park, she opens the door and steps out, leaning on the car's roof as support and repeating the calming technique. It works. She slams the door, meaning only to push it, and turns the key in the lock.

Looking around, the busy nature of the never-sleeping hospital is obvious, but there aren't any pedestrians on foot walking across the car park. She doesn't know why, modern impulse she supposes, but she checks her phone for messages. It's his rule that they don't text and she sees complete sense in this. And there's no way Drew can stumble upon any messages following the online trail. She clears her call logs every time they speak on the phone. Paranoia, she knows, is only a person's own creation. The phone's screen tells her it is 08:23.

She's ready to walk now and she's purposeful and her intentions are fixed. Conscious of her hips swinging and her breasts (small though they are) moving behind the laced curtains of her bra, she strides as lady-like as she can, for she is a lady, a trophy of everything womanly in womankind, and she is proud. Men might still think of woman's role as a mother and a domesticised creature and a thing to be possessively protective of and that doesn't bother her at all, because it's not true and more fool them.

Through the automatically sliding doors and directly ahead is a set of not-automatic double doors and she pushes the left open. Coming up the stairs from the left, just as she is about to head up the stairs on the right towards Doctor Simon Travers and obstet, is a girl with distress evident on her face.

←
→

So hollow and so numb and poetry is so fucking ridiculous.

He'd loved it, of course, but now the weight of words read but never felt are suddenly felt and regretfully known to be true. God how she fucking hates them. In a way, she hates him too, but that's wrong and she can't feel like that but then it's unfair and confusing and fuck.

An indelible image is beneath her lids and he's there lying supine on the slab and he is a slab and the grey pallor of his skin and purpled impact marks are a morbid, dull kaleidoscope of the macabre. What makes it more so is the unblemished state of the face, given away to death only by the lifeless colouration of the once rosy cheeks. As much as smells can linger eternally, the clinical cleanliness of bleach and rubber will remain forever, too. She is sure of it.

She is outside of the automatic doors and has already lit up a menthol. The taste of something not quite there and conjured by the morbidity of the situation needs to be overpowered, but the cigarette makes her feel sick and instead of retching she chokes staccato sobs, shuddering and shaking in time to the sounds.

Every blink is an afterimage and she throws the cigarette on the floor. Fuck the law and slap her a fine. See if she cares. She is angry, definitely angry, and at what exactly is the mystery. She hates him for doing it and herself for feeling it and her mum for her role in it all. She hates the prick on the phone and the mortuary assistant and the fat bitch that looked at her on the stairs. He was just lying there, looking frostbitten for the strange monotone of colour and speckled blue-black-purples with rings of yellow. Less than twelve hours they said, dredged fresh for want of another word that they hadn't used.

Reasons are and are not there and she is not stupid. She does not try to piece together the series of events, although they seem obvious, and she does not try to think of why it happened, although those reasons seem equally obvious.

These things are witnessed with perverted, voyeuristic pleasure on the television where people are invited into the morgues to watch dissections and the identification process and what a bunch of fucking animals to do that. Hypocrite she, she thinks. Whoever expects the call when still in bed after a regular night in catching up on the soaps? She'd spent the day with friends and had watched the three recorded episodes back to back, as a result having a later-than-usual night. Another hour and she would have got up to do her make-up, ready for work.

But no.

For some reason the poetry he had been reading keeps entering her thoughts and the dark aspects to them seem opaque now. He dead after his obsession with it and his nose constantly buried in the elegiac writings of centuries-old saddos; there seemed to be the same saturnine poetry about it.

Conscious that no one is coming to blanket her sadness with an unwanted arm, she looks to her sides and sees that she has had an audience, heads shifting direction as she looks up. She is grateful for their lack of interference, but equally directing her animosity towards them. Why the fuck doesn't anyone comfort a girl so obviously distraught? And another question comes immediately that softens her anger and replaces it with what she knows is the natural, probably more appropriate, sadness: how the fuck is she going to tell her sister? To her credit, she does not feel weak or burdened by the responsibility that it is her duty to break the news. She does, however, feel weak for being angry at a man whom she has loved, and this anger centres itself on her. Maybe she could have done more. There must have been ways to prevent this from happening. When was the last time she saw him – and say it, bitch – alive?

Perhaps it is her fault. It is her fault. She decides to do it in the car and makes her way to where she parked. It's her second car. The first one was a birthday present that he had bought for her. Fuck.

In the car, she unlocks her phone. It has been idly and subconsciously in her hand for the last five minutes. She types a message that reads less dramatically than it could have, not wanting to worry her sister or create in her that horrible feeling of something impending.

> Hi jo, I've got some
> big news that I need
> to tell you. Not the
> best but you need to
> know. Come round
> mine after work.

Knowing her sister, she won't text back and will turn up with a bottle of wine assuming there's a need for a drink in a girlish capacity. It'll be white wine, as well. She starts the engine and reverses out of the space. She does not know if she'll say it outright or if she will gradually reveal it. A glass of wine might be the right idea. Her sister will have lemonade with it, obviously. There is an almost smile for the flash memory of their great debate as to what makes a genuine spritzer, but it is gone in an instant and leaves no humour. Straight out: fuck the wait. That's the only way. They'll cry and hug and it'll be messy, but then at least it won't be prolonged or repressed.

A car in front of her has not started to drive past the green light and she pushes down the horn until they start to move. Her patience is brittle and close to shattering. She swears under her breath, slagging off the system that allows such people to drive. She pulls out a menthol cigarette from the left pocket of her jeans and pulls the top of the carton with her teeth. In the same manner, she slips one of them between her lips and tosses the packet on the passenger seat. She uses the lighter that she keeps behind the gear stick and presses the button to open the window. There's no wind for the speed she's driving, stuck behind a slow-moving car, but she likes the heat. She misses the passenger seat when she throws her lighter at it.

He'd liked his cars. He had at times treated her like a stereotypical boy, what with the nature of their relationship, and he would recite the specifications of engines and explain the models that predated the ones pointed out. Her knowledge of cylinders and spark plugs and cooling systems is entirely down to him, and the more practical side to maintaining a healthy engine and not getting ripped off by the thievery of the garage is confidently understood. Not that she has ever needed that, not with the garage at which she gets the car serviced; the owner is one of his old school friends. More people to pass the news on before the grapevine takes over and extends its branches to speed up the process. How many times will she have to tell it, explain it, relive it?

And back to the fucking poetry. Every piece an elegiac mnemonic of death, stamped over his moments until this. She hates it so much that she wishes as true as she knows anything that all poetry be burned. There is no place for sadness in art, just as there is no art to be found in sadness. The realism captured in those simple lines and words, those conjurers of bleak images, the power over the depression-corrupted mind: these things are no tonic to any mind. Not when of sound mind or when of darkness. She recalls the pining. He would wallow in the writing and agree with whatever poet he would read, yet only poets whose work was of sadness and loss.

She is finally on the motorway and she pushes her foot down and shifts gear. Once. Twice. She changes lane and accelerates faster until she is just over one hundred miles an hour. The speed is a calming influence on her and demands her focus. She has never been one to drive slowly but has always adhered to the law and its limits before. The window is still open and the hurried whoosh of the air is loud to her ears and takes over her head, pushing out the cycle of thoughts that has taken residence over the last two and a half hours. She slows intermittently, caught behind an eighty before they pass to the middle. Once, she is what seems only inches from the car in front before it hastily moves to its left. She is focused on nothing and everything simultaneously. She swerves her car without indicating and is from the outside to the inside in two seconds, slowing down as she takes the exit. A horn can be heard from behind her and she puts her right hand out of the window, middle finger extended, chucking the butt of her cigarette out at the same time. The lights at the end of the slip road are red and she keeps her hand out, goading the horn-blower to some sort of retaliation. The lights go green and there is no car in front of her. She puts her hand back on the steering wheel and presses the window back up. She drives slowly away, holding the cars behind her in a trail of congesting traffic and frenetic horns. A few yells can be heard too, as they overtake her.

Problems, it seems, are what makes the world what it is. Those stupid fucks are probably what they believe to be angry because they have been slowed down for thirty seconds of their day. It's all gradable, of course. Their response has tempered her anger, replacing it with a mischievous malice. She wants to piss them off and siphon her suffering onto them. She has never in her life felt this angry. She has lost people before, but the manner of the death has been different. Unjust, but different. Not even six months ago had she felt such hatred.

She rang work after the call and Tara, her manager and friend, accepted without any questions the statement that something massive had come up. Work. Another thing that so frustrates everyone she knows – well, not quite everyone – bringing out the moaning diatribes against time and money. One of the least important parts of life to lose life to. Today, she is not going to work. She knows that the distraction would be good but also that her temper and body are not up to the task of managing idiocy. Her self-control is currently compromised.

She is pulling up the lane at the back of a row of terraced houses, driving sensibly and breathing slowly. She stops outside a green painted garage, turns off the ignition, and gets out. The little metal fence to the side of the garage door is white. It is painted white but the peeling reveals a rust-coppered silver. She lifts the latch from the metal catch that juts out of the stone beam on the left and lets it swing behind her as she walks down the garden path to the backdoor of her house. It is a regular, pebble-dashed walls, ex-council, terraced house. The mortgage was cheap and the family help made it cheaper and at her age she is a proud homeowner. The word family resonates painfully.

Entering the house, priority is shifted and her role in being the world's most shit-upon person has stopped. Her news is old news, news that a million people everywhere else are being told as each second turns to a minute turns to an hour, the news that will become the harbinger of sorrow for her sister in the hours to come.

Pull yourself together she thinks, before panic, the opposite of those late-to-come words, joins the fray. There, on her slender shoulders, really does wait the weight of the world.

She has eight long hours until her sister will be there after work. Eight long hours to stew and plan countless times how she would deliver the words. Eight long hours for two words. There are a million phone calls to make but she does not want to make them. Nothing changes if she makes them anyway; the facts remain the same.

A complete whim leads her to walk up the stairs and she goes straight into her bedroom where the curtains are still pulled closed and the sheets are rumpled. She is fully clothed and she curls up into a ball with the covers pulled over her shoulders and clenched in her fist and she cries. Sleep is far away but it is what she wants: the sweet oblivion of unconsciousness and the freedom from thought. To be back in the world before waking this morning, comfortable in bed and enough in life, trivia-determined emotions back on track, sleep-encrusted eyes and the desire for more, is all that is wanted. What is too much to ask? An inactive and resting body but not a mind, she turns thoughts over and over, a renewed cycle of fear and sadness and shame, and of tangents of potentials and glimpses of positives that disappear, sometimes resurfacing to be caught and sometimes resurfacing to disappear yet again. Questions posed from a spectre and from an imagined sister and from a mirrored self argue inside her and she whispers aloud, knowing that talking to one's self is madness. Audible whines as if from stomach cramps come from her mouth and sobs intermingle to play the tune of grief and self-pity. She is on her back and on her side and on her belly and with the duvet pulled over her head or cast aside or tucked between her legs. She wants tiredness, but tiredness does not want her – a cruel relationship of desire and reality.

It is a stupid fucking idea and she can take no more. She cannot detach herself from her mind by giving it nothing to focus on.

In the living room, she turns on the television and there are the usual mid-morning housewives' and students' programmes on. The black screen fades grey into a chat show. A man paces between a warring couple who each claim the other is sleeping with somebody else and the inanity of it enthrals her and occupies her enough to sit down. The carrot-crunching couple resolve their issue by promising a baby will be symbolic of their love and the audience lap it up in a surreally violent applause. The show comes to an end with a smug-faced presenter lauding his own talents as a psychologist, wishing the audience goodbye and the viewers at home a promise of more riveting TV. Another channel shows a day working at a nursing home and the sight of elderly people is wrong and off-putting so she switches to one of the many music channels. The song is one that's on the radio all the time. It has been for the last three weeks and at first it had sounded good. It had died from overplay over a week ago and now it irritates rather than anything else. Another change and an old game show from ten years ago is on, the basis of which focuses on dividing the contestants to make them play against each other to their own detriment. It is absorbing.

Time goes slowly and it is midday when she wakes back from her television voyage. It has served its purpose well and she is much calmer. Routine has made her calm and, not for hunger, she gets a slice of chocolate cake from the fridge and pokes it into crumbling pieces with a fork. She scoops these up as a spoon and eats them in front of the television. The news is on and she turns it off by using the remote, preferring to switch her laptop on instead of watching the world and its catastrophes.

Endless uploading anything and everything enables her to

lose herself in videos, pictures, blogs and words. Cute animals and children are paraded as equals, intentions of gaining warm messages accomplished. A helpless man falls flat on his face followed by a series of other unfortunates to varying degrees of pain and humiliation.

Time ticks by.

New films flaunt their best parts in quick montages and inform her when they are out and that one actually looks like it's worth going to the pictures to see. Links to competitions and dieting secrets are popping up and leading her to a free nugget of priceless common sense or impossibility, before telling her the full package of even better chances or miracles is a steal at whatever prices they are. Meet new singles in a million fucking names are around every click and turn, which leads her to her favourite, FAFAF. There are twenty-seven messages waiting for a reply. She clicks on the little envelope icon and smiles at the opening lines that are scanned. Nearly every person on the site is after one thing, as would be expected, but the brazen nature of the hotblood lacks any kind of subtlety. The second word of the first message is cock and the sender, it is kind to inform her, has never sent her a message before. This happens a lot and it is always amusing. Some people, she is sure, get offended by it. Get off the site if it's so fucking offensive. Her pun usually makes her giggle but not today. Other messages that she has include a few longish correspondences with potential dates alongside the majority of 'Babe-you-are-stunning' and another overtly obscene, yet slightly arousing and straight-to-the-point, 'let's fuck' message. She replies to the three men in whom she has interest and they are pretty hot. One of them says he is a trainer and by the pictures of him in front of the mirror, there is no reason to dispute this. The other two are business-yuppie types who are young and into what they think is a lot of money. They're handsome though, if a little bit boring in their approach. She messages them back and includes an inviting line in each, a separation technique to see who is strong enough to ask her out for a drink or food or back to theirs. If they falter here then they miss out and she wastes no more time. You either want her or you don't. It's much the same with the first few messages from a man who wants to arrange a date by phone. During the evenings and nights in the nightclubs and bars, she and her friends get approached countless times. Numbers inevitably get collected and promises are made, but when the 'I'll call you' turns into a text-typed message she loses interest; man up and talk to her or fuck off and think of her.

After this she makes the mistake of hitting the news. Her temporary reprieve is over and the first story is of genocide in the Middle East. The second is of a toddler who was run over, by accident, by his own father. The third is of representations of death in artwork, with a vaguely familiar television critic staring morosely next to the link to the programme. It is unavoidable, this presence of death, and as it had not escaped her but merely been buried further inside her, it resumes its dominion. She had been lying to herself by carrying on with this pretence of normality. He is in every aspect of the house and in every word she reads, memories of him and the feel of him. The stubborn image of his prone blanched body. And oddly, his smile. He had a full mouth, her mum said, and when he'd smile it was large and spread all across his face. For that, it was never sinister. Not until it was forced upon his features in broken bones in his death. She was outraged and asked if they found it funny in a sickening way, toying with the dead as a pastime to relieve the boredom and the inherently depressing shape of the job. They had genuinely looked upset at the suggestion. It was clear that they were professional and had some weird respect for the dead. Fuck-off back to Egypt with your canopics and mummies. Freaks. But that smile that was once such an honest image of love is now so tainted as to never be positive again. In all likelihood she will only see him once more, too. This is the last state that will be attached to every memory, every reminiscence, every reference to him.

She breaks off for a very short while to wonder how there is so much fluid behind her eyes and whether her eyes will shrivel up, a hark back to the wild imagination of her and her sister as children: telling her sister that if she didn't stop crying after she pushed her over, her eyes would turn into the dried plums their gran would always make them eat when they visited on Sundays.

It is only four o'clock on a day hitting the high twenties. She switches off the laptop by pressing the shutdown button. In her state, a state where it seems she believes the television is based on us and not us on it, she does what she has seen them do so many times and opens a bottle of wine from the fridge. The top is a screw-top and she twists it off and does not bother with a glass. A quarter of the bottle is sunk in the first tilt and she stops only to acknowledge the arrival of the shock of cold. She gasps a response to the cold in her forehead and drinks another rough quarter. The effects come instantly. Magnification of every detail makes everything seem worse than it is but also the heightened emotion is the emotion attached to her thoughts, all of which are painful and sombre. Her mood worsens and she finishes the bottle with a back-of-the-throat burp that changes into a hiccough. Studying the bottle and drunkenly proud of her achievement, she gently places it under the sink and next to the evidence of the last weekend's nights with her friends.

And where are her friends? No one has reached out to console her and comfort her. She has been there for all of them when they have split up from their partners or when their pets have died or when their grandfolks have been admitted to hospital. Everyone is so self-centred, so egocentric, so fucking obsessed with themselves to give a damn about anything else or anyone else. Even her friends. After everything they have been through together and the times growing up and...

A tirade is born and put to early death as she realises the reason why they have not been in touch with their words and embraces of warm consolation. The fridge door is open again in synchronicity with her tear ducts. There are no sobs and the water on her cheeks is faint, a motion of her eyes that is against her will. Genuine sadness. There are six bottles of white wine in her fridge and three of rosé. She selects another white. This time she decides upon a glass and speaks aloud *Get a grip on yourself* and clumsily opens the cupboard mounted on the wall, making it slam shut before succeeding in opening it and getting herself a glass. In her right hand, the wine glass: in her left, the bottle. She slips and as well as pouring wine into a puddle on the kitchen table, she cracks the glass without shattering it. She is too drunk on grief to care. She leaves a towel over it and sways up the stairs to the bathroom where she opens the bathtaps on full and pulls the lever for the plug. The soap she adds to the basin is a toffee-brown and smells of rose, forming bubbles as the water splashes against it. She stumbles as she slips off her clothes, getting her right ankle caught in her jeans and tugging to extricate her foot. She bangs her knee against the side of the enamelled bath as she pulls the foot free and it feels both horrible and good, gaining a yelp of surprise and pain as a welcome distraction of respite. It feels as if there is a bruise there already but she looks and sees that there is not. Because it seems right she presses the wine glass against her knee but it hurts less and she doesn't like it. She drinks some of its contents instead and puts it on the fold-out, slatted table, resting the circular bottom over two of the slats. The water is coming quickly from the taps and the bath is half-filled with piping hot water. She puts her arm into the basin, up to her elbow, and brings it back out with a *Fuck*. It is stinging and acts as a direction for her to turn the hot tap off and place her hand under the cold tap. The intermingled heat and coldness sober her.

God it hurts. Strangely, it is pleasing too. She is tempted to get straight into the water but knows that her feet will feel it the most and will result in her jumping out. For some reason, one that she can explain with no conviction, she wants to do it. What she wants and what is bearable are two different things, though. Instead, she absent-mindedly drinks the rest of the wine. The bath can run on its own as she wants another glass. Why didn't she just bring the bottle up? On the way down the stairs, she can feel the pain in her knee each time she puts her weight on a step. Her face winces in unison. It's like being a geriatric. She doesn't know whether she should pick up another bottle, alongside the half-empty one, or just the half-empty. The amusing idea that she can squeeze the towel out like a sponge and refill her glass makes her smile, but her glass is still in the bathroom. She brings the half-empty bottle with her and steadily walks back to the bottom of the stairs. She sees the silhouetted figure through the translucent leaf-patterns of the front door's glass at the same time she hears the knock, and it only just makes her jump, startled.

As she is naked and her clothes are upstairs, she is suddenly made self-conscious and she runs up the stairs with fast little steps. The person at the door is not her sister as it's too early and the shape is definitely that of a man. A tall man. *One minute.* She deposits the wine next to the bath on the rack and takes the dressing-gown that is hung at the back of the bathroom door and ties it around her waist, ruffling the heavy-rimmed neck to cover her collarbone and the area beneath. She wipes her eyes and looks at her face in the mirror, adjusting the faintest of black smears with the third finger of each hand. She doesn't really care what she looks like at the moment; it's a habit, that's all. Slowly now, she walks down the stairs and feels the same dull throb in her knee as she did a few minutes ago. Something pleasant still comes with each step, unaccountable but for her loose ideas. She is at the bottom of the stairs in front of the door and she unlatches the catch that is attached to the chain, pulling the door inwards and open. She realises that she needs to urinate. There is a tall, acned late-teen standing with an awkward smile in front of her.

→

←

A delivery for you, Miss. Damn she is hot in her fluffy white bathrobe. *You don't need to sign or anything.* The box is very big but it weighs next to nothing. Probably a sex-toy or something, disguised as something else through a too-big box. She looks at him in a strange way, as if scrutinising him. Maybe she's thinking of inviting him in, a horny housewife from the telly ready to fuck him behind her limp husband's dick. She doesn't have very big tits, though. But he would regardless.

↓↑

Thanks. Now fuck off.

↑↓

No problem. Is there anything else he can help her with, like maybe his cock? He smiles his best Hollywood and tries for a spark in his eyes. She closes the door. He walks down to the little piece of shit tin-can van that he's been driving since last year.

He is happy enough with his job but can't say he likes or enjoys it. The hours available are open to flexibility and more often than not he gets the dayshifts, which are always preferable. He is unlucky if he pulls one night a fortnight. The lady's house is the last of his shift and he is on the way back to drop off the van and pick up his car. A traditional nine-to-five.

There really isn't a less cool heap-of-shit on the roads. If he'd pulled up at the girl's house with a million-pound car or summat then she'd definitely have been interested in a little bed-springing. Although, for her hotness and the lack of clothes, she had smelled funny. It was like a sour bad breath or something. He puts the ignition on, starting the car on the third turn. The more he thinks about it he knows that she is probably a cheap dirty baby-mummy, scrounging for her screaming kids and doing nothing. Agreed: he wouldn't have touched her with a stolen cock. She is down the scale. He's glad she had resisted his stupid and generous flattery. He would have without a doubt caught something from her, if not that thing that was like really bad breath or rotting gums, then a fucking STI.

He pulls straight out into the road after looking in the rear-view mirror. The van is too hot for him and it has been heating up in the sun all day. The old vehicle has no air-conditioning system to cool him down. His forehead is forming a thin film of sweat that will continue to grow and then drip down the sides of his face. The windows are open, but he can't drive at any real pace as the school-commuters and people leaving work are heading back home and the roads are filled with cars, vans and buses. He doesn't like the black taste of the air, but any breeze that blows through is better than none in his mind.

He wipes the sides of his face and his forehead and then dries his hand on the thigh of his trouser leg. The booming bass from a car and the heavy rattle of doors is heard from somewhere in the queue that he is in. Other radio sound and music add to the orchestra of car engines.

It is really irritating when people do that. He likes music but he doesn't go around blaring his CDs out as loud as possible. And door rattling? Surely that's a sign that it's too loud for their shitty can? It's not just because the CD player in the van is broken either, or maybe it is, but they're still irritating. Two years ago, when he had passed his test the day after his twentieth birthday (first time, natch), he had blasted some good ole rock'n'roll as loud as he could. What with it having been saved from the scrapyard, the doors rattled too. A bit hypocritical there mate, but he was a kid and the joys of driving were at their strongest. He still likes driving. It's just never the same as the first time you sit behind the wheel and drive without anyone staring at your every move. The man he'd had, had had a way of speaking that seemed to come only from his nose when he corrected a bad manoeuvre. One second, normal-speaking voice, whilst the next, oops, he had made a mistake, and then nungh-nungh-nungh. Nasal: that's what it's called. Like a temporary cold. Fair play to the four-eyed noseman, though; he passed him first go with a handful of minors.

The depot isn't far away from his last stop and all he has to do is park it up, lock it, and then sign out. He used to collect his jobs for tomorrow when he finished, but after a policy change that benefits management, he and every other courier find out their deliveries in the morning when they come in. His car is parked at work. He thinks about the cars that he will buy when he wins the lottery and every one of them is expensive and what he calls a fanny-magnet.

Fast. Très expensive. An engine like a jet engine. Leather interior. These contribute to making the magnet what it is. He knows he's not ugly and has a way with the ladies, but money on display has the same desired effect. Money is what they all want. It doesn't really matter what he looks like. He could be the best-looking man on the planet and poor, and then no chick would glance at him. At least not for long. He had the gift of the gab, too. He does not want a girlfriend, switched on to the fact that they're demanding and change their minds all of the time. He has never wanted one really, but he does like their company. They only have one use for men anyway, and that's for their cocks.

In a strange and colourful blend of filth and romantic notions, these thoughts pass through him as he enters the grounds of the logistics company, the mechanised arm at the entrance sensing the built-in scanning-unit on the van and automatically lifting. He parks up with a smile at the lewd act he has put the woman from his last job in. He finds the children crying in the backroom strange and snaps out of the reverie, disgusted and aroused, equally. He locks the van, ritualistically cursing the fucking lock, and walks through an open door in the side of a large, windowless, grey, steel warehouse. He heads up a steel staircase and into a small office with the rotas pasted on the rear wall. An empty desk is beneath it, a large computer monitor atop the desk. He looks at his watch on his left wrist and writes 5:02 next to his clocking-in time of 8:50. Matt will not get twelve minutes' overtime.

↓↑

How's it going, Matt? Work seems quiet to him today. Matt's the first person that he's seen since parking up. He wonders where everyone is. *Where is everyone?*

Apparel

↑↓

He turns around and sees it's Andy. *Alright mate?* Andy's all right. They talk about the football a bit and they've always got on at the staff dos. *I don't know. I've just got in.*

↓↑

How's work today? He goes to the board and signs in his time as 17:00.

↑↓

Was good thanks. Some right babes who're well up for it, too. He gives him a wink and grins at him. *You watch the game last night?*

↓↑

He played the new computer game last night. *Yeah. Good goal by Holbrook.* He had read it on the internet before he came. He can't stand football. Being separated from Athene, especially now her skill points and strength were pretty high and the interactivity was getting better as they progress together, there can't be anything worse than watching grown men act like kids kicking a football. Surely? *And a win's a win, eh?*

↑↓

Too right. Yeah. Well have a good one mate. He's a good bloke, he is. Nice trainers, too. Pretty damned expensive.

←

→

He looks at Matt's back as he leaves and shakes his head, deliberate and genuinely disbelieving. The kid is the least macho person he's ever met, covered in acne that resembled a butterfly's wings in a spotty dot-to-dot (Jones's words), gangly and gawky, and his breath tells the tale of his coffee-induced halitosis. He is a smug bastard for all this, and can talk a good everything, too. Matt doesn't really seem like a bad kid, and so he feels a bit two-faced for thinking this, but there's something creepy about him. A sinister aspect to him. And for his constant bullshit he is just annoying. Be yourself, man. Not to say planning on killing someone ain't sinister.

Andrew walks out of the office slowly, taking his time to run the clock as he hasn't seen any of the dickheads around. The dickheads consist of John, Will, and Jones, who each comprise the management tier directly above Andrew and Matt and the others, but sit directly below the difference in wage that 'real' management earn. They are good people, but they still have a remit to carry out. The problems come from the top and filter down to the bottom, so whatever aggro he receives is half of what the assholes get. His job is secure. Stealing is commonplace and jokingly cast around as a prerequisite for the job. The job itself is referred to as the unsackable, due to the amount of times people have been caught and kept on.

At the bottom of the stairs is the yellow-chevroned gangway that leads to the double doors that harbour the conveyers and the reason for his earnings. Well, one of them. Since the big score he hasn't been out with any more product – he's got the plan to work out. Funny, really, how he uses the lingo from the box. It's like it's taboo or something to actually call it what it is. A spade's a spade and a drug's a drug. You're a dumb fucker for doing them, either way. Three workers are already at the belts, probably having copped the twelve-eights. Probably Polish. They're skinny, surly types, and he's seen them a few times and hasn't ever had a problem. They're as lazy as anyone else and as committed to working shit jobs much the same. He can't work out why people seem so inherently or easily racist towards them for being the exact same. Why hate someone just because they speak a different language? Black people are the same, too. People seem to hate them for no reason other than they think they should. If any race has a reason to hate another, surely black people to white people for the years of abuse and ownership. One of the Polish nods to him.

Andrew steps behind conveyer three, directed by the rota. He will be sorting parcels by the labels stuck on their sides. The conveyer slowly brings them down in a random collection, at times all bunched up and at others, only one in ten minutes. He is required to send fragiles through one plastic-curtained door whilst the others, internal and external, go into two separate chutes whose small incline is deemed not deep enough to damage the contents of the boxes and packages. The first items are at the sorting station and he puts all three into the external chute, where in turn they will be shipped to various locations by the drivers. Mainly post offices.

The other week was a good one. A container with hundreds of the latest super phone had been sent to their depot. Cranky, a workmate and genuine friend of his, had hoisted two of them without leaving any marks on the edges of the prised-open heavy cardboard box. Lost in Transmission couldn't be applied if or when it was found out, as they hadn't left any tell-tale signs of theft. In those cases, the retailer is told that it is a factory error and they accept complete liability. Cranky had given him one of the phones as a return for the sunglasses he'd hoisted last month. Two hundred quid it will get him. He has no need for it and showing it off at work wouldn't be the best idea he'd ever had.

As a way of habit, his portable music player will not be played before the first two hours have gone. His reasoning is that it breaks the shift into quarters. For the first, slowest and most bearable quarter, no music is played and it quickens the slow-going time. The second quarter is filled with music and his earphones are plugged in. The third quarter includes his half-an-hour break for lunch, where he takes a little under forty minutes and leads into the final stretch, where the music again acts as a measure through three-minute, four-minute and five-minute songs. He isn't sure if it's a placebo or not, but his mind is tricked more often than it isn't.

The sounds in the warehouse are monotonous and rarely change. It is cool from the air-conditioning and the motors of the fans and the belts combine to make an insectoid droning that does not bother him. Andrew is not fond of silence. Depending on the people who are on the shift, conversations often break the non-silence. The only issue that he finds with this is that the topics become set and there isn't much that is different to say a lot of the time. If Cranky or Dave are working, there is the guarantee of a mini-game of catch, kick, chuck, or do-whatever-you-want with a miniature American football. Andrew enjoys this, which for a self-ordained sports-hater, surprised him at first. Schoolground games and P.E. lessons were the least favourite part of the school day. What continues to surprise him is how he never drops the ball, either. Unless the throw is crap. Cranky and Dave aren't working tonight.

The packages and parcels coming down the belt are in ones and twos and the offloaders seem to be considerate today. Most of the time they dump, which in turn merited their sobriquet of dumpers or stiggers. The older men working at the warehouse refuse to explain and he still doesn't understand.

Sounds really negative either way, and ever since he didn't get the internal to be a stigger full-time, the switch from using the term dumper to using the term stigger was easy, whatever-the-fuck it means. The interview had nearly made him quit the job completely and he had seriously weighed up the options: new job or bigger packets to sell. He'd come in wearing a three hundred fucking pound suit and cleanly shaved and with his CV and records of achievements and as polite as could be. Shake your hand sir and please and thank you and Mr. Formal himself. In walks a newbie, three months only, wearing the same casual shit he wears on the belts and holding nothing at all. Rocket scientist he isn't, but ever since he was sixteen he's had a job and never received a complaint. School grades are average-to-decent and he's never failed an exam. Passed his driving test first time, too. Two years here (sixteen months at the time of the interview) and nothing but positives from the regional don of operations whenever his appraisal was up. No finger could seriously be pointed his way for any lost-property parcels, either. But no. No job on the road for him. Pretty much why he hates Matt so much. He'd only been there three months and he casually walked into the job. Wanker.

A series of same-sized boxes, red-labelled fragile, comes slowly through the translucent rubber curtains. It is the first time tonight where Andrew has needed any alertness and he likes the break-up of monotony. The job is far from active most of the time, exceptions being when a bulk container arrives or festivals are approaching. With consideration and gentle hands, he directs each box onto its designated path, waiting with hopeful anticipation for the last of the series to come without anything behind. The seventh box is the last and no items follow it along the conveyer before it reaches him. He quickly picks it up and it feels just as light as the others. With the same consideration as before but ever so slightly gentler than when guiding them away from the chutes, he shakes it. Whatever contents are in the box intrigue Andrew and he pulls a thin-bladed knife from his right trouser pocket and neatly swipes it around the corners of the taped box. The blade of the knife is blunted but it puts no strain on his wrist, easily breaking the ochre tape around three sides. Still gentle, he opens the two halves of the box's top as a single lid, a strip of the tape joining them together in the middle. There is a lot of tissue paper and an object sealed in a thick bundle of bubble wrap. He cuts a small slit in the bubble wrap and works it away from a tiny, blue and white floral teacup. He turns it upside down and circles his lips to blow air through them. He knows the mark from the television and with a not-too-distant estimation reckons the value, undervaluing it by two hundred pounds. Before slipping it cosily into the bubble wrap and burying it under wads of the white tissue paper, he switches hands, breathes on it, and rubs his right sleeve on as much of it as he can. Placing the box on the floor and glancing quickly at the top of the belt, he turns and jogs to a table next to the double doors. There is a couple of rolls of tape and he picks up the most used one and jogs back to the conveyer, already pulling a two-foot stretch. He places these over the tape already on the box and cuts the ends with the knife. The box belatedly follows its companions after a seventy-second detour.

There's nothing coming down the belts, so he gets his battered mobile phone out and checks the time. Halfway there. He has never been and will not become enamoured with phones and the access into the gameways that they bring. The screen is too small for starters and after playing on his highly-defined, big, surround-sound television, with the best consoles available and the biggest interactive community of anything in the whole world, he knows as sure as he knows anything that it will be a cheaper, weaker substitute. Why eat magic mushrooms when he can have LSD? He muses over the phone that he is going to sell and the sum of two hundred pounds leads him in the direction of Grant. The fucker's Matt-times-ten or Matt-times-a-million and the final payback will be sweet. Two hundred pounds spent with Charlie will be well worth it. The look on Craczynskis' face will be priceless. What will it actually be like? He'll pull it out of the box and make sure the fucker sees it and then he will just die, he supposes. It'll kill him.

There is a lot of doubt in him and he isn't entirely sure he can do it, but he hates Grant. Y. Craczynski more than he has hated any single person and this fuels him to want to destroy. He feels that he wants to destroy the man's soul: to take away the biggest, most drastic thing that he can. Two hundred pounds is not a small amount of money in Andrew's mind, but it is cheap in comparison to what it can bring in its destructive aftermath. That, he thinks, will be priceless.

He has been thinking about how evil he is a lot over the last week and has reached many temporary conclusions. The time he blamed his cousin for stealing his uncle's tobacco is ranked high up the list of evils and convinces him for short times that he was a sinister shit at age thirteen and not quite a decade later he is worse. His cousin had been smacked red-raw across the face by Uncle Dave's backhand and even when he'd started crying, the wailing heard from the bottom of the stairs, he hadn't spoken up or out or said a word. Then there was the murder in The Streets on the twenty-third of March last year. His old game-name was still mentioned in whispers across the community and not a single person knows it was he who had killed Phat Man. He hasn't played The Streets since and with a lot of will power, managed to refuse buying the subsequent game, the second in the series. The only reason he had done it anyway was because it was supposed to be impossible. It was probably a glitch on the interactive server, but either way, no more The Streets. Another asshole occasion was when he'd snogged his grandmother's neighbour's granddaughter's friend, who was two years below him at school, too. She was fourteen, which was weird and he'd felt like a dirty old man. Yep. There is no doubt Andy, hell awaits son.

He is snapped out of his routine deductions on the demerits and punishments of his actions by the sight of a series of sealed envelopes. There are twelve of them by the time they reach him and he has to scan the post codes and stamps to ascertain to which chute they will be directed. At a time like this, it is easy to assume that they are all from the same source and therefore all for the same destination, and in this case, it is true. Andrew checks every one of the envelopes as his job demands and feels no annoyance that they are all going towards the exports chute. He figures they're exchange letters similar to the ones that he and his classmates had written when studying German at school. He still finds it funny that Louis turned out to be a boy. He hadn't bothered to ask his teacher. Behind the letters to Germany comes a steady stream of other, varying packages and parcels. A van must have just offloaded and to the stigger's credit, he has placed them in single file, facilitating Andrew's work.

It's funny how the workplace still seems quite sexist, what with not a single member of the staff being a girl. A woman, correction. It is amazing how even with all the news and the rights and the female faces on telly, women are still pushed into the corners of the past. Women are stronger than men, no doubt. His mum was always a better person than his dad. She could rule him much better through the love that she gave rather than the fear of pain promised from the old man. The fear of upsetting her was worse than that. His mother had never hit him, and his cousin, when Uncle Dave hit her, never once told the truth or held a grudge. She's just started university too, which adds the whole brains dimension to the equation. He's often heard it said that men's brains are bigger. If that's the case and what with women being just as smart, surely the insult was on the men? Fuck all of his friends who'd called him gay for saying it, plus they would just joke back that women's left and right are confused and that they can't drive and all the usual claptrap. He doesn't mean strong on the physical side either, because once again it's equal. Men are naturally bigger but on an equal weight footing there's no difference. Nine stones against nine stones could be six feet against five feet five, masculine against feminine or strong against weak, regardless of whether it's a cock or a pussy between the legs. He's heard the difference between sex and gender but can't remember it. It sounds right, whatever it is. So why are women stronger? Because they have to deal with men. Simple.

Someone enters the room, seen from the corner of Andrew's eye. They're wearing a parka with the fur-lined hood pulled tight concealing their face. Andrew turns and sees that the person is walking briskly towards him in what can only be described as in an aggressive manner. Andrew starts to panic and is ready to plead his innocence to whatever he is supposed to have done. The faceless anonymity of his attacker is really unnerving him and he splays his fingers with his palms outwards, innocence incarnate in simple gesticulation.

↓↑

Ssij mi kutasa, pedal. Angry face. Angry face.

↑↓

It's one of the Polish. Shit, what's he fucking said? *Look mate, I don't know what you're saying.* Stay calm. Calm voice and calm face and don't look scared.

The man pulls off his hood and starts to laugh. Andrew is chagrined. *You're a twat, Mikey. I thought you were a Polak. What did you say, anyway?* He relaxes and starts to laugh.

↓↑

Glad I got you mate. *Pawel told me it's suck me off or summat gay. Hey. Did, you like my dumping?*

↑↓

Damned right. I didn't know you were doing a shift today. Driving, too?

↓↑

Yeah, covering for Steve. Holiday wasn't booked or summat so I said I'd take it. Lazy and easy really. Nowt to it. How've you been?

↑↓

Pretty good thanks, mate. You?

↓↑

Might have the goddamned clap. *Yeah, not bad. Same old, same old.* Clinic test sometime with the good news. *You managed to get your phone gone?* He whispered it, just to be safe.

↑↓

Not yet, but I've been offered two hundred for it. Two hundred quid to kill a man.

↓↑

Not bad mate. I got two-fifty for mine, but not to be sniffed at. Two hundred each, actually. Tried for five hundred for both. *Keep your eye open for any more good stuff, Andy. I'd better check out before Jonesy or whoever else is on thinks I'm trying to squeeze overtime.*

↑↓

Overtime. He smiles. It's the same old joke. *Catch you later, Mikey.*

→

←

That was funny. His face was genuinely frightened. He was just on his way round from dumping when the thought came to him. It was like the last Halloween party when Andy was really pissed and he'd pretended to be paralytic or dead. Andy had shaken him repeatedly for about a minute and Andy's voice was about to break before he turned round and made a blaah kind of noise and the orange contact lenses and plastic fangs and the blaah had made Andy near enough shit himself. Hilarious. He knows Andy is a bit intimidated by the Polaks so thought he'd try his acting and language skills. Pawel is his swear-language teacher for all things Polak. The current count is fifteen phrases along the lines of lick his nipple and fuck your own ass. Priceless.

The coat he is wearing is not his and he takes it off and drapes it over the chair where he found it in the loading bay. He walks through a single door and then, two steps at a time, he gets to the top of the stairs and enters the office. He writes his time of 18:45 on the forty-eight-hourly clocking-in rota and has a quick scan to see who has worked what and who is working at the moment. Nobody on the current shift makes him want to stay for a chat, apart of course from Andrew.

Andy is a good kid. He says kid, but he's only five or six years younger than him at most. There's a very innocent, need-to-be-protected vulnerability to him and that is endearing in its own way. He's game for a laugh and isn't too serious, either. Plus, they share a joint joke with Matt at its centre and the kid can't half catch the fucking mini-Yank that they chuck around. He's been tempted countless times to ask if he wants to go for a drink but doesn't want him to think he's coming on to him.

And therein lies the paradox of Michael Pullman. For all of his brash talk about Andrew being gay and the rebuke to Andrew's feminist-defensive stances, he is confused as to his own sexuality.

Now, he's never put his cock in another man's ass or

mouth or even kissed one, but he can't deny that he finds them attractive. Andrew is a handsome enough kid in a tempered, modernist geek way, and he definitely finds him attractive. He also has a girlfriend that he finds attractive and his girlfriend's mum is pretty fit, too. What does it all mean?

At his car, he opens the boot and pulls out a can of carbonated soft drink from the three of the four pack that is left. He pulls the ring and drinks the whole can in one slow motion and attempts to dropkick it into the narrow depository on the bin that is around three yards away from the car, perched on a curb next to a hedgerow. He misses by some distance and gently pushes down the boot, walks to the driver's door and opens it. He steps in but immediately steps back out. The sun is still high in the sky, perhaps two hours from sunset. Allowing the car to cool down, he picks the can up and puts it in the bin.

Culver. It's hot. He finds it hard not to use the most commonly heard Polish that goes around the workplace. The combination of the beating heat and the recently shaved pubes – yep, they were completely gone – is making the area directly above his penis itch like crazy. His girlfriend had told him to do it in one of her kinky-change moods and he, the sucker, had gone along with it. The stubbly area looks rashed and he semi-seriously told her that he's got crabs. The irony isn't lost on either of them and it's burningly, irritatingly funny. Funnier for her though, definitely. Only problem now is that he can't stop thinking that he's got crabs when he knows that all he has is a severe lack of pubes. And that goddamned fucking stubble.

Swearing aloud and conscious that no one is around to hear or see him, he slips the four fingers of his right hand down the elastic waistband of his jogging bottoms and the Y-section of his boxer shorts as he steps in and sits down in the driver seat. The relief is as transient as the length of the rubbed scratch. He slams the door in a burst of irritation and starts the car's engine immediately after. He presses a button in the partition between the front-side passenger seat and driver's seat and both the front windows go all of the way down. There is no breeze. For no real reason apart from annoyance and habit, he shoots a violent spit out to his right and lands it squarely in the gap of the bin. He does not notice where it has landed, instead pulling the car into reverse and stopping to turn left and towards the entrance/exit.

What must it be like to have an STD? Shame on you, son. He's only been with the one girl and it's been ten years since their college days. The only way he can get an STD is if she does the dirty and the crabs joke is almost a way of indirectly getting her to confess to something that he doesn't think she's done anyway. She is a very quirky – that's the word – type of girl. They'd shared the same mentor at college for their business diploma and he had found the pierced lip-nose bit (no matter how many times she tells him, it doesn't stick) really arousing, which was odd in itself as he's always been kind of non-sexual. Her hair was shaved on one side and a blue thumb-print-sized tattooed spider sitting in a web was visible under the grey fuzz. The other side was long and the tips were dyed a deep red and she was only describable as being alternative. Yep. Quirky in appearance and in her mannerisms. She liked the word spontaneous when they'd first met and had made every effort, it seemed, to do odd things out of the blue. One of those was university, after two years of swearing she wasn't going to go. Turns out she was just trying to worry her old man and it worked. She has a Masters now to add to her First Class Degree in Business Studies and works as a junior or senior or semi-senior consultant or one of those high-status business jobs: has done for just over two years. She takes home the big bucks and doesn't look down on him at all. Quirky girl. Definitely not asking him to shave his pubes for fear of infection. Just a quirky ask from a quirky girl. Does he love her? Not at all. But he likes her and finds her attractive and they rarely argue. They've never split up just to get back together later, or thrown a slap or punch. They are good together. Plus, let's not forget ever, her mum is hot.

Speeding at a good eighty miles per hour down the motorway and he's half of the way home. The traffic is light, as is the evening from the sun. The air is rather heavy.

But there's nothing to worry about. He's not gay and he's not got crabs and so he might not be in love but he's damned happy. He tells himself this like a repetitive tune. He knows he's confused and fine, he admits it. Maybe it's just because he has a constant feeling of being incomplete. Unfulfilled. He's the way God's made him. Then again, he's an atheist, so what can he make of that?

A shadowy feeling comes over him and he thinks for a second, then another, a thought that he has mulled over much in the last month: is it denial? He believes that recognition of denial is itself the final declaration and indication of his homosexuality. If there is nothing to deny then it's fine, he believes, let it blow away. The doubt will go after he proves his manliness in all the typical ways. If there is something to deny, then by mutuality it requires him to be the very thing that is denied.

But. But. But.

And he stops himself from falling into the trap of rotational thinking. He focuses on everything that is around him: the children with their chins on their chests in the back of the jeep that he passes in the middle lane; a flashing sign reading SLOW DOWN in orange letters; the exit and the traffic lights and that they are green. He is still going eighty past the green lights and there are no cars waiting at the red lights opposite. He looks at the clock on the dashboard and it is not the quickest that he has got home. The lights being green gave him a good chance to beat his record, but as he takes the next turn into the cul-de-sac he sees that he is a full minute, give or take a few seconds, off his personal best. The drive of the semi-detached has a little red car with black spots on it, as if mimicking a ladybird.

She's not gone out. That's good. He'll make her some supper if she's not already made it for them. As usual, she's not given him enough room to fit on the drive. She can be a funny girl; she's a better driver than him, one hand tied behind her back. Running joke, her car being automatic.

He blocks her in, which is the usual riposte to her deliberate manoeuvre. They both think and believe that it is cute and loving. She always leaves the house at the same time in the morning. They both wake up and get up at the same time, so they spend time together in the morning if only briefly. Sometimes he works until six in the morning, and on these occasions he gives her enough room. She chides him over this with words like you don't love me really, do you? and two hours for love is always enough.

No, two hours' sleep is far from enough, even if he can go back to bed until mid-afternoon. She keeps pestering about catching her on her lunch break but he isn't really fond of her friends and the blonde one makes him feel uneasy, to be honest. It's alright for her; she gets to take her break very leisurely and can go out for up to two hours. All the vans have got a tracker anyway, and more often than not he's on the belts. Like the fucking secret police with their spy navigation satellite monitors.

The door is ajar and he pushes it open. The key for the

front door is attached to the same key ring as his car keys, but these were tucked back into his pocket as soon as he locked the car. The logic behind this is that the area in which they live, and in fact the whole part of town where they live, is one of the safest communities in the country. According to the police reports it is an area where crime is virtually non-existent. Home burglaries are regarded as something of a myth and the stabbings and shootings of the capital take place in a different world. Add to this the stiflingly powerful sun and the warmth that does not abate even at this time in the evening, and that is why. There is no wind to create a draught, however.

The sound of the telly greets him and he knows what is on already. The voice of the old dear at the launderette screeches the moaning rant that she always seems to do. He can't hear the words but he guesses it's about her son who does drugs that she doesn't know about, but he's a nasty piece of work and causes her trouble, or how she doesn't know why she doesn't just sell up and move to Barbados as she always wanted to before husbo died. He has to admit though, he does quite like the soap. Not that he'll ever tell anyone that, not even his girlfriend.

He has an idea. The television is situated in front of the patio doors, with the sofa facing both the television and the garden (seen through the large panes of sliding glass that are the patio doors), and with a bit of luck the volume was just loud enough to drown out the sound of the car as he parked.

She always listens to the telly really loud. He'll creep up on her, cover her eyes and tell her she's gonna be raped and then start laughing in her face.

↓↑

I heard the car, Mikey. And she could hear his footsteps, too. Plus the door made a little clang. *Plus the door clanged. How was work?*

↑↓

Shit. *Shit, but quick. I was gonna pretend to be a rapist and growl in your ear. How romantic is that?*

↓↑

She chuckles very girlishly. *You are such a darling cutesie-wootsie. Flowers are so lame; you are way more romantic.* He cracks her up. He really does.

↑↓

What's she rabbiting on about now, anyway? He kisses her on the lips and she tastes like very sweet tea. *Not her dead husband again? Or retiring?*

His hands are planted on the hardened ridge along the top of the sofa and his cheek is pressed against hers, eyes casually and non-committally scanning the interior of the launderette and the silver-haired ancient perched on a bench.

↓↑

No no no. She's just found out that her son is the one who stole from her. And that it was for heroin. Dee-ram-at-ic or what? Her voice is suitably sarcastic, but it really is enthralling telly. *And it looks like Kelly's affair with the stripper has been noticed by Benny, but I can't remember seeing that in the last week.*

↑↓

Hey, did your friend still want a phone? It's just Andy, you know the kid at work, still has one and I could probably get it if she wants it. Just thought. Andy.

↓↑

Um, I'm not sure. I'll ask her when I see her next. I'll ask her tomorrow. She's not going to cry, is she?

The television shows the silver-haired lady screeching a shuddered series of tears into a milky-coffee-brown handker-chief. The other lady in the launderette, to whom the tearful owner had just been speaking, pats her lightly on the shoulder and says the exact words there there. Michael has stood up and extended his spine by leaning backwards, audibly receiving the cracking sound of bones and their pockets of air. He heads into the kitchen, which is through an archway to the right of the sofa, television and patio.

Their life is often like a soap opera. So much shit happens to them that seems so over-the-top and surreal it's insane. The two of them are good. They hardly row, bitch, moan or anything. What she means is what happens around them. One of her friends had a jealous ex who decided to get smashed on drugs and pummel her face in. She had visited her in hospital and at one time the doctor said her friend was blinded in one eye. Thank God it was temporary. Then, not long ago, another friend's mum had been run over and the driver hadn't even stopped. It's like the stuff that she reads on the news but never expects to be on the doorstep. Shit, that was without the failed IVF Sammy had had or Rach's mum's death, too. Just as well that she is lucky and has Mikey. He can be messy and needs looking after, but he's a simple guy and never overcomplicates anything. His passion and compassion (he hates it when she tells her friends this in front of him) makes him understanding and really easy to relate to. And of course he makes her feel good in bed. He is the most unselfish lover she has.

Although she had only had sexual intercourse with two men before she had met Michael, her tally, as she calls it to no other but herself, is at twenty-three. In the world of business, whether man or woman, the adage on which she was taught and continues to be taught is that it comes with the territory. Ventures are undertaken, promotions are secured and partnerships are cemented by the simple horizontal pleasures that are offered and in equal measure gained by the flesh. She is not, in her mind, cheating or being (although out of wedlock) adulterous; these escapades are merely of a transactional nature and fulfil a mainly transactional purpose. At first she had felt like a whore and rather cheap, but when her promotions came and she used it as a simple tool-of-the-trade, it became just that. It is more often than not a pragmatic, unspoken acquiescence and brokering of a deal. Much like a handshake but mutually more pleasurable. The guilt of the first three times was expunged by the rapid progress in which her stock rose. Metaphorically, primarily. And apart from the time early on when she had had her advances rejected and she had cried to Mikey with the hardest lies she had ever told, there has not been any negative repercussions.

Yeah, she enjoys it really, in the way pleasure and orgasm cannot really be anything but enjoyed, but it is never romantically attached or better than what she gets at home. It isn't really cheating for that reason; there is no love involved. If he shakes hands with his friends is that really any different to stroking their cocks? Not, of course, that he'd do that. Whilst not homophobic, his gay jokes can definitely be offensive. Full of funnyisms, is Mikey.

And then there is the music of a well-known heavy-metal band coming from somewhere that muffles its sound. The band must be well into their fifth decade, but this song sounds like one that could be taken off their first LP. Her right hand strokes her right thigh and right ass cheek, trying to feel the shape of her mobile phone. Instinctively, when it is not found in either of the usual two pockets, she slips her hand into the crack between the sofa's cushions and the sound becomes CD quality and much louder. She unlocks the screen without thinking of the routine and sees that RACH is ringing her.

Hey Rach. Immediately not good. Her voice sounds strange,

kinda like a man's. That can't be true. *Oh shit. I'm so sorry.* Why did she say that? Why does anyone say that? *Of course.* It's not their fault and sorry changes nothing. *I'll be there now, of course. Straightaway. I'm so sorry.* And again. *Be strong.* She should have said stay strong. *Stay strong. Five minutes.* She looks at the phone and sees that the call has ended. Fuck me. Imagine if that was her. The feelings would be insane. It's crazy how she's still holding it together. She's never been close to her dad but if he suddenly drops dead, she'll be devastated.

In a state of shock from the news of tragedy that her friend has briefly, monotonously told her, she leans forwards with her right hand in her lap (phone still clasped inside it) and her left hand toying with the two metal studs that are screwed into her philtrum. This is a habit that she has; whenever she is uncertain of what to do, which is quite infrequent, she twists the balls against their threads. Even when at work and when all visible piercings and tattoos are concealed, she twists phantom metal and looks as if she is sniffing the ends of her fingers. Deep in thought now. Rachel, her friend, has asked her to go to her house. Her sister is there and some other friends are on their way over.

The poor thing needs some comfort and needs to be distracted from whatever darknesses are zapping through her head. Should she bring some wine? Of course not – it's not a celebration. Should she say sorry or what should she say? Definitely not that. Should she arrive late or leave right now? What should she wear? *Fuck me.* This is hard. How can she reduce the impact on her friend? What the fuck is she supposed to do? Just go, like this, now. Easy. Be natural.

She sighs from what she regards as the hardship of her situation and stands at the same time. The television is left on and she about turns, leaving a group of rowdy revellers and a disconsolate publican arguing over beverages and other such things on the screen.

Mikey. Mike. The shower's on so she's better off walking to the top of the stairs. Quick little steps like a gothic ballerina. Oh God: ballet. Her feet are still crippled by her childhood. *Mikey.* She taps her index finger on the door three times. A nasality that means yeah or what is his response. Probably got gel all over his face. *Something really crazy has happened with Rach's dad. She just rang me. I'll tell you more later but I promised her I'll be round.*

Intelligible now, he asks her what's wrong but she only tells him *Leave me half the pizza if you're gonna have it. I mean it.* Two steps at a time and heavier than on the way up, she is at the bottom of the stairs and putting on some tan-leather ankle boots, cream-coloured fur adorning their edges. She picks up her faux-tan leather handbag, larger than the purse-sized ones that she finds so pointless. Halfway down the path and she is about to turn around and tell Michael that he's a prick in a light-hearted but genuinely frustrated manner. She doesn't though, as he has not blocked her in. She figures that he must want a lie in tomorrow. Just as she pulls the keys out of her handbag

↑↓

Hey. I hope everything's alright. Love you.

↓↑

He's standing there in just a towel, his belly and chest white where his arms are bronzed. He's probably goose-pimpled, but it's too hard to see at this distance really. *Thanks. I hope so too. Love you too.* He's such a cutie, really.

←

→

He wonders what's happened and whether she'll be home before he goes to bed. He's not tired but he wants to curl up under the covers and enjoy a long sleep tonight. It's still light and the weather forecast said it'll be twenty-three at its coolest. He can't get to sleep very well unless it's dark, and the heat always causes him problems. When he was a kid – that was funny but bloody ingenious – his ma had put a thick dark-green curtain over the railed curtains that made the room pitch black. The only problem was the bloody heat that took over the room, but as his bedtime was eight o'clock, it did the job of acting as night. It will start getting dark in twenty minutes.

Removing the towel just before the door closes, Michael yawns as a result of his somnolent thinking. The net curtains are a decent enough barrier to prevent any pedestrians seeing more than his silhouetted shape. He heads to the kitchen and thinks of the pizza. His dilemma is twelve minutes of hassle-free cooking or ripping open a couple of bags of crisps. His girlfriend seemed to know that he will choose a lazy option in her absence, and it seems also that she was right.

If she was here now, she would steam some vegetables: probably some green beans and carrots alongside little potatoes, new potatoes. He doesn't like oven chips because they don't taste or even feel like the ones his ma makes, but he'd still rather have them than vegetables and boiled new potatoes. Since when did pizza become anything like a healthy meal? She's good at that, mind, looking after him in all ways like, as she harped on about, the traditional maternal wifie. She always goes on about her feminism, but he has no clue what that really means if not diving downstairs and cleaning the carpet and all that kinda stuff.

He takes out two pieces of white bread and drops them into the slots on the toaster. He doesn't push the handle down. A saucepan is placed on the front-right hot plate. Next, he opens a ring-pull tin of a cultural icon and he switches the cooker on and the hot plate to maximum heat, six. Into the saucepan go the contents of the tin. Now he levers the bread in.

In the usual circumstance when he is allowed to make the crap, her words, she will tut at him for not slowly heating the beans or the hoops or the ravioli. She does have a point; the shit sticks to the pan when he blasts it to piping hot, but why wait for longer than needed just for the sake of an easier load of dishes?

One more minute later, lost to daydreams of confusion and what he is deep down inside, the toaster pops and as an alarm, brings him back into the kitchen and he pours the saucepan's contents on the toast and grates some cheese and takes it in the living room to start eating.

Shit it's hot. His mouth is tingling and he hoohahs, trying to make it cool down. Keep doing it and it'll be okay. He tilts his head back and hahs until he reckons he can swallow it and he does. His throat is tingling and the inside of his cheek is definitely burnt. Hopefully the top of the tongue won't be – that's a real bastard. There's probably tears in his eyes. He digs into the soggy toast with the fork. A spoon would've been better. She ain't here to tell him off so he should've just grabbed a spoon.

The lack of beratement changes nothing and he makes the semblance of a child's mushed dinner out of the food on his plate. He eats it quickly and makes himself chuckle silently when he thinks of the menstrual quality of it, but then the image does not leave his mind and he knows that he probably will not finish it. He does not. He leaves the plate on the side after locating all the strips of cheese and eating them. The red stuff has now lost all of its appeal. The lady's voice narrating the programme on the television informs him how Claudia has been volunteering as a mystery shopper for four years and how she is responsible for the dismissal of seven employees from various retail outlets. He is also informed of the techniques she likes to use, such as the push-to-shove, where she deliberately attempts provocation by acting stubborn and demanding, or the wrong-right game, where she repeatedly tells the sales assistant that they are wrong when they indubitably are not or vice versa. Claudia's favourite, which she tells him she should have copyrighted, is the haggler. Of the seven dismissals, five of them have come from her haggle technique, a routine where she dupes the naïve by claiming damage to items and/or getting the price reduced by her incessant pressing. When managers find out that the assistant has sold the item at a reduced price, all of which is written up in her report, they react by getting rid of the weak link within their staff. As Claudia happily tells him, she wants to get rid of the retail runts. It's a job where only the toughest survive. In Michael's opinion, the forty-year-old woman is a bitch, and all of her ingenious plans to lose students, struggling mothers and fathers their jobs are one and the same. It doesn't matter to him that she looks attractive; her nature is horrible.

So how can he be gay? He finds the bitch attractive in that older-lady way. He just doesn't like what she does or who she is. It's getting boring now and each time it seems worse. He has a fucking girlfriend for Christ's sake. What's worrying is that a lot of the time he thinks of hard-bodied men and muscled backs. He wanked over Andy the last few times, too. If those aren't signs then he doesn't know what is. But no. He ain't a faggot. He's got a girlfriend and he's never put his cock inside a man. Or, damn that's disgusting, had one in him. After all, thinking about things and doing them are not the same. He's watched people's heads get hacked off and some nasty shit on the telly, enjoys it too, but he doesn't want to go and fucking do it. Shit.

Idly and subconsciously scratching the stubble where only five days earlier he had a tangle of wiry pubic hair, the television is turned off with a forceful and deliberately dramatic flick of his wrist to coincide with the thumb-press of the button. His face is angry, acting as a mask of masculinity to cover his doubt. He tosses the remote control on the sofa and picks up the plate. He walks a diagonal to the kitchen and registers that the room is now fully in the dimness of dusk. Without switching on any lights, he slowly fills the sink and squirts enough washing liquid into the sink that the bubbles rise nearly two inches above the water.

Cricket has been placed in his mind and he doesn't quite know why. It's to do with the bitch and that shitty programme, something she said. The time when he played for the school against the Brains, a team from Braithwaite or a name like that, was his first ever match. He'd hit about forty and the teachers had gone crazy, tipping him for county and other things. He can remember every detail. He watches it every now and again, mainly the tests or the twenty-twenty. Football was what he had wanted to do and distracted him from playing cricket, and football is what takes up most of his sporting life. Not that he plays it. It's been three years since he'd had a kick around in the five-a-sides. More evidence to his straightness, as sure as. Sport, as his dad says, is the Heterosexuality Express.

He leaves the dishes on the side to dry of their own accord. There is little light in the house now, the rapidity of dim to dark noticeable against the slow transition of light to dim. He turns the living room lamp on and draws the thin curtains across the patio doors and the thick ones across the front window. He makes himself yawn to coax tiredness into his body. It works.

He's showered, had some food and he's in no mood to sit

up with a film. If she'd been here he would've, but the best thing for him now is definitely sleep. He can't be bothered to brush his teeth. He can't say that he's not tired because he is and regardless of the heat, he'll sleep well. Fingers crossed. If she was here he would have the guarantee of a good sleep; they're like a human jigsaw, slotting into each other and changing the spooner or the spooned based on what feels right and who wants the belly or the back. Man, he really sounds gay now. Next thing, he'll be saying he loves her. If she was here he would tell her that, next to an update on his STI, before jigsawing with her and going to sleep.

In a happier mood at the turn of his thoughts, he does brush his teeth. He speaks a few phrases of Polish whilst his mouth is full of minty suds, translations being lick my nipple, shit, lick my penis, and what are you doing tonight? To his credit, he does know what he is saying and has not been duped by the Polish men he works with. He is in a good mood, as if he has reached a final solution, a revelation, a decision as to something highly important and sought after and now finally found. He had forgotten about the towel that lies discarded over the table in the hallway, but noticing it now he does not go down the stairs to retrieve it. Instead, he rubs his right palm over his lips and gets rid of the toothpaste. He walks into the bedroom and jumps, twisting in the air one hundred and eighty degrees and landing on his back on the perfectly pouffed duvet. The cool sheets feel great to him and he luxuriates on them for a while, making him think of a cat.

Cats are safe. Cats are sound. Cats are feline and sleek and sexy creatures, female in everything they do. Silky smooth skin or fur and even the male cats, the toms, are perfectly feminine. Girls are even said to be catty and a girl-fight is a cat-fight. But then there's the way they stroll across the rug or street and shoot their tails up in the air, hard and rigid and like a hard-on.

Phallic images return to him, all in an erected, aroused, erotic condition. Frustration and fear seem shadowed on his face, reclaiming their earlier territory. His penis remains unswollen. He starts crying and in this manner falls asleep.

And he wakes.

That's a nice feeling, the tingling fuzziness across his neck and shoulder muscles. Through slowly opening lids it's light. This doesn't tell him anything. It has to be earlier than eight because his alarm hasn't gone off, but it could be anywhere from five thirty onwards. The stretch feels just as good as the hunch, sending the tingles all the way down to the toes. Out of habit and because that's what he always does, he makes the grunting yawn that he knows means he won't go back to sleep. Voice engaged. Ready to go. A few minutes of lazing on top of the covers ain't gonna hurt, though.

There is a shuffling sound and a bang from the bathroom.

Everything okay? His voice is a bit croaky. He forces a throat-clearing cough and tries again. *Hey. Morning. Is everything okay?*

The reply from the bathroom says that she's okay. She tells him that it's nearly nine and he is confused for a few seconds. He remembers that he didn't put the alarm on because he doesn't have work today. It's a Friday. This alone does not mean that he has not got work. His shifts are flexible and he rarely has any definite day off other than Sunday, and even that is not unalterable. The rota has his name down for Saturday, which explains the Friday.

Some questions need to be answered, however. She hadn't got into bed last night and it seems that she's just come home. He isn't suspicious, but she'd better not have done anything.

Did you just get in? he asks, and the answer is known. A weird feeling is in his chest and it's like being sick, the time just before when the mouth waters.

She walks into the bedroom, standing at the door and tells him all about it: she'd gone round to Rachel's house after the phone call and it was far from easy. It turned out that Rachel's father was found dead in the early hours of yesterday morning, apparently from suicide. It seems that he jumped from the bridge that adjoins both sides of the gorge, landing on the hard, mud embankments during a shallow period or low tide or whatever it is. Rachel found out in the morning when she'd had a phone call and they'd asked and said are you Miss Redlaw and she'd said yeah and then the routine kinda I'm sorry and all that. Imagine it: over the phone and all, as soon as you get up before work. Anyway, she gets there and her and Rachel's friends are there, as is Rachel's sister, and it's obvious that she's drunk. She keeps going on about some old dead country singer and poetry and how he's a selfish prick and all this stuff. It's obvious that she's been drinking too. So they spoke to her and decided that the best thing to do, you know with not having any grandparents and stuff, was to have the funeral straight away. It's going to be the day after tomorrow so she was gonna help her organise it, but she and her sister are doing it today. It's mental. She stank of alcohol, too.

Michael forgets his previous thoughts on pre-marital adultery and throughout the recounting of the last twelve hours, he sympathetically emits a few damns and shits and Gods, shaking his head for the most part from side to side. He is genuinely shocked by this and he does as he has been told. He imagines himself in the same scenario as Rachel.

His dad's a good man and if he had received the news first thing in the morning, he'd be useless for anything. He'd cry, like men aren't supposed to but still do, and he'd probably get drunk too. He hadn't really cried last night. No way. Rachel's alright as far as her friends go and he feels bad for her. Imagine it. Shit.

That's messed up. I hope she's alright. Know she won't be though.

↑↓

Yeah. It was mental. Thanks for saving the pizza, mind. I noticed it in the fridge.

↓↑

She's mad like that. On one subject that's pretty damned deep and then wham, someplace else. *Would I have?* She grins at him in a very sexy way and plants a deliberately sloppy kiss on him. Self-conscious of his breath.

↑↓

Thanks cutesie-wootsie. I gotta go, anyway. Working today now to have tomorrow off. I'll be back for six latest, so keep me that pizza 'til then. Ciao.

↓↑

I'll go to the clinic for the good news. She kisses him with a peck on the nose, not preferable to her first minty one. A little tut-tut and she leaves, her curvy ass the focus as she smiles over her shoulder with favourable acknowledgement.

→

←

She walks down the stairs, puts her shoes back on and slings her handbag, the same as yesterday's, over her shoulder. The shoes are different: black slip-on pumps. She finds her keys and walks to her car.

She'd had to tell him the news, but she feels a little bit naughty for waking him, but the compassionate soul that he is, Mikey would've wanted to know.

She starts to pull out into a smooth u-turn when she sees a car in her right-wing mirror. She presses the brake pedal and looks out of her mirror to the man going the other way to her.

←
→

It really has been a long time since he'd last had some chocolate. His wife would be happy to know that, not that he's going to tell her. Might treat himself to some tonight if he feels like it. Why not? The darker the better. What with a hearty slosh of the old fire water and some acid, what could be more perfect? It's times like these that he feels most childish. He's had a veritable lie in on a weekday and is off on a business trip. He sure as hell is off for a trip of some sorts. As part of the business world and a highly educated and successful member of it too, let's not forget, he is in demand for these weekend trips across the continent. Does he feel guilty for leaving his wife? Of course he does. Her cooking is exquisite and for any fault that she might possess, she is still compliant in the old four-poster.

He is driving towards the airport in the neighbouring borough and is going to leave his car there. Traffic is light where they live, but as soon as he accesses the motorway and heads west, he'll most likely be held in a slow treacle of a queue for an hour before exiting. His vehicle is over two tons of silver sports car, less than two years old, nought-to-sixty in a near-enough-round five, twin exhausts, and still worth forty or fifty thousand pounds. Added to this the interior boasts two twelve-inch flat screens for the driver and passenger, pure-leather seats (cream), a stereo system that is worth two thousand pounds alone and in-built navigation system, top of the range. It is not that he enjoys driving, more that he enjoys having luxury items and such a large amount of disposable income. On anything that can be shown or even inadvertently seen, he will purchase the most obviously expensive items. For example, on his left wrist is a watch worth five thousand and two hundred and fifty pounds when newly bought, or his shoes, real leather, cost three hundred and twenty-nine pounds and ninety-five pence. At the time of purchasing, he had laughed at the five pence margin, as if people carried that amount of money on them and would expect to be humiliated with a small round silver coin.

He's feeling cold, which isn't bad. Even with the suit jacket. The damned heat gets in to everything and just won't leave. Summer is an angry beast, contrary to what the poets say. The one who spoke in favour of autumn was right; bridge the gap and have the better of both seasons. Winter and spring, or at least the early spring, can disappear altogether. Countless times Charlotte had said she'd be happy to relocate with him, and an equal amount of time he had replied that he couldn't leave. Could leave, can leave, don't want to. Holidays over Christmas are fine and he'd even thought about taking her and the kids on their first family holiday abroad over the winter, and he's heard of stories from ex-pats that went all over the world, in an antipodean accent now, a common irritant to the ears, saying things like Honest mate, you really miss the cold and damp and snow and all that. But even that's not the real reason. He likes it here. The weather is the forever-and-always moaned-after part of life, but the good things here are undoubtedly not as good anywhere else on the globe. Business trips, for one.

He turns the dial on the air-conditioning onto white and away from blue after noticing the hairs standing straight on his arms.

The time he's taken off work is on his mind. As a family

man it's only one whole day, but it opens up so much possibility. One day, or two if he takes a Monday, makes four, and a four-day weekend is a long and lovely one. She's still got a car in which to travel. Relativity sounds all right by him, in a more simplified manner. Rather than moving quickly to achieve timelessness, the more easily accomplished method of successfully rendering time obsolete, is to not work and have lots of money. Either way, time is rendered obsolete. Just by removing his watch, this is achieved, or at least for the majority of those four days it is. Death, the dirty old man, is absolute. So whether zooming through space on the Nebula Ten Space Shuttle or treadmilling through a dead-end job until retirement, the end result is the same. Six feet down and a last dinner of dirt. Unless, of course, you get incinerated, then you don't even leave a fossil.

But for the lying, he has no immoral or corrupted conscience. Or maybe he does; he just doesn't care. And right on cue, old boy. Hands-free is a wonder tool. *Hello you scumbag. What's the sitrep?* Guessing he's just left and has parked his ass on the seat. He can never wait to call, juvenile that he is.

The voice on the phone tells him that it's just got in the car and through a rant of lurid obscenity, expresses its delight in the forthcoming, now officially under way, business trip.

Your way with words can be no more poetic, oh filthy one. You must leak shit like a snail trail.

The voice laughs in a chuckling manner, almost pronouncing an onomatopoeic heh-heh-heh. It continues to explain the cover story that it told and obviously enjoys the fabrication.

No guilt, no conscience. Sinners are we all. *You're a candidate for sinner of the year, chum. Anyway, what time's likely?* Get there earlier than him. God in heaven, such a sweet God. He'll be there an hour earlier, most likely. There's nothing he can stand less than lacking company.

When he is at home, the phone prevents him from talking to himself in an otherwise empty house.

Ah, that's good. Well I'll be there around the same time as you, maybe even a bit earlier. Definitely not. *Get us a gee-un-tee if you are before me. Should probably be one-ish, near enough lunch.*

Affirmative, says the voice from the other end of the phone-line, before adding an over-and-out and a genital-related swear word.

Stu's a top guy, he really is. Even if he'd rung when he was in a bad mood, he would still be smiling to himself like an inane moron. Getting a call from Stu always makes him smile. Being in a good old disposition makes it even better. The traffic is his friend too, and even though the entrance to the junction is clear enough with only two cars in front of him, it's as definite as death and facts. Today, the more traffic the better. The six-CD changer and the radio can't fail to fill the time, though in all honesty the radio stations on FM are a travesty and the AM is filled with lectures or discussions that remind him of university. Or classical music.

The lights turn in their limited rainbow pattern, bottom-green to highest-red, and the cars in front lead up the slight incline and slowly wedge themselves into the stop-start juddering of barely moving traffic.

Most people have their mobile-phone updates or satellite-advisory systems informing them of the places to get on and alternate routes. Doesn't bother him; slow is good. Impatience is not a part of him, so therefore he is virtuous. Vestal, in fact. Now that is funny.

He is smiling as he turns the radio on by pushing a button. The song is in *media res* and it's from where he last drove, a few days before. The song is an eighties' classic, with a strong, low-toned female vocal bellowing notes and holding them for lengthy periods. It is upbeat and tells a message of the strength of love, about how it can never be broken.

Nonsense.

He concentrates as he drives and lets the compact discs randomly change from song to song. He likes all of the records on every disc that is in the stereo. Each of the records is a Greatest Hits of the Decade compilation, starting from the fifties and ending with the eighties. There are two discs for what must have been the goldmine of music in the sixties and eighties. The tracks end and new ones start and the cycle goes on as he constantly checks his wing mirrors and drives forwards, unhindered for passages of a minute or two. He thinks about music and wonders what bands would be like if their members hadn't died and why heroin and cocaine always seemed to be every musician's favoured drug. Why is every rock-popper's doctor cocaine or heroin? Still buzzing from the acronymisation they'd done on the last business trip. Drug of choice to obtain radicality. That's a good one. The R had taken a good old bloody age, mind, but was made easier with the amount of beers they'd drunk. Initially, docs was good, but it was just for the challenge really.

Sporadically, he looks in the rear-view mirror to see what is behind him and also to act as Narcissus. He makes sure that he looks as good as possible. Every morning after waking, he exfoliates the skin on his face with a mask, flosses his teeth, plucks any noticeable hairs on his glabella and brushes his teeth, all before breakfast. Always in that order. He is, to a degree, what people know as paunchy, but solidly so and a naturally broad-shouldered, weighing fourteen stones, which for his five feet eleven, is not a body at higher risk of angina, high cholesterol, or arrhythmia than any other. His hair is black, satisfactorily to him, with faint lines of silver spreading in straight lines from his temple to just past his ears and he has mastered what he calls the art of stomach sucking. What is more important to him, is that he finds himself attractive and is happy with what he looks like and who he is. He likes looking in the mirror because he knows that he will like what he sees. There is also a tiny imprint of paranoia and goading, as if he is afraid that he will one day find some fault with what the reflection shows or that he is mocking the mirror's lack of ability to challenge him. And if it has gone unnoticed, he loves a challenge.

With these actions time passes quickly and the destination becomes closer. Drew is calm and has not let the excitement of his trip overtake him. He knows that what he feels is a mixture of the same stuff that everyone feels: eager excitement from the illicit, a childish sense of rebellion, a gleeful naughtiness from the duplicity.

It's the feeling of really tightening your sphincter and the warm, quasi-erotic buzz that floods the body after having done so. It's fuzzy, he supposes, as far as the internal senses can be said to feel fuzzy. The restaurant that they had been in was a high-high, full of earners who made his salary look like peanuts, and there they were making hyperbolic orgasmic sounds, clenching eyes tight and making a rictus of their faces.

He reflects upon this and sees himself in the third person, a floating orb or an external eye, conjuring an image of what he thinks they (including him) must have looked like. He imagines five simian shapes with large mouths rocking back and forward with hands on little pot-bellies and then sees himself laughing next to four suited, undistinguished shapes. Stu's face is also laughing, although the conjectural image flashes intermittently between his and Stu's face. He then focuses on the trip that is ahead and thinks of his socks in the suitcase in the boot.

The deal-breaker and deal-maker and signature of all of his business trips is tucked into one of his lovely, ironed cotton socks. She really is a priceless woman, ironing his socks and every inch of fabric that he deposits in the basket. The socks are the reason why the trip will happen, and without them there's nothing. Well, there is, but it really wouldn't be comparable. And he isn't paranoid and he isn't overprotective.

He lifts the brake pedal for the umpteenth time and decides that he wants to see what is about him. Pushing his foot back down after seven seconds he looks to his left at what he guesses is a retired jazz musician. The man has a ginger-grey beard, making him think of old people's homes and the stained facial hair that their residents possess. The hair on his head is russet, pulled into a loose ponytail, and there is a lot of forehead on show. Dark sunglasses cover the upper parts of his flushed cheeks and his forearms are thick at the elbow, with small biceps before they reach the cut-off sleeves of his T-shirt. On the right, two feet behind him and making him crane his neck slightly to look from the corner of his eyes, is a woman about the same age as the bearded man to the left. This woman has white hair in perfectly straightened curtains, making him think of wigs, Egyptian pharaohs and their queens. Her lips are small and pursed and her eyes are lined with the creases of age. Her cardigan is beige and he thinks that everything about the woman is as bland as her clothes. In the rear-view mirror, there is a female shape that he can't quite make out. Perhaps she is a twenty year old university student. He assumes that she is pretty and this makes him think about the girl he saw earlier when he was only a minute away from his home.

Maybe he will have some chocolate tonight. It is a business

trip, after all.

The twelfth change of song takes place and nearly perfectly coincides with a twang in his bladder. He has an urge to urinate and this brings about impatience. He knows that by the time he gets to the airport, parks the car and then bustles his way to the public toilets, it will have built up to be one of those pleasurable bursts that goes on for over thirty seconds. He also thinks that it is his fault for making himself want to urinate; if he had not clenched his sphincter and sent the electric tingle along his perineum, he probably would not have required a toilet.

Cross his legs, think of England and crash. Why had his teachers ever said that? Interesting language at times. He'll have to find out where it comes from. The old etymology and onomastics are bloody interesting things. But Christ he needs a piss. And as is always the case, don't think of it or it'll be worse. Thinking of England doesn't help. How far from the exit? Just under a mile. At this rate that'll be at least twenty minutes. And another twenty to the airport. And another twenty to find the lavatories. Well, not that long. Three-quarters of an hour realistically. Damn.

What he decides to do is to focus on memories and his memory. Each song carries with it the faces of people from his past and where there is no recollection of the events surrounding all of the songs (although most), he imaginatively associates certain people to them by the way that they feel to him. He thinks back to a time when one of his friends had been in love with a woman who every single one of the university cohort knew was having sexual intercourse with at least another two students. On one night in the Students' Union Bar, he had given a long, would-have-been-moving, if she had reciprocated his feelings, speech, stating very romantically how much she meant to him and how she was unquestionably pure. To him, Peter Farnham, the ballad being played now is allocated. The song immediately after is one that was played at a dead uncle's wedding, a time when he was only six and he had spent most of the ceremony sipping from as many different champagne flutes as he could. Following this is a song that was first played on the radio when he was twelve, and he can remember thinking that the music that his mother listened to was for old people. He had thought that his mother was too young to be listening to that. The last song that is played as he exits the motorway is a punk song that had belied the traditional roots of the genre, and he can clearly recall the way that he had played it repeatedly in college, gaining a new admiration for music that he had never enjoyed.

That isn't too bad. Much quicker than he'd forecasted. The cars seemed to have sped up as they got nearer the exit, which is usually the case. To think: would've been happy to spend another hour in the traffic but now, because bladder complains, he's desperate to escape the slow movement and get there. He'd deliberately not drunk a large amount at breakfast to compensate for the expected length of the drive, and now, with each interminable minute of being aware of it, he needs to go even more. England it is. Not helping much, though.

Drew gently bites the inside of his right cheek and teases off layers of the skin, contemplative of the effects of distraction. It doesn't hurt him. The action is subconscious, a reactive process; it is the same when he is expectant of things, nervous, worried and excited. He consciously thinks about the accommodation in which they will be staying, a place that has hosted many of their business trips over the past four years.

The eighty-foot front of the airport can be seen to the right, or at least what is usually assumed to be the front of the airport. Bloody old nuisances, airports; a million terminals and nobody knows where is where. A quick deposit, get a ticket and oh damn yes relieve himself and a taxi.

There are three sets of lights on the four-hundred metre stretch of road that leads into the airport proper. They are all green as he drives past.

Good old lights. Sometimes they can stay on red for ages. He really needs to go.

He drives past the open barriers, machine arms saluting the sky at a forty-five degree angle. His speed is limited to five miles per hour, due equally to the markings demanding he does so and to the narrow, speed humps that are spaced at intervals of ten feet. With each even slower movement of the car, wheels rising and falling with only the softest of feelings, his eyes twitch once at the corners and his cheeks rise. He gets to the end of the road after fifty seconds and turns off into the first available car park, red diodes informing him that there are sixteen spaces free. The people carrier that was in front of him has left his field of vision and he looks to his left as he turns, noticing its absence. He nearly reaches forty miles per hour in two bursts as he locates an empty space. Not considering reversing in, he tidily slots between two other, much less expensive cars, pockets his phone, and slides from the seat when the door is opened. He walks around the car after prostrating himself and the pressure on his tightened abdomen brings a gasp. He arches his back as he opens the boot and pulls out his suitcase and a black leather briefcase, gold-coloured metal ringlets attaching the handle. With the boot closed, he presses down on his car keys and receives a confirmatory electronic beep.

Ah no. He'd forgotten? He'd forgotten. How that happened he doesn't know, but his card's in his wallet and there's the machine. Quick son. Come on. Quickly. Twenty-five pounds for a week, not that it's a week. Seven two one one. Here it is.

After returning to his car and making the parking permit visible, he projects the image of an impatient man: one who needs to be somewhere else in a hurry. He also looks more angry than happy, although it is unlikely to be mistaken for aggression. He skips up and down the curbs to the pavements and regrets it both times.

Come on. Quick.

He enters one of many huge doors that welcome everyone into Terminal C and immediately finds the iconic little man on a sign outside a corridor entrance. The airport is busy, but not more than what is usual for the place, and he works out the quickest route to the toilets. He sees that the door to the disabled toilet cubicle is ajar and he pulls it open with his fingers, not thinking of staring eyes or feeling self-conscious, pulling it behind him and pulling the handle lock anticlockwise. Turning quickly and already with his fingers bringing his zip down and tugging his penis from behind his boxer shorts, he openly vocalises his coming content in an elongated sigh. The toilet seat is down and he has no intention of touching it, his urine splashing droplets of pale-yellow translucence from its velocity against the basin. He pushes from his sphincter and deliberately tries to make it pour as quickly as he can, enjoying the relief that it brings and blinking more rapidly than necessary. From the first to the last sound of water against water, he stands above the toilet for forty-six seconds before dabbing the end of his penis with toilet paper. He scrunches four pieces of toilet paper together and wipes the wetness from the seat and swipes it into the toilet and then takes another piece and cushions his fingers as they push down on the circular flush that sits atop the cistern. He drops the last piece of tissue into the swirling basin and washes his hands. He likes the smell of the pink soap; it reminds him of sherbet and childhood.

That is much better and it definitely cannot be said to be anything other than pleasurable. A good old piss after the build up of pressure is just as good as clenching the sphincter. It was probably why he needed to go so badly anyway. Funny.

He walks the opposite way to what he entered five minutes earlier, knowing where to find the rank of taxis that will get him on the way to the hotel. The wide corridor of the building has moving walkways that extend for twenty metres at thirty metre intervals. He stands on one that leads to a pair of automatic doors on the right side of the airport terminal.

There are four taxis parked along the curved edge of the road meeting the path. He walks up to the first one, whose window is open.

Hi buddy. Are we alright to get to The Gryphon? Of course he is. At least thirty pounds for the trip.

↑↓

Yes that's fine. It's on meter.

↓↑

Cheers. Maybe forty.

He opens the front door and notices that his armpits are damp. He stands with the door open and removes his suit jacket. He doubts that the driver has the air-conditioning turned on in the car, the open windows informing his deduction. He is right.

Not an uncomfortable seat, actually. Suits rarely crease so he'll keep it folded over his lap. There: that'll do. Should ring Stu and get the sitrep on his whereabouts, although it'll be surprising if he isn't there already. Maybe get an order in. Gin and tonic with lime on the rocks. Summer it is and summer shall demand it. He did ask for one earlier? Incalls and outcalls are navigated.

The phone rings five trills before Stu's recorded voice tells him that he is probably weighed down by paper in the office, but if you would be so kind as to leave a message then he'll get back to you as soon as possible. An afterthought is that if it's the apocalypse, thanks for calling but you aren't the most important person in his life. A beep comes three seconds later.

Just on my way now, Stu. I can't remember if I asked you to get a drink in for me, but I'll be twenty minutes. Traffic was awful on the old twenty-three and I'm in the taxi now. Cheers. Over and out. Bloody answerphone. He hates leaving spoken messages. There's something so impersonal about them and not getting an answer is annoying even more when within earshot of other people. So what if he's self-conscious?

He notices that the taxi drives twice as fast as he did over the bumps and he credits the vehicle's suspension and comfort of the seats. He is rocked slightly but not irritated by it. The sounds of a busy place are loud to his ears and the stillness of the air's movement covers his head with a thin film of sweat. It does not trickle down his temples or onto his brows and he doesn't wipe it away. What he does, is unbuttons his shirt twice from the top to reveal dark curly hairs. On his lap is a rested stomach of an inch and a half. His posture is good and unslumped.

Immediately outside of the airport, is a golf course that makes the area seem bucolic. It's a picture of quaint beauty. There can't be much better a day than this to be swinging a good iron. Maybe he'll pass the idea on to the others. No. Wouldn't want to bump into anyone else on this trip. He doesn't think that any of them are members of the course but why risk it? Yuppie central just behind. Never would have went there ten

Apparel

years ago, let alone as a fresh postgraduate. Now, though. It isn't too dissimilar to where they live. Overpriced. Without a doubt it wouldn't be cheap.

At the end of the stretch of road past the golf course, the taxi turns in the opposite direction to the newly established hub of youthful ascendancy, heading towards the centrality of the bustling city. Traffic is light for the post-lunch stupor that hits the roads. The heat has rested a languid blanket over the roads, he thinks, and wonders where he's heard that before.

Radio. Can't be the television.

The car picks up speed and hits thirty-one miles per hour, creating a light breeze that feels cold against the sweat on his forehead.

Both occupants of the vehicle are directly facing forwards, the rear end of a steadily moving chain of traffic the focus of each man but for different reasons. The driver is thinking of the quickest way to get to the hotel, which is rare for him; he usually finds the most circuitous route as to make the trip more profitable. Today, he just wants rid of the man he is transporting because he doesn't like him. The passenger is looking through the windscreens of cars to make out the contours of the people within them. He is trying to see if there is anyone that he recognises or if there is anyone who he would like to be acquainted with under the duvet of an unknown room.

Unzipping the back of a dress whilst pressed against plump buttocks, slowly growing and uncoiling like the nasty naughty little serpent it is. Pushing forward with hands and call him the king when he thrusts, grinds and lifts that hem and hide the sneaky snake under it (it's red) and put it inside her and pull her over it. Sheath it.

His trousers faintly twinge unnoticed by the driver. He is conscious of his lubricious wanderings and their effect on his penis, lifting his right leg to displace what he sees as an obvious prominence. He focuses on thinking of golf and swinging clubs against tee-balanced balls. Repetitive images of an unidentified player driving the ball with a satisfying thwack and then following the ball through the air until landing but not bouncing, are forced into him for seventy-six seconds. He really feels the shrinking of his penis. His right leg is placed back to its prior position.

That gee-and-tee is looking damned good. Nearly taste it. Just don't think of the chocolate he's subconsciously promised himself. He has promised himself, hasn't he? Yes yes yes. Right here and now he just did.

A familiar stretch of road, lined on each side with buildings that contain no fewer than sixteen storeys, is being driven up. On this road, the antepenultimate building is The Gryphon Hotel. On the digital counter situated directly above the rear-view mirror, the numbers read 0026:20.

That's not bad at all. Maybe he had been slightly harsh on the chap. Forty, expected, or thirty?

He pulls out thirty pounds and when the taxi stops he gives it to the driver who says thank you and he puts his suit jacket over his shoulder and walks up the pillared steps that lead into the entrance lobby of the hotel with his suitcase swinging in his right hand and his briefcase in his left. Without looking at the reception desk to his left, he heads forwards and into the bar. There are thirty people in the bar, all but two of the tables occupied by couples: business types, mainly.

There they are. That jet-black hair can never be natural. Befitting for the unnaturalness of the man who owns it. Stu the conspicuous. Didn't expect the others here so early. Only Pete is missing. He greets them and they ask after each other's families and each other's individual health.

↑↓
You not getting a drink? says Stu.

↓↑
Probably a coffee says Carl

↑↓
A coffee: good idea. Think I will. Just be a minute. He really does not like Carl. He walks to the bar and is served by a young man of twenty years. He orders a gin and tonic and asks if the young man will bring it over when it is finished and the young man says *Yes, of course. No problem. Won't be a minute.* He rejoins the table.

↓↑
Hey, Drew. We were just talking about the laws or rules or whatever they are, of adultery. We've got never see the same girl twice.

↑↓
Never buy condoms.

↓↑
Never save a number.

↑↓
Always delete log lists.

↓↑
Well it's the same really.

↑↓
What rule or law do you want to add to our bestselling guide to successful philandering?

↓↑
Don't shit on your own doorstep. Wise words said by a million wise men, and probably by another billion who couldn't stick to it.

↑↓
Well, that's good advice, but He's married *if you get*

married, you've basically gone and done it times ten. Complete colonic irrigation all over the patio. That was good. *You've shit on your doorstep by building the doorstep and placing the angriest night-watchman on constant lookout.*

Everybody laughs.

↓↑

Who said that? The silly old boy could never've come up with that himself. Drew is doubtful of Stu's creativity regarding the coining of his aphorism.

↑↓

Who said what?

↓↑

That joke. Who said it? What's it from?

↑↓

Well, me. I just made it up. He's a damned comedian. *I am, in case you didn't realise, a genius.*

↓↑

You haven't got the IQ, old chum.

↑↓

And you're a scumbag. Everyone's laughing. *But that's not business; it's only personal.*

The laughter reaches its loudest and everyone raises their glass. Drew lifts his cup and in two large swallows drinks his coffee, leaving only the dark-brown dregs at the bottom.

↓↑

Touché. Quick-witted git. And Carl can stop laughing like the dick he is.

He is smiling as the bartender leans over to place a cylindrically shaped glass on the table next to him. The bartender says There you go, sir and Drew *Thanks,* which is followed by their combined silence before Drew gets a muted wolf-whistle from Al with the young man halfway between them and the bar. They all laugh quite loudly.

↑↓

Dah-ling. You've pulled. Rule number thicth - only perform adultery with thothe of the thame thecth. Fucking tongue-twister.

↓↑

Don't get jealous, Stu. I'll hook you up afterwards if you want. If Ferdy laughs any harder he'll be choking on his spleen. Good kid.

The talk turns to work and Al states how he has recently sold one of the fifty most expensive homes in the city to a retired bank manager. They all agree that his work is taking him places and they lay claims to various expensive gifts that they all want for Christmas. Carl says that his work is the same old same old and moans about his immediate superior. He is, according to Carl, the only reason why his promotion has not come through yet. Ferdy is employed by the same company as Stu and is combining his studies for a Masters in Economics with his junior position in the firm. Stu teases him about sleeping together and that he won't need his education. They laugh at this. Drew then details how working from home is easy and that he can do no wrong with his work. Selling knowledge and acumens in a world full of dumb people is easy, he tells them. They like this and laugh. Stu goes last and says that work is easy when all he has to do is make sure young whelps like Ferdy are working. Overseer, he says, is a mighty fine job, and he'd take it easy for Ferdy's first time against the head-office desk; he'd be walking in a week, no problem.

A genuine son of a sophisticate like Ferdinand, all public school and old-fashioned mannerisms, he probably does swing his cricket bat whichever way the wind blows.

↑↓

Ferdy asks *And have you brought the party, Drew?*

↓↑

Of course he has. Never hasn't.

↑↓

Of course I have. Likes his good stuff, too. First to ask. Ruined his quip too. *When have I ever never?*

A briefly-lived pang of guilt makes him think of his children in the park, collected early from school.

Stu tells the other four men that he needs to use the bathroom and Ferdy says that he needs to as well.

With the three of them left there, Drew initiates a conversation with Carl.

The self-righteous cunt can talk to himself. *So work's been treating you the wrong way then, Carl?*

↓↑

Yeah. Same old same old. The work itself isn't bad, obviously. It's just, you know.

↑↓

Not really chum. *Yes. That bloody idiot of a manager keeps passing you over. He's a dinosaur though, right?* Carl answers that yeah, he is. *Then his time can't be long and you'll be in. What about your family? How's Sara and the kids?* Scott? Tommy?

↓↑

Yeah. Sara's doing really well and the kids are doing fine

↑↓

How're Char and the twins, Drew?

↑↓

The twins are as mad as ever. There's some strange new Polish cleaner or something at school and there's this game that they play which involves them acting Polish, and even though it's pretty funny, my kids are not Polish.

Al looks up and laughs, joining Carl.

It's not funny. Really. He joins in the laughter. *I'd rather they were acting Indian. Anything but.*

↓↑

Let's be honest. You probably wouldn't.

↑↓

Who's asking you, pleb? *No. I really would.* Pleb.

↓↑

Funny, kids. Aren't they? You heading anywhere in the holidays?

↑↓

Well. I was thinking of

Carl's phone rings loudly from his breast pocket on his shirt, blue-white light visible through the white cotton. Carl pulls it out, right forefinger and thumb from the pocket against his left pectoral.

←
→

Sara. That's odd. *Hullo love. You okay?* Calm down. It can't be anything serious. *Uh huh.* Shit. Stay calm. *Where. I mean when?* It's not too bad. She likes to overreact. *Okay. Uh huh.* She's their mother. Every right to. *I'll be there as soon as possible. They'll be fine. I know I know I know.* Shit. *You too.*

↓↑

Shit. This doesn't look good. *Everything okay, mate?*

↑↓

Sam's had an anaphylactic at school and his pen's done the job. Jen's crying scared. I better leave.

↓↑

Is there anything I can do? You need anything? I can

↑↓

Cheers Al, but it's alright. I'd better be there to pick them up with Sara is all. Got about forty minutes to get there. Jen'll be more shook up than Sam and it won't be easy.

↓↑

You're not going? Party's not even started old chum

↑↓

I gotta. He stands up.

↓↑

But she knows you're here?

↑↓

Yeah. Clients' business meeting. Tour of the vicinities. She always knows where I am, I just don't tell her I'm with you reprobates. A small laugh. Perfect timing, too.

Stu and Ferdy return to the table as he is pushing his chair under it. Al explains the situation and Stu and Ferdy adopt serious expressions.

↓↑

Shit. Send Sara my best and I hope Sam's alright.

↑↓

She doesn't know you're here.

↓↑

I ain't married. There's no one to tell.

↑↓

Carl laughs politely and shakes everyone's hand. *Thanks gentlemen. Don't act sane without me. That wouldn't be fair.* This receives a restrained smile from everyone at the table and he nods his head and leaves.

That asshole didn't seem too concerned. My wife and kids, for God's sake. More worried about the night ahead than Sam, Jen or Sara. Some people. His wife was a bit too frantic on the phone and yes she has rubbed a bit off on him. The last time this happened, the first time, everything was fine and the school got the ambulance and no harm done. He has the pen and they used it so what the problem could be he can't tell. Last time she was hysterical but the doctors had said that there's nothing to worry about. The school had said the same, that they all train with the pens and know how to use them. So why was he so nervous? Anxious? Anxious, okay. It's her fault. Fair enough though. He can understand what it must be like for her. She's his mother. And what is he doing, trying to apportion blame. He's scared and it's his fault. Don't blame his wife. She was actually quite calm on the phone. Imagine what he'd have been like. Christ.

It is very hot outside and the glare of the sun on the pale grey pavements makes him squint. He sees white blotches in the corners of his eyes that he squeezes out with his wincing expression. He is wearing a white cotton shirt, pinstriped-grey trousers and leather shoes. There is a black-leather-strapped wristwatch on his left wrist that has already begun to accumulate a ring of sweat around it. He suddenly realises that he has left his suit jacket on the hanger in the lobby of the bar and does not give it a second thought after patting his trouser and shirt pockets and feeling his wallet, keys and mobile phone.

Bus or taxi or tram or. He hasn't been on a bus for over a decade and the tram can never guarantee getting anywhere on time these days. Taxi it is. There's one and he's. No he's not. Shit.

There is a row of three taxis parked on the other side of the road in front of another hotel, all glossy black and advertising their newness. He stops on the path and pushes his opened fingers through his hair, powdering the dried gel. Twelve cars go past before the traffic starts to slow to a halt and when they are stopped with their engines kicking out visible spumes of exhaust fumes, he walks between the bumpers and stands on the concrete divide in the middle of the road. Two cars go past and he runs quickly across. On the pavement he walks up to the furthest taxi, crouching so his face is looking at the driver through the open window. A pop song is being played on the radio station to which the car's radio is tuned.

Any chance of a lift?

↓↑

Why d'you think I do this fucking job? *F'course mate. Where d'you want?*

↑↓

Arlington Primary. He says it as a question.

↓↑

Thirty up front. You rich twat.

↑↓

Sure. Cheers. A bit steep.

He gets out his wallet and hands the driver two notes. The driver reaches out with his left hand, a faded blue tattoo of a football club's badge proudly on show on his thick forearm. Getting in the car, Carl thinks that the driver reminds him of someone, but cannot recall who.

He looks younger than what he is. Must be the hair. He looks older in the photocard identification. Steve Hughes. Looks like a Steve. Forty-six.

↓↑

You picking your children up then, eh? Spoilt little cunts, he bets.

↑↓

Yeah. Just had a call from my wife saying my son's had an allergic reaction to something at school. Should be okay.

↓↑

That's a shame. That's a. Sorry to hear about it. Hope the little shit carcs it. *Hope he's okay.* Middle class cunts.

↑↓

Cheers. Thanks.

That's more than he got from that other asshole. Didn't even ask. Irritating asshole. And the way he ends his stupid remarks with chum or chap or old boy and all those stereotypical World War One expressions. The asshole doesn't even have a posh accent. No accent, in fact.

The music in the car does not gain his attention and he watches the shopfronts and parking meters and people go passing by as he looks out of the window to his left. With his eyes, he focuses on nothing and no one. With his mind, he thinks of his love for his wife, his son and his daughter.

He's only thirty-seven. Christ. Mid-life crisis in a taxi? They're good guys, regardless what they choose to get up to in their evenings once a week. They never pressure him about doing any of what they do or. But why would they and how could they? He's thirty-seven. Christ.

The fans in the taxi are blowing out cooled air and he feels cold and doesn't like it. He does not ask the driver to turn the air-conditioning off because he is being reciprocally respectful for the comments that were made about his children.

About Sam. He's fine. No doubt. Lots of kids have nut allergies and such and how many did you ever read about that were killed by it. None. Like the doctor said. Has he heard of any kids who died from it? Well, no he hasn't. That's what the doctor said. No anxiety. Nothing to be worried about.

Familiarity assuages his fear as he sees that they are only five minutes' distance from the school. He knows that in the modern world of inescapability, if there is a problem it will be made known. He calms himself by the silence of the phone and that he is ten minutes early for the school bell. The world is a good place to him, a place where he can evade the social expectation of socialising with assholes and where his son will be okay. His wife is a woman whom he doesn't deserve but loves him and he her and two beautiful children can cause real feelings that, whilst not always wanted, reassure him of his love for them. It is a place where the kindness of strangers gives him a fond outlook on the regular once-met people that are so frequent in life. He is very much a person who instead of looking for the shit-ended side of the stick, aims to find the side that doesn't taste so bad. What about that asshole at work? Well it ain't like he's after his blood. Individuals like him, stuck in the past can find it hard to change their ways. An extra thirty kays isn't much to grumble over, anyhow.

And they arrive in the grounds of a very beautifully landscaped primary school. The topiary has been cut into the shapes of ducklings and rabbits, each neatly aligned inside the red-painted metal fences that run around the perimeter. The red paint is bright and there are no signs of rust or the flaked indication of age. The buildings themselves are of smooth sand-coloured stone with long verticular windows reaching from waist height to a metre or so from the edge of the roof. The ledges are a deep brown and wood-stained. There are seven adults standing outside the main entrance to the school, three in a conversational group, another two discussing something and two others looking into their mobile phones, thumbs changing direction just slow enough for the eye to follow each movement. One of them, a woman, pushes a perambulator back and forth two and a half inches, its occupant asleep.

Carl opens the door and steps out of the car when it stops, immediately aware of his reacquaintance with the sun and with the summer. He pats his pockets and shakes and jingles his keys, emphasising his point to the taxi driver. *Cheers again mate. Have a good one.* He closes the door firmly and without slamming it, and walks along the mosaically designed paving slabs that lead to the main entrance.

In the reception area through the window. Sara and the kids. They all look fine. Who's Sara with? Looks like Mary and Chris. That'll do her good. Stop her panicking. He's not sure though. Damned contacts need changing, hopefully not the prescription.

He walks past the girl with the pram and she smiles a full smile at him

$$\rightarrow$$
$$\leftarrow$$

he does smile back. And why shouldn't he?

She looks down at the baby in the perambulator. Her smile remains exactly as it was. It is full and makes her round cheeks curve below her eyes. The baby has the creased eyes of all sleeping babies and the wispy hair is thick enough to suggest eight months of life.

She feels warm all over. Like some of the bad poetry she wrote that her teacher had pretended to like in school, she is warm inside and outside. Metaphors. She didn't get a B for not listening. Little twitches under the eyes and the funny twitches of the mouth are so cute. Like every time, it's the lashes that are the most attention grabbing. She'll be a supermodel when she's older, no doubt at all.

Her eyes go back to the phone positioned by the handles of the pushchair.

She'd better say no. Just in case they've got her some work. The agency hasn't rung for four days and until they get her a job, it makes sense to be unsociable for a few days. *C'est la vie.* Especially with her brother's visit, too.

Her thumbs tap out a message declining the invitation of a few drinks at a club, and after pressing send she checks the time on the screen, locks the phone, and wedges it into the left pocket of her tight-fitting, stone-washed denim shorts. The ends of her shorts are three inches above the knees, and a safe three inches from the rounded curvature of her buttocks. She is wearing a near-plain-white tank top, with a logo situated in front of her left breast. Her white brassiere straps are visible over each of her shoulders, where the neck muscles extend in little slopes and meet the jutted contours of her scapulae. She is wearing ankle-strapped sandals and her toenails are finely-polished red. Her fingernails are lacquered to an unnaturally glossy sheen. Hooped silver earrings are worn, one in each ear.

More parents and buggy-bound babies fill up the front of the school over the next six minutes, glancing at watches to check the perfection of their timings. She studies each of them for a few seconds, catches smiles and happy faces, as well as a few flushed faces on the larger women. She finds it amusing that even in this day and age, it's all women. Apart from the man who went inside.

The bell rings, muffled yet still loud and audible to all who are standing outside. Twenty-two seconds later comes the shuffling little-legged run of the children. Rolled-up trouser legs show the typical pink knees of children's clumsiness, bright-red polo shirts have crusted milk stains dotted below the collar, and faces unfettered by the woes of a disgusting world giggle innocently with the genuine glee of seeing parents and siblings. The two-day break doesn't bring them any more joy than being in school, but they look forward to it as they look forward to everything at that age.

There he is. Handsome little devil.

And how are you, you cheeky little devil?

A boy skips up to her and gives her a hug around her left leg. She ruffles his hair with her right hand and puts her left on

his upper back. *Did you have a good day at school?*
  ↓↑
We made paintings of rockets we did. And we got them in our bags.

He slings the bag from his back and his fingers slide over the semi-circle of the top of it, trying to find the zip.
  ↑↓
Wow. That's really amazing. Show us when we get home. Gran will want to see it too. Children are easy.

He nods his head up and down really quickly with his smiling mouth open.
  ↓↑
Do you think she'll like it? It's a big rocket and I made it for her.
  ↑↓
Yeah. I know she'll like it. Did you not make one for me?
  ↓↑
I only made one. She's sad now. *But it's for both of you. I made it for you and gran.*
  ↑↓
Thanks Tye. That's really sweet. She is laughing lightly at the look of concern that was on his face. His smile is beaming once more. She always finds it strange how he doesn't give much thought to the baby.

He says something to a girl as they leave that makes the girl smile and they walk out of the opened gates and down the path to the left of the road that leads into the school. She lets the boy talk about all of the amazing things that he has done in school and she listens, encouraging him to detail some activities when he fails to explain them to her, and interjecting with words of theatrical wonderment that completely convince him. It is only a short walk to their house and they are home nearly four minutes after they left the school gates. Before they are home, she learns about tie-dyeing and how to spell rhythm, what rhythm means and about tea and coffee and silly balls. She does not correct him when he is wrong.

The front door to the house is open, exactly as it was when she left. Grandma is probably still complaining about the lack of a decent breeze to air out the house after all of her cleaning. Chemical aftersmell and that stuff. She's probably right, mind. Grandma's right about nearly everything. Tye's shuffled sprinting is really cute and he zips across the garden lawn like always and in through the front door. Better not tell that he didn't wipe his shoes. Then again, the cut grass will tell on him anyway. She knows she will clean it up.

Still outside of the front door, she rests the perambulator in the shade under the porch that extends five feet to the left of the doorframe and crouches down with her knees against her breasts. Her backside feels tight in her denim shorts as she uses her hands to sweep the cut and sun-blanched grass from the carpet and foot mat. In the back garden, Tye's voice is heard unintelligibly from this distance but unmistakably expressing his excitement and delight.

Probably at the rocket pictures. He really is the sweetest kid. She's heard somewhere that jealousy plays a large part in young children when they get a new brother or sister. It's not even like he does anything horrible to Leanne, or looks angrily at her or handles her roughly; he just doesn't seem to care. Lost in his own bubble of innocent fun, she supposes. Then again, it can't be easy when your dad disappears suddenly. There's a really good chance that Tye links the two together, what with Leanne being born a month before he went inside.

The word inside has always irritated her. Growing up with James was a fight against the stereotypical expectation that the whole world seemed to cast upon them. Their mother was single shortly after she fell pregnant with her, James being five months old. Their father, who James has actually cast eyes upon but, as with all infancy, will never remember, had decided that he didn't want a young family or a pregnant wife for another nine month tenure, and had absconded with a prostitute. At least, this is what the account given by their grandmother would state. Not long after she was born, their mother had met another man whose love owed more to physical possession than anything else, and when their mother had had enough and threatened to end the relationship if he didn't allow her some personal space and free will, he in turn reciprocated the act of threatening but finished it off with murder. The stigma would remain. A black brother and sister raised by their grandmother due to their parents' murder and unfaithfulness, they received a lot of overt ostracism from the schools that they attended. Their grandfather was a successful property developer and they had educated their only daughter at prestigious public schools. The schools that they attended were also outside the state system, much the same as Tye's will be when he leaves primary school.

James, however, grew up with a determined enmity towards the subtle racism that their teachers and classmates and classmates' parents would hide quite well. He consciously retaliated against the men of his past by becoming somewhat akin to them. Whenever a boy would show an interest in his sister, he would intimidate or beat them up in what would always be a successful attempt at warding potential suitors away. In his own way, he was possessive of her. He managed to get through school and then found easy ways of making money which was why he ended up in prison.

She sees that Leanne is asleep in the shade under the porch

and the baby does not wake as she is picked up and gently walked into the house and up the stairs and into a small, pink-walled room and gently placed into a finished-pine cot. She tucks her under a thin, white cotton quilt. Before she leaves, she looks at Leanne's face with its creased eyes and pursed lips, seeing her squeeze her closed eyes even tighter in some sleeping recognition of being watched.

Maybe one day. Who knows? Not much luck with men in the family though. The good ones get rich and die from unexpected heart failure, and the bad ones kill, cheat and go inside. Inside. Not that her brother's bad. She thinks she needs to use the toilet.

She walks into the upstairs bathroom and unzips her shorts before unbuttoning their solitary button. She pulls her black knickers and shorts down to rest just below her knees. She defecates and wipes her sphincter with toilet paper before standing and fastening the button on her shorts. She runs the hot tap for twenty seconds before it gets warm and then presses liquid soap into her hands and washes them under the water. Then she goes down the stairs and out of the front door.

She doesn't know why they don't just get a fold-up buggy. Much easier to bring indoors. It's pretty heavy and she's not weak. Not by a long way.

Back inside, taking care not to touch the carpets with the hard rubber wheels that have rolled through the dirt of the streets, she walks through the short hallway and through the doorway to the drawing room and out of the opened double-doors that open into the garden.

↓↑

Did Tye tell you about the rocket that he painted? He's going to show us after dinner.

She is a lean, thin woman with peppered silver-black hair

and what many people describe as a trendy dress sense for a woman of her age. Her granddaughter is proud of her for being removed from the variety of stereotypes that befall people who are rich, black, old, or a combination of all three.

You will be here for dinner? No work called through?

↑↓

They could call at any moment. *Yeah. I'll be here for food. Don't think there's a shift going tonight. And yeah, he showed me; Tye's a little artist. Ain't that right, Tye?* She pushes the perambulator gently near the garden wall to her left.

↓↑

Yeah. And a musician. I can do lots. Tea, tea, coffee, tea. I know silly balls and how rockets fly and where space is.

He is inspecting the stones that border the shrubs along the high wooden fencing, looking for insects to throw into spiders' webs.

I learnt that just today. And we played on a zile phone.

↑↓

Maybe we'll have to get you one for your birthday, eh?

↓↑

Awwh Gram, yeah. Birthday. Birthdays are brilliant. *But we can't get a rocket can we? Missus Fletcher said they were real dear. But if I'm a astraut I can have my own.* My own rocket. Brilliant. *You could visit me on the moon or I could drive you there.*

His grandmother starts laughing.

↑↓

You don't drive rockets, dear. Astronauts fly them. And maybe we can get a smaller rocket, to fly in the garden. Has your birthday not already been though, Tye?

↓↑

·*No. No it hasn't. No it hasn't.* She's forgot. *It's the third of*

August. I can member it. Third of August. It's close. It hasn't been.

↑↓

Oh yeah. You are right. Well, we'll wait and see what you get. There's still a week left of school yet.

↓↑

Gran, my phone's just started going. It might be work.

She raises her eyebrows and looks diagonally left to signal her annoyance, before taking the phone out of her left pocket and walking through the drawing room and hallway and turning left into the living room. She falls back into one of the two armchairs, the one closest to the television by the curtains, and hits the button directly below the digitally written ACCEPT.

Hello. Oh, hi Amy. Wonder how much. *Yeah, I'm free to work tonight.* Hmmm. Okay. *Uh-huh. Yeah. Okay. Uh-huh. Uh-huh. Yeah that'll be good. Text me the details.*

She lets out a deliberately lengthy breath and stares at the blue glow of her mobile phone's screen for twenty-two seconds.

There's plenty of time. Nearly an hour until she'll have to start getting ready. A couple of hundred is good money too, and not to be sniffed at. Would always be nicer if it's more, but c'est la vie. She'll help gran with the dinner before she goes. Maybe have a quick bite during it.

On the armchair, she reaches her arms back past her head and puts her legs, crossed at the knees, over the left arm and stretches. A stifled, low-throated yawn comes out of her opened mouth. She stands up and puts the mobile phone back into her left pocket and then walks back the way that she came to lean against the jamb of the drawing-room doorway.

↑↓

I've got a shift, so I'll probably not be back much before midnight. Amy's called in sick. I'll give you a hand with the dinner, if you like?

↓↑

Don't be silly. Relax before you go to work. I'll get something else on now and you can eat before you go.

↑↓

Always the same. Bless. *It's no problem. I'll have some soup or something.* Can't eat before work. *What are you making? I'll get it prepped.*

↓↑

You don't need to. I was going to make a casserole with the chicken from Wednesday. Dumplings are already made. Such a good girl.

↑↓

I'll do the vegetables for you then.

She walks to the kitchen and takes a wooden chopping board in the shape of a duck from the rivet in the wall above the central worktop, and a short-handled and long-bladed knife from the knife stand. From the vegetable rack at the end of the kitchen's ground-level units, she takes out two celeries, four carrots, one potato and one *rutabaga*, which she washes and peels and prepares. When she finishes, a thin sliver of orange is stuck to the back of her left wrist, adding to the pink petals of the tattooed violet.

The tattoo was inked on her two summers ago. It was not because she was afraid or worried that she did not have it done when she had first thought about and committed to the idea; it was because she was still in school and the hassle that she would have received from her teachers would have been a nuisance. Violet was her mother's middle name and she had thought about getting all three of her mother's names written in a loopy, archaic and sombre type, before she matured artistically (in her eyes) enough to choose something less obvious and slightly more symbolic.

What will tonight bring? It's always unpredictable and she never knows what she'll have to do. Definitely meet some interesting types, though. Alcoholics, drug abusers, depressives, violent types, adulterers. The one thing that they seem to have common is that they all have some sort of problem. Or three.

She laughs and starts to whistle a tune that she has become attached to over the past four days. In her pocket, a vibration buzzes against her left thigh and she dries her hands on her tank top. She pulls it out with her left hand and passes it to her right. She unlocks the phone by pressing her thumb to 0 and then 3 and then 0 again and then 8, and then presses VIEW.

That's good. She knows the place and there's a bus that will take her to that part of town. She hasn't worked in the place, but then she hasn't been with the agency for long, so why should she have? One of the better places in the city too, so maybe won't be too bad. Plenty of time too. Better leave before five for gran's sake.

She puts the phone into her right pocket without locking it and then gets out a heavy, thick-bottomed saucepan, into which she slides the vegetables, with the exception if the celery. from the lifted chopping board. She places the saucepan under the cold tap and fills it so that roughly an inch of water rises above the assorted contents. After putting the saucepan on the draining board, she picks up the salt grinder and grinds salt into it, swirling around the water and dissolving the salt until the water has no dusty semblance. Her tank top is used once more as a hand towel.

What to wear? Or should she just bring her bigger handbag and put clothes in it? Decisions decisions.

She is in her room and standing in front of the open double doors to her wardrobe, sliding the clothes hangers with her palms flat and fingers curling to her left with her right hand. She pauses at the light-blue nurse's uniform and smiles subtly with a faint contraction of her lips.

They didn't say she needed it tonight so she isn't going to wear it.

It is twenty-nine degrees Celsius in the room and she feels okay. Not sweating on the way to work is a self-imposed rule. The dress that she selects is black and light polyester, and she believes that it is and will be perfect for keeping her as cool as possible in the late-afternoon-and-evening sun. The hem of the bottom reaches to show only the lower half of her knees when standing up, and the shoulder straps at the top are perfectly aligned with her brassiere straps. She takes three steps to a wide, pine chest of drawers and pulls open the top drawer with both hands on the brass handles. Inside the drawer is a gallimaufry of underwear: brassieres, French knickers, g-strings, folded pyjama bottoms, briefs, socks, tights, stockings, rolled-up leggings, thongs, a single vest top, stockings. She pulls out a black, silk-cotton thong, and smiles as she thinks about work.

Perfect.

She takes off her clothing apart from the black knickers and brassiere, throwing them on her double bed, and walks from her room to the bathroom. After closing and locking the door, she pulls her knickers down to her ankles and as she steps out of them, slides the back of her brassiere around to her front and pulls the hooks from their little clasps. She has no pubic hair above her vagina and her legs have been shaved in the last twenty-four hours. Her hair is straightened and she pulls it into a bun, knotting it into place as she steps from the bamboo and cotton-topped bath mat and into the bath and twists the tap of the shower, just off from the centre of the wall and directly beneath the bracket in which the showerhead faces down. She flinches as the cold water shoots at her. As the water warms, she enjoys the cleansing, preparing herself for the usual difficulty of finishing with her feet.

Damned tickly feet. Odd horrible pleasure. Her teacher had liked that. An oxymoron.

There's no way she's putting the showerhead against the bottom of her feet. That really isn't bearable. Just move it around in the bath and it'll do the same job. Take two.

The same routine is carried out on her right foot, but this time she is rougher and quicker and does not giggle. It is still pleasurable and her mouth is fixed in a bitten-down smile for the nine seconds that she does this. She stands after shaking her foot spasmodically from left to right five times, the showerhead in her right hand pointing away from her. She slots it into the bracket and turns the dial from red and into blue and the water stops abruptly, droplets immediately forming against the small rubber nodules. Without drying, she stands on the soft bath mat and enjoys feeling the water on her body start to feel cold against her skin. It is only temporary, but it is a minor delight.

Bliss. Warmth is great but so's being cool when it's hot. Leaving cool keeps you cool and she'll not sweat before work.

There are goosebumps on her skin and her skin tightens. She takes the green towel from the top of the rack and dries the back of her neck and shoulders, moving on to her thighs, legs, stomach, back and breasts, and then her buttocks and vagina. She dries her feet by placing the towel spread and flat against the bath mat and then standing on it. On a shelf above the towel rack is a collection of various cosmetic products and she right-handedly picks up and left-handedly uncaps a cocoa-butter body moisturiser, applying it on her face, legs and arms, rubbing the excess on her buttocks, breasts and stomach.

Her dress routine starts with her thong, followed by her bra and then the dress.

Three piece suit. Always used to confuse her when she was a child and gramps had talked about getting the new sofa and chairs.

It had become a joke between them even before she knew what it meant.

Her skin is warm, the coolest it has been since waking up, and the usual hollow feeling in her stomach has started. She will not eat before work and she knows this, hence her placatory comments to her grandmother earlier.

That's one stereotype that she does live up to: the doting and concerned grandma. That's why the lies. Not because of shame or guilt, but to make gran's life easier.

At the bottom of the stairs there are three pairs of slip-on shoes that belong to her and Tye's school shoes and a pair of ankle boots that belong to her grandmother. She turns around and quickly, lightly, walks up the stairs and into her room to grab her work bag.

Get to work earlier than usual. Why not? It might take longer anyway; doesn't know the bus times for that route.

She always gets to work early. She has never been late and takes the factors into account that stem from her lack of a driving licence and vehicle. She is rarely in the same place for long in her job and depending on where she is, the distance is a variable that she deliberately overcompensates for. Back down the stairs, through the hallway and study and leaning against the doorframe, she says goodbye to her grandmother and her nephew, whose slumbering head is resting against his grandmother's seated legs on the grass.

I'm going to head off out now, gran. I've done the stuff for the casserole.

↓↑

Such a sweetie. *Did you get yourself something to eat?*

↑↓

I'll get something out now. I'm going to meet Rach for something to eat. Probably shouldn't've said that. *I'll be okay.*

↓↑

Okay. Just make sure you do get something to eat. Have a good night at work, Tasha.

↑↓

I will do. Thanks. Bye gran. Bye Tye.

Her grandmother says goodbye and Tye mumbles what she assumes is the same. She smiles, turns and walks to the bottom of the stairs. She slips into the pair of white plimsoll-shoes that is between the other two and picks her bag up, opens it, and looks inside from habit. She knows that everything she needs will be inside it and does not look for anything that is or is not there. She walks straight out of the doorway, noticing the faintest breeze against her skin and smiling, thinking that her grandmother might finally be contented with the aerated rooms. She walks down the path and considers humming a song that she has heard recently and enjoys, but decides to soundlessly think it. Her feet make only the softest clap against the pavement and her walk is slow, enjoying the minute cooling of the air from the dustless breeze.

Out of the two bus stops it's probably the 84 or 85. It's been a while since last taking it. Electronic timetables will tell all anyway.

There are three boys twenty-two yards down the path and they are chatting animatedly amongst themselves, hands clasped to miniature silver scooters and pushing themselves along in a neat horizontal line. The boy in the middle of the line sees her first and scoots faster whilst saying something. He is quickly in front of the boy that was to his right of the pavement and the left of her sightline, with the boy opposite falling behind both of the others to make a single-file convoy. Scooting past her, eleven or twelve years old at most, they look at her from the corners of their eyes, appraising the slender and curvaceous flesh of young womanhood. Childish minds imagine vividly graphic images of bare flesh, huge breasts and alien vaginas, little semblance to the woman for which they stare over their shoulders to prolong their fantasies, giggling profanity to one another.

Kids. They couldn't be more than ten.

She has a smile fixed on her face and she imagines herself from a different perspective. The third person, as Miss said, allows omnipotence. Or omniscience.

And she creates the image of a spring-step gait. The song has finished its loop in her head and she stops at the edge of the pavement, waiting for the cars to stop being driven up or down the road. After twenty-one seconds, she quickly walks across and after three metres takes a right turn on a Y-shaped path, leading past a series of lawns on the right and a green to her left. She sees a woman coming towards her in tight, pink, thigh-hugging three-quarter-length shorts, jogging with a blue bottle in her left hand and headphones on her ears. The jogger's grey vest top stops above her navel and a lineated abdominal is apparent.

Wouldn't be bad. Effort though. It's not jogging alone anyway; it's the sit-ups and gym work and everything else. Hers isn't that bad. Just about pinch some skin.

There are six people standing at the bus stop: five women, one with a perambulator, and a man.

Ooh, a baby. Bet she's a sweet little cutie. Or he.

She smiles at the mother who smiles back with a kindness to her expression and then she slowly looks in at the baby, allowing the mother to follow her eyes' direction and enjoy the predictable responses to the baby's adorability.

She's so cute. Absolutely adorable. Smile back up at her.

↓↑

Thanks. Her name's Rose and she's a little angel, isn't she?

↑↓

Yes. Completely. She wonders how old she is. *How old is she?*

↓↑

Four months. And a bit. Can't sleep in this heat much, so it's a rare occasion.

The woman looks down at Rose and then smiles again and looks at the girl that she is talking to, noticing how beautiful she is.

Do you have any children? Or are you too young?

She laughs.

↑↓

I'm twenty-three. Is that what you mean by too young?

But I don't have any children. Baby-sit a lot for my brother though. She's eight months. Lashes like a model, just like yours. Rose's.

She feels embarrassed for what she has said, regarding her own words as those of a challenge or competition: hers is prettier than the woman's. She smiles again as the woman starts to say something, catching the briefest glance from a man who

←

→

averts his gaze when she catches him looking at her.

Twenty-three. What a babe. Always had a thing for black girls and Diane would even say the same. Her black dress works wonders on her body. Twenty-three, hello. He's twenty-seven and you're fit as... Just don't tell Diane because she'll kill him.

He fixes his eyes on a seagull that is hopping along the edge of the pavement on the other side of the road, jerking its neck and pointing its beak and beady eyes in his direction.

Fucking inquisitive little shit, ain't you? Where's the bus and God he wishes it would stop, although it's not as bad at the moment. Overnight relief.

He consciously stops himself from scratching at his crotch, where regrowing pubic hairs are proving less torturous than before, but torturous nonetheless. His train of thought digresses between seagulls eating crabs and black girls...

He blames the heat for his libidinous feelings and random arousals. The slightest feel of wind has been noticed, but it is only the faintest of coolnesses that does not diminish the heat by more than two degrees. He listens in on the two women's conversation and wants to join in. He looks over again, sure that she is not looking in his direction.

She looks familiar but from where? He's sure she's a friend of Diane's. No she's not. Well, maybe she is. He's not sure. He'd've asked her if the bus hadn't appeared.

A double-decked bus with an electronic sign reading 84 in orange, dim against the glaring sunlight, is coming towards the bus stop. The people standing at the bus stop shuffle into a politely formed queue, allowing the woman with her baby to head the line and then facing the slowing-down bus intently, watching as it leans towards the curb and then swings out, automatic doors opening with the hiss of pistons lowering suspension. The woman at the front of the line pushes down on the handles of the perambulator and the front wheels lift into the air. She moves it forwards and lets it back down, lifting the rear wheels to get it on the bus.

He knew she'd do it easily, otherwise he'd've offered to help.

He lets every one of the people step on the bus before him, receiving thank yous from two of them.

Return to the centre please mate.

The driver tells him it is three fifty and he thinks that he has detected a Polish accent. He wishes that he knows how to say something other than what he knows.

Culver. Probably won't impress him.

He pays with four coins and pulls his stub from the machine to the left of the plastic glass and walks down the aisle, taking a seat at the back-right of the bus. He is disappointed that the black woman has gone upstairs. Three seconds go by. He wants to move upstairs but he thinks that it would be obvious to everyone that he is stalking her. The real reason is that the seats at the back of the bus are hot.

Why did he sit next to the stupid, boiling engine? What on earth was he thinking? At least the windows are open. Someone had a bit of common sense. And now he's goddamned thirsty, too. Half an hour's distance at the most, then a couple of beers. Perfect. It'll just taste better, that's all. And whadya know? There is a breeze coming through too. Won't stop the crabs or his sweaty lower back, but relief is relief.

It does provide him with brief respites, coinciding with the acceleration of the bus and then stopping when passengers embark and disembark. The traffic is slow moving, so moments of speed are infrequent. At every stop there is at least one more person who gets on the bus. When a person walks down the stairs and appears at the bottom of the flight, he peers at them to see if it is the woman from earlier.

If it says anything it is that he is pure hetero. Checking out the asses of sexily dressed chicks can say nothing else. She's still upstairs and maybe but no. She reminds him a bit too much of Diane, which isn't a bad thing, even though she's totally different. Something about their asses that does it every time. And Andy sure as hell has one. Damned fucking heat making him horny. Can't be anything else. Maybe he's not as non-sexual as he thinks. The rock of the back of the bus and the jerk each time it hits a pothole or crack makes his dick twinge. When are they gonna do anything about them? They moan at work like anything because of the state of their vans. And when you stop trying to think about it you zoom in and he's definitely feeling it. Don't look at it. Crappy news this morning about bombs, civil war, the peace treaties, the football on today and oh the shitty host nation against the last winners and...

Gradually, his engorging penis, visibly expanding beneath the loosely fitting three-quarter-length shorts that he wears, starts to shrink to its usual flaccidity. The football matches that are to be played today have the complete attention of his primary thoughts. He pulls out his phone and unlocks it by pressing two buttons. He then presses a button that has a blue-globe icon and he is online. A quick navigation to his BOOKMARKED FAVOURITES and he is on a sports news page. All of the day's fixtures are shown and he clicks on each, reading every name that is listed under the team sheets. When the loading screen briefly flashes into a rapidly filled empty bar, he glances outside the window to look at nothing in particular.

The bus stops with a slow yet sharp lurch forwards and he looks up to see who is leaving the bus or getting on. A grey-haired woman with a tartan-patterned trolley pulls herself from her seat at the front of the bus by using the handles on the trolley as a hoist, before she slowly limps past.

Hunchbacked unlucky old waddler.

It makes him feel sad when he thinks of the inevitability of life's natural ending. In his mind, he and all of the youth that come into contact with the aged are surely mocking reminders of everything that has been lost to them. He finds it difficult to imagine being old, reflecting on times when limbs would do what they no longer could, when bodily functions once taken (rightfully) for granted would struggle to accomplish the most basic of actions, when the passable beauty of whatever ugly face had been bestowed on them in their early adult years was still much more desirable than the withered, vacuum-sucked masks that hung loose from fragile bones. To be old and to have the presence of the dumb young forced into proximity at every juncture is cruel.

Nope. Not for him. Old age can go and fuck itself. Don't the good die young anyway? Maybe it's God's way of getting revenge on whatever sins they've done. Rape and they'll live to be a hundred; murder seems like a ninety; stealing and it's gotta-be a pretty good seventy. What else is there? Lying gets a month for every time. No, that can't be right. A week or a day or something. This stuff's definitely worthy of a book or a film, and there's a shit-load of God conspiracies about at the moment.

He is scrolling down the list of tomorrow's football matches. Only one of the games interests him: a match between the team who was the runner-up four years ago and the favourites. He finds it odd that the hosts are not favourites. He can't remember a time when a team from South America was not the bookmaker's tip to win. He thinks that is an elaborate ploy designed to earn more money, but as the extent of his betting experiences involves buying lottery tickets, he does concede that he has no idea what it might be.

The next time the bus stops, he looks up and sees what he has been wanting to see since getting on. Her black hair is long and straight and her daintily wide shoulders are a deep, rich brown. There is no evidence of a brassiere's strap, and he entertains thoughts of loose breasts brushing against the black dress.

It's like God's heard him.

She sits down on the seat that was vacated by the old woman with the trolley. He presses a button on his phone, one with a red old-fashioned telephone shape on, and slips it into his right pocket. He really wants to move to the front of the bus and sit next to her, to engage her in conversation and to idly talk about anything.

I know you, right? Where have we met before? Usual flirty lines but meant at the same time. He's never been shy when talking to the girls, and Cranky and Dave always said he was pretty wordy, but when has he ever just sat down on a bus and starting to chat. It's not even because she's stunning, really. How does he know her? He does know her.

His mouth is moister than before for the sucking of his lower lip, but his thirst is heightened and he notices it, swallowing drily twice and pushing his spit from the front of his mouth to his throat. He knows that he is not going to move up to her and initiate an interaction. His foot stops its tapping, resigned, and his fingers tap his knee, across from his little finger to his index in one liquid movement, before resting immobile.

He pulls his phone a little over halfway out of his pocket and presses a random button. The time is illuminated in white against a black screen reading 17:51.

Shit. He's late. They'll be late anyway and he'll be there by twenty past. Could really do with a drink though.

Diane had sent a text message earlier to say that she was going to spend the evening with Rachel but would be back before eleven. When Ross had then sent him a text message inviting him for a beer in Druids Bar, he had thought why the hell not? and committed to it in his response. He does not start work tomorrow until seven. He rarely plans on staying out for long and tonight was no exception.

See how it goes, but the first one is being well and truly sunk. A fruit cider will be perfect. Wonders what her name is. Looks like a Becca or a Rhian or a Rochelle. Definitely an R-rated girl. Really really fit. Her straightened long hair is really nice. Wonders what it would look like on Diane? Like her fit mum. Now that's funny.

Smiling, he turns to his right and looks out of the window, purposefully trying to distract himself from further erotic thoughts that he deems perverted whilst on public transport. He looks up at the blue sky, eyebrows rising.

It can't be. It's been ages since he's seen a cloud in the sky. Might start pissing it down on the way home.

He silently laughs and is amused by his weather forecast. The cloud is a solitary, small white shape in a pale and dusty blue sky. The sun is not in his vision, the magnified heat of its rays warming the bus through the glass windows to his left. Looking at a slight angle above eye level, he reads the names above the doors of shops and sees the red and white swirls of a barber's sign next to a charity shop, followed by nothing (the entrance/exit of another road) and then a large miniature version of a supermarket. Another charity shop comes next, then a florist and a baker's . After the glass windows displaying cakes and breads, is a series of five different cafeterias. Each one has a different name and décor, and is full of customers. The bus stops and he does not know why. He turns his head and faces the front of the bus, casting a brief glance over the neck and shoulders of the woman while looking out of the wide windscreen.

Red lights. For God's sake. What should be two minutes will probably be ten. Should've just drove. Then again, I shouldn't've.

He knows that he is going to drink until drunk, as usually happens, and his reflection that not driving is the best option is the one that he knows to be true. Two years ago, he had been at a party at Dave's shared house and had driven there with the intention of spending the night. Everyone there had joined in with the drinking games. The music and drinks were just as loud and just as frequently being drunk at one o'clock in the morning as they were at eight in the evening when they had started. Diane had phoned at 12:34, a time that made the memory even easier for him to recall. She had been in tears complaining about a mess of a business trip that she was on, a problem with a client who had made advances, or as she put it, the dirty prick had come on to her. Could he please come home, she needed him, she had said. Of course, he had replied. He had made his genuine excuses to Dave and the others, got in his car and within five minutes was blowing into a plastic tube, a serious-faced policeman reading the results with a disdainful voice. That was the first three points. He does not know if the penny that he placed on top of his tongue without the policeman noticing had actually done the supposed trick, but the twelve miles per hour over the speed limit for a residential area merited three points.

His stop is the next one and though he notices the glowing turquoise lettering of BUS STOPPING on the board by the bottom of the stairs, he idly presses the button on the bar in front of him and hears the buzzer in response. Having felt a vibration signalling a text message, he gets his phone out from his pocket and expectantly looks down to find a text message. He presses three buttons in sequence and reads the message from Ross.

Were here mate. The second bar by the piano. Last booth

He quickly thumbs a two-letter message, presses reply, and slides the phone into his right pocket. He stands up and puts his hands on each of the bars that rise from the floor of the bus. He looks to his left and down when he gets to the last one, admiring the shape of the woman's breasts that push out against her dress. She is looking into her handbag as if she has lost something.

Small and pert, just as God meant them. Perfect. Fit. No cleavage lines, but the rounded shape next to the armpit. Yes. Kind of like Diane's mum's.

Cheers drive.

The blue-spoiling white of the cloud has disappeared and the faintest trickle of wind is felt. The path that he steps on is a large paved area that separates two sides of the city centre, the fronts of two gentlemen's clubs on the other side, next door to a convenience store, a healthy-eating sandwicherie, four restaurants and a scaled-down version of a large supermarket-chain store. In the direction that he walks is a series of miniaturised botanical gardens, a statue of a naval figure from history standing proudly in each, spaced exactly five metres apart on diagonal lines across the wide piazza. It is a busy day and many people are walking and cycling along the flat slabs between the shrubs, leaves and stone.

Ridiculous how they're allowed to whizz along. Shouldn't be on the roads. One little kid and woomph, the knob'll most likely kill him.

He concedes that he has never seen a cyclist knock into anyone, either on the road or on a pavement, and thinks a thought that he has thought many times before: he just does not like them.

Stupid posers most of them in their tight spandex or their wives' tights or whatever it is, helmeted up and feeling as if they're on a bloody tour, hogging the road and limping out hand gestures as if they're directing the traffic because they're unkillable. As if they're bionic. Yep, he doesn't like them much.

He has seen the statuary many times and he tries to remember who they are. The last one that he walks past is the only one that he remembers without having to guess. The man represented in the sculpture had circumnavigated the globe four centuries ago and discovered a land populated by an indigenous people. Most of the times that he walks past the figure, he thinks silently of the murders and of the confused indigenes that welcomed the ships and this hero now cast in stone. Past the statue, he stands at the curb and waits for the red shape of a stationary man to fade and reappear directly below as a green man .

Across the street is the theatre, displaying a large billboard face of a man wearing a Venetian eye-mask above its grey-stone exterior. The traffic lights follow their three-coloured pattern and the red man fades. He walks across the road looking to his right at the stopped vehicles and then in front, at the pale legs of a floral-dress-wearing woman whose age he cannot determine.

There's something about the absolute whiteness that does something to him. She's got a mole right above the legpit, too. Really sexy. Wonders what her vagina looks like and if she has ginger pubes because that's what all really white-skinned girls have, isn't it? He's sure Cranky said something about them having no eyebrows and really pink orifices. And being real dirty in the sack. Cranky's ex-girlfriend was a ginger so he's the one to know. Wild in the sack, he said. Wild. Same thing anyway.

The girl in the floral dress veers right and up the sloping path that leads to the popular high street. He walks directly forwards, up the alley to the side of the theatre, looking to his right at the pale legs until the side of the building obstructs his view and he focuses on the cobbles, aware how easy it is to trip on them. Along the side of the street opposite the theatre is, in order as he walks, a chip shop, a pub, another chip shop, an arcade, two restaurants, and a tenement block. The street is hemmed in by the cars parked to his left and a big transporter, engine rumbling, in front of the theatre's side entrance.

Just past the tenement block is a turning to the left, which leads out on to the high street. He looks up it and then crosses without slowing. The Druids Bar is at the end of the street, facing him. Noise from the people outside carries up to him and he smiles in anticipation of seeing his friends. He does not know who else is going to be there other than Ross. It's gotta be Marc and Pritchard.

Two men walk past him in the entrance, moving broad shoulders inwards and away from him to allow him room to pass and with the second man palming the door open.

Thanks. Sound.

There is a bar in front of him which he walks around to

the right. Sixteen people line the bar, ten with drinks in hand and in various stances, either perched on stools or straight-backed or resting one elbow on the worn sapele wood, two in conversation casting glances at the bar staff, and the other four watching the bar staff's movements with varying levels of patience. He squeezes past them in the narrow space that is left him, conscious of his buttocks rubbing against others'. At the end of the bar are three steps that lead down to a rear room, a speak-easy from decades past that has an antique piano in the far-right corner, next to the jukebox. The room is large and well lit, containing five alcoves along the left side and a bar opposite. In the middle are eight long tables of the same wood as the bar at the entrance. The bar in the back also has the same dark colour but is mahogany. He walks past the tables, noticing that not one of them is empty, and looks into the last of the alcoves.

↓↑
Mike. Alright mate? He stands up and shakes his hand.

↑↓
How's it going Mike?

↓↑
Alright Ross? Sam. How's it going? Shakes Sam's hand.

↑↓
Not bad thanks mate. How about you?

↓↑
Alright.

↑↓
Yeah, I'm alright. Thirsty as hell, mind. Bus seemed to take ages. You need a beer? He'll get them a round first as he's just arrived.

↓↑
Nah, it's alright. I'll get these. What you having? Me

and Sam've just about finished these, so we'll get in a round now, yeah?

↑↓

Alright mate. Thanks. I'll have a fruit cider thanks.

↓↑

Same again, Ross. Fruit cider. *Actually mate, get us one of them as well. A fruit cider.*

↑↓

Fruit cider? What the hell?

↓↑

Yeah, it's alright. He must've heard of it.

Ross walks off to the bar.

↑↓

So how's everything going mate?

With Ross heading to the bar, he sits down on the other side to where Sam sits down.

↓↑

It's alright thanks mate. How about you?

↑↓

Yeah, I can't complain. Saturdays off work are always good. How about you?

↓↑

It's good at the moment. Lots of work coming in and being outdoors in this weather isn't a problem. The winter's a real killer.

↑↓

Yeah, I can imagine. Looking good though mate. And he is; tanned to fuck and muscled like a bodybuilder.

↓↑

Cheers mate. Brickies' three Ts: tanned, toned, and tired. He laughs.

↑↓

Fair play. So still with the missus, then? That's been about ten years, hasn't it?

↓↑

Didn't you know? We're engaged now. I asked her about a month ago.

↑↓

Nope. *Yeah, I thought I'd seen it posted.*

↓↑

Cheers Mike. Pretty sure they're still together. *How's Diane?*

↑↓

She's good. Been promoted again since we last saw you. She'll be the boss before Christmas at this rate.

He sniffs a laugh through his nose and Sam smiles.

↓↑

Not bad mate. Marry a rich bird; you can't go wrong. He laughs and Mike joins him. They both look over their shoulders, Sam his left and Mike his right, and see that Ross is carrying three drinks from the bar and past the tables in the middle of the room. In his right hand is a pint glass of amber lager and pushed against this, fingers of his left hand curled around two necks, are two bottles of the same drink, purple labelled.

Ross puts them on the table and Sam says cheers mate.

Thanks mate. He's drinking the same as him.

↑↓

What the fuck is that you're drinking?

↓↑

Fruit cider. It's really nice. Tastes just like a fizzy juice or a squash.

↑↓

Fruit cider? What's apple if not a fruit?

↓↑
I know. But it's actually pretty good. Haven't you tried it?
↑↓
Let's have a swig then. It's surely a girls' drink but then again quite a few of his friends drink it. Hmm. *Yeah, it's pretty good. Bit sweet though, but good. Bit gay.*
↓↑
Fuck off is it. Cheers Mike. He drinks a third of the bottle in two mouthfuls and holds it out to Mike, who clinks his against it. *I've seen you drinking rosé, and if that ain't full-blown homo then I have no idea.*

↑↓
Sorry Ross, but he's right. My girlfriend drinks that shit. They all start laughing. Ross puts his hands palm out towards them, fingertips raised to the ceiling in concession.

They all face towards the end of the table that is closest to them upon hearing the sound of loud voices slowly getting more audible. A group of five men place their jackets over the bench of the table and four of them sit down. The one standing is called Pete and he is being chided for being late.

In this weather? *Jackets in this weather,* he says it under his breath and Ross nods. Pete is being sanctioned for being late, no doubt.

↓↑
Image to maintain, right? Business suits are all the same. Both Mike and Sam nod in agreement, facing each other but eyeing the table with suppressed smiles on their mouths. One other of the men is called Stu and the remaining three men around him seem to vie to impress him.

↑↓
Mike's girlfriend is a suit. *Only the men though. The women are alright.*

↓↑

Yeah, exactly. Power-trip suits 'n' ties. *Power-trip suits 'n' ties. Diane never gets like that.*

↑↓

Nah, she's sound, Mike. Like Ross said, just the men.

↓↑

She's alright then, yeah?

↑↓

Yeah, was just saying when you were getting the beers. She's earning a shed-load, doesn't stop getting promoted. They nod, impressed. It is impressive. *Boss by Christmas.*

↓↑

Hold on a minute. You must've been with her for nearly ten years, yeah?

↑↓

What's he thinking? *Yeah, it'll be ten exactly this November. Why?*

↓↑

Look, if Sam's done it and that's been what – ten years?

↑↓

Near enough, yeah. Is it ten?

↓↑

Then why don't you do it as well?

↑↓

I probably would if I wasn't such a fag.

↓↑

Get fucked. I ain't had a girlfriend for over a year. If anyone's a homo, it's me. Seriously Mike, haven't you thought about it? Be marrying a rich girl, too.

↑↓

He laughs. *I said those exact words to him earlier.*

↓↑

I dunno, it's ju-
↑↓
Honestly, mate. Was it that hard asking Corinne?
↓↑
Nah. It was easy. Even did the one knee.
↑↓
See. What's to lose?
Sam speaks first.
↓↑
A house.
Then Ross speaks.
↑↓
Custody of the kids.
Mike joins in now, all three of them smiling.
↓↑
The fucking bank account and all the savings.
All three of them laugh and raise their drinks, drinking immediately afterwards. There is cheering from the table of businessmen.

They have been rejoined by Pete, who is holding a round black tray in both hands. He places it on their table to two expressive and jovial remarks about times and appreciation.

Why do they have to be so loud? Honestly. *They're like school kids.*
↑↓
They're alright. Can't handle their beer and it's what, quarter to seven? Must've left their office at four and are probably pissed. Real men, never lifted a fucking brick in their lives.
↓↑
Mike puts his phone in his pocket. *Ten to seven. They're hammered.*

Sam starts to talk about the football and who will make the last sixteen, Ross enthusiastically responding. He makes a few comments and nods in agreement at what they are saying at times, chewing the inside of his cheek. He is listening to what the large man at the table is saying, the one with the silvered lines above his ears.

It is loud but the murmur of dozens of voices drowns out certain parts. The man says that Oh you can't beat some fucking chocolate with their big everything, old chap. Big asses and big tits and big lips. Made for sex, I'm telling you, absolutely made for it.

They all start fucking laughing and he lowers his voice as if whispering a secret to the one they're all asslicking and the asslicked fuck raises his eyebrows to which old silver fox nods like a fucking child, cheesy shit-eating smile on his ugly mug.

Did you hear that?

↑↓

Hear what?

↓↑

Huh? He doesn't look happy.

↑↓

Those business fuckers. The smarmy one's mate is a fucking racist.

↓↑

Shall we move somewhere else?

↑↓

I wanna fuck him up. His hands are shaking, irritation and anger his dominant thoughts.

↓↑

Yeah, but shall we go someplace else?

↑↓

Yeah. Sure.

↓↑
Come on mate. Leave those tossers to it. Shit. Soft Mike's never been like this before. *Never seen you like this before.*

↑↓
Just can't stand it, Sam. They're cunts.

Ross finishes the last half of his pint in eleven seconds and squints whilst gasping. Sam drinks the last mouthful of his fruit cider. Mike doesn't think about his. Ross leads the way, walking behind the backs of Pete and the two nameless men who had exchanged a whispered, clandestine message. At the end of the table, at its edge and with his back turned to an alcove containing a man and a woman, Mike turns and looks at the man who has angered him. His eyes meet the man's for two seconds, enough time for him to mouth the word cunt.

→
←

Some gay kid just blew him a kiss. *Hey, Stu, some queer kid just blew me a kiss.*

↓↑
Shit. It's really your night. At this rate you're going to need to cancel lady fondue.

↑↓
I would tell you to fuck off like a good little chap, but you'd try it on with me.

↓↑
And you'd probably want me to, dahling.

↑↓
It is funny. Everyone seems to be staring at him, wherever he looks. There's an ocularity to everything. The backs of the heads are eyes and the people's hands are eyes and it's funny. Someone's saying Locky, Drew, and so *Huh* he turns to his left, away from the place where the kid had been standing, the

place that he had been looking toward, and a big iris blinks into semi-normality.

↓↑

The girls behind us are alright if you don't mind those Goth girls. Just behind us. Who doesn't mind them? But she is hot. Al agreed.

Nearly with synchronicity, the five men look at the three young women on the adjacent table. He has to turn round to join the three men opposite with their lecherous observations, as does the man sitting next to him.

↑↓

Get lost. Whichever one you're on about will probably eat you whilst you screw her, listening to that weird satanic stuff at the same time. They must be out of it. *What do you think, Drew?*

↓↑

He thinks that they are terrifying and then laughs and says *I'd fuck them with your little dick, Pete, but not my own* and laughs again. The others laugh and after Pete's retort of fuck off, they continue to laugh.

The one with blue in her black hair is so tall it's amazing. It's like she's not real and she's on stilts and it would be really funny they would think he is a legend if he just...

And he stands up, his friends knowing what is coming and the two that are to his left slap the table in a discordant rhythm as a gesture of motivation and encouragement. Pete looks up at his face and his smile

Seems to be a squinting Jap's eye. What is the lame old dog looking at? *Hey hey, chum. This is how you bag a dragon. Watch and learn and just watch and...* Shit. *Learn.*

He walks to the right, past Pete, and sits heavily down at the women's table. All three of them look at him with various expressions. There is a woman with straight black hair, cut at the length where it just avoids touching her shoulders. The colour of this woman's clothing is black and she is wearing a dress with netting across her torso. The bottom part extends into a series of light skirts, layered over one another in the fashion of a bridesmaid's dress. Her brassiere is visible through the netting. She looks nervous and bites into her bottom, red-lipsticked lip. This is who he sits next to. The other two women share the same expression of bemusement and withheld demands, repressing what comes naturally to them in the form of a blunt welcome to see if they are right with their expectations. The woman to his left has black, straightened hair like the girl next to him, with the addition of a blue streak that curls past her left ear. It is longer than the other woman's, falling across her clavicle. She is wearing a skin-tight T-shirt with an unreadable jagged font that is the logo for a band that she likes and a pair of faded once-black jeans. The last woman, sitting opposite him, has short-cropped bright-blonde hair and a denim jacket with the sleeves cut a half inch before the elbow. The jacket is unzipped and a large bosom is evident under the white T-shirt that she wears. This woman's shorts reveal plump thighs and pale legs.

Closer, they look alright. The eyes are gone and the blonde one has a really nice figure. A fuller figure, as his wife would say. As he would say. As he is saying. He turns away from the blonde-haired woman and looks at the red-lipped woman to his left.

Ladies, I am an envoy from the preposterous wealth seated behind me, an emissary of the pigs with all the money. I have been sent to convey their admiration for such beautiful girls. That was not the best he's ever done, but you can't blame him.

He is surprised when they laugh and he smiles at each of

them in turn, lingering on the short-haired woman with what he thinks is a pleasantly alluring smile that projects his sexual thoughts in minute detail.

Flummery. Just like the old university days. Jonesy and his words of wise old wisdom. *But seriously, I'm just here to mediate. The gentlemen behind me might be rich and avaricious, but they want only for me to tell you that you are elegant creatures.* Blondie, yes. *Absolutely cherubic ladies, they did in fact say.*

↑↓

What a complete weirdo. *Why didn't they come and tell us that themselves? They can't be too shy, can they? I mean, you're businessmen, right?*

↓↑

Well, Pete He turns to his left and points with his left hand, arm extended, *was the one saying how he thought you were like a modern-day Aphrodite, and that the blue line of your hair only complements your angelicness.* He turns to the right, looking forwards. *But we think that you are all three the perfect picture* shit *of* what? *pulchritude.* Yes. That was it.

↑↓

I reckon it's because it's you that fancies us.

↓↑

The blue one is really starting to scare him now. It is spreading across her face like a vein on a soft cheese. Pale and crumbly and rotting and he can't smell it, let's be serious, but he can. He fucking can. *Not you.* It's worse when she smiles. It throbs all along her face. *You fucking freak.*

Her face holds the smile for three seconds, and after her eyebrows lower towards her eyes it remains for a further two seconds. Following this, they furrow deeper and she tells him to fuck off you weird old pervert before I throw my drink over you. She is joined in abusively deriding him by her friends, whilst he sits there and smiles as lasciviously as he can at the short-haired woman. She slaps him across the left side of the face.

Ouch. *Fuck.* The fat one just hit him. *You fucking cunt. You dyke bitch.*

There are hands on his shoulders and Stu and Pete are shaking him, pulling him up and directing him away from the table. When he looks at the two men, he sees that they are his friends, but it appears that they have too many eyes. His vision is mottled by translucent patches and he finds out that he has tears in his eyes when he blinks. *She hit me. The bitch.* He is sat back in the seat that he left a little over two minutes before, Stu's hand over his right shoulder, sitting next to him on his left.

↑↓

We saw them turn on you and were coming over just as the slap came. Madman. *What happened? You were doing bloody well before it, you know. Chatting them up a treat.* Funny.

↓↑

Funny though, right? They were angry. *They were really angry. It wasn't my fault really, was it? Started alright and I was doing quite well.* He smiles at them with a deliberate grin, aiming for the look of an innocent schoolboy facing remonstration.

↑↓

Yeah it was and of course it wasn't. You are a mad bastard though, completely an'utterly. Two laughs follow and he shakes his head from left to right twice, smiling. With a quieter voice and leaning in to a half inch from his friend's left ear, he says *What time did you arrange to meet her? Time for another before you leave us?*

↓↑

I'd look at my watch but it doesn't seem to be acting straight with me. He squints with his eyes and his expression adopts a concerned tone. *I'll have to leave for half seven, so how'm'I looking, old boy?*

↑↓

It's not even seven. Why do you have to leave at half past? It's just around the corner.

↓↑

I have had four pints on top of the rest and fancy making a real trip of it, so I'd better freshen up before she gets there. Better had too, chum. Not just saying it.

↑↓

My round, gentlemen he says, taking his right hand from his friend's back and addressing those that are sitting down. *Same again or you can buy your bloody own.* A chuckle comes from Pete and he sits down on the seat of the bench closest to where the women have left.

Drew's grabbing his arm. Quite firmly too. *Whoa boy. Steady on.*

↓↑

Stu. Make mine a shandy, eh? More lemonade than lager. And don't tell the others, yeah? Wouldn't hear the bloody damned end of it. He sighs into a nasally exhaled laugh, then strokes Stu's arm whilst smiling. Stu then smiles back before walking to the bar.

At the bar, Stu pushes the five pint glasses together and tries to pick them up with his fingers wedged between the glasses. He mutters shit under his breath and leaves two of them on the bar, his fingers clamped around three. He places them on the table and puts one in front of Al, Pete and then Ferdy. He tells them that they ran out of damned trays behind the bar. He walks back to the bar, taps a man on the shoulder and politely tells him that he has left two drinks there. The man stands sideways and Stu reaches past to pick the two drinks up. The drink on the right is Drew's. At the end of his order, Stu had asked the woman behind the bar with the pierced lip for a pint of lager with a small dash as well, please. He did not and does not think that Drew will notice. The room is busier now and people are standing wherever there is space between the alcoves and the benches. He passes the drink in his right hand to Drew and then sits down. He raises his glass to the table and says sláinte. They each clink their glass against one another's and say sláinte before drinking.

There's no bloody lemonade in this pint. The cheeky old pissant. He pulls his right hand back and puts his fingers around his pint glass. He is still smiling as he looks down at the straw-brown fluid and drinks forty percent of what is left. Putting it back on the table, there is less than a half pint remaining.

Ferdy and Stu are now nattering on about films and he has to take this as a cue, surely? Down the hatch, old boy. He picks up his glass again, the burning feeling on the back of his throat from the carbonation tingling from the previous mouthfuls. In seven seconds and with slow swallows, the glass has only the white dregs of spittled lager at the bottom. He puts the glass on the table deliberately clumsily, creating an audible sound of hollowed contents and gaining the attention of Ferdy and Stu.

Right. Well, I'd better be off. Awf. How sophisticatedly spoken. *Never keep a good looker waiting.*

Ferdy says what the hell is he on about and Stu replies that he does not have a clue and looks at his watch and then taps it with the index finger of his right hand.

↑↓

You've still got fifteen minutes. I'll get a round of shorts for the road if you want? You eager dog. He smiles and predicts the response as no, that's very kind old chap but I'd really better freshen up because...

↓↑

Thanks, Stu. But I'd really better be off. Need to sort myself out a tad and another drink would really bugger me. He stands up and Stu and Ferdy stand together. Stu places his left hand on the top of Drew's right bicep and shakes his right hand with his own.

↑↓

You're off now then, are you?

↓↑

I sure am. Places to go and people to meet.

↑↓

What's she like, you old dog?

↓↑

They always know. Except Ferdy, who looks positively bemused. *I haven't the faintest what you are on about.* He turns to Ferdy. *Rather uncourteous suppositions, I imagine Ferdy. I've a round trip to the Dominican Republic, if you want to know.*

Ferdy smiles boyishly, confused, and Al raises his eyebrows in mock innocence, feigning confusion, standing up with Pete as they extend their right hands. After he has shaken their hands, he extends his farewell to Ferdy, who is taken aback by this sign of respect and successfully hides the pleasure that he feels. A round of goodbyes is routinely carried out as he picks up his suit jacket and puts it on. He turns and leaves, the four men that are staying in the bar all turned in his direction and sitting down with hands perched on the top of the bench to ease their return to their seats.

The bar is really busy.

He does not feel like an animal and the people around him do not appear as animals, but he thinks that they are, consciously imbuing the features of animals onto the people in front of him as he walks past and against them to the front of the building. With the effects of the hallucinogenic chemicals in his brain, his imagination effects the lens from which he sees and, depending on the animal that he thinks, the people around him animalistically theanthropise: a rotund man who stands taller than he erupts in hair, becomes to him a hirsute boulder; a tall woman with wide hips rising into a tapered waist pulled tight into a bodice becomes a hybridised, undefined marsupial; the three women that are standing against the wall to his left, the last that he walks past before reaching the door, are talking at the same time, repeating the words that are being said in high-pitched agreement, and the sound translates in his brain as geese. The image of cartoon-orange beaks stays with him until he walks six yards out from the door.

Taxi. Quickest route to a taxi. Down the road and up the steps to the main road. There's a rank there if he remembers correctly. And of course he does. Feeling bloody hot and nauseous because of the heat. Was cooler in the pub. The sound of traffic isn't helping either and the echo of those bloody geese-girls isn't helping.

He has walked down the side alley from the pub, taking a right after having taken a left. Tucked behind a building on his right is a heavily-graffitied wide set of steps that leads up to a main road, which he moves up quickly, springing from step to step and lifting his arms in a jogger's position. Loose change jingles in his right pocket.

At the top of the steps, the sun is wholly visible above the tall buildings that line the opposite side of the wide road, which rises on his right in a steady gradient to reach thirty-seven degrees at the top. The pavements on either side of the road are lined with a variety of shops and bars and cafeterias and two self-titled clubs. They are busy with pedestrians and on the road is a stop-start line of traffic going down into the centre of the town, and free-flowing vehicles heading up the hill. He squints and looks away from the sky-and-brick horizon, looking at the parked taxis that he thinks are twenty yards to his left, blinking rapidly and wiping sweat from his forehead and walking down the sloping pavement.

There are so many obviously beautiful women out and wearing little that he doesn't need to go back to the hotel and pay for it but it's there waiting for him so it's better. He clenches his back teeth, stopping himself from smiling overtly. Dinner, drinks and dates were, in the long run, more expensive than simply just paying to fuck anyway, which is all he ever wants. Plus, being married old boy, poses its own problems if you don't pay for it; the transaction is the transaction and it's part of the unspoken but mutually assured contract of secrecy. And lies, of course.

With the same thought-pattern cycling in his thoughts as the previous eleven times, his logic remains as sound to him as it did the first time. He has had many long discussions with himself on the nature of philandering and though he is not in ignorance of the dubious nature of his self-inquisition, he has accepted his rationale as sound.

Always the one at the front. Bloody cabbie etiquette. A rather good-looking car, nonetheless. He bends forward so that his face is visible to the taxi driver through the opened window, hands on his knees to facilitate his position. *The Gryphon Hotel, please.*

The driver, a balding and round-stomached man with a white T-shirt and sports-brand navy-blue shorts cut off above the knee, reaches down to the series of buttons situated between his and the passenger's seat and presses a door-release button. He notices how big the man's forearms are and tries not to think about elephant's legs. The driver says *hop in mate, door's open,* so he does.

Don't think about animals. Think about where he is heading and what he is going to do and think about. No, don't think about her. Think about the night ahead and the pinkness of a ripened vagina sitting between Nubian thighs, wet and watered and accepting him. She'll moan a sweat-drenched song of pleasure. He'll match it. Fucking time. Fucking time. He is on fire. What a night ahead and there's a sure-fire way to make it even hotter by melting some chocolate. That hot shaven-headed girl earlier is the reason for his craving and why should he not? What's the point of a business trip if you don't get fired? so he's gonna get immolated. Fucking yes, old boy.

He presses his hands against their opposite armpits and wipes against the hollows, his fingers meeting dampness. Folding a shirt neatly into the suitcase that he left at the hotel briefly interrupts his mental endeavours; he is playing out various scenarios and enjoying positioning a physically mercurial black woman into acts of unrestrained sexual licentiousness. He is looking out of the window to his left to avoid tainting his imagination with the taxi driver's countenance and to express his unwillingness to engage in uninteresting and countlessly-rehearsed verbiage. He can feel his penis move slightly against the inside of his left thigh.

The taxi has come to a stop and he thinks that he sees 0008:80 on the metre and he pulls his wallet out of his right pocket and pulls out a banknote that he thinks is a twenty pound note. The taxi driver's voice is audible and he pays no attention to it. He cannot be sure, he thinks, in his current state, so to avoid any confusion, he puts the purplish note onto the tray beneath the plastic partition and tells the driver to keep the change. He puts the wallet in the left pocket of his suit jacket. The driver says thanks a lot, look after yourself mate.

Three Ts there, old chap. *You're welcome. Thank you.* He pushes open the door and steps out, clutching the jacket in the same hand as when he entered and cautiously placing it over the crotch area of his trousers. He thinks of his wife.

He cheats on his wife almost as an unspoken challenge: to love, to her, to himself; what is love if it allows people to do what he does? and she would find out if she loved him enough to tail him or was jealously protective to the correct extent and he has to be unscrupulously careful so as not to leave clues or evidence as to be nocuous to his maritally secure situation. The girl at the desk's an attractive beauty of a damsel, isn't she just? and he gives her a nice smile. Perfect white teeth right back thank you. He should invite her up.

The two elevators are past the reception desk and to the left and he walks towards them, his eyes lingering on the receptionist who has occupied herself by looking at the nails on each hand. He walks through the open doors of the elevator furthest down the corridor, turns to the buttons that are situated to the left of the doors upon entry, presses the button marked 06 which illuminates, and stands to the right of the only occupant, an aged woman who he assumes is in her nineties and who makes him think of dinosaurs. He is pleased that she does not suddenly cast off her flesh and erupt in a visceral fountain of mutated flesh and transform into a tyrannosaur or diplodocus.

Probably make him sick.

He thinks about trying to engage her in conversation, but all that he can think of are vulgarities and sexually related interrogatives, and he concedes that the shape and colour of her vulva are not really such pertinent objects for discovery. He feels childish and giggles briefly and quietly. The woman in the elevator does not move and he stares at her from the side, arching his neck to the left. She has a raised bump behind her neck and focuses on this. It appears to swell and after seven seconds he blinks and it returns to its real size.

Floor 12. Why don't they stop at the first one on the way up rather than go to the top first just because the button was pressed first? Stupid system, really. No sense. Diana's out. Dino Dana's out. Off you scuttle, little old dear.

Fuck getting old. Older, old boy. You're already old. Well, middle-aged.

The doors close of their own accord and the lift judders faintly as it descends. He squeezes his penis through his trousers three times and combs his hair with his nails and sucks at his front teeth. He wipes the index finger of his right hand in the corner of each eye. The elevator stops and a second later, the doors open. He walks out and down the corridor (the only direction is ahead) and pulls his key card out of his right pocket. Stopping and standing at the door marked 186, he swipes the card against a red light by the door's handle, which turns green with the mechanical sound of a lock being opened. He pushes the door open and walks into the room, flicking the lightswitch on the wall immediately to the right of the door upon entrance. The room is well lit, even with the blinds pulled closed, but he had closed them when he arrived from the airport. He falls backwards on the double bed that takes up most of the space in the centre of the room. The door's weight announces its self-closure as a thud.

A long, loud and relaxed sigh is pushed out and he unbuttons his shirt. His suit jacket is lying next to him, above his head across the pillows. With the button at the bottom of his shirt undone and a lightly dark-haired stomach rising an inch above the waistband of his trousers, he unbuckles his belt and unzips the front of his trouser. He slides his left hand down past the elastic that rings the top of his boxer shorts and cups his testicles, pulling his phone from his right pocket. He connects to the internet and accesses his recent history. He clicks ENTER on the link that will direct him to Escortia Services and in eleven seconds is looking at a blurred-face image of a slender, curvaceous woman. Her name is Dominica and she will be here in twenty-three minutes.

Be punctual, Dominica. Let him conquer you, you sweet little minx slut.

He looks at the five images of the escort: in the first, she is standing against a wall with a straight-backed posture, a shapely right leg bent at the knee with her foot against the wall; in the second, she is sitting on a chair with the back of the chair pushing her breasts into a constricted cleavage, her legs wrapped around the chair's back legs; in the third, she is on her hands and knees, arching her back down and lifting her buttocks high; in the fourth, she is standing with her arms bent at elbows raised a little higher from her shoulders, pushing her hip out to the left; in the fifth, she is standing with her back to the camera, seemingly looking over a veranda. She is wearing a pink brassiere and g-string in each of the photographs.

His penis is erect and he holds it firmly, not moving his hand. He releases it after pushing it down and away from his body, and it springs up, hitting his stomach two inches short of his navel. A loud sound is made as he pushes himself from the bed and into a standing position. He cuts off his connectivity to the internet and places his phone on the table beneath the window (which also has a plain vase). He kicks off his trousers when they fall to the carpeted floor and pulls down his boxer shorts, arching his back as he bends over to step out of them. He shrugs his shoulders and pulls at the left sleeve of his shirt with his right hand and removes his shirt. Then he pulls off his socks, leaving his clothes scattered on the floor, and walks to the bathroom. There is a basin in front of him as he enters and a bathtub to the left. He steps from a dimpled and white rubber bath mat and into the bathtub and turns the dial that is built into the shower anticlockwise towards the red markings, leaving the arrow pointed at the number 7. The showerhead is facing to his left and against the wall and he leaves it for eleven seconds, feeling the cold water splashing against his shins from the wall, which pools at his feet. He pulls the cable attached to the head with his right hand and closes his eyes before the water starts to pour over his face. He puts his hand by his side, symmetrically standing and enjoying the comfort of the heated water as it hits his face and neck.

He does not think of anything specifically, but he is aware of the relaxation and of the enjoyment. The muscles in his face slacken and his head is held much looser forwards, the chin an inch and a quarter from the hollow at the bottom of his neck. His penis goes limp.

Wash, old man. She'll be here soon.

He raises his right arm and pushes the direction of the water downwards, splashing against the slightly pronounced rise of his stomach. He picks up from the dish a peach-coloured block of soap that has not been used before. In its centre is a black and silver label. He lathers the soap to a thick foam and takes just more than fourteen minutes to cover and rinse every part of his body, taking longer with his penis and intergluteal cleft.

That'll do. He doesn't want her to fall in love with him. Although there's a film title in their somewhere. Like the businessman and the hooker or business with hookers or an escort's business. Or maybe not. He turns the dial clockwise until it can turn no further and then steps out, water dripping from him, on to the bath mat. Stupid fucking idiot thought that would be nice to stand on after a bloody shower?

He pulls the top towel that is draped over a larger towel from the solitary metal rail against the wall opposite the bath and slings it over his shoulder, imagining being a savage Neanderthal or an ancient patrician in a toga. He walks in the bedroom and roughly dries himself, throwing the towel through the opened bathroom door and walking to the other side of the bed, the side closest to the window, and picks his suitcase up.

Can he? Should he? He has done it before and it was very bloody good. But but but, old chap, never before sex. And ever since this morning you've been waiting for this really, like a birthday treat that's not quite on your birthday. Fuck it.

He opens the clasps on the front left and right of the case and pulls out a cream-coloured pair of folded socks. He pulls the two socks apart and tips them upside down. From the sock in his right hand falls ten strips of paper the size of a standard plaster from a first-aid kit. On each one is stamped with a red circle and a black-stick figure.

There are four rapid and rhythmic knocks on the door within a second.

Shit. It can't be eight yet. The stupid dumb bitch's early, no doubt. Stupid bitch.

He pushes the suitcase and the socks and the strips of paper under the bed, as close to the middle as he can estimate. Then he kicks his shirt under the bed and throws his trousers and boxer shorts and suit jacket under it, and runs to the bathroom, bends down, picks up the towel, folds it around his waist and then rolls the highest edges over each other to keep it in place, before flattening his palm against the top of his head and walking to the door. He opens it.

Hi. Come on in.

↑↓

Hey. Straight to business, looks like. *Thanks.*

↓↑

Excuse my current condition. I mean, my state of undress. I didn't expect you so early.

↑↓

She couldn't be any closer to perfectly on time. *Sorry. You can get dressed if you want.*

↓↑

She's flashing a very naughty smile, the little minx. The dirty bitch. The whore. *Can I get you a tea or a coffee? There's nothing stronger. Hotel provision, sorry.*

↑↓

I'm okay, thanks. Can I sit on the bed?

↓↑

Yes. Of course. Sure.

↑↓

Thanks. She observes his body quickly and look at his face. *It's a nice hotel, this one.* He's not ugly at all. A bit heavy, maybe.

↓↑

Yes, it's rather nice. Yes. First time that I've been here but it came recommended. I'm out of town. I mean, from out of town. Business. Just do it. *So, uh. Shall I give you the money now?*

↑↓

Yeah, okay. That'd be good.

He laughs at his own joke that his trousers have not been stolen and that his wallet is in his trousers under the bed. He

Apparel

clumsily gets to his knees and rests his shoulder against the wooden frame of the bed, reaching under to pull something out. Ah. It's his trousers. He stumbles back to his feet. He must be drunk. First time courage and all that.

↓↑

Two hundred for the hour. Like a question but not. He puts his hand into both of the pockets of his trousers and feels confused. Where the fuck is it? For fuck's sake. He crouches down and assumes a kneeling position, against the bed with his right shoulder. *It must have fallen out.* With his right hand, he feels the carpet under the bed and the clothes that are above it. He does this for eight seconds before his knuckles bump against the obvious and familiar shape of his wallet filled with change. He pulls out his suit jacket. *Here it is.* He smiles at her. She is stunning.

↑↓

I hate it when that happens. It's always the last place that you look. God, he's totally blitzed.

↓↑

Of course it's the last fucking place you look, you dumb bitch. *Yeah. Always the last bloody place.* He stands up and pulls out ten notes, sitting on the bed next to her and holding it out. She takes it and puts it in a compartment in her large handbag.

So. He's in command. He can tell her to do whatever he wants because he has paid for the next hour's entertainment *Can we start by kissing?* but it's not seemly. He should tell her to finger her asshole or something but it's always the same. The command's in his head but he can't speak it. The spurious love that they ordain in order to satisfy his satyriasis makes him feel empowered. The commodification of the flesh, especially the flesh of such beautiful and perfect women, which they are to him, permits him dominion and makes him masterful. If only he was a tad more immoral, then he'd make them do everything he wanted.

↑↓

Of course. I'd like that. He's clean shaved and that's always preferable. Hairy faces are such a put off. And she rashes with her sensitive skin.

↓↑

Come here. She'd like that? He likes that. He puts his right arm around her and his fingers pull a firm waist in towards him. With the top of her left thigh against the top of his right thigh, he places his left hand on her left breast and pushes his lips against her lips. Fucking soft lips.

He likes to build towards what he refers to as complete arousal. This is the gradual ascension through the erotic rituals, starting with explorative fondling and the meeting of lips and ending in the act of intercourse. Softly caressing tongues in a slow motion comes second, with the act of mutual masturbation and stroking of each other's sex. The removal of clothing will follow and firmer hands will trace spontaneous patterns on flesh, the tongue, lips and teeth doing the same, but avoiding the genitals. Oral sex precedes the act of finality, however long its duration dependent on stamina and will power.

His tongue is lapping against hers and his breathing is more audibly being pushed through his nose. A small bump in the crotch region of the towel indicates his erection. Get your hand off his dick. Too early. He puts his left hand on her right hand and directs it to his chest, where he pinches his right nipple with her forefinger and thumb. He brings his right hand to hold her head and pushes her mouth against his. He doesn't move his lips against hers and pushes his tongue into her mouth as far as it will go, raising and lowering it rapidly.

He's a fucking wolf. Shit. Thank fuck his eyes are closed.

Her mouth is clamped against his, both open, from the pressure he is putting on her head with his hand and from his neck pushing his head forward. He can feel the bicep start to twitch on his right arm and he removes both of his hands: one from her hand and the other from her head. He pulls his mouth away from hers and keeps his eyes closed, moving away around an inch and then kissing her abruptly on the lips. He does this four times in quick succession. Her mouth purses and cheeks rise in a subtly coquettish smile. Her eyes are closed. His hands go to her shoulders and he slips the middle finger of each hand under the straps of her dress, pulling his hands apart in opposite directions and pulling the top of her dress down forcefully. He hooks the same fingers underneath the straps of her brassiere and pulls downwards, leaving them resting at the top of her forearms. He unfolds the top of the towel, allowing it to fall to the floor. He opens his eyes as he is kissing her and looks down at her small breasts, tracing the shape of their bottoms by placing his fingers together and spreading his thumb to cup each, and bringing forefinger and thumb together in an inwardly stroking movement. He feels a prolonged pulse in his penis and thinks that it feels like a truncheon and one worthy of a pornography actor and then leans his right cheek against her left cheek and waggles his tongue against hers from the right corner of his mouth, looking down at his small and erect penis. He stands up and holds her right hand with both of his, tenderly, before sitting on the bed and pulling her towards him, she still standing. She is bent forwards with her face positioned above his penis. She slips the brassiere straps from her arms and then puts the top of his penis in her mouth.

Fellatio Nelson is arriving. She looks up with distain, almost like the bitch understands the pun. Might be a university whore, one of the ones who supplement their maintenance allowance by fucking on the side. Either way, with a body like hers, he doesn't care. She can't be that smart because she didn't even mention a condom. Looking back down at his erect, average-sized penis and opening her mouth slightly, she is a Nubian goddess and her tongue hits his cock before her lips and why not. Hands on the back of her head and maybe that was a bit forceful but already his cock has yeah it's disappeared and she isn't choking or anything. Her lips are on his crotch and her eyes are opening wider than saucers little alien eyes and he can hear her blinks like in the cartoons. Take the hands off the back of her head and let her suck it like an ice-lolly and he has hips like the rock-and-roller coaster and he is staring at the purple swollen head. It's a plum in the orchard in her mouth and she is meeting it halfway good girl. Hands on the back of her neck and the cable ties nearly cut his hand. But it's her bra what a silly old fuck and he pulls it now but it snaps back elastic. Finger-thumb   technique remember? and it works a treat. Yes. Her back opens dromedary she's a fucking dromedary and her humps shoot up and it's scary.

Smiling in fear but in some subconscious, understood-from-experience way, also knowing that he is safe, he emits a barked laugh with a simultaneous clenching of the eyes. He looks upon her and the hallucination is gone. Replaced on her visage is an image of a molten waxworks that flitters between a famous supermodel and a ruined plastic figurine. Strikingly salient against the range of drug-induced visions but unsure as to its reality, a pink flower perches on one of her wrists that rest on his thighs.

The acid's working treats on his system and the kaleidoscope is phenomenal. A phucking phenomenomenon.

He starts giggling and the escort pulls her face away from his penis and raises, very elegantly, both of her eyebrows, pursing her lips in a mock frown of bemusement.

←
→

Honey. Would you like to fuck me? He is coked up out of his face and all his energy has gone to his cock. He says that the honey bee would love to, which is sweet.

The escort giggles her most seductive giggle and crawls on her palms, hands and knees, positioning her belly directly above his. She puts her hand around his slim penis and guides her vagina down upon it. Evidence of her arousal is found in her lubrication and she slips easily over him.

On cue *Oh bay-bee. Mmmmhm.* Really very much like a pornstress.

His cock disappears inside her and can be seen again in slowly ascending movements of her hips. She pushes her hands quite forcibly on his chest and lifts her head back as if to stare directly at the wall, if her eyes are not shut. This doesn't last long as he firmly clamps her head in his hands and pulls her mouth onto his, sucking on her lips and licking her tongue. His hips now take over and he thrusts upwards and downwards and upwards and downwards very quickly, letting go of her head to place his hands on her hips and breasts and then to grab her backside and finally to cup her face, this time with gentleness, guiding her lips back to his and kissing them in a puerile manner. He murmurs that he's gonna come and he ejaculates inside of her, his inarticulate murmur becoming an elongated sigh and his toes curling until close to cramping. His hands slide down to the middle of her spine and he pulls her flat-stomached, small-breasted torso against his, willing her to feel his trembling repercussions from the orgasm.

Well, he didn't last long but in his blitzed condition, fair play he came. Only problem now is what he wants to do with the rest of his time. Couldn't've been more than half an hour.

It has not been. He places his hands on the bed with the palms against the duvet and with his eyes closed. She is not sure what it is that she should do and rolls to her left and lies on her back to his right, placing her right hand on his chest and stroking down to his stomach and back up to his collarbone languidly. The man's breathing is quick and his stomach and chest rise beneath her hand. She can feel the wetness of his semen against her thigh and the cooling sensation of it from where the room's conditioned air meets her labia, legs slightly opened.

Stupid allergies and inflammation. When she had first had intercourse three years ago, the venereal acts had been amazing to her (and still are now), contrary to what she had read and what she later found out her friends had lied about. The problems came afterwards, where, in a panic-stricken thought pattern that initially revolved solely on infections and immunodeficiencies, she had cried in the lobby of the young persons' clinic and waited for the diagnosis on her sore and distended vagina. Given an ointment to soothe the pain and told that she may have a sensitivity to latex, she had been led in the direction of using condoms made from substitute materials. After more trial and error, the irritation still occurred and she had given up. Contraception just isn't the same, but she has the piece of metal in her arm and so far so good. Eight clients in and no problems either. She's pretty good at telling and knows that she'd flat out refuse if they looked unclean.

The man sits up suddenly and makes a noise of exertion.

She flinches and moves her hand away, startled. Her thoughts of salubriousness are broken with this movement and he says
↑↓

Well. You had better be on your way. I must be out shortly and, you know, have not got much time. What rises must fall and every time is the same.

The woman smiles, which he does not see as he is looking into the opened door of the bathroom, far from absent-mindedly but with absent thought towards his body. She says okay honey and then that she hopes it was good for him. He does not want to reply, not in this mode of regret, and so he does not say anything in response. He feels the weight shift on the mattress and hears as she dresses, adjusting her clothes with the whip of elastic straps against skin and the subtle rustling of light fabrics, barely audible for their delicacy and the hum of air-conditioning.
↓↑

He's obviously one of those types. Better not be intimate or touch him. *Thanks honey. I'll be off then.*

She picks up her bag and walks to the door.
↑↓

You were good. Why the fuck didn't he just say that? What is he thinking? But he is lucky; she turns to him and smiles rather condescendingly and opens the door and closes it quietly and she's gone. Why do you do these things, old chap?

He thinks of the same things that he has thought on every occasion when he has paid for, aimed for, or talked his way to having sexual intercourse with a woman that is not his wife. The celebratory aspect still remains, but this only materialises whilst in conversation with Stu and the others, where plaudits are bandied and respect given for pure, stereotypical masculinity. Men were made to fuck, as all men know, but he knows that this is not true and that a man worth any respect would either a) not marry or b) stay faithful. Faithful itself is a stupid term, what with his not being religious and the whole matrimonial aspect merely a relic of tradition. If he cannot respect himself completely, then how the fuck can he expect anyone else to? He thinks about how the before is always tainted by the after and how the idea is often, if not always, the better part; the disingenuous perspicacity of committing something forbidden (by whom?) is more enjoyable than the commission and realisation of the fantasy.

So he sits on the bed, elbows rested on each knee, blinking infrequently and eyes fixated on the towel that lies closer to him than it does the bathroom.

They still have sex and she is still fulsomely attractive, even if she has put on a bit of weight over the last half a year. Another in-joke and he feels guilty now for saying it: a joke that's in between her and him. Guilt.

Guilt. That dirty old bastard. But guilt is not needed and it's self-created and self-inflicted. He is the harbinger of the guilt, not the girl or his wife or the other women.

He thinks that he knows that he loves his wife, and also that as much as anything that he knows, his wife would never be adulterous: married for eleven years and together for years before that. Neither of them have considered divorce through the marriage. They have two sons.

Flowers. He will buy her flowers, his horticultural queen. Whore. Botanical queen. Better. But what if she does know? What if the last times after his business trips, late evenings, affairs and clandestine rendezvous have made her suspicious (and rightly so) and now flowers are symbolic of his shame, as sweetly pungent as the evident and odoriferous sweat of sex secretions?

Apparel

The smell of vanilla, chocolate, malt or butterscotch is noticeable to him and heightens his feelings, in turn coaxing his body to action; he leans forwards, picks up the towel in his right hand, stands up abruptly and walks into the bathroom and turns the dial and after the water is pouring hot, he steps under it. He lathers the soap until his hands are coated in off-white bubbles and rubs his soaped hands with hard-pressing palms over every surface of skin on his body. He repeats this three times and with each occasion of lathering, he takes water in his mouth and rinses, swishing it around before dribbling it down his chest during the process of covering his body with soap, reluctant to touch his penis, thinking accusatorily of it as a utensil of weakness, the reason for his infidelity. Turning clockwise slowly, he allows the water to fall upon him and rinse him of soap, finishing his rotation by stepping backwards an inch and a half and pushing his hips forward so as to push his penis under the flowing water.

Not satisfied, he turns the dial and the water stops pouring, steps out of the bathtub and spits in the sink. In the condensation that has collected on the mirror that is screwed to the wall above the basin, he uses his right index finger to write the word TWAT in neatly formed letters. His self-deprecation brings a caustic single laugh, breathed through his nose. He is looking at an asshole, and an asshole is as he is branded.

He should ring his wife, tell her he loves her and that he misses her, promise her a trip away next weekend just the two of them, they'll get a sitter or the boys can spend the night with her mum and dad. No, can't do that. Too obvious. She would probably smell the aftersmell of come or more seriously not fail to detect an odd tone, the tone of guilt, in his voice. He should have just stayed with Stu and the others. It's too late to head out again now. Well it isn't really, but he feels knackered in the most literal sense. Tomorrow night, without any chemical other than alcohol, he'll ring her and spend the night in the bars. Carl'll vacuum his share of the acid.

In the bedroom, he crouches by the far side of the bed and opens his suitcase, takes his toothbrush and an unopened tube of toothpaste from the bottom right corner, stands up and walks to the basin. He puts the little finger of his left hand up his left nostril and scrapes dried colloidal mucous from the cartilage with his nail whilst turning the cold tap with his right. He wriggles the finger and then puts it under the water, flicking the nail of his thumb under the nail of the little finger to dislodge what has deposited before brushing his teeth.

Absolutely knackered. Should sleep well. Turns off his phone and then gets into bed. He's basically dry. He walks past the towel on the floor and pulls his clothes from under the bed, remembering that he placed it on the little table by the window. He sees that he has no messages and turns it off, thinking that he really should ring his wife. He switches off the light. The bed sheets feel cold as he lifts up the duvet and half rolls on the mattress. He likes cold sheets when the days are hot and it reminds him of the impossibility of sleep as a young child; the summers were scorching and his room would face due east. Bed time was between eight or nine (he cannot remember) and his room would be illuminated by the glare of a magnified sun.

In bed now, he is quickly comfortable lying on his right side, face towards the hotel room's door, placing one of the pillows between his legs and another under his right arm and head. The hum of the air-conditioning is peaceful for him and its constancy lulls him to semi-consciousness. He is still aware and his thoughts flit between his wife and his children, work and the woman that he had coitus with less than an hour earlier.

The unwilled adding of weight in his penis irks him enough to alter his position, moving to rest on his other shoulder and bringing the pillow to his chest.

He is comfortable and the comfort brings an easy peace, dispelling his thoughts and allowing him to think little, which leads to the nothingness that brings sleep.

He sleeps.

Down the corridor and the office is the last door, only it's straight in front of him and the door's usually on the left. Or the right. Definitely not directly in front of him. The brass plaque has Marston's dickheadish name on it, so he's wrong anyway and he knocks once before going in. He's dressed in regal-red robes and holds a sceptre in his hand for an instant before readopting his business-stereotype attire. Expensive, too.

You've fucked up this time, Andrew, he says. He points at him with a long finger. Scary bastard, when like this. There's no way the company can afford to retain you now you've lost the loans department, he says, a frown now painted on his cheekless face. That's a whole lot of money flushed down the drain, he says.

He should probably say something but fuck it. Marston has always been a jumped-up cunt. He will tell him that he's a cunt. You're a cunt. He grabs him by the collar of his shirt with his left hand and punches him repeatedly with his right hand clenched into a fist. His punches are slow and he does not connect well. Marston's face bloats with the taut-skinned pink of bruising, but he smiles at him and tells him that he is fired and that the security team is on its way.

Cunt. His hand feels broken and his fingers ache from pulling tightly against the top of the man's shirt. He lets go of the shirt and the man falls to the floor. He runs out of the room, looks at the empty corridor and decides that the door to his left leads out to a balcony that has a fire-escape ladder attached to it. He twists the door handle and pushes the door open and sees the railings on the balcony through the window opposite. The top of the ladder is visible. From behind him, the crackling of distorted radio messages informs him that his pursuers are close. He runs to the vertical windows, sliding the left window to his right and stepping on the balcony when the gap accommodates his size. A gunshot smashes the glass behind him and he jumps over the edge of the railing, fear clogging his throat as he falls and falls, flapping his arms futilely to try and beat against the fast-approaching ground. Or fuck this. He'll just wake up.

His body spasms and he draws a quick intake of breath and his eyes open quickly. He is facing the window and strobes of light filter through the slits between the blinds. He yawns with his eyes closed and mouth wide open, sniffing a repressed yawn in a juddering series of in-breaths that leads to a pleasurable sensation in his groin.

It cannot be any later than eight and he could stay in bed all day. The bed is really rather good and he has no noticeable aches in his joints. The warm smell of freshly-washed and ironed linen and the coolness of the sheets in the warm room and the calming buzz of the air-con and the muffled life of early-morning weekend labour outside the safety of these walls: bloody lovely. If only he brought his face masks.

He closes his eyes and drifts in and out of roughly minute-long instances of sleep, sometimes finding himself in the office whilst at work, one time not conjuring any dreamscape, and one time in the park with his children, meeting the man who sold him the little slips of paper tucked in one of the pairs of socks in his suitcase. When his stomach starts to complain audibly, he relents after a little more than four minutes and gets out of bed. He turns on his phone and stands naked in front of the blinds, pulling two apart from each other with his left hand to peer out to the street six floors below as he waits for his phone to initialise. The drop to the unseen pavements leads him to think of his dream and self-interrogate his feelings towards his manager. His children's image also brings a pang of guilt.

He looks at his phone. It flashes three times over the next thirty-one seconds and tells him that he has 3 MESSAGES. The first two are from Stu, requesting that he join them (the second text is logged as being sent at 22:40) and the third is from his wife, expressing her hope that he isn't bored senseless as he usually is when on these business trips. That's good. He can say that he was tired and in bed before eleven. Works out pretty damned well, all in all.

He thumbs a message with the phone in his right hand.

> Hi love, all is well,
> conference didn't
> send me to sleep but
> you're right, it was
> bloody boring.
> Hope you and the
> kids are well x

He presses send and with the message details that appear on the screen, notices that the time is 06:26 am. He makes himself yawn and then enjoys the warmth and tingle of a natural yawn. He turns and enjoys the sight of the scrunched-up duvet and creased covers. His house is always impeccably clean and ordered, for two reasons: his wife believes that he has an obsession for neat arrangement and tidiness, and his wife ensures that any mote of dust, cobweb, strand of bleached grass or smudge on the mirror-glass has no tenancy longer than two days. The vacuum comes out every other day and although he is grateful and proud of the standards of his home, the childish part that remains in him enjoys the nature of the unkempt and the uncoordinated. Mess is fun.

He tosses his phone on the bed and cups his hands over his mouth, exhaling deeply from his lungs. He thinks that his breath is passable and dresses himself in the clothes scattered on the floor and under the bed. He puts his socks on last and then tucks his phone in the pocket of his shirt, changing the settings of his message receipt to vibrate. He checks that he has the card key in one of his trouser pockets and then leaves the room.

Walking out past two different receptionists than yesterday, the early-morning coolness hits him. The pavement is shaded, the sun not high enough in the sky to fall that far down. The pavement is yet to bake and the carbon monoxide yet to amplify from midday heat.

It smells of summer. Pity for the grass. Great smell, freshly-cut grass. Reminds him of the park with dad and the soggy sandwiches that mum made, tasting better, somehow, for the perspiration's effect on the bread. Or the water from the tomatoes or whatever it was that made that happen.

He gently brushes away the dried rheum of sleep that has collected since waking. He walks past a woman whose heels make a sound that he likes. She is dressed in various shades of grey and is in a hurry.

Where to have breakfast, is the question. There was a café here somewhere, he's sure. Not far from the hotel, if it's still here. He pauses, turns his body to face the road and looks back the way that he has come, glancing towards the quickly distancing shape of the grey-clothed woman. He doesn't think that it is that way. Pretty sure it's further up the road. If it's still there. He continues in the direction that he left the hotel and after a little over a minute, decides that the cafeteria that he is in front of looks good enough. It is not the same as last time.

Most of the tables are taken by men in construction colours: fluorescent yellow-greens and faded denims; sleeveless arms. A logistic's worker looks at him

$\rightarrow$

$\leftarrow$

probably still got a good twenty minutes. Should just beat the shitty traffic and zoom up the motorway. There's never much point in clocking-in early, or on time. It's not like any of the poor bastards get any more money. Good coffee.

He drinks the last of the dark-brown coffee and leaves a one pound coin on the saucer next to the nearly-emptied cup. He stands as tall as he can with his trainers flat to the ground and tenses the muscles in his legs, leaning back very slightly and forcing his back to make a popping sound. He walks out of the café and looks up at the sky. Two small clouds flank either side of the sun.

No twat in a red cap around. One hundred percent record maintained. He has not received any paper detailing parking violations and has three points on his driving licence, just like Mikey. It has become a part of the rules of the game that he and his co-workers play at work. The game does not take any specific form, but after countless discussions during the early stages of its inception, the collective decision was that the game was to break the law as much as possible with the equipment provided at work. The hard part is the secondary rule, the one that they decided should entail that the aim is not to get caught. As a result of this ruling, the leader board was topped by the worker who had the least points, points being accrued based on the severity of the misdemeanour. He is second.

He tries to feel disappointed that he does not have a piece of paper tucked under the windscreen wipers of his car. He feels disappointed and then he is amused. He walks out on the road and opens the driver's side door with his right hand, getting into the seat. It is pushed not quite as far from the steering wheel as is possible, but it is close, and the angle of the backrest makes his spine angle over one hundred and twenty degrees from his legs. He regularly tells people that he is not a huge fan of cars before detailing the mechanisms and parts of engines, the modifications available to hundreds of different types of car, and the prices of the newest nearly-affordable vehicles on the market. He is a regular purchaser of magazines that have alluring women straddling powerful supercars. The only subscription that he has is to fr33porno.net and that does not cost a penny, although it does fill his junkmail inbox. On the rear-right seat is a copy of MUSCLEmoto and an identification badge that bears the name Jason Greene: his name. His friends rarely refer to him as that, and three of his most recent acquaintances (whom he regards as friends) know him only as Cranky. The nickname was created by Jason and used to apply to one of the bosses at work; during a shift, Pawel had been fascinated by the word cranky and had decided to apply it as liberally as possible to items animate or otherwise. The conveyers became cranky, the bird that shitted on his car made him cranky, his girlfriend was cranky (as was her mother), the brakes on his car were cranky. They had all found it highly funny and when Jason said that their manager was the definition of cranky, that he was Cranky, Pawel had been shouting across to another worker that Cranky is a fucking fuck when the manager walked in the room and inquired as to whom they were referring. Pawel had pointed at Jason and when the manager laughed and said Cranky, I like it. Very apt, they all laughed. He is Cranky and has been ever since.

Cranky is driving to work and is turning over ideas of mischief with his friend in mind.

A couple of days ago was great. Mikey shit himself and thought he was one of the big angry Polaks from the trucks. He thinks Mikey's working today and is also pretty sure that Andy is as well. If they're in before him then he'll set off their alarms and run in saying that their windows have been smashed in. Or he might buy a porno on the way in and paste the images on the windscreens. Sixty + magazine would work perfect. Or maybe he could do the Polak trick on Andy if Mikey hasn't already got in on it.

He's sure there's summat going on between them. He thinks that they might be fags, but he cannot agree with himself on that because a) Mikey's got a missus and talks about shagging her nearly all of the time and b) because they don't lisp and talk about shopping and stuff. But there's something very fucking strange going on. They're alright, though. A good laugh.

He presses the play button on the CD player and the music system in the car resumes playing the song which was one minute and twenty-one seconds long. The album is one of his favourites and he taps the steering wheel to the hip-hop rhythms and nods along to the mid-paced drumbeats. He starts to speak along to the rapping, imitating a deep voice to match that of the rapper. The words come fast and he speaks each one faultlessly in order. Jimmer – used to go to school with him and smoke weed in the woods – he was always into his music and is now finally breaking through. He's been big in the local scene for quite a while, but this album is the first on a label. He chats to Jimmer every now and again over the net and promised him that he'll pop down to one of his gigs that are coming up. The music's really fucking good.

A set of traffic lights obstruct his journey by staying red for ninety seconds. Two cars go past in this time and he heads a line of eight cars when the red disappears to be replaced by its subordinate amber and green twins. Throughout the time that he sits there, he enjoys the music that is being played to him via the speakers and plans a series of actions that will trick and irk his workmates. He has discarded the idea of pasting pornographic images of sagging breasts, buttocks, weathered skin and greying hair, at least for the day. He believes that this is an idea that will not last a week before being undertaken; the best wind-ups need to reach fucking fruition when they're ripe, not when they're soggy. Sounds like something that his grandmother would say. If she was alive, of course.

The lanes on the road are almost empty of vehicles, and so when he gets on the motorway, he speeds along at a round century in miles per hour, overtaking only one car before turning off at the junction closest to his place of work. The lanes on the road heading to the centre of the city are busy. Cranky thinks that it will only be another twenty minutes or so until it starts to jam.

A few more clouds have appeared in the sky. Any more of those shitbags and it'll be pouring down before dinner-time. He is slightly amused by his weather predictions, thinking that there is more chance of having a nuclear volcano erupt in the car park when he gets there than of seeing rain this month. The bald bastard on the telly had yattered endlessly about the biggest anti-cyclops that he'd ever seen and nearly started wanking himself off over the glorious days of summer returned. Silly old bastard thought he was a poet or something. Probably right, though. He hopes that he's not stigging today as he's bored absofuckinglutely senseless with it. Not that the job is hard but it'd be good to work the belts with the boys and laze around a bit more. And play around a bit, too.

He turns the volume dial on the CD player and the music is nearly at the loudest that it can be, the doors of his car rattling with each reverberant bass note. He puts his right thumb up to the man who is sitting in the booth by the security gate and the man pushes a button that operates the gate's lifting. He drives past the raised gate and the man in the booth, nodding in the direction of both. He cannot see the man's face for the sun's reflection on his driver's side window, but assumes that he is impressed. In the car park he sees Mikey leaning on a small car that is red with black circles, talking to a girl who Cranky knows is Mikey's girlfriend.

Looks like a ladybird. It's gotta be hers: his sexy alternative chickie's. Hasn't seen her for a while.

He slowly drives his car in their direction and parks alongside them, neatly between the white demarcations on the concrete. He notices that her car is diagonally parked over two bays and deduces that she is not staying for long and that she is probably just dropping him off. He sits in the car, pretending to fumble for something in the glove compartment and then stopping the music before getting out. He does not want to start with a cliché and he quickly goes through a list of three options.

Alright beautiful? And Mike, of course.
↓↑

Such a funny boy. *Fine thanks. How're you?* She thinks it's Cranky but isn't sure. The one that Mikey seems to get all of his Polish from. And funnyisms.

Mikey says Yeah all good ta. Being dropped off 'cuz my car's fucked. Don't know why.

↑↓

That's shit. I'm all good thanks, doll. So you had to give Mikey a ride in then, yeah? Ride in. He winks at Mikey. He likes it. A good play on words. She likes it too. Maybe she fancies him a little bit.

↓↑

I like giving him a ride. What can I say? Her wink does exactly what she wants it too, although Mikey seems to be telling her off for it.

↑↓

Now you've done it. He'll take that one for ages.

↓↑

He's right, too. She's a proper dirty bitch. Just what he likes. *When you and Mikey split up, don't forget to ask for my number from him first, right?* Best movie-star face and looking smug. His eyebrows are raised and mock seriousness is his aim. Mikey says Fuck's sake, Cranky. You're mental. Her ass in those trackies is very tasty.

←
→

Well. I'd better be off. Maybe see you for a threeway sometime? That'll really tickle his fancy.

She leans over to Mikey and holds his face with both of her palms, leaning forwards with her face, slowly pushing her mouth against his and pushing her tongue in his mouth. Her neck movements are rhythmic and consciously slow, changing angles to kiss him after a series of seconds and continuing in this manner for over half a minute. She breaks away from him and then turns to Cranky, her eyes narrowed to what she is certain is an arousing expression for him. Cranky is talking to Mikey as they walk away and she gets in her car.

Her mother always said that the quickest way to a boy is

through his cock, which after having worked in the world of business for a while and having proved true, never seemed to be wrong. The first mention of sex and Cranky is hers to command. Boys will be boys. She presses the middle of the steering wheel and the car's horn sounds as she passes the two men. She blows a kiss in their direction, careful not to aim it at either of them. The funny-boy Cranky is a smug-looking arrogant sort, but he's kind of cute. Probably thinks that she is serious about the threesome. It was also funny how Mikey had lied, trying to save macho face or something. He had gone out the previous evening and arrived back past midnight, completely drunk and soon falling asleep. He said that he still felt drunk when he woke up and asked if she would please give him a lift. She made him promise a back massage later that evening and he had agreed without reluctance.

Last night. Shit, that wasn't much fun. For all of the hardships that she has seen in her life, that is definitely and without a doubt the worst. Rachel shifted between being really sad and upset and crying all of the time to moody and angry, aggressive towards her and even Jo. She can understand the way that she must be feeling, though. Can't imagine what it must be like to lose a dad or a parent, especially under the circumstances. Attending her granddad's funeral when she was seven years old was hard enough and thankfully no one else in her family has died since then. The funeral tomorrow will be only the second funeral that she has attended in her entire life. It will be her first adult funeral and she will be there almost like a bridesmaid to the grieving friend. Only it will be in black and not in white, sad and not happy and awkward instead of... Well, maybe it's awkward being a bridesmaid. Rachel will be okay in a few weeks when the funeral is a thing of the past. She supposes that what makes it harder is the fact that he was young and in good shape and that it was suicide. Shit. Suicide. But the worst is that she now has no parents. One was a road accident and the other a broken heart because of it. It's more like something from TV and not something that actually happens to someone you know. It must be so hard, losing a mum to a hit-and-run and then a dad to suicide. She is strong and that is good. Maybe her anger is a good thing, too.

She knew that she was not working today and plans to visit the shops and the clinic and buy a dress for the funeral. Initially, her plans were to visit her grandmother and recommence their knitting sessions, but she rang yesterday evening from Rachel's house explaining how she was unable to see her and briefly summarising the situation in hushed tones. The retail outlets do not open for another hour and forty-five minutes and she has decided to drive home and sleep for a while longer. She is fatigued from the emotional toll that has been taken out of her; consolation and constant, conscious awareness to the situation in which she found herself have been difficult. Every word that she has uttered and every physical action that she has extended to Rachel over the last two days has been considered and analysed before being communicated. On several occasions, her words have been undesired or the wrong things to say, and the temperamental emotive state that Rachel is currently in saw her shrug off the offered hugs or gentle hands placed on her shoulders. Her face seemed to become a mask of complete wrath at times and though she had not spoken hatefully-loaded words, the abrupt and short responses had a cutting edge. Quite suddenly though, this would change. Narrow-slanted eyes would become wide and pleading or closed and tearful. Physical closeness was kept away, at odds to the message communicated by her countenance during these bouts of hopelessness. She knows that no fault should be cast upon Rachel and is aware at her selfishness; she thinks that she wishes the event of her friend's father's suicide had never happened, because at least then she would not have to go through this. She reminds herself that she is empathetic and sympathetic, but maybe that she is not strong enough mentally to bear others' anguish. In a world of such negativity and stuck within a maelstrom of pain, anguish, horror, rape, murder, death and regret, it is only logical that she does not seek out others' torments to share in the unfortunate burden that is borne with it.

Surely?

The last time in her life that she had willingly accepted the mental confusion of an unsolicited, negative feeling, was that first time with work. She had felt sullied and dishonest. All night the man, who could only have been thirty at the oldest but had told her he was forty, an executive something-or-other with a yacht and the right connections or, as was found to be the truth, had a father who was an executive and had connections in the largest international communications networks, had been flirting with her and unashamedly asking her to go to his hotel room. Since he first asked, two hours after the board meeting closed and whilst eating the dessert that he promised he would pay for, she had relented for over five hours. He was handsome and tall and the firmness of his body when they danced hinted at substantial sessions lifting weights and exercising.

Didn't stop him being a prick, though. She'd told him straightaway that she had a boyfriend.

When he had asked her if she wanted to head out for some food, if she knew a good place to eat, she had answered that she had a boyfriend. He had responded with the words only eating, something to eat, not looking to do anything else. As soon as they had started eating, he had started referring to her hair, then braided, as being such a turn-on and that, when she walked, gravity held such a perfect respect for her tits and ass. Did she know that she had the most comfortable looking lips ever, if she knew what he meant? She had smiled, inwardly repulsed by the choice of words and brazen commentary whilst eating, and had humoured him. She would leave as soon as she had eaten, of course, but during the courses he had explained about his role in the company that hers was trying to gain work from, and had completely disregarded the tab that was accruing rapidly with each glass of chateaux-something that they drank. The conversations about power, money and assets were arousing and the alcohol was intoxicating and both coinciding made her susceptible to his concupiscent suggestions. After they had eaten, they sat in the restaurant for nearly an hour and when they left she was feeling happy and her initial plan of leaving the man was no more. He had recommended dancing in a jazz bar that he'd seen whilst passing in a taxi and she had agreed. He told her that he wanted an honest way to put his hands on her ass and get in close, adding that it would be better for everyone if they spent the night together anyway. Not Mikey, she thinks that she thought. In the hotel room, hers, he had started kissing her and licking her lips and face as soon as the door was closed. Her memory was not reliable for what happened in the room, but she knows that she felt good, that the sex was good and that he was skilful and not selfish. Only in the morning when he rubbed his erect penis against the bottom of her buttocks in search of her vagina, straddling her waking body that lay on its front, did she realise the extent of his disgrace. He had found her vagina and pushed heavily against it, pornographically murmuring yeah, ah yeah with repetition. Wholly awake and conscious and thinking clearly, headache clinging to her forehead, she had asked him if he was wearing a condom. No different to last night, adding that she shouldn't forget her pill. She had yelped or screamed or shouted that he should get off her and that she was not on the pill, which at that time was true, her and Mikey finding no issue with the ceremony of removing and putting on a condom. Chill out, he had said, chuckling and standing naked on the floor, his penis pointing towards his face a few inches above her eye level. He had dressed patiently whilst she went to the bathroom and sat on the toilet with her forehead pressed against her fingertips. She did not get out until she heard the door close and waited a further few minutes. She had regretted that and as a result, knew to what extent regret could make a person feel awful. She felt used and shameful. In the week that followed, she had come close to telling Mikey, feeling that she needed to confess but uncertain as to the reaction that she would receive. She decided not to tell him and before the fortnight was out, after her immediate supervisor had informed her of the acquisition of the account for the largest international communications network service providers in the world, she had rid herself of the majority of her guilt.

The best thing about driving at this time is easily the speed you can get to places in. Driving away from town, too. The other lane is a bit busier. Getting warm as well. A proper summer this year, which'd make a change. God she's tired.

She blows through pursed lips in an attempt to whistle, aiming at a classic rock-and-roll song that was first recorded during her parents' teenaged years. In her mind, she tunefully mimics the melody and the imagined high-pitched whistle accompanies her blowing.

The roads are navigated by familiarity. She is conscious of what is around her but pays it no attention due to its regularity and its normality. She knows where every set of traffic lights is, the two speed-monitoring units (one of which is nearly hidden by the branches of a spindly tree), and the zebra crossing. She knows where the potholes have developed from the ice-cracked roads and where the ramps are placed, driving over or around them if space permits. In this fashion she gets home, stops the car in front of the house, parking on the drive. They had pushed Mikey's car a little over two metres up the road to allow her access to their driveway.

Getting out of the car, a man is seen in her peripheral vision but not noticed. His wave of lethargic good-morning greeting is unacknowledged as she walks up the path alongside the driveway and pulls the keys out of her handbag with her right hand and presses the lock for the car, hearing the mechanisms click from four yards away. She scrapes the key against the lock of the door before slotting it in the keyhole and then twisting anticlockwise and pushing the door forwards. She has not let go of the key and steps forwards and pulls it back out. She pushes the door closed from the bottom with her right foot, and drops her handbag and key by the closed door, slips off her sandals and walks up the stairs. She goes in the bedroom and crawls across the bed on her hands and knees, grabbing the rumpled duvet and enjoying the coolness of the sheets. She changes into her tracksuit after Mikey had explained about his car and she had offered to give him a lift in return for a massage.

She really is tired. Mikey gives good backrubs. He's a good boy, listening to her directions and being perfectly firm with his hands. For a not very physical boy, his hands are rough from the packing and stuff he does at work. It's really comfy. Not too hot yet, either.

Mikey is standing before her, kneeling down now, holding

a small box towards her that has to have a wedding ring within it. She goes to take it but he brings it to his chest, smiling childishly, teasingly. He opens it up and inside is a beautiful ring, a simple ring of gold with a single white diamond at its centre. He asks her if she will make him the luckiest man in the world and she says yes. He stands up and they hold each other in a wet embrace and she is falling or gliding and wakes up.

Her phone is vibrating against her right thigh, a song playing loudly from a small output. She rolls to her right, laying on her back, and pulls it out of her pocket with her left hand before exchanging it to her right. She sees that it is Rachel from the caller identification.

She just can't take it right now. It's wrong. She just can't take it right now.

The vibrating and the music stop and she unlocks the phone's screen to remove the notification of a missed call. She looks through her messages in the conversation folder and twenty-eight seconds later, a repeated dual beep and vibration inform her that she has a voice message.

She'll listen to it later. Just can't bear to right now. It's ten to nine.

She can taste her breath and does not like it. She wants to get out and brush her teeth and then have a glass of orange juice. It is not pleasant at first, the accentuated cold and bitterness of the usual sweetness, but she enjoys it.

She pushes herself to a sitting position and slides across to the edge of the bed without thinking of her superstition and places her left foot down before the right in the same manner that she has since she was seven years old. She stands up and puts her hands on each of her buttocks, pushing into them and leaning backward. There is a popping sound that satisfies her and coaxes a sound of expelled air from her mouth.

That was a good one. Like an old woman with this morning stiffness. Get rid of this awful taste as well. Should've brushed her teeth before driving Mikey to work. Ooh: orange juice.

The bathroom floor feels cold against her feet and she likes it. In her right hand, she flips the lid of the toothpaste tube with her thumb and sucks a small amount of toothpaste out. She puts the toothpaste tube down and then she takes the electric toothbrush from the cup that Mikey had put it in earlier and slowly drags the rotating brushes gently across her teeth. After thirty-three seconds, she turns the cold tap with her left hand and puts the brushes under it, leans her mouth under the flowing water and takes a mouthful of it, and then faces the basin and spits out the froth. She puts the toothbrush back in the cup and turns off the tap with her left hand and then picks up Mikey's shaving mirror that is on the cabinet above the basin. Sometimes she wonders why the doors of the cabinet do not have mirrors on them. She looks in the small rounded mirror and bites her teeth together, knowing that there will be no remnants of food as she has not eaten this morning. On her cheek, there is the faded grey-pink of a small spot that had been tweezered. She adopts an inquisitive expression, arching her eyebrows as high on her forehead as she can make them stretch, turns her head to show the left side of her face and then the right, smiles ruefully and leaves the bathroom to return to the bedroom. Along the right upon entering, there is a shelf that extends across the width of the room. On each side is a chest of drawers and where there is a gap between them, a red-painted wooden stool is tucked underneath. Following the length of the shelf is a mirror, three feet high and stopping an inch before reaching the edges where walls meet. She pulls the stool out and sits on it.

Make-up. An early-morning girl's best friend. An any-day

girl's best friend. All girls' best friend.

She looks at herself in the mirror, unclipping the two hairclips that hold her hair back on the right of her head and letting it fall down to the base of her neck. She knows that she is attractive and she thinks that she is pretty and beautiful depending on the aesthetic that she adopts. Today, she will aim for pretty. She wants to feel as girlish as she can. With this as her agenda, she sifts through three different make-up bags that are kept on the shelf (what Mikey refers to as pencil-cases) to remove pink eyeshadow, a small padded brush, pink lip-gloss, nut-brown concealer, black eyeliner, reddish-pink blusher and a brush, chestnut foundation and a different brush, and mascara. She removes the two metal balls that are pushed through the piercings beneath her nose, unscrewing them by wedging the metal against the inside of her lip with her tongue and twisting with her right forefinger and thumb. She puts the balls on the shelf and picks the stemmed studs from her tongue and puts them next to the others. A packet of baby wipes is in front of her. With each little pot, tube, or brush, she applies the make-up with a steady right hand, proceeding by unclipping the lid of the round pot of concealer and then dipping her fingers in it. She massages the skin-coloured cream against her face, opening her mouth wide to make her skin taut and expand the surface for her application. She inspects her face with each press of her fingers and brushes the surface of the cream within its pot when she realises that she needs a little bit more. The rule of make-up, as passed on to her by her mother, is that it is easier to add more than it is to take surplus off. And that it is expensive to be wasting good products.

The spot is well and truly covered. It was massive too, but a little artistry with the tweezers made it near enough disappear. A little touch of concealer and it is concealed. Voilà. Mikey and his foreign obsession has definitely affected her. Squeezing with the fingers only bruises the skin and makes it more easily infected. Tweezers really are the best way.

She picks up her pot of blusher and then her foundation in her left hand and unclips the lids with her right, before touching the ends of one of the brushes in the foundation and lightly brushing the light-brown over her cheeks, starting with the left. She becomes satisfied with her application of the foundation and very lightly presses the end of the brush against the dark-pink foundation and dusts the powder just a little below each of her cheekbones. After this, she clips the lids on the pots and puts them in two separate bags, depositing the brushes with their counterparts.

Rouged up, baby. Looking good. She lifts her chin higher than usual and turns her head to the right and then to the left, enjoying looking at what she thinks is a perfect face.

She stands up to lean in close to the mirror as she lifts the cap of her eyeshadow and then looks at the little padded brush before rubbing it against its pink contents. She notices that she needs to buy more, which she actually realised six days ago but forgot about. The centre of the round container is a tiny circle of transparent plastic. Slowly and with careful small strokes and dabs, she covers her lids with a sparkling pink. Once more satisfied, she puts the brush and the little cylindrical container in a bag and unscrews the liquid eyeliner. The line that she draws across the edge of her left eyelash, starting from the point closer to the eye and her nose, is neat and she is happy with it.

Shit. Always a nuisance starting from inside on the right eye. Still, it's good enough. The corner could be a bit thicker. She decides not to attempt to make the line thicker. She screws the eyeliner nib and handle back in the pot and puts it in a bag.

And finally, mascara. To make lashes fantastic. Always thought that they were too short. False ones are just tacky.

She unscrews the mascara and the wiry brush that is attached to the handle is lifted in front of her left eye. She flicks the brush from beneath the eyelashes and upwards, away from her face, with quick flicks of her thumb and forefinger. She repeats this for both of her eyes, repeatedly brushing away from her eyelashes and dipping the brush in the tubed container.

She really does look good. No wonder Mikey is so head-over-heels for her. Perhaps she would ditch him and marry one of those rich sugar daddies who would look after her and give her an allowance and fawn over her and... Maybe not. Mikey's great and she probably does love him as much as love exists. If anything, he's the poorer of the two of them. Christ, she's probably classed as a yuppie in the socially and professionally mobile world of the modern woman. Why sell herself at all when she's raking in decent money and successful already? Onwards and upwards. God, imagine screwing a wrinkly old man for money and to live a supposed luxury life. Rather not, thanks.

She pushes the make-up bags against the wall beneath the mirror, having finished with the mascara. She picks up the studs and starts to screw them in.

Not really feeling them today. Don't know why. She unscrews them from the thread and leaves them near where she picked them up. She takes off all of her clothes, throws them on the bed, and stands in front of the mirror for twenty seconds, pushing her right hand against her stomach and enjoying the firmness that meets it. Nice abs, good-looker. She hardly works out these days either. Not strictly true, but it's nowhere near as much as she used to. Maybe she'll grow her pubic hair, too. Really give Mikey a reason to scratch at his recently shaved balls. Or the bit above them, if they're being literal.

She leaves the clothes on the bed and opens the wardrobe to its left, picking out a yellow, frilly-edged gypsy skirt that covers half of her shins and a black vest top. She throws these on the bed and opens the middle drawer of three that are built into the wardrobe below the doors. She rummages through an assortment of underwear, lingerie, a sex toy and a pair of handcuffs, pulling out a sky-blue two-piece bikini. She ties the back of the bikini top from the front and slides it around, holding the end of each of the neck straps and tying them in a bow behind her neck. She pulls on the bikini bottoms and then picks up the skirt from the bed and sits down to pull the skirt over her legs. The front of the skirt has a zip, a button, and a laced belt. She stands up to fasten the skirt in triplicate. The vest top has been ironed recently and smells fruity and clean, its elasticity tight against her contours as she puts it on over her head. She looks in the mirror and is reminded of herself as a thirteen-year-old, a time when she wore bikini tops and not bras, conscious of the conversations that she lied her way through at school.

Looking back, it seems a bit strange now. She was one of the girls who had always been looked at as pretty and even when she had got into rock and metal and became a Goth, the cool hard boys had still found her fit. As a woman now, she is attractive, which rules out that stupid saying of ugly kids growing pretty and pretty ones growing ugly. Those sayings are stupid anyway.

Is she hungry? Can't really decide. Maybe just have some cereal or a banana. If he's left any. He doesn't really eat badly, with the amount of fruit he eats, but he would have a pizza every day if he could. Surprising how he hasn't got loads of spots.

Midway down the stairs she has decided to eat cereal because it is quick, easy and no fuss, as well as a banana, providing that there are any. As she enters the kitchen, she looks at the fruit bowl and sees one banana, three yellow-green apples, and a bunch of stalked, similarly coloured grapes. She takes a bowl out of a cupboard and fills it with balls of dried, sugar-coated wheat. From the refrigerator, she takes out a green-labelled milk and pours it over the cereal. Then she sprinkles white sugar over the top of the bowl and starts to eat with a teaspoon.

She really is acting very girlish. Perhaps it's a counteraction against the awful news from Rachel. She read somewhere about the coping strategies of animals and the mourning of elephants. They don't leave the dead body of their lovers or family for ages. The story was about the similarities between animals and humans. Thinking about it, there isn't really much in common between people and elephants.

It's really sweet and not that nice. She doesn't know why she put extra sugar on them.

She silently tells herself that she is not nervous but does not convince herself. The cereal is not to her liking and she presses the spoon against the mulched contents of the bowl with her right hand, tipping the dregs of the milk in the sink and scraping the remains in the bin. Taking a banana, she walks to the living room and unpeels it by pulling the stalk down with her left hand, tearing the skin messily.

Shit. Hate it when that happens. Dumbest fruit ever. They never open cleanly. Now her nails will probably get banana under them. She picks at the half-split skin and succeeds in lifting the edge and sliding the pad of her right forefinger under it and peeling it all the way back. Thanks God for that. She smiles at her own silliness.

She eats it quickly, mapping out her route and looking at

various objects in the room without considering them. There is a collection of ornamental elephants on one of the pine shelves nestled in the corner of the walls closest to the patio and the television that she always thought of as elephantine Russian dolls. The wood-carved figures are largest on the right, standing at nearly six inches, and then decrease in size until the last elephant on the left, the fifth one, which stands at roughly two inches. There is an amaranth vase with wooden carvings representing flowers protruding from the top. The wooden shapes vary: sticks end in chocolate-coloured ovals, chromosomically-intertwined loops curve around each other, splayed and fibrous fronds erupt from the lip of the vase, a kernelled husk is attached to a stick. They are all varying shades of warm brown and complement the décor's rusticity. A CD rack is propped against a mahogany and glass cabinet and contains fifty-four cases, the majority of which are hers. She subconsciously thinks about fellatio but does not focus on it, her thoughts more concerned with reapplying lip-gloss before she starts driving.

She returns to the kitchen and steps on the pedal of the bin's lid-release and drops in the skin and the pulped end of the banana. She briefly sucks the end of her right thumb, forefinger and middle finger, drying them by pinching her skirts at the side of her right thigh. Her keys and handbag are by door and she walks there, ready to leave. Her sandals are there and she does not want to wear them.

Doesn't really go with the way she's dressed. They're alright, but her trainers'll be better. She quickly jogs up the stairs, skipping the penultimate stair and hitting the landing and then opening the wardrobe to remove a pair of pink and white trainers from a selection of neatly-arranged footwear. She puts them on in the bedroom, the laces already tied and so slipped on, before walking quickly down the stairs and picking up her bag and keys. After opening the door and leaving the house, she pushes the door shut and pulls the handle down and then up, ensuring that it is locked, heading down the path next to the drive and pressing the button to unlock her car with her right hand.

It takes her until she puts her hand on the door of the car and notices that the metal is not hot to realise that the temperature has cooled. Whilst it is not a cool day, the heat seems to be heavier and she looks up at all the visible sky that she can see, seeing the cloudless blue accompanied by a border of cloudy grey. The sun is covered.

Must be the first time in literally a month. This wasn't in the forecast. Supposed to be peaking at nearly a hundred for a hundred years. About forty centigrade. North African hot heat is nice, but muggy – no thanks. Not really the summer that she wants. Must be a blip or something.

Sitting in the car, the door is left opened as she searches in the handbag on her lap for the lip-gloss that she knows is in there. She looks for the lip-gloss absently, not really seeing what is in her bag. After thirty-one seconds, her left hand knocks it to her right and she registers that she has it. She looks in the rear-view mirror, unscrews the end of the make-up with her right hand and then applies a thick coating of lilac-tinged lubricant to her lips, slowly starting with the bottom and finishing with the top, before pursing them together. She stares at herself in the mirror for seven seconds, unblinking and concentrating on thoughtlessness.

She drops the lip-gloss in her handbag, takes the keys from between her lap, places the handbag on the passenger's seat, closes the door, and puts the key in the ignition. From routine, she puts on her seatbelt and turns the key, the engine starting with a low thrum and the radio station that she last listened to resuming its playing a fraction of a second afterwards.

She chooses not to manoeuvre the car in a three-point turn, the way that she did earlier, and drives to the end of the street to turn the car in the wider expanse of road available where the cul-de-sac arches to its finish. Only after she has turned and looks at the house that she shares with Mikey does she recognise the song being played as one of the few that she presently likes within the music charts.

No. That butterfly, achy-tugging period pain and dry mouth. Why didn't she get some orange juice before she left? That funny taste when you drink it after brushing your teeth would have been good, maybe. She's not sure.

The song's irritating too. Funny, really. It sounded good two weeks ago when it was first heard, but now it's been overplayed to death and sounds pretty shit. She presses the standby button on her CD player and the first notes of a song, played on piano, start to sound, replacing the radio. Each note is minor. The introduction to the song is slow, averaging fourteen notes every ten seconds until the electric guitar rings out a deep chord at forty-two seconds. The beats per minute exceeds two hundred at sixty-eight seconds.

She is driving steadily. The traffic is less busy than it was earlier in the week, the lack of weekend workers perhaps reflecting the unrestricted ability to stay in bed: the permission to do so. She is not listening to the music and is not really aware of anything specifically in her visual world. The effort not to think of what could be is requiring her to blank all awareness of the objects around her that do not form part of her second-nature, the actions and sights that have been familiarised to her to the extent that they are expected and to which she is reactively attuned. Conscious thinking leads to other thoughts.

Simple words can connote seemingly disparate memories or considerations. Thoughts breed thoughts breed thoughts and so continues the cycle.

It has taken eleven minutes and two seconds to enter the grounds of the clinic. It is a red-brick building with a flat roof. The building has been graffitied with large white lettering that Sara Has Aids and FUCK! and herpes Is a giFt and a few difficult-to-decipher tags of the amateur artistes, letters interlocking seamlessly that look impressive in their illegibility. A few crude diagrams are scattered around these, the inelegant juvenile depictions of penises and apricot-shaped vaginas discernible.

There are many free spaces in the car park and she stops her car along the area marked in the middle of the tarmacked expanse. There are two rows of marked-out rectangles in the middle section and she parks, ready to leave, with the front of her car at the edge of the rectangular space and the road.

She sits in the car and unfastens the seatbelt. She leans over to her bag and rummages for fewer than ten seconds to locate her lip-gloss, pulling it out with her right hand and taking it in her left. She unscrews the top and traces the end of the brush over her bottom and then top lip. She dips the end back into the gloss and dabs at her lips before she screws it back together, drops it in her bag and places her right hand over her stomach and gently massages it in circular movements.

Feels a bit like that time when she had dietary issues at the beginning of High School. Constipation. Probably just being stupid. Might as well get it done with anyway. Probably a perfectly normal reason for it.

Withholding her thoughts is now futile, she knows, with the only reason for her ever having stepped through the push-open doors being to collect the results of the frequent tests that she has to ascertain the state of her sexual health. She has visited the clinic for the last eleven months and this visit is the fifth. The clinic functions on the basis of sending an envelope clearly marked with the clinical services of the generous government or by sending a text message with the results of the test included. For the first time, she had requested a message to be sent to her mobile phone, but paranoia or common sense informed her later decision to collect an envelope from the reception desk. She does not and did not think that Mikey is a spouse who will invade a person's privacy, including to a much greater extent, her own, but the reality programmes that offer the viewing audience the voyeuristic thrill of Schadenfreude and the tragic finality of ruined relationships and the imbuement of the scarlet letters as a result of the amorous espionage that she assumes Mikey is not versed to, has provided her with sufficient evidence that collecting it physically from the clinic is the safest option.

She is certain that Mikey has never cheated on her, with that small amount of doubt that she knows is the intelligence of being able to think for one's self. Absolute conviction is something for scientists to prove, something that the science of human emotion is impossible to find. But there lies her problem; she knows as much as she can know anything that Mikey has not brought upon her any illness, which leaves one last explanation.

It's probably just a water infection or a rash or something. But she is not optimistic. She has read up on the symptoms of the irritation and because Mikey seems to share the same itchiness, the logical conclusion that she has reached has led her to assume the worst.

At the desk, a smiling lady who appears to be in her close-to-retirement years, spectacles fashionably thick rimmed and rectangular, dark-brown hair evidently dyed, with no roots showing, with dye, and a fulsome cleavage on show from unbuttoned buttons and a slightly-too-small brassiere, mouths one second silently whilst listening to a voice through the phone pushed against her right ear with her right shoulder.

How can she smile at this time? Stupid fucking cow knows who she is and what she's about to read. It's the same fat old bitch who sees her every week, who arranged for her to collect the results every time. What is she on about? She doesn't read them. She's not a nurse. She's alright, really. Whoever's on the phone though. Hurry up.

The receptionist looks up and moves her eyes to her left in a rolling motion, before winking her right eye and smiling impishly.

Standing with her hands against the desk, palms down, chewing the inside of her right cheek, she finds the receptionist's actions pleasing and amusing and smiles back, aiming to transfer the message that she understands with a similar movement of her eyes.

She's alright. Very mumsy. Feels a bit bad for thinking of her as a cow.

She does feel bad and she is aware that she is nervous and that her feelings are largely affecting her temperament. She thinks of butterflies as disgusting and that nervousness is weakness, which was the business adage that was framed on her tutor's wall at university. She is nearly certain that the woman was there when she was a child and would come with her own mother, collecting the inhalers that had to be renewed every six months or so in case of an asthma attack. As a child, she had known that she did not have asthma, but in a school where the majority of the children carried their pumps with them at all times and the cool children would smoke them in the way of cigarettes, she had wanted one and acted highly convincingly during exercise and physical education.

Something brushes against her and she turns to see a mother with two children – obviously identical twins because they're exactly the same and even wearing matching football tops – who smiles a mumsy smile at her and says

$\rightarrow$

$\leftarrow$

Sorry.

The little buzz of excitement from these meetings, illicit and illegal, like in one of those old-fashioned, slightly eroticised romances with the genteel long-locked hero and the fairytale-esque freedom that the captured princess receives. That is her, right now, leaving this place all flushed with excitement and not just the humidity of the accumulating cloud. It was never about plucking up courage or telling lies, rather more the keeping of a secret. Never once had she denied going to the hospital or the clinic, but in his own gentlemanly manner, he had never pressed her for details or scrutinised any of her words. Some of her friends think that that is non-committal and that it is to be attributed to the usual normative behaviour of men, but she knows that this is not the case and that it is simply, and rather pleasantly, an indicator of their absolute trust and loyalty and respect for one another, and ultimately of their reciprocal love.

She pushes the door open with her left hand, placing her back against it to prop it open for the boys to walk out. They say thanks mum and she lets them skip along the path to her right, a few yards ahead.

She knows that he thinks of her as motherly at times, ensuring his safety and comfort on his business trips and informing him of their children's activity, but she knows also that she never imposes or restricts, and playfully receives the flowers that he buys as means of apology, an apology that they both know is unnecessary after his return from his travels. She thinks that it would be impossible to know each other any better than they do.

The boys are squabbling about something in front of her. It lasts for ten seconds and then, with one of them pointing at something along the wall of the building, they both start giggling and the argument is abated with their childish and mischievous chuckling.

Simon Travers is rather handsome, and has that way of making you feel like the only woman he's ever touched, and maybe she does just a tiny little bit have a crush on him. Maternally, more than anything else, or like that term that Drew always moaned about, partners. Sound like they're going off for a game of doubles, he'd say, but it was like they were partners after the intimacy they had shared. A purely platonic love, anyway. And it wasn't him that she'd seen today anyway. She had asked if she could come to the clinic as it was closer to home and she could walk it with the twins, and he'd said it was fine. Thirty minutes was all that was needed and it took nearly an hour, the last couple of times. With Drew away, it was easier to do it now and it made sense. Straight in, business transacted, and the boys did not even become erratic through inertia. In fact, they seem more subdued than is usual: no bickering or raucous boyishness.

You okay, fidgety-fingers? The boy closest to her turns his chin and looks up at her and grins, nodding rapidly in his enthusiasm to conceal his tiredness. He yawns and he, the good young man, places his right hand slightly belatedly over his opened mouth. Good manners, angel. His grin comes back with a series of quick blinks, his top row of teeth visible and the gap of his recently fallen out bottom-centre incisor is barely noticeable.

↑↓

Where did you go, mummy? In there. What did that man do to you, mummy? She can't have been kissing.

↓↑

Doctor Black just had to check mummy's tummy and do some scans is all, sweetie.

↑↓

Malcolm said that the man was hurting you. Yuk if it was kissing.

↓↑

She laughs. *No. I'm fine. Mummy's fine. The doctor was just looking after me and making sure everything is okay with me.* It was uncomfortable at times. Maybe she had still looked a bit awkward. Dr Travers never caused her any discomfort.

↑↓

See. I told you. So there. I told you it wasn't the same as Supertaker and mum's friend.

↓↑

Now what on earth are they on about? *What was that, David? Who are you talking about?* It must be Lydia.

↑↓

He's in trouble now. *Nothing.*

They stop walking.

↓↑

David. Or do I have to ask your brother?

↑↓

Malcolm said that you were kissing the doctor and doing sex in there. He showed me the sign. He feels naughty. He feels his face warm.

↓↑

She cannot prevent the little snort of exhaled laughter from escaping through her nose. *Well, that was not happening. Who were you talking about? Who's mummy's friend?*

David is looking at Malcolm for help or advice as to what he should do next, but Malcolm is fixedly staring at a blackened stain on the concrete paving.

I'm not going to ask again. Bedtime when we get home, otherwise.

↑↓

Malcolm said that he reckoned the man was kissing you or sexing you, like Supertaker and your friend at school. It's all his fault.

↓↑

The boy stressed his brother's name in reprimand and attempted absolution. It made her want to laugh, along with the seriousness on the boys' faces and the ridiculous nature of their discussion. *Who's Supertaker?* Must be the Polish caretaker.

↑↓

Dad calls the muscly man at school that because he's really strong. Like a superhero.

↓↑

She laughs through her nose and her opened mouth. The boys look puzzled. *Dad's going to be in trouble when he gets home.* She tut-tut-tuts and the boys smile sheepishly, phewing silently at their luck and thinking happily of the future where the naughtiest of the three males in their house is going to be told off by the only woman.

The boys return to their joint musings, perceptive to each other's gentle goading and irritability. Malcolm balances his feet, right foot ahead of the left, on the side of the pavement. He looks at his brother to encourage or challenge him to the do the same, wobbling to his right.

Stay on this side of the path, boys. Away from the road.

Rails by the side of roads. She's said that for years now. If there were posts along the curb, then there would be no risk of children slipping off the curb unless...

Malcolm. I mean it. The teacher voice, as Drew says. He says that she would make a great teacher, too. The things he says. Such a good man. Magnificent with the twins, too. He's never hard with the boys, but they give him the boyish respect and have that masculine fear that she supposes all boys have for their fathers. She can't say they're not mummy's boys, either. They won't go to sleep unless it's her that tucks them in and they do what they're told: dishes, toy tidying, weeding.

She thinks that she sounds like a haughty old snob in her hubris towards the nuclearity that her family has. An old-fashioned family unit, one where mother is mother, albeit a modern mother who works professionally, who is the better cook and better domesticated, with the designer's mind and the botanist's patience, and emotionally understanding; one where father is father, whose discipline is final and who does the practical stuff, the electrics, the plumbing, the DIY, the car, who throws and kicks a ball about; one where the children are children who still find the word sex taboo, work hard at school, love each other and protect each other with warm rivalry, who do not place their elbows on the table and know where please and thank you belong within their manners.

Boys. We're crossing the road in a second. Come stand next to mummy. The two boys stop walking and when each of them flanks her, David takes her left hand and Malcolm sees that she is holding the strap of her handbag in her right. He looks up at her, conveying the message with an endearing smile. *Take mummy's hand, Malcolm.* They walk a further twenty-three feet and are near the pink concrete-curb step and Malcolm asks quickly can I press the button, mummy? and immediately after the last word is spoken, David says aw, can I do it mummy? Malcolm did it on the way. A battle of repeated noes and pleases lasts just under three seconds before she silences them with the faux-stern voice that her husband tells her was made for a headmistress. *If you two don't stop your bickering, I will press it. Now, if one of you presses it first, then the other can press it the second time.* Malcolm's eyebrows furrow slightly, confused or grumpy or perhaps both. He does not jut his bottom lip forward, which is his usual action before he becomes obstreperous in defiance. *David first and then you, Malcolm. It's important that the second one is just as strong as the first one.* She sees that he thinks about this for a second and agrees with her logic as he tells David to press it first.

As soon as they stop next to the closest traffic light, David presses the button on the box that is attached to the post of the traffic light twice and looks at his brother with a playful smile of the eyes and a slight pursing of the lips. Malcolm's mouth opens in disbelief at what has happened and the face that was very recently in his mother's mind is the face that he adopts.

↑↓

You nurbalhead. You pressed it twice. That's not fair. Mum: tell him. It's not fair. Mum. Mum. It's not fair. He pressed it twice. It's not fair. He's a smelly idiot.

He starts to cry. At this time, his brother has become the person whom he thinks that he hates the most in the world. He is never again going to share his sweets with him or tell him any of the rude jokes that Jordan tells him at school or trade football stickers with him or give him any of the biscuits that he steals from the tin when mum and dad are in bed. He is not going to talk to him ever again, actually. He wishes that his brother would die.

There is a beep-beep-beep-beep and he crosses the road, feeling his mother's hand pulling against him. He very deliberately does not look to his left, where he is certain that his brother is grinning like a monkey.

With his big dopey ears, fat face, smelly teeth and rubbish hair and no friends. Mum's saying something to him. He doesn't care. She should tell him off, wash his mouth out with soap when they get in, like she did when he swore in front of Nan.

↓↑

Malcolm. Listen to me this minute or you'll not be having a film and supper, Saturday or not. He's obviously upset with his brother. Boys will be boys. *And David, apologise to your brother. You know that he was going to press it the second time.* The stubbornness of boys. He mutters not fair just audibly and then says sorry Malcolm, who retorts with a confutatious poking of the tongue in his brother's direction, wary to the ingenuousness of his contrition. When David gasps, disbelieving that his brother would dare to do that in front of their mother, it is too much for her. She laughs at the innocence of her children and the contagion spreads to her sons, who laugh towards each other and with each other and skip along the path, shoving against each other's shoulder in friendship.

Even the sweatiness between her legs and the pits of her arms from the stifling mugginess do not lessen her happy mood. Her thoughts flit between the unforeseen whitening of large parts of the sky and the cloistering heat that it brings, and the evening to come with the twins. When Drew is out on a Saturday night, whether for a couple of drinks or due to commitments with work, it has become a custom for the three of them to watch a film. It reminds her of the times when she was their age and the same would happen at home; her father would tell her that he was going to church on a Saturday evening, and she was twelve before realising the euphemism and that he was off to the pub. The remote control was her father's domain and so the freedom to watch whatever was on the early-evening television was a shared luxury between her mother and her, and a rental film would always follow. She rents from one of the few remaining rental stores now, reluctant to relinquish the link to her childhood and past ritual. The smell of the shop, which she refers to obsolescently as the video store, lures out the excited, childish feeling of anticipation, a feeling that seems to come less and less as she gets older and closer to that fabled age when life begins. Of course, the recent months and the visits to Doctor Travers have brought the sensation in abundance, only in a more adult manner, if that is possible.

Good thing about being with the boys: they don't give you much time – any time – to yourself. If they aren't being naughty little devils or winding one another up, they're making a mess or helping her or asking her to play with them. Sure, some mothers might moan about the dependency and the constant need to be aware of everything they do, but it has never been like that, not even when they were pooping, puking and mewling in nappies. It's hard to imagine what it'll be like when they leave the nest and get jobs and girlfriends and maybe see her once a week. What will they be like? Handsome devils like their father, no doubt.

He had texted quite early in the morning and was probably asleep last night quite early, too. Flying always made him feel lethargic and he seemed his usual affable self, which is to say that he was obviously bored and would much rather be at home for the weekend. Probably get flowers. He must surely have noticed her gained weight, but as always, he was too lovely to mention anything. Probably not chocolates, anyhow.

The two boys are kneeling over something on the grass, where it meets the concrete. Malcolm picks it up and places it in line with his right eye, contorting his face in an eccentric display of inspection. His mouth opens in wonderment at what he has found and his brother reaches to take it from him. He pulls his hand away and jumps up, running back to his mother.

↑↓

He speaks really quickly. *Mum-mum-mum-look at what-I found. Mum-look at this.*

His mother asks him what it is and puts her hand palm up for him to place the object in. It is muddied and round, the size of a two pence piece and copper coloured.

It's treasure coins, mum. From pirates that used to live here. There's probably loads buried in the ground. It's so cool. He's going to be rich. Proper pirate treasure. David better not take any of it.

↓↑

Oh. It has a ship on the tails side. *It's an old halfpenny.*

↑↓

Amazing. Probably loads of them buried there. Uh no. David's digging for more. *David. Don't dig without me. I found it. I'm digging. I found it. I get to dig. I was the one that found it.* There might be a whole pirate ship under there. With swords, wooden legs, guns and that big flag with the skeleton on.

↓↑

Boys. Look at your hands. Stop your digging right this second. It's going to be a nightmare getting the dirt from their nails.

↑↓

But mum. It's real treasure. There's loads right here. We got to dig. She's mad. She even said so herself. *You even said so, mum. Hay-penny, you said. Real treasure.* Why is she laughing. She's mad. Or she wants it herself. It's not fair. She's not fair.

↓↑

It's a special type of treasure that only ever comes on its own. In ones. One at a time. He seems dubious. *It's a lucky coin and you use it to bring luck. It's not from pirates.* Now he seems happy. *I'll keep hold of it until we get back and then I'll clean it up for you.*

She is aware that David looks either jealous or upset. *David. Did you help Malcolm find the coin?* He nods five times, expectant of the soothing words that he knows are to come. The words that she is thinking of saying are not very good, in her opinion, so she decides to take what she thinks is a gamble. *Well that means you get to choose the film tonight.*

It looks like Malcolm is about to complain, already forgetting his magic coin. *I think that's fair, as your brother has got a magic coin.* It does the trick. Both of the boys look happy again. Good. Even though they squabble a hell of a lot, they are really sweet together and look after each other.

Why on earth did she decide to wear jeans today? It's been hot for ages and it's always muggy when the clouds keep the heat in. Well, she supposes it wasn't cloudy earlier, before they left.

The sky is a hazy white with a mosaic of light, pale dusty-blue specks visible behind it. She thinks that it is going to rain and that some rain would be good; drought measures are the last things anyone wants and it will help to clean the dirty paths and roads, the roads that are stained temporarily with vehicular fluids and the pavements with urine, faeces, chewing gum, vomit, blood and spit. And God knows whatever else there is. She likes the sun, the heat and the real summer that they've finally got, but sometimes a little rain is needed to clean things up. It could do with it.

She walks up a trodden-dirt path that leads to a stile, the boys already having clambered over it to get to the playing fields, and puts her right foot on the first of the two wooden steps, supporting herself with her right hand. The same as on the way to the clinic, the tightness of the jeans that she is wearing makes the task awkward for her. She can feel the dampness at the back of her knees. She steps over the top post, right foot followed by left, and hops on the prickly, dead grass. There is no sponginess to cushion the impact, only hardened mud and straw-coloured grass already flattened against the ground. The boys are running in looping directions and indiscernibly yelling with their arms out, pretending to be birds or airplanes or some other avian thing. She hopes that no inconsiderate dog-walkers have been past this way.

She walks across the field to where the boys are waiting for her. They are animated and tell her about a dogfight that they had on the field and who the fastest pilot was, exclaiming that the other was dead from their totally amazing shooting. She commends their bravery in an officious and serious tone and hurries them along the path. It is stileless where the grass meets the similarly beaten ground that marks the footpath, and they turn right into a lane, the boys resuming their roles as fighter pilots. There are various garden gates to their left and she, now with the boys behind her, stops at the sixth gate, pulls out a heavy-looking slim key, places it inside the lock, turns it anticlockwise, and pushes the gate open with her left hand whilst removing the key with her right. She stretches her arm across it and takes a small step back *Come on* to allow the boys in. She locks it standing in the garden and walks to the back door, the boys having already gone in; it's statistically the second safest neighbourhood in the city.

She walks in and drops the keys next to a fruit bowl on the table in the middle of the room, which she and her husband call the annex in front of the children and the drinking room amongst themselves, and slips off her sandals, sliding them under the table with the outside of her right foot. The boys' shoes are to the left of the back door; they have already settled in the living room and she can hear the roars of dinosaurs through children's tongues and the movie voices of hardened men imitated against the backdrop of clashing plastic coming through the wall and along the corridor.

Malcolm. David. Go and wash your hands before you start playing with anything, she says, aware that her hands are also dirty and then washing them under the hot tap. Footsteps can be heard going up the stairs and the swooshing of the plumbing behind the walls informs her that her sons have turned the taps on and probably hold their hands under the spout of water for fewer than ten seconds. The footsteps' sound descends.

She pats her stomach and is reassured by its firmness. It is not clear yet that she is pregnant, unless placed under vigilant scrutiny and she is not a person who is overtly self-conscious or unhappy with their own body and aesthetic. She is loved and she has a wonderful loving family and she adores her home, friends and family; life, in her view, is very good. She allows herself a moment of pleasant reverie.

Even if the weather is sweaty. Time to change, she thinks. She leaves her handbag near the fruit bowl and keys and walks out of the annex and to the door frame of the living room and stands between the two sides and puts her hands against them. They notice her presence and turn around, silent and expectant. She smiles at them and says *I'm going upstairs for five minutes, so no squabbling, okay? What dinosaur have you got there, David?*

↑↓

It's a stegosaurus, mum. He's trying to eat me with a T-rex, but my soldiers are killing him.

↓↑

No they're not. Their guns bounce off his skin. Don't they mum?

They talk over each other, explaining who has the best dinosaur and whose weapons are the best.

↑↓

Ooh. It sounds evenly matched. See who has the better army by the time I get back down. I won't be long. She turns to her right and walks out of the door, away from the annex and the living room and turns left up the stairs. On the third stair, she stops and calls to her children *And no squabbling.* With an unnecessary sigh, from habit and not from exertion, she walks to the top of the stairs and past the boys' rooms on the landing and in her and her husband's room, directly at the end of the landing corridor. Two steps into the room and she tucks her left thumb down the top of her jeans and presses her left forefinger against the thumb, unclasping the button with her right forefinger and thumb. She sits on the king-sized bed and lies on her back, unzipping the zip and lifting her buttocks from the bed, sliding the jeans off until the knees.

They look good, skinnies, but they're so damned tight around the ankle. She sits forward and tugs at the bottoms of the jeans, feeling the muscles tense in her biceps and triceps, pulling them off. She picks up the jeans and folds them neatly, and after placing them on the side of the bed, stands up and in the same motion as standing, pulls her top over her head. The feeling of relief comes and the backs of her knees and the upper inner thighs feel cool as she folds the top neatly and places it on the jeans. There is an antique French armoire, in the Rococo style of Louis XV, along the left side of the bed, which is placed against the left wall when entering the room. It was passed to her when her great-aunt died four years ago, the other options being that it would be given to charity or taken to a landfill site. She had been impressed by it and wanted it, rather than accepting it out of sentiment and for posterity. She opens the two doors and takes a black ruffle cami-dress from under some other clothes on the second-from-top shelf. She places it over her right shoulder and picks up the clothes from the bed, placing them on an emptied section of the bottom of the armoire and closing the doors. She takes the dress from her shoulder and holds it in both hands, walking to stand in front of the mirror in the door of the wardrobe that is positioned on the right side of the bed. Standing with her right hip directed towards the mirror, her white knickers high above her thighs and resting on the top of her hip, she looks at the contour of her belly and thinks that it is noticeable now, the weight that she's gained. Her breasts look good, too. She lifts the dress up and pulls it down from above her head, happy with the image reflected from the glass, pulls her knickers backwards through her dress with a ping of elastic, making herself more comfortable, and walks out of the room and down the stairs.

So, who's won the war? she wonders, stepping in the living room.

↓↑
You've changed.
↑↓
Yes. So, who won?
↓↑
David did.

↑↓
Did you, David?
↓↑
Yeah. It was close though. Malcolm fought really good.
↑↓

No squabbling. Who would've thought it? *Well, as you boys have just had a really big battle, I bet you're really hungry?*

They say yes or yeah at the same time.
What would you young men like?
↓↑
S'getti.
↑↓
With toast. On toast.
↓↑
With cheese as well. He is hungry. Thinking of food makes him hungry.
↑↓

Not surprised at all. *And what would you want afterwards?* Yoghurt.
↓↑
Fromage frais.
↑↓
Yeah. Fromage frais.
↓↑
Okie-dokie. And then we'll go to the park after, okay? Of course it's okay, the excitable little monkeys.
↑↓
Can we put the telly on, mum?
↓↑
Okay. But stay in the chairs when watching it, okay. No square eyes or brains like cabbages, eh? Serious expression and pointed finger. Perfect.

Smiling when her back is turned to her children, she walks to the kitchen on the other side of the corridor, opposite the living room. The first thing that she does is open the door at the back of the kitchen that leads to the annex, hoping that a wind is blowing cool air through the annex and in the kitchen. It is not. The kitchen is hot.

Every year it's the same, but not to this extent. Air-conditioning would be such a treat. Maybe mention it to Drew. He feels the heat. Tins.

The tins are in a shelving unit nailed to the wall opposite the sink and she opens it with her left hand and takes one tin of spaghetti hoops with her right hand and places it on the worktop. In the same manner, she takes a saucepan from the doored units beneath the worktop and places it on the back-right hotplate, turning the right-middle dial on the front of the cooker anticlockwise so the raised line is directed to 2. Picking the tin up with her left hand, she pulls it down and to her stomach with her right forefinger curled through the ring-pull, peeling back the top of the tin. She pours the contents of the tin, a sloppy mixture of orangey-yellow and bright red, in the saucepan, slamming the side of the tin against the side of the saucepan to remove two spaghetti hoops that are stuck to the bottom of the tin. She steadies the pan with her left hand.

What to have? Could have the same as the boys but it's got a little bit boring. It's all they seem to want to eat. Drew's economical influence. As a girl, she'd never liked hoops. Um. Toast sounds good. Yes. That'll do.

Thinking that she might as well warm the grill as the toaster only fits four pieces of bread, she turns the second-from-the-left dial to 100 and opens the upper-door of the cooker. On the shelves at the end of the kitchen's left wall, close to the opened door that leads to the annex, is a selection of neatly arrayed foodstuffs and ingredients. She removes the adhesive yellow label that bears the sell-by and use-by dates from an already opened loaf of bread and takes out six slices of white bread. Conscious of crumbs dropping from the bread, she shields the floor by walking with her left hand palm up beneath her right hand that is carrying it over to the cooker, and places the bread in two rows of three across the griddle. The air being exuded from the cooker touches her skin at forty-two degrees Celsius and she attaches the handle to the griddle pan.

In a ruminative mood, thinking of food and Drew and the future and her children, she removes two bowls, three plates, a saucer and a grater from the long shelves bracketed to the wall opposite the cooker and places them on the worktop to her left. There is no sign that the saucepan's contents is being heated and she stirs them idly with a wooden spoon that she takes from a container.

The toast. She pulls the handle of the griddle-pan quickly with her right hand and expects what she thinks as the worst. Nope. Not burnt. Time's going strangely slow today. She'll put it back in a second. They don't want their toast like their dad likes it: black.

Oh Drew. If only you knew. She's guilty for all those months of secrecy, not telling him, skulking around. Only a year ago he'd said how he would like another child, and now this. It had all seemed so easy at first but now it's just so...

She doesn't know. Maybe tomorrow. Definitely tomorrow. If she can pluck up the courage to do it.

She is neither happy nor sad as she rests with her hands against the top-front edge of the cooker, thinking partial thoughts of nearly nothing for over a minute.

She checks the spaghetti hoops. They're fine.

She picks up the griddle pan by the handle in her right hand

and turns each slice of bread over with her left, before resting the pan on the single grill rack.

She pulls out the grill pan, placing it under the shelf in the cooker and turning the grill off.

To the left of the original entrance to the kitchen is a dual freezer-refrigerator, from which she takes out a sealed block of cheese. There is roughly a third of the block in the resealable packaging. She splits clasps at the top of the package and takes out the cheese, putting it on the plate closest to the edge of the worktop and slides the grill pan towards her.

She forgot to get the butter out. What's wrong with her today? She walks to the fridge and takes out a tub of olive-oil spread and opens the cutlery drawer attached to a breadbin that she uses as a storage container for pasta. Taking a bone-handled buttering knife, she opens the lid of the tub and places one piece of toast at a time on the middle plate, which she brings to the edge of the worktop, sliding the plate with the cheese on it to her left. Too much butter can ruin toast, no matter how much the boys like it. Drew'd better watch his cholesterol, too. The things the boys pick up from him. She smiles whilst she spreads a thin layer of butter across the bread, the warmth quickly rendering the semi-solid state liquid. When she is done, she cuts four of the pieces of bread in two and symmetrically arranges them on the outside of two of the plates. Glancing at the frying pan, only a few bubbles indicate the heat of the water. Perfect. She places a bowl in the centre of the two plates and pours an estimated half of the saucepan's contents in each bowl. The saucepan is placed next to the plate in the basin and then she grates cheese on the tops of the two portions of spaghetti hoops. Should she sprinkle some pepper on them? They won't notice.

Boys. It's ready. Have they heard? She can hear the telly

from here. Can't make out what they're watching. *Boys?*
Slightly louder. The sound of the television is absent and the
shuffling and light thud-thud-thud of fast-moving feet can be
heard. She opens the door to the annex and pulls out two trays
that are tucked at the back of the upright-standing shelves. The
two plates containing the bowls of spaghetti hoops and four
halves of toast are placed on the top tray and she carries this
to the table, removing the bottom tray and putting one of the
plates on it in front of one of the chairs. There is a rectangular
cutlery basket split into three compartments next to the fruit
bowl: red napkins in one half of the basket and knives and
forks in one of the quarters, with spoons in the other quarter.

The twin boys come in the annex.

↑↓

Wicked, mum. I'm starving.

↓↑

S'getti. Yes.

He pulls out a chair and sits in it, positioning his ankles and
the tops of his feet around the bottom of the front chair-legs
before lifting his backside from the chair and sliding it forward
with his feet. He takes a tablespoon from the basket in front
of him and puts his spoon in the bowl. He is right-handed, the
same as his brother, mother and father.

Take the colder parts from the sides. Blow on the spoon.
It's way too hot otherwise. Malcolm's burnt his squidge face
already. Hahaha. Silly Malcolm. Probably thinks mum was
telling the truth when she told that fib about good luck. Dumbo.

Mmmmm.

↑↓

*Remember to take from the edges first. You've burnt your
mouth, haven't you?*

She places her tray on the table and sits down next to

247

Malcolm, who has his head tilted back and is opening his mouth wide and then narrowing it with whispered didgeridoo sounds expressing his pain.

The sides, like your brother. Okay?

↓↑

Like him. He smiles. He's happy as Malcolm is usually better than him at things: football, throwing, dinosaurs, bikes, fighting, farting. He's not better at mathematics though, or art. Dumb fat face.

↑↓

How's your food?

↑↓

They tell her that it's yummy and lush and they eat silently for the next few minutes. Malcolm asks

↓↑

Can we go to the park after, please, mum?

↑↓

She knew that's what they'd want. *Of course we can. Shall we go now?* A little mean, but it is funny.

↓↑

What about dessert? You said we'd have fromage frais. Can we have that first and then go to the park? Please?

↑↓

Their faces, you evil woman. *Oh yeah. I completely forgot about that. Of course we'll have fromage frais.* Strawberry cheese, her sister and her nieces call it. Funny language. *And get some fresh air. But no running immediately after eating because I don't want any upset tummies. Okay?*

They nod in agreement to their mother's proposition and smiling at their serious faces and humour-filled eyes, she walks out to the fridge and takes two little raspberry yoghurt pots, snapping them apart after releasing the door to close and handing one to each of her children. They peel the lids off fewer than three seconds after being handed the pots and stick the underside of the lids to their tongues, pulling down and licking in this manner four or five times.

Whilst they eat, she collects the trays and places them each on top of the other and does the same with the plates, scraping remnants into the bin. The dishwasher is to the right of the sink and she opens the door and pulls out the top rack. Before she arranges them in the machine, she rinses them under hot water.

Sometimes, after leaving the dishes in the washer for a few hours, the machine can make the dishes smell musty and slightly sewagey, so she does not like leaving them in the machine when the cycle finishes. She likes this more than leaving used dishes on the side or a filled-up machine of food-encrusted dishes.

The boys come in the kitchen and pass to her their spoons and tell her that they're ready and that their laces are tied tight and good, and she puts the spoons in the cutlery compartment and presses the switch on the wall with her right thumb and sets the machine on a regular wash. She considers closing the back door and does not, briefly assaying the predictability of the weather and deciding that no rain has been forecast and that it will not rain. She slips her feet in her sandals, pointing her toes upward and splaying them to fit her big toes past the thongs, and picks up her large handbag, slinging it over her right shoulder. They leave through the front door.

The sky is more white than blue, the clouds having become more expansive and thicker. The air is warm, with a warm wind that expounds her perspiration before she has reached the public pavements at the end of her front garden's path. The two boys are energetic in their fervour of irritating each other and their jocundity is apparent from the consequent laughter that follows the mock deprecation. They ask their mother questions at irregular intervals, retracing where they have leapt, skipped and walked. They walk from the precursory exclamations that she makes, reminding them of their frothing bellies. They ask questions about the bones of dinosaurs and which planet goes where in the order that Miss Humphreys told them and how they can remember but not after Jupiter because their demonic doesn't work and does she know who the best artist is, to which she replies offhandedly in response that requires little consideration. They admire her intelligence when she recites the order of the planets and remonstrate when she states the best artist, of whom they have never heard. They know that their mother is intelligent, just not as intelligent as Miss because she is not a teacher and Miss is.

The park is an extension of Drew's domain, she thinks, where the boys will be boys and throw things and play-fight etcetera. He'd taught them how to ride a bike without stabilisers and had got the children interested in cricket, which seems odd as it really is such a boring game. Cricket over the back fields, not in the park since they'd redone it. A new skate park with big ramps, too. God forbid when they move on from their bikes and scooters and get skateboards and skates. No broken bones between them but that won't be the case when they take up doing that stuff.

She has long thought that it is funny how her mother was one of four girls and her father one of four boys, and that her sister had two girls and she two boys. Girls are always good as gold but boys are bothersome, her mother would say to her father's feigned chagrin and playful submission. Her boys are far from bothersome, but just a little naughty, which is to be expected with a rogue like Drew for a dad.

During the walk, she tells the children to hold her hands

when they cross the road. It only takes around five minutes to arrive at the park.

The boys immediately run to the helter-skelter and climb the laddered steps to the top, fifteen feet from the ground. Their enjoyment can be heard from where she is sat, on an empty and pristinely black-painted metal bench. She watches them astutely, wary of the height at which they stand at the top before the short and looping slide to the bottom. Malcolm is first to ascend and he waves to her from the top, grinning. He sits down and propels himself forward and down with the handrails at the sides. The metal used for the chute creates too much friction for him to gain much speed.

It's still amazing. Parks were good when she was young but they never had what they have nowadays. Or, rather, what this one has. None of the other parks in the city are like this, she doesn't think. A massive helter-skelter, a sandpit, a paddling pool with a dolphin spurting water from its spout and all this is residential, too. She had monkey bars, various climbing things, swings and a roundabout, sure, but even the roundabout here is like a fairground ride. Kids don't know how lucky they are these days: holidays twice a year and maybe even abroad this year, pocket money every week, treats and sweets when they ask and, to their credit, not very demanding computer games. On top of that, no civil unrest and mad people in charge. Or war.

Back when she was a child. It seems scary counting back. Sounds like ages. The nation was at war and the unhappiness of the whole country could be felt even by her. She was only, what? Must have five or six, a little younger than the twins.

Being inactive whilst sedentary is difficult for her and she has brought a book to read. Sitting in a park like this, with nice weather, is hard to beat. Although, saying that, the weather has turned a bit. Not cold at all, but cloudy. The book is titled 'Express' and is written by a woman called Frances St Julian. It is a crime novel and she finds it highly thrilling. There is no better book on the planet than one where the hero is also the villain, albeit subtly shown to the reader as they progress through the pages. It is a page-turner and nominated for various prestigious awards, with quotes from high-profile critics, novelists and and television celebrities on the cover proclaiming it as the book of the year and how the action is explosive and the plot riveting.

She reads:

Something did not quite add up about her. It was the way she moved away from him when Holman had asked her where he was. It did not in its own right indicate that she was lying, but there was something more to the words that followed.

'I haven't seen him for three days.' The turning of her head towards the window and that step away from him.

Holman knew that she hadn't lied to him, but had skirted the question. A good interrogator knows how to frame his questions and what was he if not a good detective?

'Where did you last see him?'

'It was at his place, on West 47th.' She answered slowly, her calm voice belying nothing.

'How did he look when you left him?' he pressed.

'Like always,' she said.

'What's always?' he said. 'How was he?'

She turned to look at him, and she fixed him with the blue eyes of the cat-walk model. She really was breath-taking. Most killers were. It's how they lured the weakness of men to their deaths.

'His usual way, you know?' She jutted her chin forwards,

thoughtfully. 'Or did you never meet him?'

'I knew him.' Holman emphasised the word knew, stressing its shortness into a lengthy word. He saw her eyes twitch minutely. 'But the state you left him in made it a difficult identification.'

To her credit, she didn't run as he pulled out the garrotting wire and made it visible in the gloom of the bedchamber. He pulled the wire taut and lined it with her throat.

'What are you... what do you think I did?' Anxiety obvious in her voice now. 'You can't seriously think that I... did anything.'

'You're right,' Holman said, his voice devoid of any emotion. 'I know you did it.'

She opened her mouth to protest, but Holman's strong hands whipped the garrotte around her neck and he slid like a lover behind her, pulling her tight against him. In a matter of seconds her breath had given out, but he kept her there for a minute ensuring the job was completed.

Now she hadn't seen that coming. Earlier on, she was quite shocked when he had lost his temper with his superior officer, the chief inspector, and had challenged the man to strip him of his badge if he thought he was not up to the job due to his wife's death, but this wasn't expected.

One of her sons comes to her and repeats the word mum a number of times in a short period, pointing to the left of the bench three inches from where her left foot is with his right forefinger.

↓↑

Dad found a big dog poo right there when we were here last. It was stinky and really bad. Worse than David's breath. It was, mum. *Really bad.*

Apparel

↑↓

She looks down at the concrete platform in which the base of the bench is cemented. *Thanks for looking out for me, Malcolm. What are you up to now?*

↓↑

Me and David are seeing who can go down the slide the most times in a minute. Are you watching us, mum?

↑↓

Sure, lovely. I can see from here.

She places the opened book pages down on the bench to her right and her eyes' direction follows her son as he joins his brother on the helter-skelter. She watches them and broadens her smile to ensure that they see her enjoyment and when they walk over to the swings, panting, she picks up her book.

Resuming her reading, she continues to admire the hero, though from the beginning of the narrative to where she is now, page one hundred and twenty-six, Grant Holman has become more sinister in his actions; he is a murderer.

As she reads, she looks up frequently and locates the boys in the increasingly crowded park. When they arrived, there were twenty-one people and more than double are now here, twenty minutes having passed. Post-lunch escapades and lunch-time picnics form the periphery of her glances; in the park itself are the observing and protectively cautious parents and older relatives, partaking in the activities of their children.

On page one hundred and fifty-one, the flirtatious signs that have been building over the last seven chapters reach the start of their crescendo. She feels flushed and self-conscious as Holman starts sucking on the woman's nipples after removing her brassiere. The heat becomes more intense and she glances up from the pages at intervals of roughly twenty seconds, aware of her own arousal and sensitive to her distance from the others in the park. When Holman starts to thrust hard in her vagina, the climax described in minute detail of red-painted nails gripping the under sheet of the bed and the repetitive yeses of her sensation, a tingling arises at the base of her neck and her head is damp. She swallows drily and reads back over the description of Holman's entrance. He only enters her once.

The last time of looking up, she sees her sons jogging toward her, sixteen feet away. She closes the book quickly and keeps it in her hand, feeling strangely aroused, and when the boys see that she is looking at them and aware of them, they ask almost in chorus can we go in the pool mum?

Of course. Feet only though, so I'll keep hold of your socks and shoes. She stands up, the warmth in her face fading and her nervous shame fading. Does she look embarrassed? She sure feels it. *Sit here whilst you take your shoes off. Don't want to get dirty socks.* She stands up and picks up her bag putting the book in it. Out of sight, out of mind. Silly really; it's only a book. Can the children see that she's? The two boys start removing their shoes, sitting on the bench. They mutter something about the dog excrement that they saw three days ago, giggling and looking to the left of the bench. She asks them if they have had a good day and they say yes and uh-huh.

The socks are rolled into balls and poked to the bottoms of the boys' trainers, each of them carrying one shoe in each hand, wearing them in the fashion of gloves. On the way to the paddling-pool, Malcolm taps his beshoed right hand against the right side of David's head, telling him that he's just kicked him in the head, and David looks set to cry before laughing and then pushing his shoes against his stomach. She takes their shoes a few feet away from the edge of the pool, one pair per hand.

The pool is sloped away from them, at its deepest being

twenty-two inches, and is dusted with the living debris of kicking flies and the shells of the dead, drifting from the splashes and currents created by the pool's occupants, along with the dried browns and greens of wind-swept leaves.

Don't splash each other, now. If either of you do, you're out. Okay? She decides to place the shoes on the grass, slip off her sandals, and sit on the edge of the deepest end of the paddling-pool, lifting the hem of her dress to rest closer to her knee than her crotch. She puts her bag against the concrete lip of the pool, on the grass to her right.

That's better. The feet lead the way to the head. Her equanimity is restored. She feels better and her thoughts are only vaguely on the book. The wind is warm against her skin, though the cooling water is refreshment for the cloaking heat that she has felt through the day.

Observing the boys, who are salvaging the stranded insects by scooping them up with leaves, she does not know that a woman is walking behind her until she hears her name being spoken. She turn and looks up, squinting from habit, recognising her friend at the same time as she says

↓↑

How are you? Haven't seen you in a while. Everything okay?

↑↓

Hi Kim. I'm okay thanks. How are you? Should she stand? She turns to her right, swivelling with her hands on the side of the pool and lifting her feet from the water, pushing herself up and standing. The two women touch their right cheeks against the other's and simulate a kiss, Kim's being more pronounced. A boy of around five years stands to her left.

↓↑

I'm good thanks. Here with Theo. And there's your boys.

How have you been?

↑↓

She smiles at Theo. *I've been well thanks. You look good. How have you been?*

↓↑

I've been good thanks. You look good, too. Put a bit of weight on since, though, it looks. *Is Drew here?*

↑↓

No. He's working this weekend. They're all mine until tomorrow. Should she tell her? Doesn't really know her that well. Drew's friend's wife. *Are you here* what's his name? *just with Theo?*

↓↑

I've let Rob stay in with the football. This damned World Cup. She laughs. The stupid prick can watch that shit if he wants. *Well. Good to see you. Best be getting back.* She leans forward to brush cheeks and says, *Let's try and catch up sometime. You've got our home?*

↑↓

Yes. That'd be good. I'll give you a ring in the week. Tell her the news? *Nice to see you.*

She watches the woman walk away, her child quiet by her side. An attractive woman, Kim. Her husband, whatshisname, seemed okay when they met. Not as handsome as Drew, but very charming in his own way. That was nearly half a year ago, now. Time really does fly.

The boys are happy rescuing the drowning and floating insects. She decides to leave the book in her bag, excitedly anticipating the time later, when the boys are tired and sleeping and she can read leisurely and long in the silence and comfort of the armchair. She walks around the edge of the paddling-pool with her feet bare, enjoying the slight prickle of the dried grass against the soft, uncalloused soles. It is quite tickling. She appreciates the money that must have been expended on the construction of the park; how they managed to blend in the new apparatus within the contours of the landscape; the neat arrangement of the houses beyond the trees and the arrangement of the trees' planting.

Nearly half of the way around the second circuit of the pool's perimeter, she realises that she has not seen the boys' faces and that their backs are turned to her throughout her walk. She is sure that she knows the reason for this, and calls her children to come. Furtively looking at each other and then at her before looking at the water below them, they traipse to the edge of the pool, next to the shadow cast upon the water.

I'm pretty certain that I told you two not to splash or get your clothes wet, didn't I? In fact, I know I did. Her voice is stern. She is cross. *Out, the both of you.* The heat, probably. *Now.*

The timbre of their mother's voice stultifies their recalcitrance and they walk away from her without speaking, up the ramp and out of the pool, and to her side where she stands with her hands on her hips, fingers pointing toward the ground, lips tight together and eyebrows raised. She tells her children to sit on the grass and let their feet dry before putting their socks back on. To avoid them using their socks as towels, she keeps both of their sock-deposited pairs of shoes by her feet.

That's a good idea. If they go to the shops now and pop in the video store, they would be back before three easily and she could get some reading in before and during tea. The pretext for heading back early could be their silliness. She can't wait to see what happens next and she could finish the book tonight. Realistically, there's what? Four hours' reading time before she'll be in bed: one hour over tea, maybe an hour whilst the boys play, a couple of hours after they're in bed. Looking set to be a big day tomorrow, so not really wanting to get in any later than midnight.

When you're ready, what about going to get the film and some sweets for later? Give us a chance to dry off. She couldn't.

The responses are quick and the same, two nodded yeahs showing their affirmation. She tells the boys to dab between their socks and to put their shoes on afterward, looking at the different faces that she can see to determine whether or not she knows anyone. Three women look familiar and she is quite sure that she has seen them before, but there is no one there that she calls a friend.

The boys stand up and she shoos them ahead of her, smiling at the success of the word sweets. Children might be difficult at times, but they're no different from adults when persuasion is necessary: conditions in place for the adult male are equally simple, coming in various forms of ethanol, balls, and sexual intercourse. Using herself as pillar, she thinks of woman's persuasive susceptibilities coming from romanticism: dinner, flowers, perhaps sexual intercourse too.

Definitely a nice long massage does the trick.

The boys have left the gate open and she closes it and ensures that the latch is securely in place. The boys are waiting for her on the pavement at the side of the residential road, each taking one of her hands and mimicking their mother's left and then right-turning head in humorous synchronicity. They cross quickly, a car slowly driving towards them from their right.

The row of shops that includes the video store also has a traditional sweet shop, an independent bakery, a greengrocer's, a newsagent, and a launderette. Its local name is The Bastion.

On their way to the shops, they walk past an old woman in an electric wheelchair, four couples consisting of a man and a woman, with one couple also pushing a pram, four solitary joggers, three of whom are men, two male dog-walkers, four groups of children from the ages of eight to fifteen, seven solitary walkers of whom two are female, and one solitary teenaged girl. The boys are oblivious to most of the people, though feel self-conscious and guiltily amused by the old woman in her motorised wheelchair as they move to the side of the pavement and look at her drooping, orange-speckled skin as she rolls past.

As the smells of sugared pastry carry across to her on the light, warm wind, she sees her children enter the video store through its propped-open door and enters seven seconds after them. The immediate coolness of the air-conditioned store pleases her. The build up of clouds has made it even more sweltering. She looks out of the postered windows at the front of the store, seeing that the pavement in front of the row of shops is in the shade.

There are eight people in the store, including two workers. Video stores are a thing of the past; here's the evidence. Three people looking to rent a film. On a Saturday. And that young man over there's looking at computer games. Seems like a healthy enough young man, polite too.

←
→

Smile and make known. The world's most obvious housewife, searching for those two kids that just ran in, who looked strangely similar. Probably twins. A weirdly elvish face, seeing as it's not slender. Not fat though, but she looks pregnant. Back to the games. Three of them. He'll take three of them and set the whole thing up perfectly.

He has a hollowed feeling of tingling lightness in him as he thinks about what he considers as his master plan. There is a combative duality of emotions in him. It is akin to when he buys a new computer game and feels the partial nausea of excitement and anticipation before loading the disc in the drive.

He hasn't really thought about it before. No more than any other kid when watching films or playing a game or reading a book. Books are good; games are better. Why would you read a predetermined story arc instead of creating your own? Obvious.

He picks up three game cases from the shelves, the first of which is titled Shadowlair. He also selects the game that he has already completed from his purchase earlier in the week, and another called Furified. All of the games are certified as being suitable for, and only allowed for rental by, people aged eighteen or older.

He needs to make sure that he chats to the girl at the checkout. Make some rubbish joke or say something about the weather like everyone else or talk about the game. No, not talk about the game. Too obvious.

He walks to the counter where a man is serving the woman who entered following her children. The two boys are either side of their mother, talking animatedly about the film that the man is scanning and what sweets they are going to buy in the sweet shop. He looks at the woman in front of him and stares at her backside for eight seconds, berating himself as being a pervert though he feels no sexual gratification. The woman pays the man and thanks him, wishing him a good day and receiving the same sentiment in return, turns around, tells her children Come on, and smiles with a blink at him. He reciprocates her pleasantry and greets the man at the counter.

Alright. How's it going?

↑↓

Hi. Did you find everything you were looking for?

↓↑

Yeah. Add more. Engage. *Well. You know. There's always more that you want to get, but.*

↑↓

Yeah. This one's a good one. It only came out last week. He scans this as the last of the three game cases, pulling out a black-covered plastic folder containing plastic sheaths.

↓↑

Yeah. I've looked forward to this for ages. What sort of time is completion? Twenty-six hours and twelve minutes, eighteen seconds.

↑↓

I reckon about thirty hours. Took me twenty-eight. There's Shadowlair.

↓↑

Now that's an idea. *Are you working tomorrow?*

↑↓

Yeah, you know. Weekend. Where's Furified?

↓↑

Well, I bet I could start it at around five, today, and have it completed by the time you close tomorrow. It is seven? *Seven, right?*

↑↓

I'll be here. My time was twenty-eight-six. Twenty-something seconds. There's no chance he'd do it. He puts the last two discs in their respective cases. *Seriously impressed if you do it, man.* He takes the twenty pound note from the customer. *That's a real quick time.*

↓↑

I'll give it a go. He waits as the man puts the receipt in the bag with the games and passes him his change. *See you tomorrow.* The man says see you later and nods twice in a respectful manner.

That couldn't have worked any better. He's a genius. If this was the telly he'd never be caught. Not that he will, anyway. Somethings are just fucking meantta happen.

It's kind of ironic, the way everything is going to work out. The unassuming streeter cleaning up for past crimes against him. It reads like some sort of tag line for a film, probably called The Street Cleaner and with one of those ageing action heroes of decades past whose biceps are still as big as his legs. Or maybe a line like He came for justice, but got revenge. That doesn't quite make sense, though.

Outside. It definitely feels cooler.

He walks along the path, aiming to avoid being overtly noticed by any person that he walks past, conscious of those on foot and in or on vehicles. The clouds have now spread their whitish-grey across the expanse of the sky and pinpricks of blue are scarcely visible. The feel of the air against his skin is warm, though not the searing heat that was casually blowing over the last three weeks. Makes a nice change not having to squint so much.

Yesterday, he had finished work and was supposed to meet an acquaintance to sell him a strip. He's not really a friend as he's a bit of a knob, so it didn't bother him too much that he bailed on him. It was more important to set up the meeting and make it feel more real, anyway. Every last detail had been thought of. Plus, he hasn't got any tabs. The stupid fuck wouldn't have been able to buy some from him.

He quickens his pace, walking under a subway with the local children's cartoonish pasquinade of the constabulary foregrounded in his attentions. The usually composite sight of vibrant walls and the smell of ammonia is missing its urinary aroma, which he believes is due to the area. The offspring of the middle class becomes the middle-class rebels, he thinks; even the spray paint is a bit too perfect, too neatly organised. He is eager to get in his home and change the discs in the cases and ring work to make his excuse as to why he cannot work tomorrow. Every detail, he believes, is planned to a tee.

He thinks of Greek goddesses and what it is like to be a woman, of killing and of work, and in three minutes and eleven seconds, he skips to the top of a set of concrete steps and scans his fob at the locked gate, pushing through when the light is green. A brown-mackerel tabby pads past him when he is a step from stopping at his door, turning to look at him as he gets his key out of his right pocket and places it in the keyhole with his right hand, turning it clockwise and pushing open the door. He pulls the key out and pushes the door closed when in the apartment, removing his trainers by standing on the heels with the opposite foot, pressing them down and lifting his feet out. He slides them against the skirting board with his right foot and walks towards his personal computer, the bag containing the rented computer games in his left hand. He puts the games on the armchair as he walks past it.

He sits in the swivel-chair in the left corner of the room and at the computer desk, a desktop computer with a flat-screened monitor and slim-bodied hard drive in front of him, he clicks the mouse to retrieve the computer from its dormancy. He does not shut his computer down, leaving it on the mode designated sleep and restarting it when necessary: updates and installations. He waits for forty-two seconds, pulling his phone out of his right pocket to check for any messages – he has none – and then guides the cursor over the internet icon and clicks with his right forefinger. His connection is fast and at the top-left of his navigation bar is a favourited website called gameworld. com, in which he is automatically logged-in. He looks back at his phone and selects the application FAFAF and opens a new page through tapping the touch screen with his right thumb. On the homepage, he opens a pop-up that logs the conversation that he has been a part of for fourteen days. In it, a man whose identity is presented as TONY, 36. PROFESSIONAL MALE SEEKING FEMALES BETWEEN 18-40 FOR TIMES OF ENJOYABLE INDECENCY. DISCRETION IMPERATIVE details the location for a rendezvous in a room in a luxury hotel. The profile of Tony states how he is an active man who values the necessity for fitness and good health. He is physically fit and although he smokes, he does not drink or consume products that are not organic or low in sugars. His single image shows a handsomely-shaped face with no stubble and clear, tanned skin. He has hazel-coloured eyes and dark brown or black hair.

The second interlocutor, controlled and created by him, is a woman called Véronique and whose profile reads FRENCH SINGLE LADY WHO HAS 27 YEARS AND IS FREQUENTLY IN THE GYM. SMOKER AND OCCASIONAL DRINKER LOOKING FOR A MAN WHO IS A REAL MAN AND LIKES THE BEDROOM. Three pixelated images accompany the profile, showing a slim woman with blond hair in her underwear facing away from the camera, her body supple and seductive in the matching black items of lingerie that she wears. He thinks that he has created a realistic profile, having remembered the way in which the French state their age and order the words in their sentences. It's done a good enough job so far, with that fucking prick falling for it.

During the excitement of the execution after he had identified the man, he had pulled out the transparent plastic boxes from under his bed and rifled through his French books from when he was thirteen or fourteen-years-old, scanning for the syntactic rules that he would use for authenticity. He had imagined himself as the woman and thought about what he would like, using his profile to characterise this fictitious French woman. He had visited an internet café in the centre of the city to set up the profile. Creating a new email address and signing up for the month's free trial, he had used three images from a lingerie catalogue that he had taken deliberately under dingy lights with his digital camera and deleted them after their uploading.

He had made sure that the communication was initiated by Tony, frequenting the forums that he entered and making sure that she was noticed. He had been surprised when he started writing to her; he was not vulgar or directly propositional, instead seeming courteous and subtly funny. The man appeared to be a sophisticate. He, as her, had felt strangely excited through their subterfuge, enjoying the interaction and the deceit.

He had stolen the mobile phone from work for its untraceability and had never logged in to the website on his personal computer. When everything's done, he'll delete the account and it'll be tossed into the docks. Everything's been thought out.

There are no new messages. He receives responses sporadically, presumably as a result of working hours and the logic of not appearing too keen. Once, he received a reply within two minutes of sending a message, but more frequently he does not respond until hours afterwards: over a day on two occasions. It is important that she does not show herself as excessively keen, either; realism forbids overt attraction. He does not want to warn Tony of her fabrication, not at the stage where they have agreed upon a time and place.

He tosses the phone on the armchair and browses through a list of items subordinated under the heading New Releases, nothing interesting him. He pushes himself and the chair backward with his feet and turns, facing the armchair. He stands up and rolls his shoulders smoothly before kneeling in front of the chair and pulling out a box from under it. He opens it and looks at the contents. A black handgun is on its right side next to a magazine containing fifteen bullets. He holds the gun in his right hand, lifting it to his face, the rear sight being two inches from his right eye. He imagines the man's face in front of him, pulling his forefinger against the trigger as far as it, unloaded, allows him. Quotes from films are thought of. Computer games are thought of. Murder is thought of.

He's actually going to do it. Fuck. As easy as that, one pull of a trigger, and goodbye and goodnight. Apparently, the gun he's got isn't one to burst a man's head like a balloon or a watermelon or summat. Which is better, probably. He doesn't want to see it. Not really. Well. Maybe he does. The vile fucker's face exploding in a red mist.

He puts the gun down in the box, briefly inspecting the magazine and then putting the lid on the box. If he's going to do this, then it's time he rang work. Another part of the perfect plan.

He stands up, pushing the box under the armchair with the toes of his right foot, and picks up his mobile phone with his right hand. The games will be switched shortly. He uses his right thumb to open his contacts list and selects the contact work. He presses Call and takes the phone in his left hand and places it against his left ear. It rings four times before one of the managers at his work place says hello.

Hi. It's Andy. How's it going? The manager starts to reply with nicety but he carries on, speaking in a dulled monotone. *I'm ringing about work tomorrow. I won't be able to work for a couple of days. Food poisoning, I reckon. Been sick and stomach cramps all the time.* His voice is pretty good. Tired sounding. His manager says that's okay, thanks for ringing in. You been to the doctors? *No, not yet. I'll go when I feel like I can move a bit more.* Shall he? *I'll be fine by tomorrow, probably. It's just that forty-eight-hour thing with food poisoning. All that stuff, you know?* He says that's fine. Best thing to do, really. *Thanks, Dean. I'll ring tomorrow letting you know. Bye.* He says bye, get well soon, and they stop the call at nearly the same time.

Another part of the plan in place. Coming along nice and smooth. He knew his boss wouldn't ask him in, even when he said he could work tomorrow. Health and safety and all that.

He completed the game yesterday. It took him twenty-six hours and twelve minutes, the built-in log of the duration of play storing his time within the disc's memory. He decided that he would create an alibi that cannot be questioned, optioning for the rental of a game that he has already bought. He opens the case of the computer game after picking it up from the armchair, removing the disc from it and placing it on the seat of the chair. He takes the opened case toward the television, under which sits his games console. With his right forefinger, he presses the eject button and a tray protrudes. He takes the disc from the tray and clips it in the case, pushing the tray back and enjoying the feel as it smoothly enters.

The quick chat with the man at the shop set it up perfectly; when he goes in tomorrow a couple of hours after it's done, he's definitely gonna check to see what time he's clocked. He imagines the respect he'll receive and the very fact that he is such a good gamer will make him easily remembered. An alibi and a half.

He scours through the website on his desktop computer for around half of a minute and then looks at the conversation record on FAFAF for another three minutes, scrolling down to the first interaction and then ascending to the current culminant. This has been his habit for the last two weeks, loading the website on his phone at frequent intervals and looking if there are any new messages sent.

And it will all come to this. If he can do it. Of course he can do it. He's committed to it. No backing out now. Not after waiting all this time. It's just too perfect, like it's been set up for him. Almost like it's fate, not that he believes in that crap.

Now what to do: either head to the shops and pick up some Saturday food before coming back to sort out his clothes for tomorrow, or sort out his clothes and then go to the shops?

The clothing he wears is the decision that he is required to make before he kills the man tomorrow. It has made him fractious, deliberating on the most disguising attire that he possesses and items that are the least likely to leave evidence. He has seen countless times on the television, criminals who have committed murders, theft, torture and left dog hairs, footprints, dandruff, rubber from the soles of trainers and fibres from clothing. The most ridiculous, and what he regards as the most problematic, is the closed-circuit vigilantism of the cameras that are constantly alerted to the activities of every body in the city, the country, the world. A criminal takes many hours in planning and detailing the supposedly perfect plan, only to walk past and look at a camera. He has to travel to the hotel and enter unrecognised, kill the man, leave the hotel without being remembered by anyone and then return home incognito. Every action he takes before opening and closing his apartment's front door must avoid being noticed.

Which is impossible, hence why he's been thinking of what stupid damned clothes to wear. Hopefully there's still the slippers that he wore in hospital stuffed in the attic and gloves from when he was a kid in the bottom of his drawers and some other things for his head and face. But what else? He really does need to figure out what he's going to do. As long as no one can see that it's him from any images, it doesn't matter. The clothes'll be thrown in the docks with the phone and the gun.

He is nervous as a result of these thoughts. He contemplated buying clothes from a second-hand shop or from a charity shop, but the receipt of purchase that he would receive would be recorded on any store's database, even if handwritten as most charity shops seem to do. The nerves that he feels become catalyst for doubt and in consequence he silently declares that he can't go through with it.

Head to the shops. The decision is made. If he bumps into anyone then he can just say how he's feeling rough and seeing the doctor. That would actually work out pretty damned good. Makes the whole sick thing much more realistic and that's what's important: being realistic.

Back in the small vestibule of the apartment, he steps in his trainers and slides his right forefinger around his heels to unwedge their backs. He opens the door, leaves and then closes it behind him. He looks at the sky for four seconds before turning left and walking past the gate. It is a darkening hue of grey than earlier and the speckles of blue have left. The changeability of the weather has been the small-talk stalwart of fleeting conversations at his place of work, as well as during most short-lived interactions whilst shopping. It is one dependable topic of conversation whatever the weather, he thinks, amused by his witticism.

At the bottom of the stairs, he crosses the road immediately, quickening his step so the approaching drivers do not have to slow down and he does not get hit. There'd be some sort of divine justice in that, wouldn't there, if he was to be hit? God's intervention would prevent the killer from killing by being killed. But no. Not really. He deserves to be killed, and much more nastily than a quick bullet to the head.

He is walking in the opposite direction from whence he came less than an hour ago, the subway on the other side of the road. There is the soft, warm breath of wind hitting against him, making his face redden. The air feels still. Rain falls, spitting.

Pizza. Has to be pizza. Oven chips, pizza and maybe some lemonade. He does not enjoy drinking alcohol as much as his friends and most people seem to enjoy, and having been made unconscious through inebriation twice, considers that he does not even like alcoholic drink. Some crisps as well. Make a toasted sandwich to go with a film. He's got cheese and bread.

A group of three teenagers walk past him, laughing amongst themselves and moving to his left to allow enough room for them to pass each other. They are wearing shorts. Two of them wear vests and the other wears a football-shirt. It's a shame he can't get into football. He knows all about it and reads up on it but is nowhere near feeling what the majority feel. It's another expectation and one that, if not correctly adhered to, people will pick up on and question your sexuality if you show disinterest. He actually wants to enjoy it, but there's something a little too predictable, limiting and boring about it. Even the computer games are too simple to be enjoyable.

The rain is harder now and as he comes to the pedestrian

crossing, he hears the sextuplet beeps that accompany the green man's short-lived flashing and the appearance of the red man, and he quickens his step, catching the smiling sight of a black woman

$\rightarrow$

$\leftarrow$

who thinks that it is pretty good timing. She doesn't like waiting round for the lights to turn green again after a build up of traffic even when it's not raining. Pretty miserable weather all of a sudden. Nobody predicted this, either, apart from gran, and she always guesses it spot on; she'd had to get the washing in earlier.

She is wearing stone-washed blue jeans, tight against her thighs and knees and slightly looser against the bottom of her calf muscles and her ankles. Her white trainers have pink logos on the sides and pink laces, which match the colour of her jumper, but brighter. Her umbrella is a faded black.

She is walking to the bus stop to board the number 62 that will get her to the prison in which her brother is incarcerated. It is her ritual, even though he protests that she should not be seeing him and especially not on a Saturday night when there are a million other things, better things, to be doing. They talk about Tye, their grandmother and music, and they do not find these meetings depressing. Some strange unspoken rule seems to be to not speak of Leanne. Perhaps he doesn't want her to be inside there with him.

The best brother she could want, really, still looking out for her in his own way and wanting what's best for her. In a world filled with sickos, paedophiles, rapists and murderers, he had to get caught. It's not that she thinks it's unfair – the legal system is – but it's bad luck. Nothing else to blame but bad luck. Well, and James, of course.

Her earphones are plugged in her ears and music is playing. The current record is a classic eighties' dance song, selected randomly through the use of her mobile phone's shuffle function. As she walks to the bus shelter, she is semi-alert to the world around her, the volume of the music directly flooding her eardrums drowning out the sounds of transport, rain and people.

The bus stop is empty and she sits on the sloping, red-plastic bench, shaking off as much of the rain from her umbrella as she can in three rattles of the unfolded fabric before closing it and fastening the ribbon around it. The digital board states that the bus will stop here in eleven minutes. In this time she listens to three songs, the screeching of the bus's brakes audible over her music as the bus stops. She drapes the earphones over her shoulders as she stands and balances the umbrella against her knee, pulling her purse out of her handbag with her right hand and unclipping it with both thumbs and pulling out three one pound coins with her left forefinger and thumb. She puts the purse in her handbag and picks up her umbrella. The doors retract away from her and she steps on the bus.

A return to Wellern Avenue, please. She puts the three coins on the dish beneath the protective plastic casing before the driver can say anything. He taps softly against the touch-screen monitor in front of him in three different places and a ticket silently ejects from a slot in the cream-coloured box to her left. The driver rips the paper against the serrated lip of the slot by pulling up and hands it to her. *Thanks.* She sits on the second seat from the front, on the right of the bus.

The journey is quick and the ten minutes and thirty seconds are occupied by her listening to music and looking to her right, through the window. The handle of her umbrella is rested against the edge of the seat and a small scatter of raindrops is formed next to her right foot. She enjoys her music, thinking about the tunes as the songs play. Walking off, she pulls an earphone from her right ear and says *Thanks* to the driver who tells her to have a good day. She smiles and walks off.

The rain is lighter than when she boarded the bus and there is a stronger wind, making the rain curve closer to horizontal than vertical. She points the umbrella against it, walking quickly away from the stop where she disembarked and past a row of student houses, dozens of signs from letting-agents erected in the unkempt gardens, two of which are strewn with debris. She gives the buildings no attention, absorbed by the music and looking directly ahead. She passes no people along the stretch of pavement and does not stop to cross any of the intersecting roads. At the fourth road, she turns right, the high walls and barbed-wiring of the prison visible above the housing's skyline.

Every time she visits, she thinks the same thought: not quite a mansion, James, but you've done alright with the size of your home. She smiles and walks for eleven seconds. A free gym, too. He's already looking big compared to how skinny he was before it all happened. He's even made some good friends and says that there isn't much trouble. He might just be saying that though, in his protective mode. He hasn't looked bad or acted unhappy when she sees him, so maybe he is telling the truth. Never any depressing topics, either.

The prison is modern and its outer walls are bleached concrete, the near-white greyed to her vision by the misty rain. There are four entrance gates, one on each of the outer walls. At what is regarded as the main gate, she sees the face of the prison officer who seems always to work the Saturday afternoon shift. He smiles at her and they exchange courtesies as he looks non-committedly at her identification. During the first three times when they had undertaken this routine, he had asked her to state the purpose of her visit. Today, he does not. There are three officers at the gate and he leads her through the passage to the main building, where he asks her to deposit all of her items in a grey plastic tray, which include her phone, earphones, umbrella, and handbag. The umbrella is taken separately and placed behind the front desk. He tells her to enjoy her visit and that he will see her on the way out.

At first, unfamiliar with the system of visiting those locked away from society, she had walked to the main gate and expected to be let in. Looking back, she thinks that it is obvious that that is not the way it works and cannot believe how naïve she was. An officer says this way, please and she follows her along the memorised route to the visitors' room. In the past, she has had to wait over twenty minutes before being led to the visitors' room, but the last four times have included little waiting, perhaps as a result of her frequent visits. Five o'clock's not been a problem yet. Surprising really, because that's the time when most people are free. Maybe he has a point; people really do prefer to go out and get drunk on a Saturday than do nearly anything else.

There are five rows of benches, able to seat three prisoners and their visitors opposite them, each row supervised by one officer. James is sitting on the last allotted space to the left of the fourth row. All of the prisoners' backs are facing her. The officer escorting her opens her right hand, palm up, and gestures forwards. Here you go, love, she says. The officer waits for her to walk towards her brother before turning and leaving the way in which they came. The permitted duration of their interaction is thirty minutes, in which they have proved to be lenient. She walks to her brother from the left, saying his name when seven feet away and seeing him turn towards her voice.

←
→

Tasha.

↑↓

Hey. She sits opposite him, smiling to reflect his dimpled smile. Really like Tye's. *How've you been keeping? Alright?*

↓↑

All's okay. As good as it can be locked up in a prison. A small chuckle. Not that funny. *How've you been keeping? You okay because of tomorrow?*

↑↓

Tomorrow? *I'm okay. Glad you are.* Tomorrow? *What's tomorrow?*

↓↑

You're kidding? It's mum's, you know, day. The day she, you know.

↑↓

Oh. Of course. Sorry. Every year since their mother's death, friends and family had gathered at the cemetery to pay their respects, which meant standing at a patch of grass and feeling sad. Even as a child she had never understood why they would gather for collective grief, and at fourteen she had decided to avoid those days and follow the priest's words about celebrating rather than mourning those that are dead. Birthdays are there for celebration; death days are there to be forgotten.

↓↑

It's alright. I know your take on all that. How's Tye getting on?

↑↓

He's great. No mention of Leanne. *Looks so much like you, you know, with those dimples when you smile.*

↓↑

He smiles, trying not to smile by pursing his lips. *He can't help but be, with a dad like me. Good looks run in our family.* His smile widens, showing the tips of his teeth. She's always been like that to him. Making him feel good.

↑↓

Arrogant? She laughs lightly. *You're looking good. You were so tiny before.*

↓↑

Weights. Been hitting them each day. Working with the prison instructor, you know.

↑↓

Keeps you from getting bored then, really?

↓↑

No. *Yeah. It makes the time go pretty quick.*

↑↓

Tye wants to be an astronaut now. He's been drawing rockets and spaceships since he started learning about space in school. It's really cute.

↓↑

That's cool. Remember what you wanted to be? An archaeologist. Does he say much about me?

↑↓

Strangely, he doesn't. *Yeah, of course. He's a strong little man though. Doesn't get upset easily. A bundle of energy. Never stops.*

↓↑

Cool. He's doing okay at school?

↑↓

Yeah. Really good. He's done really well and he had an excellent report.

↓↑

Good on the little guy. He nods his head and leans forwards over the top of the bench's table. *And you're okay? It can't be easy looking after him all the time with gran.*

↑↓

Tye. No mention again of Leanne. I *'m alright. Work's going great and everything's going alright. Really.*

↓↑

I know you're okay. Good. But listen. If you ever needed anything, you know you can talk to Wayne, right?

↑↓

Yeah. I know. Thanks, but we're okay. Things are going really well. She doesn't want anything to do with his friends, anyway.

She believes that it is their fault that he is in prison. She does not doubt the strength of their friendship nor that they will help her brother as much as possible in his position, but she blames them for his imprisonment. If he had never got involved with them, then he would never have taken part in crime.

↓↑

Good. Change the tone of this conversation. It's not fair on her. *Hey. Who's gonna win this World Cup, then?* He nods encouragingly at her once, coaxing her participation. He knows that she has never liked football.

↑↓

You knob. He is the only person in front of whom she feels comfortable to use taboo language. Y*ou know I don't give a damn.* She smiles at him. *Is this your way of asking for the scores? Because if it is, I don't have a clue.*

↓↑

Sorry, Tasha. I know you don't. We have tellies in here. The first quarter-final kicked off a couple of hours ago. There's even a few syndicates. She's frowning. *Which of course I ain't doing nothing with.* He expects her reproach.

↑↓

You'd better not. He seems to be doing okay. He really does look healthy.

↓↑

Of course I ain't. Anyway, I was wondering if you could do me a favour. And before you say no, hear me out. I know you don't li...

↑↓

James. Stupid. *Think about what you're about to say.*

↓↑

What?

↑↓

Think about what you're gonna say. Remember where we are. He's never done anything like this before. Why's he laughing?

↓↑

He holds his hands up with his palms facing her. *Nuh nuh nuh nuh. You've got it wrong. Listen to me. Let me finish.* What was she thinking? *I'm not asking to break me out or nothing. Listen to me. I know you're not into the whole visiting mum thing, but you know. I was hoping you could go there tomorrow for me. If it's okay for you?*

↑↓

Oh. Of course. You go every year, right?

↓↑

Every year but this. Thanks Tasha. I appreciate it. They sit in silence for nineteen seconds, reflecting on this commitment and looking at each other. *Could you, you know, speak to her about me? Let her know I'm okay?*

↑↓

Yeah. No problem. Even though this sounds pathetic to her, she understands people's needs and sorrows and she will do what her brother asks.

↓↑

Thanks, sister he says, winking at her and smiling to break the still atmosphere. He directs the conversation to discussing the lives of their mutual acquaintances and friends from school, asking for details about pregnancies, jobs and relationships. During this interaction with his sister, he finds it easy to avoid talking to her about the unpleasant events that have occurred since he has been in prison. Once per month, she comes, and he eagerly awaits her visits, believing that they are the only thing that enables him to maintain his hold on sanity.

When the officer tells them that their time has come to its end, he nods and holds up his right forefinger as a request. The officer nods in acceptance of his proposal.

Don't forget to see mum for me tomorrow. Thanks for doing that. And for seeing me, too. Send my love to gran and the little man and... She knows he won't say her name in here. God, it sounds like he's reading a will. *Thanks. See you next month?*

She answers of course. They stand and say goodbye. He stays standing as she is led from the room by the same officer that brought her. He watches her go, before the officer standing guard at the bench that he was sitting on beckons him with a look, a quick nod in the door's direction, and by turning around with his back to him. He nods at the officer and walks toward him slowly, expressionlessly resolute. He knows that it is important not to show any evident camaraderie with the officers.

The officer asks him how everything is with his sister and he replies *fine*, considering applying thanks. He thinks that it would not be difficult to escape from the building, with its relaxed approach to prisoner interaction. The design of the rooms and access ways between sections is symmetrical, he has learnt, which makes the memorisation of the schematics easy. It's not like in the movies or on telly, where you stick a gun in their face or dig a tunnel. Disguise and concealment, they call it. That's the best way. Not that he's gonna do that, not with twenty-six months and Tye and Leanne. And there's never a time when he's not being watched by someone, so.

The officer opens the cell's door and holds it with his left hand. There you go, James, he says, as he walks past him and turns to him, nodding once more at the officer through the viewing-slat on the door.

$\rightarrow$

$\leftarrow$

The black kid's alright. Ten years' experience as a screw gives you the eye to see through them all. He's not a soft kid, but he's not a nasty bastard either. A hard face to cover the fear. Never rude or complaining. A good kid. Only got a year left most likely. Done alright as far as it goes: avoided gaining too much attention from anyone, which isn't easy. A nice steak when he gets in. Marie's are unbeatable, perfectly cooked all the way through yet still pink. Perfect end to any day's work, but especially a Saturday. And especially a Saturday when he's working the next day, too. Got a real good-looking cut: fillet. Not the cheap shit that comes covered in plastic. This is off-the-counter steak. Proper steak.

The cotton uniform he wears is cool against his skin and he is not sweating. The reapplication of anti-perspirant during his lunchbreak gives him a florally chemical aroma that he does not like, but it is preferable to him than sweating. If only they'd make something for foreheads. There's an idea. He finds the uniform comfortable, as do all the officers he talks with, which makes the heat more bearable in the workplace.

Air-conditioned prisons are yet to be sanctioned by the human rights advocates.

Finishing in twenty minutes. Probably get out around quarter past, but that never bothers him. It's a good job, not like those places abroad or across the pond where inmates are a thousand to one and they throw their shit at you. Well. It's never happened to him. One more transportation, then a nice steak and those Spanish potatoes she does. A few beers during the show – no point watching now that England has been knocked out, embarrassing – and then a midnight nightcap at the latest. Another eight to six shift tomorrow. He has no problem with working weekends. The pay is double per hour and the inmates are less depressed, a noticeable difference in the ethos: Saturday night is Saturday night.

Cell two hundred and fifty-two is where he stops. He looks in upon a young man named Calum Howard Osborne, whose common name amongst the officers and prisoners is the acronymised

Cho. You ready?

↑↓

Sure thing, boss. Time to see some titties other than your own, you fat fuck. This thought amuses him.

↓↑

Come on. Your girlfriend today? Calum is nineteen and imprisoned for causing grievous bodily harm to a man who was attempting to dance with his girlfriend by cradling her buttocks in his hands. He can sympathise with this, but blinding a person in one of their only two eyes necessitates judicial recrimination and punishment.

Calum says yeah and smirks. He's a pretty cocksure kid, that's for sure. Borstals may have closed down, but these boys are still tough. They're in here with murderers and gangsters and somehow hold their own. He closes and locks the door.

They walk across the mesh-metal of the second floor and down the steps to the ground floor, taking the same route he had taken earlier with James. They walk and do not speak to each other, courteous alrights being spoken between him and the officers they cross on sentry. Calum looks in the cells as they pass.

In the meeting room, Calum sits on the same row that James had sat on, occupying the middle space of the bench. He waits for four or five minutes and his girlfriend walks in, the door held open for her by an officer. She is gymnastically slim, with prominent thighs on show through her leggings and a flat stomach obvious beneath her T-shirt: a commitment to diet and fitness. With bouncing strides she sits opposite Calum, leaning forwards immediately to excite his attention with her cleavage.

He cannot hear what they say, both lowering the volume of their voices to aid their discussion's surreption. He focuses on them intermittently, thinking of the food his wife is cooking at this moment in their house a few miles away and then thinking about the lives that these two young lovers have in front and ahead of them. He tries to see signs in their actions and mannerisms that show their love for each other, but the concentration and inverted eyebrows that they adopt with frequency makes his task difficult. It's like a business relationship, where they're in it for some equal gain. No real love there.

He also thinks about his time in the army, posted in Germany, where he met his wife. He was about the same age as Cho, but even though he couldn't say and wouldn't say he loved her at first sight, he showed her how much she meant to him. Still does. Love's not something to be messed around with. He's a lucky bastard to have Marie to share a life and a beautiful daughter with. Even when she was pregnant so bloody young, there'd never been talk of them having an abortion or not being together and their love had grown with their daughter. He believes that he is a part of the perfect marriage and observes Calum and his girlfriend on the bench, gauging the depth of their romance and making restrained comparisons, alerting himself to the difference in generation and epochally-sculptured social culture.

With thirty minutes of the two lovers' meeting having passed, he thinks that another five minutes won't hurt anyone. Can't be easy being inside so young. A lot of these young kids have kids of their own. Thankfully, his daughter never gave him a minute of trouble growing up: healthy, happy, well-behaved. What more could any parent want? Nearing retirement with two grandkids and a decent enough son-in-law and a successful, professional working-mum daughter. And a steak to get home to with a wife who is perfect. Nearer ruby than pearl, as well.

He checks his watch four times whilst supervising the prisoners and their guests on the bench, thinking about his family and food and the holiday that he, his wife, his daughter, son-in-law and grandchildren will have in less than a month with the ending of school not far from now. One week or two? He can never remember?

That's time, Cho. Wrap it up. He is not surprised any longer with the manner in which these two separate. They say see you later and nod and smile briefly and she walks away as he walks towards him. Kids these days. Impossible to understand. Most of them, anyway.

He walks through the door for the seventh time today, ensuring that his ward is on his left side. It is an old technique that he learnt whilst boxing during his time in the army; keep the opponent circling to your left if you strike most effectively with your right hand. Bigger swing makes bigger impact. Being alert in this job prevents being taken unawares. They do not speak as they walk, and when they stop at cell two hundred and fifty two and he unlocks the door, he says

See you tomorrow, Cho. Be a good boy as usual. He receives a grin and a respectful nod. Poor young bastard. Defending his girlfriend, albeit pretty violently, but on principle it's a thing that all men can understand. A few years left for him, that's for sure. Probably be out before thirty the way they're filling up. Not enough space these days. Or money.

For what he thinks is the thirteenth time, he slowly descends the steps and then through two further security doors, requiring him to unlock them with a plastic card. Apart from when he takes lunch, this is the only time when he goes through these doors. The second door leads to the recognised front of the prison, where the entrance has been dubbed the reception. Here, he deposits his plastic and metal keys in a plastic tray that is the same one used by visitors, along with a two-piece radio and receiver. He leaves two sticks of chewing gum in an opened packet in the tray as he walks to the desk and passes it to one of the three officers who are seated on swivel chairs. He says thanks and asks if the day's been alright? to which he replies that it's been quite good, pretty quiet, and tells him to have a good rest on his shift, he's in tomorrow if he's working too? A series of pleasantries to the other staff in the entrance room and he leaves the main building of the prison.

Shit. It's bloody pissing it down. Was a bit overcast earlier but he'd thought it'd've cleared up ages ago. Wouldn't've driven even if it was raining buckets, but a coat would've been nice. Just getting used to it after what feels like a decade of wet summers. He quickens his pace by another mile per hour to reach the gate-post and hopes that the door is opened for him. The rain is thick and he cannot see the thirty-two yards to the building clearly, squinting to prevent his eyes being hit with raindrops. Bloody rain. Like a tropical storm. In all likelihood, thunder and lightning's not too far away. Shit. Right in his bloody socks. Please be ready at the door. Are they there? Looks like it. They are. Good.

Thank God for that. Cheers Pete. Bloody hammering it down. Doesn't know if he can say that really, what with Pete being a proper Catholic. Doesn't seem to mind.

↑↓

I've got a brolly you can have if you want. Car's on the main road. Won't take a minute to run.

↓↑

If you didn't mind?

↑↓

Honestly. Not a problem. He crouches behind a small desk and picks up a small, wrapped black umbrella in his right hand, offering it as he walks the two steps near his original standing point.

↓↑

Thanks mate. Like a relay. Top man. *I'm here in the morning anyway. I'll bring it back then.* Pete tells him to have a good night and says that he will be in after church and he leaves, unfurling the umbrella from its single strap and pushing the cover to the top, extending the metal arms and opening the protection from the rain. He can feel the force from the wind pushing against him and he is brisk with his strides. The umbrella is held four inches before his face and head, obscuring his vision slightly. His eyes are at knee level, alerted to pedestrian feet. Of the five minutes and thirty-six seconds that it takes him to walk to the house that he shares with his wife, he encounters no one walking on the pavement. Forty-two cars pass him. His thoughts do not vary further than the duration of the inclemency or his tea.

He can smell the fat in the air as he opens the door. He smiles, consciously and naturally, thinking of the taste of what he will soon be eating as he steps in, pulling the key from the door with his right hand. He pushes the door closed, rests the unfolded umbrella with the handle against the wall and wet top against the entrance mat, turns and grimaces with the strain of leaning without bending his knees to remove his heavy steel toe-capped boots. The belt feels tight against his midriff and digs sharply in his stomach, the weight of his belly pushing over it. With his shoes off, he pushes against his knees and stands, caressing his belly with a laugh, thinking of his wife and the food waiting for him and how funny it seems that his socks are dry. He removes his belt and carries it with him to the kitchen, nudging the closed door open with his knuckles to avoid fingerprinting the white paint.

↑↓

Hi Graham. How was your day? She walks up to him with an oven-glove mittening both of her hands, presenting her left cheek forwards, which he kisses.

↓↑

Alright, ta. You been okay? Charlie pop round?

↑↓

She's dropping the kids off tomorrow before. Oh shit. The steamer's been on full for ten minutes. She removes her right hand from the glove and turns the dial marked rear right as far as it allows anticlockwise. The flame beneath the steamer is extinguished. She puts her hand back in the glove and lifts the top two pans from the three-tiered steamer, placing them on the front-left rack.

↓↑

Too many cooks. I know. Her domain. Beans on toast or nothing with him.

↑↓

Not at all. Just forgot myself. Ten minutes and it'll be done. Go and have your wash.

↓↑

Yes ma'am. Always perfect timing. Whatever time he gets in, there's always food ready and waiting. She has some sort of sixth sense, as she can sense how far away he is. Twenty minutes late today and still timed to absolute perfection. What more can any man ask for at his age?

He pulls the door open by the handle with his left hand and pulls it slowly closed as he steps out of the kitchen, its momentum finishing the action as he turns right and walks up the stairs. He can hear the swishing grind of his right knee's cartilage as he takes each second, right-footed step, practicably inattentive to it. At the top of the stairs, he enters the bathroom adjacent immediately before him and undresses, removing his wristwatch last, leaving it on the corner of the bathtub closest to him.

His skin feels sticky, which he thinks is the rain; for a man who knows he is carrying an unhealthy surplus of weight, his body does not sweat unless physically exerting himself or bathing under a forty-degrees Celsius heat. After the day's work and the warmth of the house, he thinks that a cold wash is needed. He fills the basin to near three-quarters full with cold water and lathers the bar of orange soap that is in the soap dish, smearing the soap under his armpits and across his chest before lathering it once more and smearing it over the back of his neck, ears and face. He sucks in a sharp breath as he touches his armpits and the back of his neck and pulls the plug out to release half of the water in the basin. He turns the hot tap and runs the water until it is warm and then hot and fills the basin with a quick spurt, past the overflow. That's better. Still cool but not freezing. He picks up a crisp dark-brown flannel from the side of the bath, one of three, and sponges water with it. He wrings the flannel before cleaning the soap from his body. Leaving the flannel in the sink, he repeats the lathering of his body past his stomach. The cold water affects his testicles, tightening them, as well as enhancing the flaccidity of his penis. He wipes the side of his right hand up the cleavage of his buttocks and uses the same hand to spread soap across the surface of his upper thighs and buttocks. The flannel feels cold as he washes over the soaped areas, and colder when he steps his left foot in the basin. Still lithe and dexterous for an old bugger. He uses the nails of his right hand to scrape away at the skin of his sole and heels after soaping, repeating this with his right foot. He feels refreshed.

He lets out the water in the sink and wipes at the sides with the hot tap pouring water, removing the scum from the sides of the basin, before picking up his clothes and putting them in the washing basket and dabbing himself with the towel that is on the rack. He walks out of the bathroom and to his bedroom, where he dresses in a pair of white briefs, aged grey shorts and a navy-blue T-shirt bearing a sports-brand logo. His stomach produces a gurgling sound as he walks down the stairs and when he walks in the living room, his wife smiles at him and nods to the tray on the table by the side of an armchair. The television is on, a potential winner of a reality TV show strumming an acoustic guitar with a well-toned vocal which makes a good impression on the four judges and the cheering audience.

I'm bloody starving. Been looking forward to this all day. He sits in the armchair and picks up the tray supporting a big plate, a small plate, two ramekins, a fork and a steak knife. On the big plate is a piece of fillet steak, cooked so that it is browned and topped with fried onions, and *patatas bravas*. On the small plate are two buttered slices of white bread. One ramekin contains peppercorn sauce and the other contains English mustard. *You're the best, love,* he says as he cuts through the meat with his steak knife. He prongs the piece of meat with his fork, dips it in the peppercorn sauce and chews it quickly. *Mmm.* He closes his eyes and nods as he chews, before swallowing. With the ritual over, his wife says glad you like it and smiles and they eat.

During their eating, they talk about his day at work and remark on the prowess and talent of the hopeful contestants on this year's show and he compliments the food six times. She tells him that they are looking after their grandchildren until Monday and that she will be taking them to school on Monday morning and that there are four ice-cold beers in the refrigerator.

What a perfect way to spend a Saturday night. Thirty-odd -years ago, the pub was the best thing but now it's staying in watching the telly with a beer and the wife. He tells her this and she chuckles. She still sounds like she did at nineteen, when she giggles like that. He tells her this. She replies, smiling warmly, that flattery gets you nowhere and collects the trays. They have not eaten at the table for many years. He slaps her backside as she walks from him after collecting and placing his tray on hers with the accoutrements sensibly balanced. He likes her high-pitched response and reinforces his absolute love for her with a tingling pulse across his penis. After all these years, she still excites him. The increased size of her boobs actually excites him; they were great when small and upward, and equally now they're fuller and lower. It's like two women, seeing the girl you fall in love with become the woman you grow in love with. When younger, he'd preferred older women (or at least thought he had) and as he became older, he looked at younger women more. Now, he looks only at his wife. Never cheated, anyway. Looking is only looking, as is thinking. Sex ain't that important anyway. Not really. Not now.

He stands up, noticing the weight in his stomach and feeling satisfied with the food that he has eaten. You get what you pay for, that's for sure. He walks to the kitchen with the intention of helping his wife wash or dry the dishes (usually dry), but as he opens the door, she says

↑↓

You've had your wash. Get in there and watch the show. You'll smell of cooking if you stay out here.

↓↑

He was thinking about getting in the bath after her. *You sure?*

↑↓

Yes. Close the door or you'll stink the whole house out.

↓↑

Okay. No bath for me. *I'll just grab one of those beers.* He opens the refrigerator to the left of the door and takes a purple-labelled bottle of dark ale from the door. Closing the refrigerator door, he opens the top drawer in the side unit next to the refrigerator and takes out a gold-coloured bottle-opener in the shape of a nude with his right hand. He holds the bottle with his left hand and hooks the bottle-top off with one upward movement of his wrist, dropping the utensil near where he picked it up and closing the drawer.

Cheers, love. She's the best. Only told him off so he can sit down after work. Shame about the bath, but she pretty much pours a tank of napalm it's so hot. He's got sturdy, resilient hands, but he can't put them in the dishwater after her; she runs it ridiculously hot, just like her baths.

He sits in the armchair and drinks three mouthfuls from the bottle in succession. It's a bloody good beer. The two youngsters duetting that bloke's song from the seventies – or was it sixties? – are good. He loves it when they put a new spin on something, especially when it's as famous as this song and already been done a million times.

After around ten minutes in which he watches five more performers, there is a series of advertisements and he finishes drinking from the bottle, leaving a quarter inch of ale in the bottom. He stands again and walks to the kitchen where his wife is taking a handful of cutlery from the draining board. Went down okay? she asks him and he tells her it was a treat and then expresses how good he thinks some of the performers are and asks her if she wants him to start running the bath for her, to which she replies that it's okay, thanks. He gets a beer from the refrigerator and uncaps it and leaves the kitchen with his wife. She goes upstairs and he goes to the living room and sits in his armchair. The programme has just restarted and the presenter is talking with one of the hopeful contestants about what it means to them to be on the show and what winning would mean. He thinks that the questions are shit. Briefly, he deliberates over changing the channel and watching the start of the football. What's the point? This is good anyway, shit questions notwithstanding.

He watches the programme for around forty minutes before his wife enters the room and puts an uncapped bottle of ale on his table and then sits on the sofa opposite him, placing a glass of white wine on the table next to the end of her seat. She is in a lavender dressing-gown and wafts the aroma of citrus. From her shampoo, he guesses.

Cheers. She knows him perfectly. One beer quickly, then the next couple or so a bit slower. A lot slower: his routine. *Nice bath?*

↑↓

Lovely, thanks. I could've spent another hour in there. Elimination, now?

↓↑

Perfect timing. He smiles, picking the most recent bottle from the table and raising it towards his wife with his left hand. She reciprocates with her glass of wine and they both drink. He wants to sit next to her and hold her and put his hand under the dressing-gown across her chest but he is unsure whether she would want that right now. She looks, he thinks, lovely, relaxed and radial and then gets it: radiant. She looks radiant. *You look radiant.*

She giggles and he walks over to her, leaving the bottle on the table next to the armchair and wiping the condensation from his fingers on the left side of his shorts. He sits behind her on the sofa, putting his arms around her midriff and interlocking his fingers. He rests his chin over the back-right of her neck and quickly kisses her right cheek. She rests her back against his front, placing her hands over his. She says that's lovely and they watch the elimination of two contestants, discussing the horrible manner in which nearly-realised ambitions are quickly severed by a simple rejection of their talent, as voted for by the audience. They agree that it is cruel, but also that it makes for excellent television.

When the programme ends, he kisses her again on the right cheek and walks to his armchair and sits in it, picking up his bottle and drinking from it.

A film is due to start that he has seen twice before over the last twenty-seven years. His wife has started reading a book that she appears to be halfway through and so he's happy to watch the film again. It's not bad, if he remembers right.

With advertisements, it takes him two hours and six minutes to get to the film's final credits. In the film, a woman is convicted of killing her husband and put in prison after a trial convinces the jurors of her guilt. It follows the progress of a handsome lawyer, played by a famously attractive actor, who is determined to prove her innocence and eventually manages to succeed, both of them apparently falling in love during the process. With his skill as a barrister and his oratorical prowess, he gains her release and they celebrate in a hotel room, having sex. When he wakes, his wrists and ankles are tied to the bedposts and she is grinning at him. She confesses to being the murderess and the film ends.

His wife and he have short conversations and exchange remarks as she reads and he watches, with one visit each to the bathroom to urinate and a visit to the kitchen for her to bring in the bottle of wine and a bottle of ale. With the film finished, he provides the cue for their joint venture to go to their bed, yawning loudly and placing his hands on the back of his head, triangulating the shape of his arms with the elbows pointing outward.

I'm looking forward to bed tonight. Gonna drop off pretty quick.

↑↓

How did the film seem this time round? Better than her book, she hopes. *Could you remember the ending?* She stands and picks up her empty glass and the empty wine bottle in her right hand, the book closed in her left.

↓↑

No. He couldn't. *Kinda remembered it. It was alright.*

She walks out to the kitchen, talking about the lead actress and whether she died last year or the year before. He pulls the television's plug from the socket above the skirting-board, hearing the swishing sound of his knee, and brings the three empty bottles from his table to the kitchen.

Two years ago, I think. A couple of days before the kids' birthdays. Can't remember. It was two years, he's sure.

She walks up the stairs as he locks the front and back doors and switches the lights off, and by the time that he is brushing his teeth, she is finished and in bed. When he finishes, he urinates, spitting the last of the lathered toothpaste in the toilet. He flushes and rinses his brush under the cold water and swills his mouth out after sucking water and puts the toothbrush in the rack and pulls his foreskin back and splashes cold water over the end of his penis. Better had, just in case, he thinks.

He removes all of his clothes, switches the bathroom light off, and carries them to the bedroom, placing them neatly on the dresser positioned to the right of the bed. He sees that his wife is wearing her pyjamas and so the thought that sexual intercourse may be a possibility is at an end. There is nothing less of a turn-on than pyjamas. She has left the duvet folded, her feet and legs covered up below the knees. There is a fan blowing cool air from a table by the window. Neither he nor his wife are affected negatively by the sound it makes when aiming for sleep; the sound is relaxing to them and lulls them to sleep. He turns the lamp off and the room is cast in darkness.

N'night, love, he says, turning to his left to place his right arm over her chest and his chin on her right shoulder. She replies with night, Graham, and squeezes his hand. He thinks about the contestants on the reality TV programme for a minute or two, whilst they both subtly reposition themselves and become as comfortable as they can. He thinks about his breathing, regulating it as he has taught himself in order to fall asleep quickly. In seven minutes, they are both asleep.

His wife is next to him, sitting on a wooden bench in a park. She asks him to sing a song and he does. He never was a good singer, but he's pretty impressive. He knows this is a dream, and he will stay in it as long as he can. There's a big crowd gathered and they are adulatory. Most of them are attractive women and he knows that he could bed any of them. His lids start to filter less light as they clench and unclench, slowly opening.

His wife is not in the bed next to him and he knows that he will have breakfast waiting for him when he gets downstairs. What a way to wake up before work. He rolls from his left shoulder and onto his back, stretching with his arms pushed down against the bed, hands in the direction of his feet and clenching his fists, feeling the muscles of his forearms and biceps, and points his toes toward the end of the bed. His neck muscles are taut as he yawns lengthily and quite loudly. His left hand is slightly numb and he shakes it for just over twenty seconds, feeling the warm throb of blood coursing through his palm and fingers.

He can hear the television from downstairs and the weather outside. Another day of rain and wind. Summer had been looking like a proper scorcher. Still might. Storms come with hot weather, usually. The fan has been turned off. He'd better get out. The digital clock on the wall opposite says 07:07. Palindrome, he thinks. They have a digital clock because even though his wife likes the sound of air being blown through the rotor of a fan, the ticking of a clock irritates her.

He pushes himself quickly from the bed, standing and arching his hips forward with his hands on the back of his head, elbows pointing out. His uniform has been placed on the dresser and he smiles. She thinks of everything. He dresses in three minutes and eight seconds, starting with a pair of grey socks, then the briefs that he placed on the dresser with the shorts and T-shirt last night, followed by the prison-provided trousers and shirt and the looping and buckling of his belt. He remembers that he left his watch in the bathroom, but she must have brought it in after her bath. Everything. He sprays deodorant under each arm, past the bagginess of the short sleeves, biting his teeth from the cold, and straps his watch around his left wrist.

A nice breakfast before work and the grandkids tonight. Nice way to start and end a Sunday. Let's get some breakfast. Bet it's a bacon and egg sarnie with a healthy amount of sauce. It smells like it. At the bottom of the stairs, the smell confirms his prediction.

Mmm. That's the ticket. Couldn't ask for anything better. It smells great. *Enough energy to last 'til lunch.* The smear on the bread from where she'd wiped the tomato sauce to clean the knife. Perfect. *You're too good for me. Unless you're trying to give me cholesterol or a coronary.* He sits in the armchair, picking up the plate with the sandwich and appreciating the mug of tea. Simple things of life.

↑↓

Very welcome. The best thing about domesticity is the lack of change. He never asks, is always a gentleman, and still shows genuine gratitude. A keeper, her mother had said. Damn right.

↓↑

He didn't chew enough. Stuck in his throat. Bastard. *Any idea what time Charlie's bringing the kids round?* Stickler for manners: no talking with his mouth full.

↑↓

Around ten, she said. Something big planned for the day. I didn't press.

↓↑

Bloody good sarnie. He chews quickly and swallows. *That's good.* She goes out to the kitchen, carrying a plate that he thinks probably had fruit on; it was a half of a grapefruit. The yolk of the egg bursts as he bites and his right little finger feels it. It solidifies waxily and quickly and he scrapes it off by putting it between his teeth pulling it away. He eats the yolk with a mouthful and mops as much of the yellow from the plate that he can.

On the television, a crisis in monetary conversion rates has been announced and a correspondent stands before a bank, providing an analytical doomsayer's monologue. The caption along the bottom relays other affairs. He cannot read them. Maybe she is right and he should get contacts too. Even when squinting, it doesn't help. He watches intently, focusing on any mention of pension schemes being hit, drinking his tea in small slurps. When his tea is finished, he is quite convinced that in the financial jargon that was spoken, no reference to pensions or savings accounts had been discussed.

He brings the mug and plate to the kitchen, placing them in the plastic bowl on the draining board that contains last night's wine glass. There is a small amount of water in the bottom, in which he swishes the fingers of his right hand. His wife is making a sandwich, a lettuce being sliced as he kisses the back of her neck and leaves the kitchen, walking up the stairs and into the bathroom. He brushes his teeth. Never after, always before. Sensible. He closes the bathroom door and unbuckles his belt, pulling his trousers and briefs down together, and sits on the toilet seat. His stomach muscles contract and his stomach fat wobbles from the exertion as he helps himself to excrete. He does not use the toilet facilities at work: home comforts. No rush.

No rush. He stands, flushes, pulls up his briefs and trousers together, adjusting the briefs before pulling the trousers to his hips and tucking his shirt in. Finally, he clasps the button, buckles his belt, and pulls the zip up.

At the bottom of the stairs, his wife is holding a carrier bag that he knows contains a lunch box.

↑↓

Now you be a good boy and don't be getting into any trouble, you hear? She laughs and smiles at him and watches him put his shoes on, passing him the carrier bag and opening the door when he stands.

↓↑

I'll try. Mum. He kisses her and picks up the umbrella. *Have a good day with the kids, Marie.* He kisses her again. She says that she will and tells him to have a good day. When he is at the bottom of the path, he gives her an American salute.

←

→

She watches him open the umbrella and tuck his chin to his chest, the bag containing his lunch dangling from his right hand that is holding the umbrella.

Horrid weather. Luckily it's only round the corner. Was the reason they moved here, after all. Still wouldn't want to be out in it. It only takes him five or ten minutes, but he'll be drenched from the waist down by the time he gets in. Wonder where he got the umbrella. She'd noticed it last night. Probably from some Samaritan at work. Still didn't wear a coat. He's not a morning person, which is another reason why she sets him up every morning. Well, and she enjoys it. Being thanked for something is priceless, especially from your husband.

She shuts the door and lifts the pyjama bottoms higher, the elastic clinging to her lower back and along her navel. Sunday mornings are television mornings; the breakfast-cookery programmes are on and you can get some pretty good recipes from them. The guests are always well selected, which is a bonus as well. It's book-reading television. Or at least with the book she's reading at the moment it is. Can't leave a book unfinished once started though. She was once six hundred and fifty pages into a book that she stopped enjoying for the way it dragged after only a hundred or so pages and she still finished. And it was still trite. This is what she is going to do.

In the living room, she picks up the remote control in her right hand and flicks it at the screen at the same time that she presses the menu button. She scrolls down the list of channels advertising their televisual wares and selects Breaking the Sunday Fast, her favourite of the four competitors within the genre. It will play as an enjoyable background; she picks up her book, the top of one of the pages folded in a small triangle marking where she is to continue after yesterday's reading.

The author of the book has been a favourite of Marie's for over the last three decades, but the last seven books including the recurring (and once dead) main character have gradually become less thrilling to her. She recognises a retirement-fund cash-cow cynicism.

She reads and watches the television when an interesting idea is discussed and practised, or when the conversation becomes amusing and the presenters, chefs or guests start raucously laughing. It's contagious, the laughter. The show's a comfort programme. And Sunday comfort is a thing that she likes. The room is left once: to urinate and make a drink of orange juice diluted with soda water. An hour passes in this manner until she gets a telephone call. The telephone is placed on the little bookshelf at the rear of the living room and takes her fourteen seconds to answer it from its first ring.

Hello. Charlie? It is. *Alright, thanks. Of course.* She was really rather absorbed. *Yes, that's fine. Don't forget that they'll need their.* Her daughter's not dumb. *No, not at all. Twenty minutes. Fine. See you then and bring your coats.* Laugh. *Of course not. It is dismal out there is all. Bye. Bye.* They're on their way over in the car. One of their cars. Better get ready and put some clothes on.

She walks out of the living room and up the stairs and strips the pyjamas from her body when in her bedroom, leaving on her brassiere, and dresses herself in comfortable white knickers and a loose dress in which she admires her physique. Leaving the room, she returns to the kitchen.

She'll be wanting a cuppa. Kettle on. The boys'll have squash and ask for tea. She fills up the kettle, the markings on the outside showing the level required to make two mugs of tea, and places two mugs and the teapot on a tray, lifting off the lid of the pot and putting a teabag in it. Waiting for the kettle to boil, she tips the water from the bowl on the draining board and rinses the dishes under the hot tap. She hears the click of the kettle as the switch releases, stopping the channelling of electricity, and four seconds later there is a series of four knocks, struck in two pairs, on the door. She fills the teapot, puts a cosy over it and places the kettle on its base, before walking quickly to the door. She stands aside as she opens it, knowing that they will rush in. The boys do, but her daughter does not. One of her grandchildren says Hi, Gran and the other says Gran excitedly, hugging her around the waist and transferring the collected rain from the hooded raincoats to her dress.

Hello Malcolm. David. Lovely to see you. She's not coming in. *Charlie? Not coming in?*

→
←

I can't. Have to get back quick. She kneels down. *Give mum a kiss.* The boys each kiss a different cheek, nearly at the same time. *Now make sure you behave yourselves.* She stands up, passes a small suitcase to the woman in the doorway, and steps backwards to the path. *They've got everything they'll be needing in their rucksacks. Call me if anything comes up.* *Thanks mum.* She waves as she closes the gate and hears her mother say Don't worry about a thing and walks along the pavement to her car. She pulls the handle of the driver's door and seats herself, slamming the door in her haste to avoid the rain getting the interior damp. She turns the keys with her left hand and starts the windscreen wipers. For a couple of seconds, she considers switching on the lights and decides to do so. She reverses the car a foot and then rotates the steering wheel to the left, slowly pulling out of the space in which she parked. Her mother and her two children are standing in the doorway. The boys are waving at her, blurred through the window. She beeps the car's horn twice and accelerates steadily.

Oh but the dread is tangible. She can really feel it. It's a weight and it's an adrenaline rush and it's guilt from the lies, but it's also soon to be closure. The months of secret meetings with Simon, the lovely doctor who seems so young but has barrels of experience, can finally be brought into the open. Catharsis. One of her favourite words and soon to be her favourite feeling. How Drew will react is beyond her and she really doesn't want to, really cannot, think about it seriously. But she has to and she does. Flashes of reactions are the best that she can create and she is deliberately not focusing on them. They are there though, of course, she wouldn't be human if they weren't. Soon.

She decided last night that she had to tell him, when she was asleep all alone in their large bed, stroking the places where Doctor Travers had been touching her and imagining the warmth of his softly calloused hands probing her gently and firmly at regulated intervals. The bed had seemed huge to her without Drew's comforting presence, the proximity of his overt masculinity that she could say was hers and hers alone. Scripts had been written and cast away, words stumbled over, and mannerisms and postures etched out in her mind, all parts of the delivery of such news.

He will be back in around half an hour. He had rung from the motorway on his hands-free phone and explained how he would be earlier if it wasn't for the traffic. The traffic's never good unless travelling before nine on a Sunday. He'll walk in the door and call for the kids and be met by her, just her, explaining why the kids are at their grandparents' and letting go of her secret, making it a secret no longer. Drew, lovely Drew. How will he react? Part of her, a rather large part, believes he will be happy and at least act happy. If not, he'll be sullen and thoughtful.

The rain makes a tentative driver of her, causing her to slow down. Her husband chides her for this when she drives with him as a passenger, but she knows that it does not annoy him. What mood is he in, she wonders? She can't imagine what it would be like to get news like this delivered to her door, but if he really loves her, which of course he does, sweet lovely Drew, then there won't be any problems. Good, there aren't that many cars on the road round her so she will be home ten minutes before him. She's like a schoolgirl with a crush. If it wasn't so drastic she'd be enjoying this, but she supposes she is, in a secretive kind of way. It is exciting. He won't get angry, will he? He'd probably come out with some long, lovely, intelligent words that will make any and all of her guilt float away. There's a funny feeling in her stomach. After thinking this, the irony of the statement leads her to laugh aloud for seven seconds and to wear a humoured smile for a further ten. She's not hysterical, is she? Lord, she hopes not. That's the last thing he needs after working the weekend: a hysterical her.

She turns right from the main road and drives on a road with a row of terraced houses on either side. The space that the car was parked in earlier has not been filled and she manoeuvres the car in the space in two movements, reversing in and then straightening the car with a short lurch forward. This is it. Go in and get ready and put the kettle on. He'll be here in what? About ten minutes. She turns the engine off with an anticlockwise turn of her left hand and removes the keys and quickly opens the door, steps out, stands up, and slams it, pressing the button on the left of her keys. She does not hear the locks whirr and then click; the wind is too loud in her ears. Quickly up the steps. Horrid weather.

In the house, she brushes the hair that is stuck to her forehead and cheeks to the sides.

Cup of tea. Two cups of tea. He'll be here in a minute. Or he might want a coffee after the drive. Kettle on anyway. He can decide when he gets here. She thinks that she can hear the scraping of metal against the front door's keyhole. She looks at the door and sees the obscured shape of her husband through the steamed glass. She'll just ask him herself.

Hi Drew. I'm putting the kettle on. Tea or coffee?
↑↓
Hey beautiful. Coffee. *A coffee would be great, thanks. God it's pouring it down out there. Had to park halfway up the road and got drenched. It's come out of nowhere. Wasn't on any forecast the other day.* He walks in the kitchen, propping

his briefcase on the seat of the chair closest to him. It's quiet. *Malcolm and David at your mum and dad's?* He puts his hands on her shoulders, standing behind her, and kisses her on the left cheek.

↓↑

Just dropped them off and made my way back. Just got in, actually.

↑↓

Ah. That is why your hair is wet. Looks rather attractive, actually. I didn't know the boys were spending the day with your parents.

↓↑

This is it. Do it. Go girl. *Look. Drew.* She's going to cry. *We need to talk. That's why the boys aren't here.* Why does this feel like a confession?

↑↓

God's sake. Did not see this coming. Welcome home and here's a decree nisi. *What's up, Char? Is everything okay?* He can feel his heart beating. He can actually feel his heart beating. Bloody shit.

↓↑

Well, these last few months, you know, I've been. Oh god this feels wrong. She starts crying and holds Drew. She pulls him tight to her, sobbing. He says Charlotte, it's alright. It's alright. What is it? and rubs his right hand across the top of her back, repeatedly.

She's such an idiot. It's like those shows where they keep the suspense going and going and going and *I'm pregnant.*

↑↓

Pregnant? He could laugh. *You're pregnant?*

↓↑

Yes.

↑↓

No divorce, adultery or confession. Thanks God. Jesus fucking Christ. He laughs. *That's amazing. Wow. That's amazing. Really amazing.* He hugs his wife more firmly, then steps away and places his hands on her shoulders, looking at her face with a smile of delight. *Char, this is amazing. How long have you known?*

↓↑

Her crying and and her guilt are abating, but her voice is affected by constriction of her diaphragm. *Three months, around. I've been seeing Simon, Doctor Travers. Everything is fine with the baby, but since they said, you know, about not being able to conceive again, I didn't want to, you know.* She's regained a bit more control. *You're not angry?*

↑↓

Angry? Don't be silly, Char. This is amazing. Angry? He loves this woman. *I love you. More than anything. Hey. This needs a celebration. How about you make that coffee and whilst I'm still drenched from the tempest, I go out and get some more appropriate drink for later?*

↓↑

Okay. She nods and he kisses her, lips against lips and tongue against tongue. He smiles at her and she feels foolish for the depth of her guilt, a guilt abolished by the man that she loves with all of her.

←

→

I won't be long. He kisses her again and tenderly wipes his thumbs across her cheeks, removing her tears. He walks out of the kitchen and opens the front door and goes out, closing it.

Absolutely amazing news. Talk about a thirty-second heart-attack. It sounded like she was about to come clean on some affair of some sort, but instead it's this. A father again after over seven years, with doctors saying it was nigh impossible and. They'd only spoken about it last year, wistfully. Fucking rain. He gets the keys out and unlocks the car's doors with a pressed button. He opens the door with his right hand and gets in the car quickly. Champagne, chocolates and flowers, that's the list. Maybe some wine as well. There is still a plentiful amount of the old juniper and they are always stocked with tonic. Great, just out on the main road and stuck behind a fucking bus. Slow Sunday buses. At least he can appreciate the luxuriation permitted him in the privacy of his own car: a luxuriation of completed personal endeavour and accomplishment. What has been has been. No more from now on. Another child on the way. Three boys. Never thought about that before.

For three minutes, he convinces himself that there is to be no more philandering in the future.

The double-decker bus slows down, its red lights at the rear left and right prominent against the greyish backdrop of stormy weather. It stops and lowers, to which he imagines he hears a hissing piston sound. A shape quickly steps from the bus and opens the umbrella that it is carrying. It is most definitely a very shapely she. A very shapely black she. Shit. He recognises the elation being replaced with numbing guilt. From now on, no more. A solemn promise to the future and to Char and to his unborn soon-to-be-born son. Or daughter. He might have a daughter. A quick glance as she walks past and faces him but the moving stream of water on the windscreen blurs

$\rightarrow$

$\leftarrow$

the driver's face. Something of a naughty feeling about looking in on people when they don't expect it. As a child in the back of cars she had always peered at the other kids as they were driven past. Mum had told her off a couple of times for being a people-watcher. A voyeur. If only she knew now. Maybe she would tell her in a TV-style confessional now, talking to a stupid piece of stone. It's what James wants and he's only ever been there for her.

The wind is sweeping against her back and pushes her slightly, forcing her to walk with staggered, quick steps on the pavement. Her black raincoat reaches to the back of her knees, the denim beneath sodden and shades darker than the blue when she first put them on. Her black walking boots are tight against the top of her Achilles tendons.

She had loved her mother and still does. Walking along the walled border of the cemetery towards a specific one of the twelve entrance gates, she questions herself as to the reasons why she never visited from her own volition up to this day. A feeling of sadness, she supposes, is why she just shivered. As well as the pouring rain. But it's warm. Tropical even. It really is only a piece of stone and it's stupid, that's the real reason. Standing over some words on a slab of stupidly expensive stone and doing what? James asked her to say something to her. She's doing this for him. There really can't be any happiness in murder. At least not when it's your mum that's been killed. Is she really going to have a conversation with a patch of ground and a slab of stone? She probably is. She said she would.

At the second gate she turns in and walks past the two opened, black-painted and bronze-spiked gates. The wind is swirling and pushes against her from her left. The ponytail that she has pulled her hair into is at a near ninety degree angle to her head. The umbrella is angled against the wind, her face turned away from the umbrella and the wind.

the assaults of small children on the new arrivals (Amadou's idea). In the long march between stones and scrub under the scorching sun, Jean said that he wanted to send a fax. To which Amadou explained that in the city there was a German doctor who worked for a German cooperative organization, and this man had a fax that would be less expensive. Then, however, reaching the small post office on the edge of the savanna, in front of the clerk named Madame Arattara, Jean had the bad idea of sending a fax from there, evidently because he had not listened to Amadou telling him about the German. As soon as we got out of the post office, Amadou made sure we heard his loud moan. This because Jean had sent the fax via Madame Arattara, instead of sending it through the German doctor. But why was he moaning so much? I thought that Amadou was feeling diminished to the extent that he was a man with many connections ("J'ai beaucoup de relations"), given that he had worked a great deal as Coppo's interpreter, and for this reason everyone knows him as Amadou the Italian, and before we arrived he worked with two Brazilian anthropologists with whom he maintains contact, to whom he sends I don't know what information. In addition to the relationship with the German doctor, whom undoubtedly he holds in higher regard than Madame Arattara. What was there to say? I thought he was right, as opposed to Jean. Here I tend to think everyone is right.

9 The situation we're in still has not been clarified, that is to say, we hadn't understood that Amadou shouldn't be seen merely as the cook and caretaker of the house where we're lodged. Amadou is a public relations man, in addition to our official governess, so to speak. But I think he is very perplexed about what we're doing in Coppo's house, seeing that (1) the ones from the Center for Traditional Medicine sent us, but he did not receive orders from Coppo; and (2) we are not anthropologists or psychiatrists, which makes us completely incomprehensible, more so given than we're not even regular tourists enjoying a vacation. His nanny-like solicitude is irritating Jean, who had a

She sees a large gathering of people, the varied levels of height visible from the flatly-angled bottoms of umbrellas. Humourlessly she thinks that it is funny how the priest, vicar or whoever is also holding an umbrella aloft. She slows and she can almost feel the sadness; the garden of the dead, she had heard someone say somewhere, and that's another reason why it's a stupid old tradition.

←

→

She wonders if that's someone who's lost, on their way to the funeral. She stopped to have a look, but has carried on in a quick, awkward looking walk. Probably the wind.

Look at the different faces that are congregated. The poor girl's been ruined by all of this. It's unimaginable how she must be feeling – impossible to reflect by switching shoes. And the last time to ever see him with rain pelting down upon his cold white face. They said there'd be a cover, actually, but still. Poor girl. Diane's been different, too. This whole affair seems to have affected her almost as badly as Rachel. She cannot hear the priest eulogise even though she is fewer than ten feet from her, the noise of the rain tapping against umbrellas and stone dampening the woman's voice. The wind is a loud gasp. She looks at the priest and sees that her mouth is immobile. A hand pulls at her coat's right sleeve, by the wrist.

↑↓

Davina. We're going to see the, you know, now.

↓↑

The dead man's face. She doesn't think she can; she's never seen a dead body before. Redlaw tradition: that phrase had been uttered so many times over the last couple of days. Doesn't mean it doesn't freak her out, all the same. *I don't think I can. I'll uh, wait in the car, Di. Follow you when we head to the wake.* There is a sharing of sorrowful expressions. *Keep her strong.* Jo's holding up okay, but the same can't be said for Rach.

↑↓

Okay. See you in a few minutes. She smiles understandingly, gently squeezing Davina's right forearm. She understands. Not the nicest of things to see at the best of times and these are not the best of times. She looks at the rain, falling heavily, although it seems that she can see every individual drop plummeting to the stone, the grass and the mud in perfectly straight lines, not wavering in any direction but down. Is this her? It is. Down from rising high. A young aspirant rising through the ranks of male-dominated and male-polluted business and then ruined by those same pollutants and glass-ceiling scumbag fuckers.

The rain swerves in the fast-moving wind and the faces are dampened with it being blown against them. The marquee that protected the catafalque from the weather and which they are under is too small. She can feel her tears, coldly juxtaposed with the warmth of the rain, hoping that they remain unrecognised by the others as they squeeze against each other to stand around the rectangular excavation. On a mechanical hoist is the coffin, in which lies the corpse of the two girls' father, her friends' father, dressed in an expensive black suit and white shirt. A rose has been pinned as a broach on his lapel.

She looks at Rachel and expects her to throw dirt on the coffin. But of course she won't. Not when it's open. Stupid. Well, that's been proved recently, hasn't it? You are a stupid bitch. Maybe the dirt will be wet mud, too. Stupid. The tradition does seem strange, though. On the telly, the open coffins are always inside. Strange family tradition, having an open casket outdoors. One minute's silence. Miserable stupid day. She is not miserable for the event itself; the sombre atmosphere expounds her emotional disposition and the minute of intrinsic, vocally silent grief, accompanied by the natural destruction of nature and its drenching patina, leads her reflections to darker territories. Fuck this shit. Men: they're all assholes. Even Mikey's irritating as hell. The worst thing is that she is the biggest asshole of them all.

With the finishing of the silence, the priest nods to an assistant and the casket's top is secured. The mechanics are activated and the hoist lowers and the dead body is beneath the gathered living, the majority of whose eyes are directed towards it. The two daughters cast a small handful of grainy dirt on the casket and the younger rests her head on the elder's left shoulder, crying with eyes closed, an umbrella erected above them, the handle in her right hand. The elder looks steely at the casket, contempt struggling to be contained and hidden, before looking her way.

$\rightarrow$

$\leftarrow$

The whole fucking thing is stupid and she can see through everyone: the selfish bitch that calls herself a friend and is pent up in her own shitstorm of whatever the fuck can be wrong in her perfect little life. Shallow nigger. What sort of fucking hair is that? Suitable for a funeral? Not at all. With that stupid fucking tattoo, as well. Her boss-friend cares only about the Sunday money that she's losing with her shallow sympathy. Dad's friends are clueless idiots and probably expect free drinks, the shallow dicks. The only one with any sense is Davina, waiting to drive her to the fucking bar. And Jo, of course. She's okay. She's upset.

People try to console her as she walks clumsily through the throng, her sister against her. They say things to them that carry sensitive sentiment. She does not listen. She wants to be away from the mourners that are not her sister and away from the black sky and hammering rain and blustering wind and self-centred people and spindly trees and broken headstones. The rain has stuck the fabric of her trousers to her legs and her left thigh stings against it, reminding her of her behaviour with the broken glass on the day when she had first heard the news. She thinks it stupid now, but at the time she understood perfectly.

Behind her, Diane and Claire are walking and not speaking. Others are following her lead. Amongst the many that are walking to their cars, the words spoken are shared between the topics of storms and death.

Davina has the car started. Good. The lights are on, even though it's only just past twelve. A dark day. Windscreen wipers too. It's like that scene in that film. She opens the rear-left door of the car, taking the umbrella from her sister and closing the door when she is seated and opens the passenger door and gets in the car. As she slams the door closed, she notices the bright-green shape of the cigarette lighter that she thought she had lost, wedged in the nook. She leaves it there. There is no conversation as Davina starts the car's engine and reverses, turning to the left. She drives the car slowly across the gravelled, divotted road, leaning forwards in the unfamiliar car for what she hopes will allow her better visibility.

Out of everyone, Davina's the only one she relates to. She says what she thinks and is never a bitch and has real values. All the other fuckers are only out for themselves. She's honest. Fake tits, whatever; she's not proud of them or embarrassed by them. She's not tight, either, or condescending. She's the only one who she had felt real sadness from. Said this morning that she would drive her, too, seeing that she was in no state to drive herself and Jo. Jo's alright, obviously. Being younger, she's dealt with it worse, crying all of the time. From sadness. She hasn't yet realised that it's the stupid bastard's weak fault and that if he hadn't been so weak then all of this shit wouldn't have happened. Maybe they shouldn't bother turning up to the wake.

I don't know if I can do this wake. Was thinking maybe we should just go home, to mine. Get something to drink there.

↓↑

We have to. Her voice is choked, high-pitched. *Dad's friends are there and it's. It's.* She cries, sobbing. *It's for dad.* She lengthens the vowel in dad this time. *It's dad.* She cries for a few more seconds before saying *Don't be a bitch* and putting her face against her hands.

↑↓

Waste of stupid fucking time. Don't need to be there.

↓↑

She speaks quietly, wanting not to be heard by the crying girl in the back. *Rach, it's your sister. She needs you to do this for her. Okay?* She's not answering. *Rach? We're going to your dad's wake. Okay?*

↑↓

If it was anyone else. *Fine.*

The sound of rain against the car's roof and the dragging of wet rubber across the windscreen and the spray of puddles being driven through dominates the interior of the car. She looks out of the window, trying to identify their location by squinting at the building that they pass. They're near the centre. On the pavement is a weirdly-dressed man wearing a cap. He hasn't got an umbrella, the stupid asshole.

←
→

Keep his eyes down. With every car that drives by, it's hard

313

not to look up. Some strange habit but more than likely down to alertness and personal safety. If he keeps his head tilted towards the pavement, the peak of his cap covers his eyes from any observation, whether personal or electronic, allowing him to see six or seven feet in front of him. His hands are in his pockets and they are sweating from the warmth. Even the rain feels hot against the back of his neck and cheeks. The gun creates an imaginative weight against his ribs from its seat in his left-inner pocket. The heels of his feet feel slippery from rain water that he imagines is perspiration. He feels like shit and he feels righteous and it's happening now and there's no way he's backing out of it, not now. He'll lift the gun and point it at his face and pull the trigger and that's all there is to it. It's fucking loaded in his jacket. He cannot prevent himself from thinking about its ability to discharge spontaneously against his chest and this only excites his nervousness further, making him want to withdraw from his course of action.

He left his apartment when the first sight of the sun was visible from his window, before six, encountering nobody as he walked out of the door and quickly down the steps. The cat had mewled as he stepped down and had caused him a momentary panic before he recognised his excessive paranoia and let out a clipped laugh through his nose. He chose a wooded area named Gorse Park in which to sit, keeping only to the concrete paths skirting the climbing frames and the river that runs through the centre of the wood due to the rain and the softened mud. During this time, he played games on his mobile phone and read over the conversation that he has had with the man whom he is going to kill; every detail is now finalised and the arrangement has been made. If there are any problems, he has thought out the manner in which he can easily abandon his intent and simply walk away. He resolutely avoided scouring the internet for information on the use and loading of a handgun and for the specifications and accessibility of the hotel room in which he is to commit murder. No traces, he told himself, as well as the very realistic prediction that the gun will not fire, that he is spotted or that he cannot gain access to the room unless he is permitted entrance by a porter. Regarding what he wants to happen, he thinks that he is fifty-fifty towards successfully killing the man and a problem occurring that will impede him.

He felt tired earlier, but he feels intoxicated at present, empowered by reserves of strength and endurance. The awareness of what he has committed to doing has heightened his sense of suspicion: the increased volume of car engines as they drive past, pedestrians staring at him as they walk past, unseen cameras tracking his every footstep.

Shit. He can feel the cracking shell of a gastropod and the cushioned-living vegetation under his left sole as the bottoms of his plimsolls are very thin. It freaks him out, all that sticky, gunky stuff. He questions himself as to the difference between what he has just unconsciously done and what he is consciously about to do.

The rain blows against the right side of his face, dozens of pellets every two seconds hitting his lips and barest outline of greyish stubble. It's weird how hot it feels. Uncomfortable too. The hoody is feeling really heavy from the rain and hunching is hurting his neck. The heat from wearing shorts and a T-shirt under the outer garments has also made it stuffy. The shoes that he hid in a bush by the docks will probably be soaked through by now and if not, they'll definitely be by the time he gets there. He has adopted a stooped stance in the attempt to disguise his five feet and eleven inches of height, as well as to facilitate the concealment of his face. He looks, he thinks, like a dosser. Like the perfect image of a bedraggled hobo. There's even a hole in both of the pockets of his jogging bottoms – he can't even remember where they came from, but as they're tight at the ankles about an inch above where they should fashionably be, they're probably something that mum bought a few years ago. No wonder he's never worn them. His head feels heavy, too. The cap is soaked through with rain.

He had been tempted to walk the route that he is taking yesterday evening, with the intention of identifying where the cameras are located and how best to circumvent them. He decided that the observational trip would be counterproductive as his face would be seen on every camera and he was, and is, reportedly ill.

He's gotta be pretty sick to go and kill a man, surely? He humours himself with his quip, unsmilingly. He does not think that any countenance other than stern is befitting the circumstance. Not to say he's not going to enjoy it, though.

Small puddles have collected against the curbs, running down the road in the direction that he has come. Each ringed wave lasts the briefest of moments before being replaced by another. He focuses on these as he walks, subconsciously calmed by the repetitious patterns formed. It also helps him to keep facing down.

He visualises pushing open a door with the number 84 embossed in gold on its front, walking in a room, seeing him lying on the bed and propped against the backboard, pulling the gun from the unzipped jacket's inner-left pocket, holding it pointing at his face, pulling the trigger towards him and then seeing a red dot appear on his forehead, a thin line of blood quickly spreading up to the eyebrow and staining it a bizarre crimson. The man's head falls limply forwards and he looks as if he is sleeping. He visualises this until the hotel is in sight, replaying the projected scenario and altering small, unnoticeable details. The walk to the hotel takes three minutes and thirty seconds.

He has thought and rethought how he will enter the hotel and find the room, its door ajar and him waiting on the bed as determined in their kinkily-arranged agreement. He wants to stop and observe the building with its grandiose exterior, pillared steps, continental flags blowing in the wind and rain, and take one last moment of introspection and silent monologue and evaluate the dilemma but no. There is no dilemma.

It's the third building from the end, the corner that he'll take when it's finished. Never paid the building much attention before, but he was pretty sure it was this hotel and it feels good to be right. When doesn't it? He walks up the empty steps, past the red-cloaked man standing at the top by the opened left door, and into the hotel lobby. The reception desk is to his left and he inclines his head towards it before controlling his actions and facing directly ahead. His eyes are quickly searching out elevator shafts, which he finds. But that he can't take.

He briefly feels panicked, looking up quickly to survey the corridor and failing to observe a stairwell. This can't be right. Surely hotels must have stairs and can't just have lifts? What if there's a fire or a faulty cable or...? He must look suspicious. They're all staring at him. It really is like he can feel their eyes on him, following him, probably calling the police. He starts to swallow, four times in quick succession so that the fourth is dry and slow. He can look up a bit as there can't be cameras at eye-level. Probably those round ones on the ceilings. Black domes. Not round. Spherical. He walks past the two elevator shafts and their closed doors and feels frustrated, the same way he felt when he was six or seven years old and his friend had opened his packet of crisps to receive the plastic pog that he had wanted, and the same as the holiday where he was not allowed to buy the plastic-toy gun, and the same as the day when it happened, his reason for being here, when he...

A closed grey door is to his right. It has a circular pane of Perspex, delineated with cross-hatched green lines forming squares. Through it, he sees a staircase. His heart is beating faster, leading him to feel the accentuated pulse of his blood as he pushes through the door and imagines he can smell the cordite of a smoking barrel. The glands at the sides of his jawline and neck feel swollen and bitter water tingles at the back of his throat and across his tongue. He swallows quickly and continuously as he walks up the stairs, hearing the closure of the door as the heavy wood clicks shut against its frame. The rainwater on his sleeves drips as he ascends, his quick pace and lifted arms releasing them from him in various trajectories. The back of his neck feels hot.

Number eighty-four. The building looks like it's got about twelve floors and he's no idea how many rooms that makes. Unlucky to have thirteen floors, though. He knows that. It must be the second floor at least; there's no way you can fit that many rooms on one. Too posh for crowded sleeping. At least that's how he's always thought about it, growing up. He'd never stayed in a hotel in his life, only ever going away with his family to stay in some shitty, freezing cold tin box with the posh-sounding name chalet.

At the top of the second flight of stairs, he pushes open the unmarked door and walks past the first two rooms, noting that their numbers are 56 and 57. It could be on this floor, he thinks. His breathing is more pronounced, a consequence of his exertion ascending the stairs and the adrenaline coursing through his body because of his propinquity with the man who made his childhood a thing less than childhood. It is real. He is about to kill a man. His testicles feel tight, tingling with anticipatory fear and power. He is about to kill a man.

The numbers on the doors ascend until he reaches a T-junction of corridor, taking the left and walking to the end, his head never lifting higher than is necessary to see the numbers. At the end of the corridor, there is no 84 embossed upon a door. He walks up the corridor and ahead, finding that none of the doors along this stretch of rooms bear the number 84.

Shit. Shit. Shit. This is stupid. He should just leave. Walk out. Nothing's done so nothing can happen. What is he thinking? Just go home and play a game and forget this stupid thing because.

He pulls the door handle with his right hand, swinging it towards him and stepping backwards before walking past it. It swings slowly closed as he walks quickly up the stairwell, two steps at a time for most of it. He knows that the room he is searching for is on this floor. He was never bad at maths. It's here. He's probably wanking himself on the bed already, thinking over all the crazy weird shit that he wants to do. Surprise, dickhead.

The first room that he walks past, after having opened the door to the floor, is 72. I'm coming for you, he thinks, not impressed with his rhyming ability or lyrical prowess. Evens on the left. 76. 78. 80. Shit. 82. 84. The door is left open a crack.

He stands before the door. His arched shoulders feel heavy and his body feels enveloped with static. A slight tremble is pronouncing across his jaw and the bottom of his chin.

You can do it. You can do this. You can kill the man who fucked up your life and ruined your childhood. The vile prick is in that room. He pushes the door gently with his left palm, effortfully attempting to make no sound. This room. He is in this room. With him. It is dimly lit. He hasn't seen this man's face, actual face, not virtual or digital face, for nine years. He holds the narrow edge of the door with his left hand, guiding it to its position a half-inch ajar from resting against the jamb. On the tan carpet is a pair of shoes, abraded leather visible on the outside of the right shoe. This is it. He's in there, the man who fucked up everything. Stay calm. He slowly unzips the jacket's front about four inches, sliding his right palm across his left pectoral and in the inner pocket of the jacket. The gun's metal is warm in his hand, the glove not restricting the transition of its heat. The hand in the glove is moist from rain and sweat. The gun looks small, incapable of creating death. It shakes with the small tremors of his adrenaline and uncertain commitment, alien to his customarily pacifism. He steps as softly as possible, close to the wall, thinking earthquakes.

He does not expect to see what he sees: a man sitting on the edge of the bed furthest from him with his hands on his knees. The man wears a thulian, vertically pinstriped shirt and black denim trousers. His hair is cut neatly, trimmed where the base of his skull meets the top of his sun-bronzed neck. It does not appear that he has heard a sound.

Holding the gun up, his hand steadies. This is where he says a line from a film or speaks his reasons for being here or gets him to beg for a second chance and forgiveness. But it's not.

Hey. His voice is a dry whisper. The man turns his neck to the right, looking from his face

$\rightarrow$

$\leftarrow$

to the gun in his hand. It's a steady hand, whoever this little prick is. Something familiar about him. Maybe he'd met him when he was a kid, though he doesn't look much older than one. Well, this is it, is it? He wants to say something, but his throat feels dry. Wishes he had smoked when he'd considered it on his way here. He smiles, eyes on the young man with the gun steadily held at his face. He's not going to say anything, then? Well, in that case, he'll have a fucking cigarette. And keeping his eyes on the young man, recognition settles in him. He remembers what he did to this kid. Good on the kid. He moves his hand towards the right pocket of his trousers, for his cigarettes, and in front of him, in the most minute second of his life, he sees a dance of smoke, hears thunder boom, feels nothing. Light-ignite. All the world is a safer place.

Recommended Reading

If you have enjoyed reading *Apparel* and like innovative and unusual fiction you should enjoy the novels of Andrew Crumey and Robert Irwin. We suggest the following titles:

The Secret Knowledge – Andrew Crumey
Sputnik Caledonia – Andrew Crumey
Pfitz – Andrew Crumey
D'Alembert's Principle – Andrew Crumey
Mr Mee – Andrew Crumey
The Arabian Nightmare – Robert Irwin
Exquisite Corpse – Robert Irwin
Satan Wants Me – Robert Irwin

If you like erotic fiction with a strong storyline you might also want to read:

Torture Garden – Octave Mirbeau
Lobster – Guillaume Lecasble
Prayer-Cushions of the Flesh – Robert Irwin
Memoirs of a Gnostic Dwarf – David Madsen
Confessions of a Flesh-Eater – David Madsen

You also might like to try another novel set in Bristol:

The Romeo & Juliet Killers – Xavier Leret

These books can be bought from your local bookshop, your favourite online retailer or direct from Dedalus, either online or by post. Please write to Cash Sales, Dedalus Limited, 24-26, St Judith's Lane, Sawtry, Cambs, PE28 5XE. For further details of the Dedalus list please go to our website www.dedalusbooks.com or write to us for a catalogue.

The Secret Knowledge – Andrew Crumey

A lost musical masterpiece is at the heart of this gripping intellectual mystery by award-winning writer Andrew Crumey. In 1913 composer Pierre Klauer envisages marriage to his sweetheart and fame for his new work, *The Secret Knowledge*. Then tragedy strikes. A century later, concert pianist David Conroy hopes the rediscovered score might revive his own flagging career.

Music, history, politics and philosophy become intertwined in a multi-layered story that spans a century. Revolutionary agitators, Holocaust refugees and sixties' student protesters are counterpointed with artists and entrepreneurs in our own age of austerity. All play their part in revealing the shocking truth that Conroy must finally face – the real meaning of *The Secret Knowledge*.

'It's a very clever novel, this metaphysical mystery, but one that I fear I am not clever enough to make sense of. The answer may be that you shouldn't try to do so, but instead to surrender to it.'   Allan Massie in *The Scotsman*

£9.99 ISBN 978 1 909232 45 7 234p B. Format

Pfitz – Andrew Crumey

'Rreinnstadt is a place which exists nowhere... the conception of an 18th century prince who devotes his time, and that of his subjects, to laying down on paper the architecture and street-plans of this great, yet illusory city. Its inhabitants must also be devised: artists and authors, their fictional lives and works, all concocted by different departments. When Schenck, a worker in the Cartography Office, discovers the 'existence' of Pfitz, a manservant visiting Rreinnstadt, he sets about illicitly recreating Pfitz's life. Crumey is a daring writer: using the stuff of fairy tales, he ponders the difference between fact and fiction, weaving together philosophy and fantasy to create a magical, witty novel." *The Sunday Times*

'Built out of fantasy, Andrew Crumey's novel stands, like the monumental museum at the centre of its imaginary city, as an edifice of erudition.'

Andrea Ashworth in *The Times Literary Supplement*

£8.99 ISBN 978 1 909232 80 8 164p B. Format

The Arabian Nightmare – Robert Irwin

'At one stage in this labyrinthine narrative, a character complains 'things just keep coming round in circles'. The form of this clever tale owes something to *The Thousand and One Nights*. The subject matter is exotic and Eastern, the episodes linked tangentially and mingling one into another. Into the thread of the stories, Irwin injects discussions on sexuality and religion. However, since dreams, as we are shown, are themselves a deception, then the philosophical points must necessarily be falsehoods. The invention is exhuberant, but the author manages to keep control to stop everything lurching into shapeless indulgence. The result is a unique and challenging fantasy.'   *The Observer*

'...a classic orientalist fantasy tells the story of Balian of Norwich and his misadventures in a labyrinthine Cairo at the time of the Mamelukes. Steamy, exotic and ingenious, it is a boxes-within-boxes tale featuring such characters as Yoll, the Storyteller, Fatima the Deathly and the Father of Cats. It is a compelling meditation on reality and illusion, as well as on Arabian Nights-style storytelling. At its elusive centre lies the affliction of the Arabian Nightmare: a dream of infinite suffering that can never be remembered on waking, and might almost have happened to somebody else.'

Phil Baker in *The Sunday Times*

£7.99 ISBN 978 1 873982 73 0 266p B. Format

Exquisite Corpse – Robert Irwin

'*Exquisite Corpse* is among the most adventurous, ambitious and daring novels published so far this decade.'

Nicholas Royle in *Time Out*

'Robert Irwin's novel about English surrealism is funny and profound and hugely satisfying.'

A.S.Byatt in *The Sunday Times Books of the Year*

'The final chapter of the novel reads like a realistic epilogue to the book, but may instead be a hypnogogic illusion, which in turn casts doubt on many other events in the novel. Is Caroline merely a typist from Putney or the very vampire of Surrealism? It's for the reader to decide.'

Steven Moore in *The Washington Post*

'Robert Irwin is a master of the surreal imagination. Historical figures such as Aleister Crowley and Paul Eluard vie with fictional characters in an extended surrealist game, which, like the movement itself, is full of astonishing insights and hilarious pretensions. Superb.'

Ian Critchley in *The Sunday Times*

£8.99 ISBN 9781 1 907650 54 3 249p B. Format

Lobster – Guillaume Lecasble

Lobster will appeal to readers who like the unusual with a sprinkling of erotic in their fiction.

'On board the Titanic, a lobster is saved from death at the moment he was about to be boiled. Now red, yet alive, he manages to escape, but not before an erotic moment with the woman that ate his father. This weird and wonderful little fable is like the awful offspring of Hans Christian Andersen and Salvador Dali: it is filthy romanticism and heart-breaking smut. As the story progresses, the metaphors it deploys become apparent: without or with a shell, who is vulnerable? Can love exist without pain? Do we seek in lovers the echo of one profound moment, or aspire towards someone that unites all the failed loves? Lescables's big little story provides no answers and all the questions, beautifully.'

S.B.Kelly in *Scotland on Sunday*

'There was a Lobster-shaped hole in world literature which has now been filled by this remarkable work.'
Nick Lezard's choice for *The Guardian's Paperback of the Week*

£6.99 ISBN 978 1 903517 34 5 110p B. Format

Memoirs of a Gnostic Dwarf – David Madsen

Memoirs of a Gnostic Dwarf was included in *The Guardian's 1000 Novels To Read Before You Die List*. It is a cult classic, warm and fruity and a must-read novel for lovers of the baroque, visitors to Rome, clergymen of all persuasions and readers who like their historical fiction with a big dollop of excess.

'*Memoirs of a Gnostic Dwarf* opens with a stomach-turning description of the state of Pope Leo's backside. The narrator is a hunchbacked dwarf and it is his job to read aloud from St Augustine while salves and unguents are applied to the Papal posterior. Born of humble stock, and at one time the inmate of a freak show, the dwarf now moves in the highest circles of holy skulduggery and buggery. Madsen's book is essentially a romp, although an unusually erudite one, and his scatological and bloody look at the Renaissance is grotesque, fruity and filthy.'   Phil Baker in *The Sunday Times*

'Inquisitions, religious sects and orgies in Renaissance Italy makes for a historical caper with a blinding plot; and the eponymous street-urchin-turned-papal-envoy is an unforgettable narrator.'   Sophie Ratcliffe in *The Times*

£9.99 ISBN 978 1 909232 75 4 336p B. Format

$$\leftarrow$$
$$\rightarrow$$

$$\downarrow\uparrow$$

$$\leftarrow$$
$$\rightarrow$$